XENOGENEIC
FIRST CONTACT

LANCE ERLICK

Finlee Augare Books (Chicago)

This is a work of fiction. All of the characters, organizations, and events portrayed herein are either products of the author's imagination or are used fictitiously, and any similarities to actual persons, organizations, or events is entirely coincidental. Also, though locations used in this work exist, for dramatic effect details have been altered. Accordingly, they should be considered fictitious.

Edited by Leah Carson
Cover design by Donna Harriman Murillo

Finlee Augare Books, Chicago, IL
ISBN: 978-1-943080-22-9 (print)
ISBN: 978-1-943080-23-6 (e-book)
Library of Congress Control Number: 2016920388

Printed in the United States of America

Look to the stars, but stay alert

ONE

Dr. Elena Sweetwater Pyetrov studied the launch area below her in stunned silence as uniformed officers burst onto the scene, followed by dozens of men and women in camouflage gear carrying assault rifles. It looked like a stunt for a Hollywood movie about space invaders.

Members of her ground team scrambled in response to the unannounced intrusion. It brought back memories of anti-space opposition two decades earlier to her father's mission to Jupiter. That ended with his disappearance and a presumed crash into the Jovian planet.

Beyond the bulletproof glass of the observation deck, a Navy Seal chopper buzzed the launch pad. The Moon shuttle was being prepared for tomorrow's take-off to reunite Elena with her crew on the Moon base. In the distance, the Atlantic was calm and skies were clear for her launch.

Elena picked up her cell phone to call her benefactor, Mason Crenshaw Devereaux, the billionaire owner of MCD Enterprises that was financing her expedition. Static filled the line. *Damn.*

She used binoculars to watch her ground crew as two uniformed officers approached them. One of her assistants shifted anxiously with an armful of last-minute test equipment for the mission. A second checked an electronic pad and shook her head. Two members of her ground crew made it to the safety of a hangar with camouflage soldiers in pursuit.

This can't be happening, Elena thought, *not when I'm this close.*

Government delays had already put her behind schedule. She had a narrow window to initiate her six-month journey aboard a brand new, privately funded MCD spacecraft already stationed on the Moon base. After years of preparation, she was finally heading to the Jovian moon Europa, part of her dream to continue her father's work.

Someone pounded on the control tower's door. A commanding female voice called out, "Doctor Pyetrov?"

Elena opened the door to a slender Federal agent who forced a smile as she stepped into the control room, followed by two beefy marines who collided on their way in.

"What's the meaning of this?" Elena asked. "We've been cleared—"

"There's been a development," the agent said, straightening up. She compared an image of Elena on her cell phone to the person before her and nodded. "You're wanted in Washington."

"I was told—"

"My orders are to bring you, in cuffs if necessary."

Elena looked at the two beefy men. Backing up, she saw all of her ground crew down below, surrounded by camouflaged soldiers.

"The sooner you come with us, the sooner this can be cleared up," the agent said. "Let's go."

"Can I at least speak with my team?" Elena held up her cell phone, which showed no signal.

"That won't be necessary," the agent said. "They've already been told. You're wasting time."

Not seeing any alternative, Elena chose the non-handcuffed approach. Again, she tried to phone her benefactor. When that provided nothing more than electronic static, she grabbed her briefcase, followed the agent and her marines to the roof of the observation deck, and climbed into a sleek, new helicopter.

"Are you jamming my signal?" she asked.

"I wouldn't know," the agent said. "Buckle up."

Without waiting for Elena to do so, the agent lifted the chopper and sped north, throwing Elena back in her seat at what she figured to be 3g, zero-to-sixty in one second.

She fastened her belt. "Now that I'm cooperating, can you tell me where we're going and what this is all about?"

"My orders were to deliver you to a congressional committee," the agent said. "That's all I know."

>===>

They landed on the new helipad above the senate offices. The agent and marines led Elena into a congressional meeting room and to a seat at the focal point of a semicircular table. It wasn't her first time in this chamber. The last visit hadn't gone well. On that occasion, Devereaux had intervened. This time she couldn't reach him.

Elena scanned the annoyed faces of the six women and five men on the Special Committee Responsible for Alien Programs. She'd encountered them all before. Evidently, they'd cut short their summer break to haul her in, either to stall or cancel her privately funded mission. She needed the government shuttle to reach her ship at the government-run lunar base.

She sat, clutching a thin briefcase in her lap. When her eyes met the glance of Chairwoman Senator Christabelle Jorgensen, chills ran up and down her spine. The senator despised anything having to do with space. She'd made that clear during her campaign and during their prior encounter.

Jorgensen raised her hand, and the room fell silent. "After long deliberations, we cannot allow your mission to launch." She sounded annoyed.

All eyes focused on Elena. She felt the heat of their attention, as well as the intense lights aimed her way. "Distinguished senators and representatives…" she began.

"Cut the formalities," Senator Jorgensen cut in. "We've been sending missions and messages into space for decades. None of it has improved the lives of desperate people here on Earth." One of Jorgensen's acts upon entering the Senate was shutting down the SETI project and its search for intelligent signals from space.

Folding her hands on the table, Elena raised her voice a notch. "Just because we don't know what we'll find doesn't mean we shouldn't explore. Columbus sought a trade route to India and opened up the Americas. Nicholas Navarov found water and key elements on the Moon that will allow self-sustaining colonies to ease overcrowding on Earth."

Jorgensen smiled for the hidden cameras. "Really? Your plan is to move billions of people to the inhospitable environment of the Moon?"

"We could colonize Mars."

The senator slammed a gavel on her table. "People want to live better here on Earth. We will no longer waste valuable resources on space exploration."

Elena took a deep breath. "Dr. Alexander Pyetrov—"

"The Committee knows your father's failures, Ms. Pyetrov. If he hadn't pursued his folly to Jupiter, you wouldn't have stood over his empty casket."

"He gave his life to further knowledge." On this matter, Elena had mixed feelings. When her father missed her sixteenth birthday for his mission, she'd cursed him to a fate worse than death. With his many absences, it had been one disappointment too many. Even so, at his funeral, she'd vowed to fulfill his vision.

She studied the six attractive young women dressed in identical gray nanofab jackets, sky-blue blouses, and navy skirts. They'd swept into office in the last election, championing the plight of women and children saddled with global crop failures. While Elena empathized, she didn't believe short-term needs should cancel long-term research.

Senator Jorgensen's cat-like eyes sliced into Elena. "We would be better served if you continued your efforts with the Women and Children's Taskforce."

Elena glanced at four men seated to her left, members of the Evangelical Ministry on Alien Mythologies. They leaned back in their seats, arms crossed, with scowls on their faces, content to let Jorgensen take the lead. A wrinkled clerk at the far right made sure recordings picked up everything Elena said—no doubt to use against her later. She sighed. "While that work is vital, I believe this mission can improve humanity's future."

"Isn't it true you expect to find alien life on your mission?"

Elena's throat tightened. She did hope to discover new species in space. Perhaps they'd be as bizarre as worms near submerged thermal vents on Earth, although so far, robotic space probes had been disappointing. "Learning about new resources will benefit everyone, and all of the financial risk is borne by—"

"I've read your report," Jorgensen said. "And not all the risk is private. Your sponsor requires use of our lunar base and our shuttle."

"For which he paid."

"Nevertheless. Sometimes science wanders into places that do more harm than good, like the atomic bomb. Wouldn't you agree?"

"Fire can keep us warm or burn down homes."

"Why pursue microbes while billions of people on Earth are starving?" Jorgensen asked.

With the exception of New Mexico Senator Emanuel Montrose to her right, everyone at the table deferred to Jorgensen. In private, Montrose had been sympathetic. Now he shrank into his seat as if Jorgensen had power over him.

"Exploration has made important contributions to understanding our solar system," Elena said. "Who knows? We might find microbes to help balance our food needs."

"People don't want to eat germs."

"If we don't explore," Elena said, trying a different tack, "whatever is out there could catch us unaware. Before Columbus, the Chinese discovered the Americas. Then their emperor died and his successor turned inward, which allowed the Europeans to dominate."

"I'm astonished that you champion Columbus, given what Europeans did to your Navajo ancestors."

That stung. Elena wished she knew more about that part of her heritage. "I'm aware of the exploitation of Native-Americans, but if Columbus hadn't explored, I wouldn't be here."

Several members of the panel broke out laughing. When Jorgensen remained somber, the room fell silent.

"Our primary concern is how alien mythologies contaminate young minds," Jorgensen said. "Isn't it true that while promoting this mission, you encouraged speculation about alien life?"

Elena measured her words. "My focus was on funding and approval."

Jorgensen paused to look at her notes. "Do you believe aliens brought life to Earth?"

"I believe in God," Elena said, *just not a god who denies the existence of alien life.*

"You didn't answer the question."

"I don't know. Do you?" Elena felt like a prop to political campaigning. "With all due respect, Senator, our future depends on exploration."

Jorgensen waved her hand in dismissal. "Leave us."

Holding her head high, Elena grabbed her thin briefcase, marched out of the stuffy chamber, and headed straight for the restroom.

In the mirror, she stared into a weary face with dark eyes. Lines creased her bronzed forehead. She spotted another gray nestled among her obsidian-black hair. Each visit to Washington seemed to add more. Although men said she was attractive, she looked older than her thirty-four years, thanks to the frustrations of butting heads with bureaucrats.

Elena felt exhausted from her preparations and this latest distraction. This committee could have halted her mission at any point. *Why now?*

Gritting herself into control, she clutched an ornamental platinum comb her father gave her before his last mission, and pushed back her short-cropped hair.

>===>

Elena paced outside the committee chambers, longing for time in space, away from vicious politics and other people's expectations. Even her on-and-off-again fiancé, Captain Marc Carlisle, a marine pilot, held expectations. He had repeatedly pressured her to include him on her mission. She only had room for her handpicked crew. Besides, Elena was convinced they wouldn't survive together in such tight quarters. Their strained goodbye the night before had left a sour taste in her mouth. She couldn't permit entanglements to hold her back.

Chamber doors swung open. Senator Jorgensen emerged, her face betraying no emotion. The senator offered her hand and squeezed Elena's in a firm grip.

Jorgensen's mouth drew into a tight line. "This mission is a waste of resources. You know that."

The senator's vacant eyes gave Elena chills. "With all due respect, our future lies out there."

"Are you prepared for whatever sacrifices this mission calls for?"

Elena's throat went dry. Suddenly, Jorgensen seemed willing to let the mission continue after all. The senator led Elena into a room across from the committee's chambers and closed the door. She left the lights off, no doubt to avoid cameras. The darkness made it harder to ignore the senator's pungent perfume.

Elena recalled a previous encounter with this scent. About a year ago, a colleague pressured her to join the secret professional group Sisterhood of the Nile. Membership bound her to their code. Only later did she realize what she'd agreed to: a commitment to the Women and Children's Taskforce that, while worthy, distracted from her mission.

Withdrawing into the darkness, Elena forced a deep breath and nearly choked. "What changed your mind?"

"Your single-minded determination." The senator took Elena's hand.

Confused, Elena pulled away and bumped into a table. She straightened up. "I'm committed."

"One condition. Your mission is limited in scope. You'll report all findings directly to me and no one else. Is that clear?"

Elena pressed against the table. "This is a scientific mission."

"And a commercial one."

"My sponsors won't—"

"Then consider yourself grounded."

"Senator, any commercially viable materials we find would benefit—"

Jorgensen grabbed Elena in the secret arm grip of the Sisterhood. *That explains the dark room.* The group's support might explain the senator's rapid rise in politics and the solidarity of the five women who rose with her and sat on the Committee.

Was this a charade intended to get Elena to agree to conditions? Well, sponsors were one thing. Elena had her own reasons for going into space.

She swallowed hard. The Sisterhood's code obligated Elena to a senior member like Jorgensen. "I accept."

The senator moved away. "Go before we reconsider."

>===>

A space cruiser glided high above the Earth, monitoring events unfolding in the American capital and at a Florida launch pad. Standing before the wide screen in the command center, General Nurock Gorg tightened her well-toned stomach muscles and stifled her disgust at the pale human form Supreme Commander Viv had taken.

The general looked away from the screen before her contempt for non-gray complexions and smooth foreheads twisted her forehead ridge-crest; to snub her supreme leader would be suicide and Gorg had a score to settle. The attempts to ground the human space mission had failed, opening up opportunities for her. She smiled, hoping that would soften her image for the supreme commander, and returned her attention to the screen.

"We cannot risk exposure," Viv said in human-accented Knoonk language over the secure com-link. She adjusted her camera, which then showed behind her the brightly colored office in Viv's Washington home. The vivid colors stabbed at Gorg's eyes, an unfortunate byproduct of inbreeding among a too-small surviving population. Overuse of color was a human obsession that the Supreme Commander had acquired as part of her genetic transformation to human form.

Gorg adjusted the command ship's controls so the craft would appear to float as satellite debris to the humans' feeble sensors. She glanced at her immediate superior, Commander Jinek Zurbiz, whose bloated figure filled the captain's chair. Zurbiz was the only person between her and the supreme commander, a position Gorg coveted.

Zurbiz's ineptitude had condemned General Gorg's sister to die on Earth during a routine recon mission. When Colonel Dwentok Gorg was wounded and couldn't reach the extraction point, Commander Zurbiz refused to risk a rescue mission that could have saved the colonel's essence. In fact, to avoid letting humans capture the fallen soldier, Zurbiz had ordered her body remotely incinerated. Now there could be no ritual resurrection, no chance for life to continue in a new body. In her mind, Gorg spat at the flabby target Zurbiz made. *You're a disgrace to our people.*

Seated next to Zurbiz was little Nalon, the faithful sycophant. *You picked the wrong master*, Gorg thought.

"I share your disappointment," Supreme Commander Viv told Gorg. "I also grieve for your sister, a great Knoonk warrior." She paused, leaving only background hum for a moment of remembrance.

Then she turned her human face to Commander Zurbiz. "Where do we stand on finding the Royal Couple?"

Zurbiz bowed with her ridge-crest at attention across her forehead. "We have many leads to catch the traitors."

"You should have caught them by now," Viv said.

Gorg suppressed a grin. It was another failure by her incompetent boss and another step closer to Gorg replacing Zurbiz. If the commander hadn't been so timid … well, Gorg would handle things differently.

In fact, General Gorg would have caught the Royal Couple twelve years ago, when the remnant of her Knoonk rebels overpowered the outposts in this solar system. Zurbiz's hesitation allowed the Royal Couple to complete their transformation to human form and escape to Earth to hide among the inferior species. Despite Zurbiz's bungling, Supreme Commander Viv chose her over Gorg to command the outpost.

"I suggest General Gorg take this assignment," Supreme Commander Viv said.

The general bowed. She relished the opportunity to exact revenge against humans for the permanent loss of her sister. As a bonus, she would get to upstage Zurbiz.

Commander Zurbiz changed the subject. "We are resurrecting our fallen comrades as quickly as we can."

Yeah, Gorg thought, *the lucky ones killed in our failed rebellion.* The survivors preserved and transported their essences to this outpost at the edge of the galaxy. They were receiving the ritual resurrection denied to Gorg's sister. Never again would she stand side by side with her kin as Knoonk warriors.

"Not fast enough," Viv said. "Humans are sending another manned probe. Use it to our advantage."

TWO

"Beware what you ask for," Elena's father had once warned.

Those words rattled about her head while she squeezed out of the lunar shuttle's sleep tube. As the drug-induced fog faded, she sat facing a narrow sky-blue corridor. The bizarre encounter with Jorgensen kept looping through her brain, making no sense.

Despite her pledge to the senator, Elena would soon be on the Moon base, away from all the politics. She hoped her lunar crew had checked out and provisioned Devereaux's long-range spacecraft, though when she reached the Moon, she would perform her own checks. Then they would launch toward Jupiter. She smiled. *This is finally happening, Dad.*

Stretching, Elena closed her eyes, pictured her father before he vanished, and wished she could share this moment with him. She snapped on antiquated magnetic boots and struggled to put one foot in front of the other to reach the main cabin. Her seamless blue and red transport bodysuit was too tight, the stretchy material clinging.

Predictably, Marc Carlisle managed to finagle his way onto her lunar shuttle. At the last moment, he'd shown up with official documents showing that he was replacing one of the passengers transferring to the Moon base. That was when she'd decided on induced sleep for the two-day journey. *I'm not going to let him pester me into taking him to Europa.*

The ship lurched, tossing her against one wall and then the other. *Wretched clumsy boots.*

At least on the longer journey she'd have artificial gravity and other conveniences. She peeled one boot off the metallic floor, pushed it forward, and let it magnetically reconnect. Fighting the boots in zero gravity took all her concentration. That and the lingering haze of induced sleep delayed her recognizing the obvious. It was rare for a spacecraft to shift direction abruptly unless something hit it. The only things that came to mind were meteorites and space junk, neither of which would be good.

The boots resisted her attempts to move faster. By the time she reached the main compartment, the nineteen other blue-and-red-clothed passengers, many dazed from sleep, were already strapped in or struggling to reach assigned seats in one of five rows. These lunar miners, construction workers, a cook, and a few agrarians were all heading for the lunar base or a nearby settlement.

The view-screen before them showed a starry sky, mostly blackness. The pilot's seat was empty and Captain Zak Pavlin was nowhere in sight. Elena thought there should have been a partition separating the crew from passengers, so the latter wouldn't notice such details. To conserve weight and space, NASA had built the shuttles without dividers.

Nearby sat navigator Reese Paswitch. Her highlighted brown hair and eyeliner seemed overdone for a transit to the Moon; she was looking forward to a lunar wedding. Her fiancée sat in one of the passenger seats, gripping the armrests. Two crewmembers on either side of the controls, young recruits on a routine lunar transit, were both sweating. They looked as if they hadn't slept in days.

In the co-pilot's seat sat Marc Carlisle, looking as if he'd pulled all-nighters for a week. Elena sighed. She didn't need their personal drama replayed in public. She hated shutting him down on their last night together, but she was tired of his insistence that she let him accompany her to Europa. Now he'd moved a step closer.

After they reached the lunar base, she would let him stew while she prepared her team. Then she would bid him farewell—again. Maybe this time they could leave on better terms.

The transport jolted to the left, forcing Elena to steady herself against the cabin wall. Her attention fell on the forward view-screen, which no longer showed a starry sky.

"What the ... Jupiter?" She felt dazed, still recovering from the sleep drugs. *Am I dreaming?*

No, she was awake, all right. The magnetic boots were like

having her feet encased in concrete. She grabbed hold of an empty seat and dragged her boots toward the pilot's chair. *Have I been asleep for six months?* She checked her wrist-com. Two days had elapsed and she was still on the shuttle. "Where's the Moon?" she asked Marc.

"Good, you're up." He reached for her hand.

Elena pulled away. Weariness and frustration swept across Marc's face.

"What happened?" she asked.

"Somehow we diverted to Jupiter, months early." Marc's attempt to act calm was betrayed by his face, wrinkled with unsettling terror.

"How is this possible?" Elena scanned the jumble of controls and lights for evidence of what went wrong. The whole setup looked like something from the Smithsonian. The shuttle was a generation out of date, since the government refused to invest in space exploration. NASA had assured her that the weathered craft was sturdy enough to get them to the Earth's moon. *Not to Jupiter.*

"We don't know." Marc's face sagged. "Maybe you can help puzzle this out." His pleading look reminded her of the night they'd parted.

Approaching Jupiter should have excited her, but Elena struggled to absorb what was happening. She was near her destination without her team, no gear, in a shuttle that couldn't survive out here. Preparation was everything. She shook her head. "The shuttle can't travel this fast."

Marc returned his attention to the controls and pulled up status charts. "Agreed, but we've been approaching Jupiter for hours. I'm open to explanations."

Elena didn't have any. She stared at the image of Jupiter, with the sinking feeling that she'd survived Jorgensen only to vanish in space like her father. Only one thing made sense, yet it didn't. "Were you that desperate to be on my mission that you veered off course?"

"Whoa." Marc threw up his hands and let out a heavy sigh. "We didn't do this. The crew and I have been through forty-eight hours of hell. The controls don't work. The pilot and co-pilot are checking panels for malfunctions. Tara L'Enfant is helping them."

Elena had bumped Tara, an electronics expert, off her mission in favor of someone she deemed a better fit. Tara had taken the consolation prize, one rotation of work on the lunar base and ended up on this shuttle.

"Why are you at the controls?" Elena asked in a harsh whisper.

"I have pilot training."

"Not for a shuttle." Elena took a deep breath. She didn't want another fight. "I want to speak to the pilot. Where is he?"

"He's working on our thruster electronics. You'll have to wait until he's done. In the meantime, why don't you sit?"

"Tell me what you know." She stopped herself from adding *that shouldn't take long.*

"Not a single switch, circuit or gear problem."

Reese Paswitch sat nearby; her bloodshot eyes and knotted brow betrayed shell shock. Even her cheeks sagged, hardly the image she would want at her wedding. Passengers stared at the screen. Several got up and approached.

Elena tried to focus on the science, but her mind remained foggy. She couldn't account for traveling so far so fast. Although her sponsors had exhausted every resource to find the fastest way to the outer solar system, even their long-distance spaceship couldn't achieve these speeds.

"What do you make of this?" Elena asked, lowering her voice.

"We lost controls an hour into the flight," Marc whispered.

The bulky control panel had no flashing lights. No displays hinted at anything wrong except for that Jovian mass ahead of them. "Why didn't you wake me?" Elena asked.

"I tried," Marc said. "You must have taken extra sedatives."

To avoid you. A sharp pain stabbed behind her right eye. She dropped into the pilot's seat and immediately her eyes felt leaden, ready for sleep. She took a deep breath and clenched her fists. "Not much, though my head's ready to explode."

Marc handed her a mug of coffee. "This might help. It's a richer blend."

Clutching the mug, Elena sucked in lukewarm coffee through a tube and hoped it would do the trick.

A half-dozen puzzled and scared passengers closed in around Elena as they pushed for a closer look. Worry spreading across their faces. She stood to get air. These passengers hadn't signed on for the challenges and risks of flying to Jupiter. She didn't want to add to their terror.

She handed Marc the coffee, placed her hand on his shoulder to steady herself, and leaned in to whisper into his ear. "I want a complete assessment."

"Gladly," Marc said, "but you're not in charge until we land."

"Neither are you. You should have stayed home." Elena pulled away and stared at the growing image of the gas giant, Jupiter. *Four-hundred-fifty million miles in two days.* "Any chance that image and the instruments are wrong?" *After all, this is a relic.*

"The crew checked everything a dozen times. I'm sorry; I really did try to wake you."

Elena's knees trembled as she fought deceleration. "Any thoughts on how we got out here?" *Out here?*

Marc stood. He towered over her by five inches. "I've read theoretical treatises on space-time continuum and wormholes. I don't know. Something bypassed all of our controls and pulled us toward Jupiter."

"You're saying we have no control," said Wil Benning, the biggest of the passengers and a construction recruit hired for the lunar base. He pushed his way forward. "What the eff is going on?" He glared down at Elena.

"Are we crashing?" another man asked.

Passengers pushed closer, all shouting at once.

Marc faced the burly construction recruit. "Everyone take a deep breath. We're doing everything we can."

"Where's the pilot when we need him?" Wil Benning asked.

"He's checking the equipment. Unless one of you has electronics or aeronautics skills, sit down and let the crew do its job."

Elena couldn't make sense of their velocity: two percent the speed of light. When her sponsors had brainstormed faster means of space travel, they'd brought in a Stanford physicist who discussed the Alcubierre Drive, a specially designed engine that creates a field around a spacecraft using exotic matter and negative energy that might allow it to bend the space-time continuum and move as fast as the speed of light. It had too many technical problems and no evidence it would work, so her sponsors dropped that option. Nothing else explained this speed.

Most passengers returned to their seats, except Reese's fiancée who hovered over her. Elena sat in the pilot's seat. She scanned the usual status reports on a small screen in front of her and turned to Marc. "Get me access to the view-screen's history."

He clicked a file on the small console before her, and up came the video. "What are you thinking?"

She played the video from an hour after takeoff and sped it forward. The shuttle veered away from the Moon, which zipped by. Then it lifted above the plane of the planets. Not believing the trajectory, she slowed viewing to real time and was stunned by how quickly they passed Mars.

She checked her wrist-com. It registered a two-day lapse, yet at the shuttle's implied speed, the trip couldn't have taken more than a day. She wondered why Marc hadn't said anything. In fact, he'd mentioned two days.

To verify, she counted off a minute. The console's clock registered two. Even Einstein's relativity couldn't account for that. She counted again to be sure.

The craft lurched right.

As others fell against metallic walls, Elena grabbed her seat belt. "What was that?"

"We've been getting bursts of movement," Reese said, "as if someone else is navigating."

Elena tried to bridge the gap between Marc's feigned coolness, Reese's panic, and the possibility that someone was tampering with time and the shuttle's speed. The lights on the panel before her were either green or white. "How much fuel do we have?"

"That's just it," Marc said. "We aren't using much—only enough for electrical and life support."

"That's crazy." She decided not to share her suspicions until she knew more.

Reese tugged Elena's arm. "You guys need to see this."

Standing, Elena stared at an approaching moon, which looked pink, thanks to the screen's enhanced color contrasting. It took a moment to register that this was her Europa, the ocean moon, as she'd imagined it. Her jaw dropped. Of course, Europa was a moon of Jupiter. *Amazing.*

The image quality was unlike anything she'd seen before—the lines and angles of angry ice pushed and shoved by Jupiter's tidal pressure. Clarity was so sharp she could imagine reaching out to touch it.

Marc tinkered with the controls. "Zak!" he yelled into the communicator. "What do you have? We're on a collision course." He turned off his mike and turned to the passengers. "Everyone in their seats and buckle up," he yelled. "Prepare to crash."

"I'm on my way," Zak said.

"What's going on?" someone yelled.

"Sit and try to be quiet," Marc said. "Elena, that includes you."

Unable to take her eyes off the screen, she groped for the pilot's seat. The stark image of crisscrossed pink lines grew, demarking broken ice sheets, until the cracked and haunting image of Europa filled the view-screen. They plunged through the negligible atmosphere. Giant blocks of ice rushed toward them.

A chorus of confusion welled up behind her. Passengers screamed. A construction recruit fell against the forward screen with a crunch. Keeping her eyes fixed on an approaching brown ridge, Elena grabbed for the seatbelts. "Do you have thrusters?"

"Inoperable."

"Missiles?"

Marc glanced over. "It's a transport, not a fighter. Now get your seatbelt on and brace for impact."

Elena tugged at the seatbelt a moment too late. The shuttle slammed into the icy surface, throwing Elena into Marc's arms. Air squeezed out of her lungs. She couldn't move. Her insides heaved. She pressed her eyes shut and begged for relief. Marc held on too tight.

"Leeeet goooo!" Elena's voice trailed distant and hollow in her ears. She struggled to break free. She smelled sweat; Marc was as petrified as she was.

Lights blinked out. Elena fell against the view-screen and winced from pain in her left shoulder. Odd screams scratched at her ears, punctuated by elongated blasts and the thunderous crackling of ice … or the shuttle. Time slowed, though she knew that was an illusion.

Darkness engulfed them except for sparks from the control panel. The smell of toasted electronics filled her sinuses and left a metallic taste in her mouth. Despite the loss of power, the screen glowed reddish.

A cacophony of terror jumbled signals to her brain. Emergency lights flashed on. Red splattered. Blood choked her throat. She was pinned by deceleration as the shuttle slowly broke through the ice.

Distorted screams tore at her ears. The screen presented a yellowish glow that illuminated sheets of ice flowing past. If the impact hadn't destroyed the ship, ice pressure should have, yet they continued descending. Three bodies lay crumpled nearby. Elena couldn't see faces.

Another body slammed against the view-screen: Captain Zak Pavlin, the pilot. Unable to lift her body, Elena slid closer to check his pulse. Nothing. Other bodies hit the screen. Acrid odors of blood, vomit, and electronics attacked her sinuses. Elena was amazed that she was still conscious, still experiencing all this.

Onscreen, the wall of ice turned into a brackish-brown slurry: a liquid ocean, as predicted.

Astonished by her own calmness, Elena strained to see. If only they had lights to penetrate the murkiness. *I'm here, on Europa, Dad.*

She sensed the sides of the shuttle bulging inward.

The shuttle continued its descent. The cabin filled with smoky haze. Her eyes misted and burned. She no longer saw Marc or Reese in the flickering lights. She drew her knees to her chin. Guilt tightened her chest, the nightmare of finding her brother Leo hanging by a rope after their father vanished. She hadn't been there to protect him.

The ship stopped. Metal creaked. Everything fell forward. Voices echoed around her.

"Help!" someone yelled.

"No!"

Elena covered her ears and cried out. She couldn't hear her own voice. Icy water swept into the compartment. A thousand needles stabbed her flesh. She couldn't see through the fog. Her entire body was on fire with frigid stabs.

Lights went out. Sparks flickered from the controls. Then even they vanished.

Darkness enveloped them.

THREE

Screams ceased.

Elena's heart raced. Shivering, she tried to keep her head from spinning and nausea from tearing her apart. No one could have survived that crash. They couldn't have traveled so far and so fast, or withstood the ice or pressure.

Her eyes teared up. Lying on a hard surface, Elena gagged on syrupy air she recognized from college swimming days: chlorine. When she filled her lungs, her body didn't rebel, which was a good sign. Other than the hint of chlorine, she didn't detect poisons in the air. *I can't be dead and feel this alive, can I?*

Queasiness faded, yet her mind remained foggy. The sleep-inducing drugs should have worn off, but she couldn't shake the haze.

The icy water was gone along with the shuttle, and she was dry. She couldn't recall moving. Her lungs adjusted to musty air; her eyes stopped watering. Bright light glowed from above against walls and ground, gray as the overcast winters she'd endured at the University of Michigan. Uneven wall and floor surfaces gave the impression of a cave though too smooth and monochromatic for a natural formation. Lights covered the entire ceiling as if painted on with a bioluminescent coating. There were no natural formations—no stalactites, stalagmites, or anything she would associate with a natural cave.

Elena smiled. If this cave wasn't natural, someone created it.

It reminded her of a game she and her father used to play. They pretended that aliens hid among us, observing our behavior from UFOs. He made her guess what first contact would be like and how she would act. Now she wished she could tell him what she'd found.

She stopped shivering; vertigo eased. There was no hint of the frigid world or the shuttle and debris, only Marc and Reese. Both groaned and stirred on the pastel-gray ground nearby. The others were gone. Elena rubbed the back of her head, wishing she could puzzle out how they got from the crash site to this chamber.

Marc rose unsteadily and braced himself. His jittery movements told Elena that he was petrified. *That's not good.*

He offered his hand. "What a rush." He tried to make it sound cheerful; his voice fell flat.

Elena got to her feet. "I'm fine." Her throat felt like sandpaper. Her voice echoed off the cave walls. She took a deep breath and willed her headache to stop. She felt shaky, trying to process all that had happened. It didn't feel real, except for the restored gravity.

Standing tall, Marc scanned the bland cave walls.

"Someone's trying to gas us," Reese cried out. With bloodshot eyes, she seemed in shock.

"Stand up and breathe slowly," Elena said. "It's worse near the ground."

Elena slipped her belt-bag off her bruised hip and was surprised to see no blood on her navy blue pants. They weren't the same uncomfortable bloodstained pair she'd worn on the shuttle, though she couldn't recall changing. Marc and Reese also wore clean uniforms with none of their earlier coffee stains or blood.

Marc offered Reese his hand. She just sat, sobbing, her body rocking back and forth.

Marc's eyes darted around. "Any idea where we are?"

"Four-hundred-and-fifty million miles off course," Elena said in frustration. She wasn't even convinced of that.

"You know what I mean. This place. What is it?" Marc had gone too long without sleep, even for him. Moreover, he'd had too much caffeine, a bad combination.

"A cave," Elena said, unwilling to share her suspicions until she knew more. *We aren't alone.*

Her first steps felt light. She guessed they were subject to one-third to one-half of Earth's gravity, much too high for this to be Europa.

Her spaceship would have used rotation to create artificial gravity, but the uneven walls hinted not at a spacecraft or satellite but rather a cave in a rocky planet or moon. The time distortion—one day instead of two—and the fascinating video had to factor into this.

Reese struggled to her feet. "Where's Howard? Where's everyone else?"

Her fiancée had slammed into the view-screen. "Maybe he's in another chamber," Elena said.

While Elena felt calmer than circumstances would warrant, Marc looked unusually agitated. "The first principle of survival is to face facts," he said. "I don't know how we survived. I guarantee no one else made it through that ordeal."

Burying her face in her hands, Reese sobbed.

"Do try some empathy." Elena hugged the navigator. "We don't know the others are gone. We shouldn't have survived, yet here we are."

Nodding, Marc stumbled toward a wall, adjusting his pace to the light gravity. "Elena," he said, "you're right. Our first order of business is to find resources, food and water, and a way out. Do either of you have communicators?"

Elena shook her head. Marc had always been high energy and action-oriented, but she'd never seen him this frantic. "You haven't slept in days. Why don't you lie down? Reese can keep watch while I look around."

"Not until I know what we're facing. Look for ways out of here."

"Suit yourself." Elena glanced around this astounding alien cave and wished she had her equipment to analyze the rock composition. That might hint at where they'd ended up.

The calm she felt made no sense after their ordeal. It felt as if someone was manipulating her emotional responses. It couldn't be a lingering effect of the sleep drugs. Even her hands stopped trembling from the icy cold.

At first, Elena had perceived the chamber as nondescript bland shades of gray. A closer look revealed milky gray, coal gray, mellow gray, stark gray, edgeless eternal gray, and claustrophobic gray. It reminded her of how Silly Putty looked when you blended colors, but all of these colors were shades of gray. With the exception of the lit ceiling, other surfaces blended into one another with no sharp corners and no evident exit. The ceiling was some fifteen feet above them, though the grayness made judging distance difficult. In any case, she couldn't reach that high.

Rubbing her sore shoulder, Elena took it all in. "This is magnificent, don't you think? It's like Navarov finding ice reservoirs on our moon."

"Let's focus on finding a way out," Marc said. "We've got oxygen. That's good. I don't see any food, water or an exit of any kind."

"Why bother?" Reese wiped tears from her cheek. "The ship's gone. There's no way home."

Marc took Reese by the arm. "Get a grip, Lieutenant. It's my job to get us home."

"You're not her captain," Elena reminded him. She stopped herself from replaying the remarks they'd made during their last evening together.

"Look, Elena, I'm the senior military officer. This just became a military survival mission. We need to pull it together."

"We've been spared death by some intelligent being."

"I know you believe in aliens," Marc said.

"How else do you explain surviving the crash? There's light, heat, and air to breathe."

"Where's my Howard?" Reese ran her fingers through her hair and tugged at a clump.

Marc placed his hand on Reese's shoulder. "Let's look around while we still have our strength."

Elena pulled Reese away. "I'm sorry about Howard. Why don't you rest while I look around?"

Reese forced a smile. Her eyes brightened for an instant.

Marc joined them. "I'm sorry we fought over my wanting to join your mission. I just didn't want to lose you like you did your father."

Elena patted his shoulder. "I know. Your concern was so sweet, but it no longer matters. We're here now."

"Exactly. We need to treat this as a survival situation. That's what I've trained for."

"What if our hosts put us here for our own protection?" Elena asked.

"I'm not saying I buy your alien hypothesis, but if they exist, I doubt they mean us well. We could be their food supply."

"You've watched too many science fantasy movies. This could be first contact."

"I'd feel safer with my sidearm," Marc said. "What if this is an arena and they expect us to fight to the death?"

Elena shook her head. "They didn't let us die on the shuttle."

"Then why don't they show themselves?" Marc spun around, his weary eyes searching out threats.

"I don't know." Elena crossed the uneven floor with Reese, wishing there were at least some natural features to help her puzzle out this cave. If the ship's video was bogus, they could have gone in any direction. She doubted they'd reached the Moon with its human settlements. Mercury and Venus were too hot. The gravity was about right for this to be Mars.

In any case, someone had gone to a lot of trouble to give them shelter without exits, except possibly the sky rim, which was out of reach. Smooth gray walls had no handholds or footholds. Whoever had spared their lives didn't want them peeking above the rim. She could barely calm the butterflies in her stomach over such a potentially momentous discovery.

Reese shuffled beside Elena. "Do you think we'll find Howard and the others?"

"Anything's possible." Elena studied the rim. There was a thin line of darkness. She couldn't be sure if it was merely the seam between the wall and ceiling lights or a gap large enough for an opening.

"How do you remain so calm?"

Elena pondered that. Again, she wondered about the chlorine smell that had diminished now that she was standing. The gas hadn't affected her breathing though it implied a different atmosphere than on Earth, with different chemicals that could affect mood. "Would it help if I panicked or despaired?"

"I guess not."

"Look around. There's intelligence at work here."

"What if they're insects or lizards?" Reese made a face.

"Then we'll find a way to communicate."

Marc joined them. "Find anything?"

Shaking her head, Elena examined the wall. Nothing was this gray in its natural state. She tapped the surface, which had the texture of polished rock and was cool to the touch. Hearing whispers, she peered up but saw no movement. She scanned the ceiling rim for any way to climb. The walls were too smooth, too polished.

Hands shaking, Marc reached into his belt pack and held out a pack of cigarettes as if seeing it for the first time. "There has to be an exit. How else did we get here?"

"Transporter." Elena glanced at the rim. Someone was watching; she felt eyes on her.

"Aliens and transporters," Marc muttered as he fumbled with a cigarette.

Elena was worried. He never trembled like this before a mission. "Don't even think of lighting that," she said. "You have no idea what's flammable or what might explode." She grabbed his cigarettes, tossed the pack onto the gray floor, and crushed it beneath her clean leather boots. This was another puzzle. These weren't the magnetic boots she wore during the crash. "Besides, I thought you quit."

He held up his hands. "I swear these aren't mine. I have no idea how they got into my pack."

Elena walked the perimeter with Reese, examining the smooth walls and the ceiling rim from every angle. "They could have technologies to cure disease. And think how quickly we could colonize planets to relieve population pressures on Earth."

Marc crossed the cave floor to join them. He took a deep breath and grinned, which came across as a thin veneer. "If these aliens are benevolent, why keep us penned up here?"

Elena recalled her father's game. "If we brought an alien species to Earth, we would first observe to see how they adapted to our atmosphere, how hostile they were, and whether they brought diseases before meeting them."

"Then what?" Marc asked. Since he hadn't trained for space travel, no one had briefed him on mission protocols, including those pertaining to encountering other species.

Elena noticed faint shadows that moved along the wall across from them and vanished. "We're being observed," she whispered. "We should be on our best behavior."

Marc spun around, reaching for a sidearm he didn't have. "We need to watch each other's backs."

"Stay calm." Elena said. Marc's erratic behavior had to be more than caffeine and lack of sleep. Maybe something in the air they were breathing brought this on. If so, somehow it had the opposite effect on her.

Marc sucked in a deep breath. "You have no idea what they're planning for us."

"Neither do you. We're their guests." Elena turned her face toward the sky rim and called out, "We've come a long way. We're hungry. Can you provide us food and water?"

"Right," Marc said, "What if we are the food?"

"Chewed mood food." A high-pitched girl's voice reverberated off the walls.

Reese covered her ears. Elena looked for the source of the sound.

"Show yourself!" Marc struck a fighter's stance.

"Show yourself, throw yourself, bet you cannot grow yourself." Giggling resonated all around.

"Can you help us?" Elena said.

The shrill laughter rang louder, mocking them.

Elena spotted a shadow and whispered, "At my two o'clock."

"Two o'clock, crow the cock, time just flies, oh what a shock." Giggling resumed.

When the shadow moved, Marc tore after it. Elena and Reese followed. Marc paused at the wall. Then the wall absorbed him, like a marble pushed into Silly Putty. Elena poked at the wall and ran her hand across its slick surface, finding no gap. She tapped on the gray rock, which felt solid.

Marc emerged nearby. It was an optical illusion, a hologram. Elena sank her hand into the wall and struggled to reconcile the illusion of feeling her arm as it disappeared. *How clever.*

"Come on," Marc said. "She's getting away."

He took her hand and led the way into the rock. Darkness enveloped Elena. Even the entrance shed no illumination, as if the hologram could absorb the cave's light. As Marc pulled her through, Elena wondered about the source of the mocking shadow.

>====>

After twenty paces, Elena stumbled out of the tunnel into a wide-open space. Bright lights from above blinded her. A glowing brilliance covered the ceiling and filtered down over a vast cavern perhaps a mile long.

Air wafted with sweet fragrances of flowers, pine needles, and vegetation of almost every sort she might expect on Earth. Here, green ivy covered the gray walls. In a valley spread out before her, conifers, elms, and palms clustered together. Greens were deeper shades of jungle forest and yellows brighter floral delights than anything she remembered on Earth.

On the left stood a cluster of tall cacti that reminded Elena of her former home in New Mexico. This was a living paradise in a light gravity environment, far more than she could have hoped to find. Whoever transported them and created this fantastic ecosystem had to be very advanced. Interacting with them might be like Neanderthals meeting twenty-first century humans.

Marc tugged Elena's arm. "Come on. We have a phantom to catch."

The high-pitched voice responded in singsong from behind a hedge of thick yews. Marc sprinted toward the sound.

Reese nudged Elena. "Do you think it's safe?"

"This seems to be her world," Elena said. "If we scare her, she might not guide or help us."

From up ahead came the sound of rushing water, a chirping bird, crickets, and someone whispering above them. She studied the glowing sky, much larger than in the first cave, with only a black line separating the gray walls from the light.

Marc returned, out of breath. "Come on, you're letting her escape."

"And you're frightening her. I have a better idea." Elena's lips were as parched as the desert on her left. She headed toward rushing water, parted a tangle of reeds, and knelt in a clearing by a stream six feet wide. It vanished into tall grass on her right; to her left, it disappeared under a wooden bridge.

Marc caught up. "Don't drink. It could be contaminated."

Something resembling goldfish swam nearby. "It might taste different," Elena said, "but this is the only water we've found." Elena scooted to a slab of gray rock for a closer look. The water appeared clear and didn't smell foul. It carried none of the chlorine odor from the first cave.

"Wait!" Marc pulled her away from the edge.

Frustrated, Elena tugged at his arm. When she couldn't break his grip, she twisted and pushed, evidently too hard in this low-gravity environment, for he flipped into the water.

Cool liquid refreshed Elena's face; the moisture on her lips carried a hint of sweet flavor. As she leaned over to drink, a dark creature swam near where Marc treaded water. He saw it and thrashed his way to shore.

Elena helped him out of the water—and froze. Across the stream stood a wild-eyed girl, wiry, poised like an animal ready to flee. The girl's brown ponytail bobbed as she swayed side to side.

"Please don't go." Elena said.

The girl looked to be in her early to mid-teens, with a sweet, young face. Her ponytail dusted her bright-blue halter as she knelt and cupped her hand to the water. Her emerald eyes fixed on Elena. The girl's jeans looked like they'd been bought at a department store on Earth. *Are you human?*

Marc leapt to his feet. "What are you waiting for?"

"Waiting for, can't find door, hop around with a scare in store." The girl broke out laughing. She rose to her feet and cradled the water to her lips.

Marc approached the stream. The girl laughed harder as an eel-like creature slid by. Drawing back, he stumbled toward the wooden bridge. Reese hurried after him.

Elena remained. "Do you live here?"

"Here, there, and everywhere," the girl said in a singsong.

"My name's Elena. What's yours?"

"Tea for two, down the flue, mother left me for the zoo."

"Shall I call you Tea?" Elena said.

The girl darted away.

Marc appeared across the stream, out of breath. "Could you help?"

Reese joined him. It disturbed Elena how the shuttle's navigator followed Marc's orders, since he wasn't her boss or even part of the crew. On the other hand, Reese wasn't doing well after the crash and the loss of her fiancée.

Elena hurried across the bridge. She headed toward the far end of the long cave and the sound of falling water. Scanning plants along the way, she identified nothing edible. So where did Tea find food?

Frantic rustling came from behind some yellow forsythia as Marc chased his phantom. Elena followed a different path around the bushes. To her right, a fifteen-foot waterfall emerged from the gray rock face. No bridge crossed the stream, which spanned the cave and flowed along the wall to her left. Across the stream was higher ground. The shadow darted from behind the waterfall.

Elena approached a narrow path, crossed behind the falls, and spotted Tea atop the hill. Emerald eyes stared back. The girl's body was poised to spring. *Are you welcoming or setting a trap?*

Tea darted away. Elena followed, yet when she reached the hilltop, she stood alone. Glancing back, she saw Reese across the stream.

"Wait there," Elena called out.

She moved along the ivy-covered gray wall as it narrowed into a dead end with no gaps. Remembering the first cave, Elena worked her way back along the wall and almost missed it—an opening in the rock that she couldn't see.

She pushed through the masked opening.

FOUR

Elena closed her eyes and counted eighteen paces before the dark tunnel ended. She emerged from darkness into a well-lit cave similar to the first, except...

A white picket fence surrounded a two-story colonial that looked familiar. Rows of vegetable crops filled the space on the left. To the right were fruit trees: apples, oranges, cherries, peaches, and pears. She froze. The fresh fruit was tempting, but this was too good to be true.

The girl emerged from the front doorway, stepped aside, and waved her arms to invite Elena to enter.

The previous cave, which Elena thought of as Paradise Cave for its bounty of vegetation, didn't compare to what now lay before her. She wondered if this was a holographic illusion like the cave entrances.

No, she'd smelled the flowers and tasted the water in Paradise Cave. That was real. This was a cruel joke: the very house where she'd grown up. She inhaled the sweet fragrance of orange blossoms. Nearby were ripe tomatoes and tall beanstalks like those she'd harvested with her father the summer before he left on his mission to Jupiter. Her mother had been so distraught after his spacecraft crashed that she'd sold their home. Then Elena's brother, Leo, committed suicide and their mom died in grief. Elena had never returned to that home.

She glanced back for Marc and Reese and didn't see them. She was alone.

Elena hungered to reunite with family memories. This house's roof didn't bow, and the shutters and fence didn't need paint. Other than that, this was her childhood home. The setting reminded her of Ray Bradbury's *The Martian Chronicles*, a story about aliens who read thoughts and created a virtual reality. *If so, then who is Tea?*

Elena crossed the threshold. *This can't be real.*

The living room looked like her childhood home the night her father had left. A tapestry depicting Columbus' voyage hung over the sofa. Above the fireplace floated the image of Navarov planting the UN flag on the Moon.

Every detail was exact, right down to a man resembling her father sitting in his armchair, poised to regale her with exploits of his latest mission. The man before her was much older, his smile tinged with sadness. "Come, my daughter."

The frail man pointed to her favorite chair and a pitcher of pink lemonade. "It's wonderful to see you. There's much to say and little time." He reached out to her. His hand twitched and dropped onto the armrest as if even that simple effort exhausted him.

Elena studied the wrinkled face. "You're not my father. Are you the one in charge?" The aroma of peanut butter cookies made Elena's mouth water, though she didn't see the actual cookies. It had been two days since she'd had any nutrition other than the hibernation IV. She bit her tongue, hoping pain would bring this into focus.

"Being in charge, higher than sarge, rarely around and not very large."

Elena turned to face the slender brunette. "Are you in charge?"

Tea ran upstairs.

"You'll have to excuse her," the old man said, his eyes fluttering. "Thelma is a special child. As you get to know her, you'll find she's a remarkable young lady." He held out his wrinkled hand, touched hers, and tapped with his index finger.

The door flew open and Marc barged in, dripping wet. "You okay?" He wiped his feet and moved closer.

Reese stumbled in behind him, still looking shell-shocked by all that had happened. Whatever helped Elena remain calm wasn't working for the navigator, whose skin-tight uniform clung to her body. Her streaked hair dripped water onto the hardwood floors. The bags under her eyes looked ghoulish.

Elena pulled away from the old man and took a deep breath to let go some of her tension. "There was a dry path."

"You could have told us." Marc stepped closer. "Who's the old man and where's the girl?"

"I asked Thelma to fetch you," said the frail man. Then he raised his voice. "And bring something to eat." He reached toward Elena; again, his arm slumped onto the armrest. Even in the light gravity, this was too much for him.

"Thanks for your hospitality." Marc shook the man's hand. "Can you tell us how to get back to Earth?"

The old man shook his head. "No one leaves. I've been here eighteen years."

"This can't be real," Elena said, staring at pictures over the fireplace of her. A chessboard at the man's elbow looked like the setup eighteen years ago, the night she ran off. She fought off the memories. "Who built this place?"

"They call themselves Knoonk," the old man said, his weary eyes fixed on Elena. He seemed to be having trouble keeping his eyes open. "They've monitored Earth for thousands of years and were content to leave us alone. We kept sending probes. I've watched you these past eighteen years—getting your PhD, becoming a fine scientist, and single-handedly pushing for a new mission to Jupiter." He squeezed Elena's hand with a weak grip, and squeezed again. "I've prayed that you would avoid my foolishness, but you were born to explore, my daughter."

"Where are the Knoonk?" Marc asked. "Maybe they can help us get home."

"They rarely show themselves, and only here," the old man said. "I have no idea where they live." He squeezed her hand again, several times.

Disturbed by the connection she was beginning to feel, Elena placed the man's hand back on the armrest. To challenge the old man's similarities to her dad, she withdrew a crumpled picture of her father from her waist pack. If someone wanted to pluck her memories to create a virtual reality, why make him so much older? "Daddy?"

Marc touched her arm. "Come on, Elena. Your dad died eighteen years ago."

Elena considered the facts. Her father had been on a collision course with Jupiter when Houston lost contact with his spacecraft.

He couldn't have survived that crash, yet she couldn't have survived her crash, either. "How have you watched me?"

With difficulty, the old man craned his neck and moved his hand closer to hers. "The Knoonk tapped into your wireless comlink."

"Then we can send word to be rescued," Marc said. "Where's your network connection?"

"It doesn't work that way," the old man said. "I can only watch. The Knoonk won't let me transmit."

"What can you tell us about the Knoonk?" Marc asked. "What do they look like?"

"They're a lot like us, bipedal, technological."

Nearby was the plaster sculpture of an eagle Elena had made before he left, decked with a silver necklace and a turquoise stone like the one her mom had. Her dad must have snuck it on his mission. This was the fate worse than death that she'd cursed on him. For years, she'd suffocated under a blanket of guilt that her curse had caused his death. Here he was alive, watching what happened to his family—his son dead and his wife dying of heartbreak. Elena touched his arm. He felt real.

"Think about it," Marc said. "This can't be your father."

The old man shook his head. "I wanted to warn you to cancel your mission. There was no way to send a message."

Elena searched for a way to verify what she saw, heard, smelled, and felt as if this might be one of her most vivid nightmares, or maybe a near-death experience. Thelma didn't fit any of those possibilities.

Still dripping onto the wood floor, Reese trembled like a cornered mouse. Marc paced. Confronting someone who might be her father, Elena barely knew where to start.

"Why did they crash our shuttle?" she asked.

The old man's eyes darkened. He seemed to shrink into his chair. "They feared you would find their outpost. That was why they captured me, why they've doomed every probe sent out this way."

"Why not take me?" Elena asked. "Why kill the others? They were heading for our Moon base."

The old man shrugged. He looked up and blinked rapidly. She looked away.

On a nearby table rested James Fenimore Cooper's *The Last of the Mohicans*. Even here, her dad maintained his quaint practice of reading paper books. "My mission was to figure out why all our satellites to Jupiter had failed and try to repair some of them," he said. "The Knoonk made sure I failed because my mission could have detected their presence."

"Are you sure?" Elena asked.

"The Knoonk admitted as much. Afterwards the opponents of the space program shut it down. Your mission failure will halt the program for another ten years, delaying discovery of the Knoonk."

"What exactly do they want from us?" Marc asked.

"They want to remain hidden," the old man said.

"They've held you prisoner all this time?" Elena asked. The special love she'd held for her father began to attach to this old man. "How inhumane."

"Elena, think," Marc said. "There's no way your father could still be alive."

"Let me handle this." Elena stared at a framed press photo that sat beside her father; a photo taken two days ago as she departed Earth. "How have you coped?"

"It wasn't so bad," the old man said, squeezing her hand.

His index finger tapped several times, as if sending code, and then his arm slumped onto the armrest. "I regret not sharing your life," he said. "When my ship crashed, I didn't expect to see you again. They let me watch you grow into a strong, wonderful woman." His voice caught. When he swallowed, it looked as if his Adam's apple would punch out. "After your mom died, I had a daughter here with the only other survivor, Natalie." Elena knew her as a crewmember on her father's mission.

"Thelma?" Elena asked.

His jowls pulsed as he chuckled. "She's your half-sister. She's thirteen and every bit as hyper as you were."

"I have a sister?"

"She's been a treasure to a weary old man."

He took Elena's hand again and this time pressed his thumb into her palm, a warning of sorts. His finger tapped out several short and long strokes, Morse code. Then he slumped back in his seat and closed his eyes. The letters spelled out 'e-v-i.'

Elena moved closer and smelled cherry pipe tobacco in his clothes. She stopped cold. Only immediate family knew he smoked a cherry blend. She couldn't find a single flaw. Except for being two decades older, he was the father she'd lost and missed for too many years. He'd even been the one to teach her Morse code. What was he trying to say?

"You need to hold on for your daughter's sake," Elena said. *Did I mean myself, or Thelma?* She didn't want to believe but already she felt a strong attachment.

"I'm tired," the old man said. His eyes narrowed into slits and he blinked as he talked. "Our hosts keep me alive with their marvelous medicine. They can only do so much. I haven't the strength to carry on. Thelma needs more than I can give her." This time he spelled out 'e-v-i-l."

"What about her mother?"

"She died eight years ago. They couldn't save her."

A cloak of responsibility engulfed Elena. After her father disappeared, she'd felt the same need to protect her brother, Leo. She'd failed him. She'd been too absorbed in her own pain to see how suicidal Leo had become. She looked toward the stairs and caught a glimpse of Thelma before the girl hid herself. Elena returned her attention to the old man and his message. She blinked out 'w-h-o.'

Eyes nestled deep within his wrinkled brow grew red and puffy, swelling shut. Again, he reached for her. He couldn't hold up his arm. "I wanted to see you. I never wanted you brought here."

"Dad?" Elena touched his arm and felt a stronger bond. She tapped out on his forearm her question.

"Heartless old creep, in very deep, little old man talks in his sleep."

The old man turned to Thelma. "I'm sorry, honey." Then he reached for Elena and tapped out 'k-n-o-o.' "The Knoonk heard me call for you in my sleep. You and Thelma are all I have. Soon you'll be all she has."

Elena blurted out, "You can't drop a sister on me and leave."

"Drop a sister, pop a blister, soon you'll leave me just like mister."

"I'm sorry Tea ... Thelma. I'm not angry with you. It's just a shock."

A cauldron of fear, anger, and hurt swirled across Thelma's young face. Elena couldn't abandon her as she had Leo. That responsibility crossed over. With it came resentment. She took a deep breath. "Thelma. That's a beautiful name." Elena reached for the girl's hand. Thelma withdrew toward the stairs.

"I'm not upset with you," Elena said. "Please understand. They kidnapped us. It's so sudden, and we can't leave."

Thelma's eyes scrunched up and she crouched into a fight-or-flight stance.

Elena reached for her sister's hand. "Thelma, please talk to me."

"She only talks in rhymes," her father said. "It's her way of communicating."

"I'm sorry," Marc said, "but I don't plan on spending the rest of my life here. What can you tell us about the Knoonk?"

"They leave us alone, providing what we need as long as we cooperate. They won't let you go. Already you know too much; you know they exist."

Reese approached the old man. For an instant, her eyes showed clarity, as if she woke up and remembered something. "Are there other caves where other survivors could be—where my Howard could be?"

"After my crash, I woke in this cave with broken legs," the old man said, the swelling in his eyes going down. "The Knoonk transported me to a medical facility where they fixed me up, but my legs weren't the same."

"Have you been to the cave with the desert and the stream?" Elena asked.

Her father laughed. "At first I explored it. In time I've grown weaker and can't get around."

With that news, Reese's eyes clouded over.

Elena knelt next to her father. Cherry aroma filled her nostrils. "Were there others?"

"Only Natalie and me," her father said, touching Elena's arm. He tapped out more letters before his arm dropped: 'k-e-v-i-l,' K evil. "Thelma joined us, and now you."

"What are the Knoonk like?" Elena asked.

"Like us," her father said. He tried to blink and went into blinking spasms. "They—" His left arm stiffened; his jaw locked. His eyes bulged, and his head slumped against his chair.

Holding his head, Elena felt his pulse racing. "How can I help?"

The attack ceased; his body relaxed. "I'm okay." His eyes betrayed this claim. They were puffy and filled with pain. He reached for her hand and tried to use his index finger to mark out another message. His hand cramped and he pulled it to his chest.

Elena wrapped her arms around him. "Are we really on Europa?" she whispered into his ear.

His body stiffened. "Focus on the gravity of your situation." His voice trailed off.

Marc butted in. "Excuse me. How can we talk to our hosts?"

Her father turned toward Marc. "Empty your hearts of anger. They offer food, supplies, and use of the com-link. It's not a bad place to retire." He managed to tap out on Elena's arm: 'n-o.'

"I'm not interested in retiring," Marc said. "This place sounds like hell."

"There's no escape, no way to the surface, no ship, and no way to communicate with Earth." The old man said this as if reading a script. "All I can offer is my home. After you get to know our hosts, they can change the environment to suit you, though not if you threaten them." Her father stared past her, his eyes almost swollen shut. He twitched but in no pattern that made any sense.

His coded messages and looking past her were his way of warning her. *The Knoonk are watching, sizing us up, and they may be evil.* The last bit ran counter to the first contact game she'd played with her father. Elena would have to use every opportunity to sort that out and to make them pay for her father's suffering. She realized he hadn't moved much since she arrived. His legs had withered. He was small and frail.

He coughed with difficulty. "It's time." He said it with emotional detachment as if describing an object on the shelf.

Thelma looked ready to bolt, so Elena went to the stairs, took her hand, and pulled her next to their father. This time Thelma didn't refuse.

"Promise to care for Thelma," their father said between shallow breaths.

"I promise. Please don't go. I'm sorry I ran off that night. I couldn't bear you leaving again."

"It's okay, hon." He smiled and for a moment, his puffy eyes lost their grim look. "I didn't blame you. If anything, I blamed myself for the misery it caused you, Leo, and your mom. I'm glad to see you again, just not under these circumstances. Promise you'll care for your sister as you cared for Leo during our trip to the Huntsville Space Academy."

Nodding, Elena turned to Thelma. "If you follow me, I'll take care of you." The words flew out before Elena could consider the commitment, or the responsibility.

Thelma threw her arms around Elena's neck and clung with a tight grip.

Elena hugged the girl. Their father's pending death must have weighed heavily. Thelma would have contemplated the dismal prospect of living alone in the only home she knew. *You must be terrified.*

Reese touched Elena's arm. "I'll help in any way I can."

Marc placed his hand on Elena's shoulder. "You can count on me."

"Right now I need friendship," Elena said. "No strings."

Marc nodded. "I understand."

"You two need to stop bickering," her father said. "Family is everything. It took me too long to realize that. I've watched you two bumbling about, pretending you don't need each other."

Elena was stunned. She knew her father's outburst pointed at her. She took a deep breath and held her father's arm. He appeared too weak to send any more coded messages. Then it hit her. Leo wasn't with them during their trip to the Huntsville Academy. She and her dad had traveled to visit him. She stared into the old man's swollen eyes. His other arm reached toward her. His mouth opened. His eyes flickered. He fell back, limp. The message about Leo was another coded message not to trust the Knoonk.

She buried her face in his shirt and wept. It had to be him, warning her in the coded languages they'd used when they didn't want Mom to catch on. She tried to send him Morse code, but couldn't find a pulse. He wasn't breathing and she had no way to help him.

Elena clung to her father, seething with anger that the Knoonk had separated him from his family. At least she got the chance to say goodbye this time. She'd become so like him. Now she had a piece of him to cherish.

She placed Thelma's hand on their father's arm. "Forgive an old man who knew he was dying."

A quaint smile crossed Thelma's lips. "The piper is paid; your fingers can wade in cookies and lemonade."

That odd reaction brought a smile to Elena's lips. Then reality sank in.

FIVE

Elena hugged Thelma and studied her father. She considered and discarded one hypothesis after another to account for their surviving the crash and the subsequent discoveries: the wondrous caves, her childhood home, and her father.

Logic said this was an illusion, yet in her heart, she knew. It wasn't what matched but what didn't that convinced her. He was older and frail. The house was newer and in better repair. Moreover, he'd reversed the chess game with her to play his role, no doubt a reference to needing to take care of Thelma. Elena resented having that responsibility thrust on her, but Thelma had no one else.

Elena missed her father again. For years, she'd prayed to be able to beg for his forgiveness. Now she felt relieved, empty, and angry that they were stuck on a strange world and she couldn't even trust that she knew which one: the gravity of their situation.

She wiped a tear from her cheek. Before she could indulge her need to learn about their hosts, she needed to give her father a proper burial. The ache to honor him swelled up until her heart wanted to burst. Burying required a casket and tools to dig, which might require help from the aliens.

Elena studied Thelma; her sister stared back. Elena sensed other eyes watching them.

"Okay, ladies," Marc said. "Let's put our heads together and sort out our options."

"Really?" Elena caught herself before she said something that might spook Thelma.

The girl moved away. Elena held her sister's hand. "We need to bury Dad," Elena said. "Do you understand?"

Eyes watering, Thelma looked past Elena. When she opened her mouth to speak, no words formed. Elena clasped Thelma's other hand.

"Okay," Marc said. "We need tools. Where do you keep those?"

Elena held her gaze on Thelma. She saw her father's eyes in the girl. "To bury Dad, we need to contact our hosts. Can you help?"

Thelma's head floated back and forth in childlike nonchalance.

Marc drew nearer. "Ask her where they keep the tools to tend the garden."

Thelma withdrew further. Elena held tight and rotated to shield her sister from Marc. "Help me bury Dad."

"Okay." Marc turned away. "Reese, let's find some tools." He led Reese outside.

Elena let go of Thelma's hands. "Promise you won't run."

Thelma stared, not blinking, almost as if she couldn't see. When Elena sat back on the sofa, Thelma sat across from her and cocked her head. Rather than talk, Elena looked for non-verbal cues. The girl didn't give much, yet her eyes flicked up for a split second. *Cameras?* Thelma darted upstairs.

Marc burst into the room followed by Reese. "The ground is solid rock," he said. "The garden is shallow. There's no tool shed. So how did they plant the garden?"

Elena stood up. "After building these caves, a garden would be child's play."

"Speaking of which, we need answers from the girl." Marc headed for the stairs.

Elena blocked him. "Leave Thelma to me."

Nodding, Marc reached for Elena's hand. "Then please talk to her. Find out what we're up against." He lowered his voice to a whisper. "Do you think ... I mean, since we're stuck here together..."

"No!" Elena backed up the stairs. "I said friends only, and I meant it."

His shoulders sagged. "I didn't mean to upset you. I was just thinking about what your father said."

"Oh, so now you agree that he's my father?"

"Yes." Marc raised his hands. "We'll give you and Thelma some time alone. Reese, let's hunt for some tools." He turned to leave.

"Wait," Elena said. "That came out harsher than I meant. We're all on edge. If we manage to get back to Earth, we'll revisit everything. Okay? I promise."

"Thanks," Marc said. He held the door open. Reese shook her head and followed him.

From the living room window, Elena watched Marc lead Reese out of the cave. Even though she and Marc often fought, mostly over her career, Elena still cared. The hurt in his eyes tore at her. For him, life was simple: meet girl, settle down, and start family. Elena didn't want to worry every moment whether someone dependent on her would come to harm, as Leo had. She hadn't found the right time or place to share that with Marc.

Elena headed upstairs, looking for Thelma and found an open window. Elena ran to it and gazed outside. Thelma was running toward the tunnel entrance.

Elena leaned out the window. "Thelma, don't go."

Thelma stopped and turned.

By the time Elena reached the front step, Thelma had retreated to a cluster of orange trees. The girl tossed an orange to Elena and picked another. Ripping open the fruit, Elena inhaled the sweet fragrance. Biting into the orange filled her mouth with syrupy juice. She wolfed it down and didn't stop until she was gnawing on the peel.

Elena glanced at the sky rim. If Thelma couldn't give answers except in her nonsense rhymes, maybe Elena would have to look up there.

From the house, she dragged out the dining table, coffee table, and both end tables, which she stacked against the cave wall. She scrambled up the wobbly arrangement, aided by the light gravity. When she reached the top, she peered up. The ledge was still too far away. She clawed at rock, but her hands found no purchase in the smooth wall. Climbing down, Elena tumbled the last few feet, hit the ground, and rolled over.

"I just want to bury him." Her words echoed off the walls and faded.

Getting to her knees, Elena glanced up and froze. A small humanoid stood beside the vegetable garden. Her father had hinted that the Knoonk were evil, but Thelma approached the newcomer as a friend. Pale blue-gray tights hugged the alien's slender waist and covered what might have been breasts. The outfit covered all but two gray hands, a pair of feet, and a head the color of the walls. Except for its grayish color, lack of hair, and the ridge crest on its forehead, this being could have passed for a young woman.

Thelma bowed and bobbed her head left to right. "Father's dead, not in bed, now it's time to rest his head." Her words seemed far too cheerful for someone who'd lost her father, her only human companion. Her sad eyes didn't match that joy.

The gray oval head nodded. "His time." The sparse gray mouth barely moved as it spoke in guttural tones. The sound also had a nasal quality behind a miniscule nose.

"His time?" Elena clenched her fists to control her outrage. She didn't want to begin first contact on a hostile note. "He's only sixty."

"You wish to grieve?" Narrow eyes betrayed no emotion. Elena would have to work hard to understand these beings.

She lowered her head. "It's customary to have a funeral and bury him. Can you transport us to Earth so we can do this properly?"

"Dr. Pyetrov explained that you may not leave."

"You listened to our conversations?"

"It is efficient." Even the ears were diminutive on the sides of the hairless gray head.

"Why can't we leave?" Elena inched closer. She kept her head down, trying not to appear threatening.

"You must have children and families as you would on Earth." Beneath the tight-fitting outfit, the alien's slender arms and legs appeared almost anorexic. "Shall we mummify or recycle?"

"He deserves burial."

"Mummify, plummify, stick around and you'll zombify."

Elena approached the alien. "If you can't bury him here, please send us home."

Thelma danced, hopped, and skipped in tight circles around her sister. "Mummify, bumbify, say you naught if you dumbify." She bumped into Elena, twirled, and became more erratic with each turn.

"I don't want to cause problems," Elena said, "but you kidnapped him and held him prisoner. You owe him a proper burial."

Thelma dropped to the ground, convulsing. She croaked, as if choking.

"Can you handle or shall I help her?" the stranger asked.

Dropping to her knees, Elena placed one hand under Thelma's head, turned her sister on her side, and held her close, hoping the seizure would stop. Her father had neglected to mention this aspect of being "special."

Thelma's muscles relaxed. A barely-audible utterance reverberated against Elena's chest cavity. "Mmmmm." Thelma went limp, yet she was still breathing.

"Shall I medicate?" the alien asked.

"No! I'll manage." Elena glanced up. "Why can't we bury—" Her throat closed.

"Body putrefies unless we mummify. Or we can recycle and put body to use."

Elena released Thelma and stood. "I choose mummify. When can we start?"

The alien pointed her slender arm toward the back of the cave. For an instant, the ground glowed, a flash of light or plasma almost like a halo. Where there had been gray rock, a rectangular opening appeared thanks to some kind of technological magic.

Elena approached the hole. It seemed about six feet deep. At the bottom lay a casket with cherry-stained wood and gold trim, the same style they'd used eighteen years ago, except that one had been empty.

Fighting tears, Elena asked, "Is … is Dad in there?"

"He is," the alien said with a head nod. "Shall I cover?"

Thelma stood up and approached Elena.

Elena's gut churned from the memories of eighteen years ago and today. "Give us a moment, please."

Fighting the temptation to run into the house to check if her father was still there, Elena studied the alien's vacant eye slits. She wanted to understand the technology that dug this hole, but she couldn't stop the flood of emotion at seeing her father again, watching him die, and attending another funeral. It seemed appropriate to bury him with his dream of extraterrestrials, yet she wanted to take him home and lay him beside her mom and brother.

Thelma took her hand.

Elena sucked in a deep breath. A tear slid down her cheek. She wiped it and looked down at the casket. "Heavenly Father."

The alien watched like a statue, no movement, not even an eye blink.

To keep from breaking down, Elena studied the alien's hoof-like feet capped with a toe ridge. "Do you have a name?" She returned her attention to the casket at the bottom of the hole.

"Nalon Krok. Finished?"

"No." Elena placed her hands together in prayer, which Thelma copied. "Heavenly Father. Nalon Krok, Thelma Pyetrov, and Elena Pyetrov are gathered to pay last respects to Dr. Alexander Pyetrov and ask you to take him." She spoke about what a good man her father had been and of his tireless pursuit of knowledge, all the good things she remembered about him. She took a deep breath and could almost smell the cherry pipe tobacco.

Then she glanced at Nalon. "Thank you. It's time to cover him."

In a flash like the one that created the burial site, the hole filled with gray rock, leaving no evidence of the grave. A glow lingered for an instant and vanished. It happened so fast, it lacked the satisfaction Elena had hoped for, the closure that she needed. Anger rose up inside her that she'd gotten a chance to see her father again only to lose him.

Still, she was face to face with an alien her father had come to know. That brought her back to her youthful games with her father and learning about first contact. The only thing that came to mind for creating and filling the burial site was a transporter like what had brought them to the dry cave after the shuttle crashed.

She glanced back at the house, as if her father might get up and walk out to greet her and continue their first contact discussions. He couldn't; she'd watched him die. Now she felt a stronger connection to the grave than to the house. Her head was ready to explode over the crash, seeing him, and meeting an alien. Steeling her nerve, she tried to concentrate on connecting with their hosts. "Can you show me how you do this?" She swept her arm toward the smooth gray rock of the burial site.

"Maybe someday."

Thelma spun around in a dance. Elena turned to see Marc and Reese returning from the tunnel with bundles of sticks.

"How can I speak with you again?" Elena asked the alien.

Thelma fell to the ground, muscles twitching.

Dropping to her knees, Elena comforted her sister. Marc dropped the sticks, stumbled, and ran between Elena and the alien. Nalon stood, frozen to the spot.

Midstride, Marc's body convulsed. He fell spread-eagle onto the gray cave floor. Nalon stepped around the body, holding a tube the size of a pen. The alien pointed the device at Marc. An electric spark arced toward the middle of Marc's back; he twitched as if having a seizure.

"Stop, please." Elena set Thelma down and crawled to Marc.

His muscles stopped twitching. He stared up, displaying more terror than defiance. Like Thelma, he curled into the fetal position, which made Elena wonder if the aliens had tortured her sister— evil.

Nalon stepped aside. "Violence will not be tolerated. You must settle down and have children. If you behave, we will supply your needs."

"That's not how it's done," Elena said.

"It is required."

"And if we don't?"

"You will," Nalon said. She vanished in a blue flash.

SIX

Elena knelt between Marc and Thelma, while Reese shuffled over. Two days earlier, Elena had been anxious and hopeful. Now she wasn't sure what to expect. They needed time to recover, but things were happening too fast, tearing her between grieving for her father, the implications of taking responsibility for Thelma, and understanding the alien world.

She despaired at Nalon's disappearance. Their transporter capability was beyond anything Elena had imagined. Her inability to talk to their hosts was infuriating.

Marc got to his feet, spun around, and fixed his gaze on Thelma, still curled up on the floor. He looked like a wounded animal anticipating another attack.

Elena held her sister. "I'll protect you," she whispered and glared up at Marc. "What were you thinking?"

"They kidnapped us." He spun around, still searching for danger. His hands twitched. "I didn't want it hurting you."

"They spared us."

"Maybe, but you let our first real alien escape."

"Guys!" Reese looked as if dragged through hell. "Let's work together."

Thelma's body relaxed. Elena set her down and stood up. "Our host helped bury Dad."

"You had the funeral without us?" Marc's shoulders sagged.

"Nalon offered to assist." Elena helped Thelma up and sheltered her from Marc.

44

"You're on a first-name basis?" Marc took a deep breath and offered Elena his confident look, which wore thin with his lack of sleep. "As senior military officer, I'm in charge of getting us out of here."

Elena folded her arms. "Then try to build better relations. We need our hosts in order to survive."

Marc nodded. "You're right, but please include me whenever you communicate with them again." He drew closer.

Elena backed up to protect Thelma.

"Did you get the girl to talk?" Marc asked.

Thelma ran into the house. Reese followed her.

"It'll take time," Elena said. "She lost her father. Her world is changing."

"We don't have time." Marc glanced over his shoulder.

"Maybe the mission is way off course, but we came to learn."

"Our first priority is to warn our government."

"Warn them of what?" she asked, though she shared his sentiment.

"Let's find a way to communicate," Marc said. "Maybe your sister can show us that communicator your father mentioned. We have a job to do."

A headache formed behind Elena's eyes. "What job? You didn't just happen onto my shuttle, did you?"

Marc touched her hand. "I couldn't miss sharing the greatest mission of our generation with you."

She withdrew. "Don't BS me. You've been against this from the start. Then you sign on. Someone wanted you to keep an eye on me. Senator Jorgensen?"

"Don't get any wild ideas."

"She did, didn't she? That bitch." Elena advanced. "What were your orders?"

He backed up. "I ... you know I can't tell you."

"You'll gamble our relationship on that? Look around. We aren't going anywhere."

Marc sighed and closed his eyes. When he opened them, Elena glared back.

"Very well," he said. "I was to contain anything we found to prevent contamination of Earth."

She burst out laughing. "You still don't get it. You aren't in a position to contain or control anything."

Elena hurried into the house to look for Thelma. The girl wasn't downstairs or in her bedroom. If she had another attack, Elena wanted to be there to help. The bedroom began to spin. Elena braced herself against a dresser that looked like the one she'd had as a child.

With her field of vision narrowing, she moved toward the bed. Everything that had happened was catching up with her. She couldn't get over her father being alive all these years. She resented Marc's need to be in control and the thought of Jorgensen and Marc working together. Elena gripped the bed frame and slumped onto the mattress.

>===>

Commotion outside Thelma's window drew Elena's attention. Her sister stood by the tunnel entrance. Marc jogged and stumbled toward her, still adjusting to the lighter gravity.

Elena leaned out the window. "Don't touch her."

Marc glanced up. "Can you stop her nonsense?"

"More to come, not the sum, less to place within your tum."

"See what I mean!" Marc shouted.

Thelma darted past him and into the house.

Shadows appeared at the tunnel entrance. "There!" Elena pointed.

Two shuttle passengers wearing fresh transport uniforms emerged from the stark gray wall. Reese ran to greet the couple as they staggered along the path. "Is Howard with you? Have you seen Howard? Is he okay?"

Looking as if someone had dragged her through the desert, the woman passenger collapsed to the gray stone floor. Her male companion dropped to his knees to help her.

More passengers shuffled in wearing transport uniforms that showed none of the trauma of the crash, which was more than could be said of the occupants of those outfits. Four women and five men arrived in pairs and a threesome. They didn't appear to have physical wounds, though they staggered along the path as if none had slept in days.

Had it been that long? Elena checked her watch. No, it had been less than a day since the crash, maybe half a day given the earlier time distortion. She imagined that they, like her, would be hungry after two days in hibernation and their time here.

Elena hustled to the kitchen and brought bread, cheese, and

water to the newcomers. While Reese asked each for news on Howard, Marc helped the new arrivals to the front porch, grilling them on what had happened and whether they'd met the alien. None had.

Marc tried to help Wil Benning, the construction engineer. The big man pushed him away. "This is your fault. You took over and did something to the shuttle."

Marc backed away. "I had nothing to do with the crash or with this." He panned his arms out to take in the entirety of the cave.

One of the women Elena didn't know gave a similar description of the crash, ending up in a barren cave. Then Thelma appeared and led them here. Other passengers nodded in agreement.

Elena looked up at her sister in the window above, wondering what other secrets Thelma held and how to get her to talk. Thelma looked vulnerable and scared. The commotion was upsetting her quiet world.

While the newcomers ate and shared similar stories, Elena offered first aid. Amazingly, none of the new arrivals had any physical injuries from the crash, though they appeared traumatized and in shock.

"How did we get from the shuttle to the cave?" one of the women passengers asked, "and how do we get home?"

"What happened to the others?" another asked. "Are there more caves?"

"What do the aliens want?" a brunette asked, brushing frizzy hair from her face. "Will they send us home?"

Wil Benning pointed to Thelma, standing in the doorway. "Is she one of them?"

Elena decided not to explain her sister. It was more than they could handle. "She's one of us."

"How do we get to the Moon base?" Benning asked. "I worked hard for that assignment."

Elena decided to level with them on this. "We can't leave, because we know about their outpost. They promise us food and shelter if we settle down and don't make trouble."

"That's bull."

"Perhaps, but that's all we know," Elena said. The passengers' bedraggled faces betrayed their shock. So far, Reese was the only member of the crew to turn up.

"I say we hunt them down," Benning said. "Search cave by cave until we find them."

"Maybe there are other survivors," Reese said. She turned to Elena. "Find Thelma. Tell her to bring my Howard."

Elena hugged Reese and hurried into the house. By the time she got upstairs, her sister had escaped through an open bedroom window. Along the side of the house, the first couple to arrive picked apples.

"Stay away from the fruit," Marc yelled from the walkway. "Wait until we take inventory. We might need to ration."

From Thelma's bedroom window, Elena watched the couple disappear behind the house.

Marc stood in the clearing out front. "Everyone gather around."

Here we go again. In college, Marc had swept her up in his enthusiasm for doing things and going places—taking charge. She'd spent three years trying to convince herself she wasn't in love and the next eleven breaking it off whenever he got too serious. As usual, he stepped forward while others, including Elena, avoided the burden of responsibility.

When all except the couple had turned their attention to Marc, he climbed onto the porch to address them. "Until we have a better idea of what the aliens are up to, we should organize, gather resources, and learn to rely on ourselves. Who's with me?"

Eyes betraying shell shock, Barry Wellington was the first to raise his hand. A mouse-faced man barely taller than Elena, he'd been miffed because Elena hadn't invited him as lead microbiologist. No doubt, he was casting his lot with Marc to snub her.

While Marc sorted out leadership, Elena worried about Thelma. Her sister might know her cave surroundings, but she wasn't accustomed to strangers. Living with their father, she wouldn't have seen what competition under stress could do to people.

"In order to survive, we need to work together, all of us," Marc said, the last part louder for Elena's benefit. "My Marine training includes survival under extreme circumstances. We have military protocols to handle stressful situations. Follow me and I'll do my best for you."

Elena shook her head. Marc had no clue, yet people listened because he sounded confident and they wanted to believe. Reese was so distraught over losing Howard she would have followed the Easter Bunny.

When she looked out another window, Elena spotted tall, leggy Tara L'Enfant, the electronics engineer who had tried to talk Elena into making room for her on the long mission, and by accident got her wish. She hung on Marc's every word while glancing up at Elena. If Tara expected Elena to challenge him, she didn't understand Elena's aversion to the messy side of leadership.

Wil Benning stood on the gray path between Marc and the others. "He was at the controls when we crashed. He got us into this mess. We need new leadership."

The others moved to the side and looked to Marc, waiting for his response. They seemed drunk with exhaustion and resignation.

Elena searched the rest of the house for Thelma and the com-link her father had mentioned. She located neither. The second floor appeared like the one in her childhood home, right down to the women's clothing hanging in the master bedroom closet. That freaked her out. At least there weren't any of her mom's colorful Navajo outfits. These clothes probably belonged to Thelma's mom.

Elena withdrew to what would have been her room. None of the pictures, dolls, knickknacks or other personal items was hers. An empty space on the desk might have held the communications link. There was no sign of the device.

She glanced out the window in time to see the first couple head toward the exit, arms full of fruit and other food. She spun toward the hall, hoping to catch them before they left.

Scowling, Thelma blocked the door.

SEVEN

Elena stood aside to let Thelma enter. "I don't mean to pry. I was worried about you."

She placed a finger to her lips and led her sister down the creaky stairs. Looking confused, Thelma followed. By the time they reached the front porch, the couple was feeling around for the hidden tunnel entrance. Elena headed toward them.

"We should stick together," Marc yelled in Elena's direction. Then he addressed the others. "Let's inventory supplies. We'll make headquarters in the house. Reese, Wil, let's talk."

Elena turned to see Thelma bar the door, bracing herself against the frame.

Marc moved toward her. "Please step aside. We need to check supplies."

Elena intervened. "Don't touch her!"

"Please, Elena," Marc said. "We need an inventory so we can ration what we have. That's standard protocol."

She stared up at him. "Protocol? This is our father's home. You may only enter as our guests." She was surprised at how attached she felt to this place.

He sighed. "Okay. Can we use the house as guests? I don't plan to stay long." He motioned for Reese and Wil to go inside.

Reese hesitated. Wil climbed onto the porch.

Elena backed up toward the doorway with Thelma behind her. "You don't have permission."

"I've got this," Barry said. He ran around the back of the house.

Thelma hurried to intercept him. Elena glared at Marc. "Why are you doing this?"

Marc closed his bloodshot eyes for a moment. "I'm sorry." He lowered his voice. "Let's not fight over this. We're in a military situation. We need to control our limited resources."

"Take a deep breath," Elena said. "You're not thinking straight. The Knoonk supplied Dad and Thelma for eighteen years."

"You're too trusting."

"And Jorgensen sent you to sabotage my mission."

Marc's face reddened; he hung his head. "I never intended to hurt you. Promises made on Earth mean nothing out here. All I care about is protecting you and these people."

Thelma screamed and ran back to Elena's side. "Broke the door. Glass on floor..." She clung to Elena's arm.

"See what you've done!" Elena hugged her sister.

"I'm truly sorry, Elena, I am," Marc said. "We need to ration supplies. Wil, take inventory. Barry, check the garden." Marc held out his hand. "Please join me."

She backed away. "You have no right to desecrate Dad's home."

"Come on, Elena. This isn't your childhood home."

"I know, but it is Thelma's home."

Thelma tugged at Elena's arm and led her toward the stairs.

Leaving Marc, Elena followed her sister. "Can you show me the com-link?"

When they reached Thelma's bedroom, Elena looked more closely at the shelves: a single doll, gray rocks, and a 3D chess set. Elena examined a cube, wondering if it could be the Knoonk com-link. It lacked anything resembling a keyboard, screen, or communication device.

Beside the shelves were paintings done in broad strokes. The longer Elena looked, the more depression filled her, as if the painting could reach deep inside.

"Where's the com-link?" Elena asked.

Thelma grabbed a backpack from her closet, tossed some clothes inside, and headed for the doorway.

Elena blocked the way. "I see you play chess. So do I."

Thelma swung her backpack behind her in an arc that swept the chess set off the shelf and scattered her stones and doll across the wood floor. Then she jumped out the window, landed nimbly on her feet like a cat, and ran.

"Please don't go," Elena yelled.

Not wanting to take her eye off the girl, Elena climbed out the window, lowered herself until she was clinging by her fingertips, and dropped. She landed on her feet and rolled to her side, a soft landing. When she looked up, Thelma lingered by the tunnel entrance, waiting.

Elena ran and joined her sister. "Do you want to talk?" she whispered.

Thelma led the way into the tunnel. Elena felt her way in darkness along the cool walls and into the burst of light inside Paradise Cave. Thelma ran toward the back of the cave, to the dead-end. Elena followed and glanced around, hoping to find the couple who had snuck off. They were gone or in hiding.

Leaving the rest of the shuttle survivors made Elena anxious. Her growing attachment to Thelma harkened back to her own losses: her father, her brother, and her mother. Elena's only other relative, Uncle Donald, couldn't stand the way she reminded him of his brother.

Elena focused on her scientific quest. "These are magnificent caves," she said when she caught up with her sister. "Do you know how they were made?" They were too smooth for natural formations.

Thelma tilted her head toward Elena. "Caves, waves, slaves."

"Slaves? What about our hosts?"

Thelma scurried up the sheer cave wall, grabbing at handholds Elena couldn't see. It seemed this was another holographic illusion. The girl disappeared into the rock wall eight feet above the ground. Elena ran her hand over cool gray stone and couldn't find the handholds Thelma had used.

She glanced toward the tunnel to Father's Cave and up to where her sister had vanished. Thelma's hand reached down from the hidden opening. Elena explored the smooth rock-face above her until her hand grasped a hidden crevice below Thelma's hand. Elena rubbed her palm across the smooth wall until she located another. Hand-over-hand and foot-over-foot, she inched her way up the wall. With her sister's help, Elena scooted up into a dark tunnel, just big enough to allow her to crawl. In the inky darkness, surrounded by cool rock, there was only one way to go.

After some twenty paces along a rough, gritty pathway, she squinted at a brilliant sky of light. This cavern was the size of Father's Cave with a dark rim between the bright ceiling and gray walls. Along the sides of the cave stood fruit trees and rows of tomatoes, corn, and beans.

"Do things grow year-round?" Elena asked.

Thelma headed toward the back of the cave to a small boxy white house. Elena followed. Inside, her sister danced in tight circles through the four modest rooms of the sparsely furnished home. The furniture looked Early American, cut from large, rough logs unlike any of the trees in Paradise Cave.

"Is this your house?" Elena asked.

Thelma hurried outside. Elena ran to catch up and stumbled in the light gravity. She tried longer strides, regained her balance, and almost caught Thelma before the girl scampered up the wall like a monkey.

"Please come down. Father put me in charge."

Thelma glared down. "Leave me alone, or never come home, won't find on dresser a platinum comb."

Elena backed away. *Do you have a comb, too, or have you seen mine?*
"I want us to get along. We need to talk."

Thelma disappeared into the gray wall.

Frustrated that her only contact to this world wasn't helping, Elena looked around. She was alone. The white boxy cottage stood like a Monopoly house centered between trees and the garden, which offered more than enough food for the two of them.

It hit her like a slap to the face. Marc had taken Thelma's home, and the girl had provided Elena another, away from the hostility. Elena had expected to take care of Thelma, but her sister wasn't helpless. Despite her fey manner, it had been Thelma taking care of their father. *What other secrets lie hidden in that young mind of yours?*

>====>

General Gorg waited until Zurbiz was preoccupied with the regeneration process that she'd promised to Supreme Commander Viv. *Never promise what you can't deliver*, Gorg reminded herself. It was a failing of those too eager to please.

She took a transporter jump to a Knoonk spaceship that floated in orbit around Earth, hiding among abandoned satellites and spacecraft debris. Accompanying her was Major Narn, one of the sharpest middle officers in her command.

"What's with the veil of secrecy?" Major Narn asked as they materialized on the orbiting spacecraft. "Should I be concerned?" Her eye slits were tight as she maintained a rigid calmness.

"Have you done something to be concerned about?" The general stared at her junior officer. She trusted her read that Narn was merely acting cautious. "We're here to meet with Major Burb and one of her Earth-bound trackers."

If Major Narn relaxed, the general couldn't tell. *Good. She's only being alert.*

Gorg put on special eye shades that would turn the pink complexion that Major Burb had taken, the blonde hair, and the colorful clothes into shades of gray more comfortable to Knoonk eyes. Narn did likewise. Then Gorg activated the transporter from Earth.

Lieutenant Debra Telet appeared in a bright floral outfit along with her similarly attired boss, Major Burb. They were tall, slender, athletic, carrying the human genes selected to blend in and dominate the human race. To Gorg they looked hideous, reminders of those who had murdered her sister.

"General," Major Burb said. She and her sidekick bowed. Without their forehead ridge-crests, they looked disrespectful.

Gorg reminded herself they couldn't help it. Ridge-crests would make them stand out on Earth. She pointed for the pair to sit so she didn't have to look up at them and had Major Narn sit in the corner as an observer. "You should have acquired the Royal Couple by now. What's taking so long?"

Major Burb fidgeted, as humans tended to do. "They remain off the grid. They altered their appearances from the images we have, and we lack any other identifying clues to help us hunt for them. It is no excuse. You asked for an explanation."

General Gorg turned to Lieutenant Telet. "Tell me straight. Nothing needs leave this room."

Telet looked at her major and then at the general. "We lack clues."

"More," Gorg said, inching closer.

"Commander Zurbiz demands daily meetings," Telet said, hanging her head. "She fears the Royal Couple might make an alliance with the humans."

"So?"

"Every time we close in, she transports us here." Telet bent over almost to her knees. "I'm sorry. I mean no disrespect."

"I asked for this meeting because I'm taking over the hunt for the traitors. I don't need face-to-face meetings or even daily meetings. I need facts and I need results. What resources do you need?"

"We could use four more trackers," Major Burb said.

"I'll get you two immediately," Gorg said, "and work on two more. The royal traitors are your top priority. They are not to be harmed. We need them alive."

"We understood that from Commander Zurbiz."

"Just being clear. I sense that's not all." Gorg had to look away because even with the shaded glasses there was too much color emanating from the Earth-bound trackers' clothes.

"The lieutenant is a bit free with advice," Major Burb said.

"Then perhaps I should promote her. For over a year you and your teams have failed to capture the traitor."

"We're under strict orders from Commander Zurbiz."

"Lieutenant Telet, do you have anything to add?"

The lieutenant looked from her boss to the general and back. "With respect to Commander Zurbiz, we have a limited number of trackers. We lost two in a skirmish three months ago. The commander refused to give us more."

"Why?" Gorg asked, moving closer so she was standing over the major.

"Commander Zurbiz doesn't want to risk losing any more Terran-adapted Knoonk until she can raise more," Telet said.

"Despite the risks the traitors present?" That meant the regeneration process really was behind schedule. The Supreme Commander needed to hear about this, but Gorg didn't want to tip her hand with Major Burb.

Telet fidgeted and looked up. "Something has slowed the production of new trackers. Commander Zurbiz told us to do what we can with the resources we have."

"That changes right now. You're to report to me and only me. If Commander Zurbiz asks, tell her I've sent you down an undercover path that requires complete communications blackout. Is that clear?"

"Absolutely," Major Burb said.

"Then go."

General Gorg pushed the two trackers up onto the transporter platform and sent them back to Earth. Then she sent word to another pair of trackers to report to Major Burb.

"With all due respect, General," Major Narn said. She waited for the general to look up from sending out messages. "We've been hunting the Royal Couple for ten years and nothing dire has happened. So I can best serve, what has changed?"

Gorg looked over at the major, who was showing proper respect with her body and ridge-crest submissive. "We're close to having the gate in place."

"My sister and others will be able to join us?" Narn lifted her head in delight and then resumed her respectful bow.

"Tell no one until we can verify that it works. If Commander Zurbiz can get her regeneration process on schedule, we will be in position shortly to move our people to Earth and enjoy wide-open spaces. Of course, you and I will have to undergo regeneration first. After we take over, we can complete that process on Earth."

"Then why is it so important to capture the Royal Couple?"

"Because, my protégé, if we hold the Royal Couple, the Confederation of Counterrevolutionaries can't interfere."

>===>

Elena surveyed the two-bedroom cottage for anything to help crack the mysteries of this world. The gravity here was three times that of Europa. Her best guess was Mars, but she lacked the tools to prove her hypothesis.

Throughout the house, she found only bare walls, with no mementos like those in Father's Cave. The cottage was equipped with beds, dishes, and food for two, as if Thelma had specifically arranged this place for the two of them, since their father couldn't climb the wall and Thelma couldn't carry him. All of this amounted to data, clues, but nothing upon which to base a conjecture, let alone a conclusion.

Elena entered a bedroom with a small bed, a plain dresser, and a closet full of the latest fashions for girls Thelma's age. They looked like things she could have bought on Earth. The other bedroom held only a bed and an unfilled dresser. Not even a hanger hung in the closet.

Outside, Elena walked the perimeter of the cave, feeling the walls for openings, handholds, or anything with clues about the nature of this habitat. She came up empty, no new openings and nothing but smooth gray walls. Hungry, she gathered tomatoes, cucumbers, and lettuce from the garden beside the cottage and chopped up a salad. She added vinaigrette from the refrigerator. As she returned the bottle to the fridge, suddenly it hit her. The house had electricity.

With no evidence of wires outside, the Knoonk must have buried them in the rock below the cottage or they used microwave receivers or some other means to transmit power. That got her to wondering about their power source and the unwelcome implication of superior Knoonk weapons.

Watching for Thelma, Elena ate on a front porch similar to her New Mexico home, the one she'd sold. Except this horizon was close and dismal gray instead of bright ochre. She closed her eyes.

Coyotes dogged her vision, darting in and out of view as they had while Leo hung himself. She'd been walking the New Mexico desert, trying to ignore their howling, when she should have been helping with his grief. She'd been fighting an intense headache that accompanied her father's funeral on Earth. She'd attempted to conjure up the Night Chant of her mother's Diné (Navajo) ancestors. She'd gotten it all wrong. The real ache had been in her heart.

Brushing aside those memories, Elena finished eating. Trying to understand the Knoonk by studying their caves was like staring at pictures of pyramids hoping to learn about those who had built them. She set her dishes in the kitchen and tried to scale the wall where Thelma had disappeared. She couldn't find the handholds Thelma had used. The girl was clever, of that Elena was certain.

Out of frustration, she followed the tunnel to Paradise Cave and hung over the ledge. She saw no trace of her sister. Marc and two of his crew were scouring the cave for anything edible or useful to survival. The overhead lights dimmed and went out. Stars dotted the ceiling. *A nice touch.* She headed to the cottage, alone except for coyotes howling in her head.

Returning to the cottage in the dark took her back to the Navajo's Long Walk. During the American Civil War, Colonel Kit Carson and the New Mexico militia attacked Navajo settlements, driving the survivors on a march of 300 miles to Ft. Sumner. After this arduous trip through the arid southwest, they met overcrowding and lack of food and water.

>===>

At first light, Elena woke on the thin sofa she'd located in the dark the night before. She checked Thelma's room to find her sister asleep beneath a thin gray sheet. Relieved that Thelma was safe, Elena curled up on the floor next to the bed and dozed off.

When she woke again, Thelma's inquisitive face stared down. Elena wanted to reach up into that mind to understand her sister. Instead, she touched Thelma's hand. The girl gave the briefest of smiles and hurried into the bathroom.

In the guest bedroom, Elena found clean clothes on the bed: a pale green halter and short plaid skirt. She looked for jeans, pants or anything more practical in the dresser and closet. All she found were similar outfits in slightly different colors. She peered up at imagined cameras and stepped into the closet to change.

When she emerged, she studied her image in the dresser mirror. The outfit was far too revealing. She would have to find a way to make something more practical for cave exploring.

By the time Elena reached the kitchen, Thelma had whipped up a full English breakfast, their father's favorite. Elena checked the refrigerator for something to drink and found it stocked with items she could have found at her local grocery, though with generic labels that only announced the contents. She poured herself some grape juice. "Where did you go last night? I was worried."

"Go last night, see their plight, can't describe this kind of blight."

"Thelma, I don't understand. Please, tell me about our hosts. I want to meet them and understand them better."

Thelma got up and danced toward her bedroom.

By the time Elena reached Thelma's room, music blared with heavy bass and a droning rhythm. Elena knocked and opened the door. Thelma danced and sang to the music.

"Nyak, nyak, nyak." Thelma stretched the sounds with a variety of tonal qualities, with the melody rising, falling, and then holding steady in ways that reminded Elena of Chinese. The girl's head bobbed back and forth. "Kyek, kyek, kyek."

The noise aggravated Elena's headache. "Can you turn it down?"

Thelma continued to dance and mutter different strings of sounds. Elena lowered the volume enough so it didn't hurt her ears. Thelma ran from the room.

Elena forced the window open, climbed out, and caught up

with her sister by the tunnel that led to Paradise Cave. "Dad should have warned me that you're having problems. I can help. I want to, but we need to work together. I can sit outside while you listen to music, but we need to talk."

Thelma fell to the ground. Her body convulsed. Her arms flailed and twisted. Her legs twitched. She panted, gasping for breath. Her irises floated up, leaving the ghoulish whites of her eyes.

Elena knelt down and tried to comfort her sister. She didn't see any obstructions keeping Thelma from breathing and so just held her.

Thelma's body relaxed. Elena stroked her sister's shoulder-length brown hair. "I didn't mean to yell at you. I don't understand and I need your help."

When Thelma's body went limp, Elena eased her onto her side.

Thelma rolled over, clamored to her feet, and ran for the tunnel. Elena wasn't quick enough. By the time she reached the passage and dragged her bare knees across rough stone to Paradise Cave, Thelma had vanished. The attacks were too intense to fake. Something was triggering them. Whatever it was, Thelma didn't trust Elena, not yet.

EIGHT

Elena rubbed her scraped knees, leaned over the ledge into Paradise Cave, and listened for activity. The cave was too quiet for her liking. In her mind, coyotes scratched out a sad melody.

She eased herself down to the cave floor and moved along the wall, testing for secret passages and handholds to other elevated tunnels. Her coyotes' melancholy tune rang in her ears. She pushed onward until her feet ached, and her head pounded. She stopped at the stream and leaned over.

The reflection showed her puffy face. She couldn't deny that seeing her father again brought back memories of his first funeral and losing Leo and their mom.

She splashed water on her face, which didn't help. It was hard not to despair. They were at the mercy of the elusive Knoonk, and exploring seemed futile. No matter what she learned, they wouldn't let her tell anyone back on Earth.

Elena sat on a rock ledge across from the waterfall and scanned the cave and sky rim. Seeing no evidence of her sister, she removed the wrinkled picture of her father from her belt pack. She forgave him for missing her birthdays and hoped that, wherever he was, he could forgive her. She stuffed the picture into her pack, took out her harmonica, and played.

Thelma's head poked out of the wall some eight feet above, from another elevated tunnel. The girl seemed to enjoy the music, though she refused to come closer. *It's a start.*

A hand touched Elena's shoulder. She jumped.

"Thank God you're okay." Marc squeezed her hand and sat next to her. "I was worried sick all night when I couldn't find you."

"I'm fine," Elena said. She looked up to where Thelma had been. The girl had vanished.

"I love that you're independent, but we should stick together."

"Do you have everything under control?" She looked over at Marc and noticed that he was nursing cuts, a black eye, and looked even more exhausted. "What happened to you?"

Marc sighed and scooted closer. "It's nothing."

"Don't tell me that." She examined his eye.

"I'll be fine." He kissed her hand and squeezed. "People are scared. Wil and some of the others blame me for bringing us here. I swear I had nothing to do with this."

"I know."

"Thanks for that."

Elena pulled free of his grip and studied a makeshift bandage. You want me to look?"

Marc shook his head. "It's chaos. Last night, more passengers and crew showed up."

"Reese's fiancée?" Elena asked.

Marc shook his head. "Zak Pavlin is back."

"What? He was dead."

"The last thing he remembered was hitting the view-screen."

"Who's missing?" Elena asked.

"Three passengers, the doctor, and two crew members."

"Poor Reese." That meant Thelma must have disappeared last night to fetch the other survivors.

"Have you seen the couple that left?" Marc asked.

Elena pulled away and faced him. "They didn't return?"

"No." Marc lowered his voice. "Elena, I need you."

"Why? What's going on?"

Marc took a deep breath. "I have twenty-three mouths to feed and not enough food. Thelma must know where we can find more."

"We have a small garden," Elena said. "Enough for two. If you remove us and the couple, you have nineteen."

"We did inventory. We can't last a week on what we found. I laid down martial law, but … there've been thefts. I need your help. We can share leadership. You can be responsible for the house and supplies. What do you say?"

"Thelma needs me, too. She doesn't need the fights. Remember, you took her house."

"I'm sorry," Marc said. "There's no good excuse. I'm used to dealing with soldiers trained to follow orders and deal with emergencies."

"We're civilians."

"I know. Everyone is terrified." He looked at her. "You don't seem scared."

"I am, but it won't help to dwell on that." She touched one of his bruises, and he winced. "We need to show our hosts that we're peaceful."

"That's why I need your help. We have twenty-three lives to consider."

"Nineteen."

"Okay, nineteen. Have you gotten Thelma to talk?"

"She's traumatized," Elena said. "It'll take time."

"We don't have time. Our best shot is to work together, teamwork."

Elena stood. "Dad said if we act peaceful the Knoonk will work with us. After all, they provided for him and Thelma."

Marc hung his head and sighed. "You heard what your alien friend said."

"Nalon?"

He looked up. "She returned and insisted that we mate or starve. I don't want our people to starve, but I don't like them telling us what we have to do in order to eat. I certainly don't want anyone but you."

Folding her arms, Elena glared at him. "I have no intention of mating like animals in a zoo. What else did she say?"

"If we don't do as we're told, we'll face famine and plagues."

Reese approached them from the right, wearing a thin beige top and a plaid mini-skirt. Her hair was a rat's nest; her cheeks had sunken into her gaunt face. Reese's eyes pleaded; she must have been crying all night.

The construction worker, Wil Benning, stood on the other side. Elena backed away.

"What are you doing?" Elena asked.

Marc stood and hung his head. "Wil and the others will only follow if you return and agree to lead. Besides, I can't protect you on your own."

She stared at Marc. "Thanks, but I don't need your protection."

Marc reached for her arm. "I need you to come back for everyone's sake, including yours."

Elena moved between Marc and Reese. As Marc followed, Elena heard a thud behind her like a bat hitting a ball.

Wil slumped to the ground. Thelma stood over him, holding a thick branch.

"What the hell?" Marc glared at Thelma.

The girl held the stick over her head. When Marc moved toward her, Thelma threw the stick at him and sprinted for the wall.

Elena grabbed Marc's arm. "Leave her alone. I think she believes she's protecting me."

"What?" Marc asked.

Thelma hit the wall at full speed, scurried up the rock face like a squirrel, and hung ten feet above them.

Marc pulled free of Elena, ran to the wall, and tried to climb. He couldn't find a single handhold. Elena wondered where Thelma would have learned this behavior, certainly not from their father.

On the other hand, Thelma had come to Elena's defense. That was encouraging, though misplaced.

Marc turned to Elena. "What's the matter with her?"

"Stop acting like a college freshman and leave her to me."

"Please, Elena, don't make this difficult. We've got to stick together." Marc reached for her hand.

She moved away. "You're not my boss. We're not even engaged anymore."

"I don't want to boss you, but if you don't return, we starve. Your alien friend made that clear."

Thelma jumped onto Marc's back, knocking him to the ground. She grabbed Elena's hand and pulled her toward the waterfall. They crossed under the falls and hid in the foliage on the other side.

Marc yelled after them, "You don't know what's out there. It's too risky!"

Maybe so, Elena thought, but her sister didn't belong with the scared shuttle survivors.

Thelma ducked down and watched. She'd taken significant risks in attacking Wil and Marc, though she had an escape route each time. This wasn't a helpless child.

"Thanks," Elena whispered.

Elena watched Marc help Wil to his feet. They did put on a poor show for their hosts. Any chance she had of connecting with the Knoonk wouldn't come from hanging around the others.

She turned to try to get answers from Thelma, but her sister was gone. Elena avoided Marc as she made her way around Paradise Cave hunting for more tunnels. Short plaid skirts might have been useful in attracting boys in high school; they were impractical for cave exploring. Her knees had no protection and she didn't need a mirror to know that when she bent over, her black briefs showed.

She returned to Cottage Cave for her transport uniform. It was gone. The Knoonk must have taken it. Thelma, on the other hand, had jeans and tops in her size.

Frustrated, Elena returned to Paradise Cave and looked for the high cave from which Thelma had spied on her and jumped Marc. She covered a ten-foot section of wall and located holographically hidden crevices. She pondered the science behind such large-scale illusions and the Knoonk motivation for doing this. She couldn't figure how Thelma had found them when she ran at the wall. That indicated a high level of familiarity with the caves and the motivation to find quick getaways, inconsistent with a lonely life with their father.

Using her knife, Elena chipped off a chunk of the wall, cracked open the fragment, and crushed it with her shoe. The powder was as gray as the wall. Whatever the Knoonk had used to build the caves was a dense, uniformly gray material like concrete, though with a more crystalline consistency. She wished she had her geologist, or any of her team, to better figure this place out.

She climbed, got a foot off the ground, and couldn't locate another handhold. Thelma scurried up beside her to the invisible ledge. Elena dropped down, moved to where Thelma had climbed, and located holds all the way up.

Entering a new cave, Elena saw another garden and wondered if Thelma knew of enough caves to feed everyone. Toward the back stood a house that was bigger than the cottage yet smaller than the one in Father's Cave. Elena entered. The living space and kitchen were larger and more comfortable than the cottage. *So, why didn't you bring me last night? More important, who is using all these caves and homes?*

Something gray darted by. Expecting Nalon, Elena bowed her head. The object stopped and twirled—a heavily damaged hovering robot.

"Party, hearty, tardy," the robot said and smashed into the wall. Something fell off and rattled across the floor.

Elena stepped around the crumpled robot and headed upstairs to the dense drum of music. She found Thelma in a bedroom, sitting at a table with a virtual keyboard and holographic images that floated in front of the wall. Earth-based com-link newsfeeds flew by too fast for Elena to read.

"Thelma, please slow down."

The image froze on a news report: *Houston lost contact with the lunar transport after launch. Mission Control won't comment on the fate of the crew and twenty-five passengers.*

Thelma resumed flipping screens so fast Elena barely glimpsed headlines. When the images slowed, one caught her attention: *United Nations Poverty Relief Emergency Program Administration for Redistribution, Education, and Development demands governments redirect space funding to fight poverty.* It was just as her father had said. Another headline flashed: *Evangelical Ministry on Alien Mythologies condemns search for extraterrestrials as defaming the word of God.* They were halting space exploration when humans needed it most.

Thelma flipped from screen to screen, mixing comics, sports, music, and history in no particular pattern. All the while, she hummed in a low, annoying drone.

Elena wanted to see more without provoking Thelma to run off. "Can I use this when you're done?"

Thelma's head bobbed back and forth, letting images and music distract her, as if content meant nothing and rhythm everything.

"Can we send messages?"

Thelma turned up the volume.

"Thelma, please!" Elena yelled. Not knowing how else to reach her, Elena pulled out her harmonica and played it.

Thelma stopped, turned off her music, and listened, her head still swaying. Elena moved closer to peer into the girl's eyes, which glazed over as if in a trance. Putting down the harmonica, Elena opened her mouth to say something.

The girl turned on her stereo full blast.

Elena turned off the music. "It hurts my ears."

Thelma hopped in circles.

Elena grabbed her sister's wrists. "We need to talk. Now."

Thelma fell to the floor.

Elena held tight. The attack was too convenient, perhaps a pretext not to talk or Thelma's version of a temper tantrum. This faker must have exhausted their father's patience. Well, if the child wanted to play, Elena would match her. She lay next to Thelma and wrapped her arm around the girl's waist. When Thelma rolled over, Elena moved with her.

Suddenly, Thelma sat up. Elena clasped her forearms. The girl couldn't dance, couldn't escape.

"What aren't you telling me about the Knoonk?"

Thelma stared back, not moving a muscle.

"Please talk to me. I can't help if I don't understand."

Thelma cried out and began convulsing. Elena moved to lay her sister down. Thelma pulled free, turned on her stereo, and returned to flipping images. That seemed to calm her down. Then her sister got up and motioned for Elena to sit. She did and tried to imitate some of the hand movements Thelma had used to call up screens. The images flashed faster.

She looked up to ask Thelma to help and her sister was gone. *Damn it, Dad, why couldn't you tell me more about Thelma?*

Unable to get the images to slow down, Elena stepped out to the porch and glanced up at the rim. "How can we meet to get to know each other?"

NINE

After a week of holding the group together in the caves and trying to get Elena to return, Marc despaired. He was proud of Elena's many accomplishments, yet she took too many risks. She needed protection, even if she didn't think so, which was why he'd leapt at the opportunity that crackpot senator had offered.

Morale was deteriorating. Despite his training, he didn't know how to get home or how to handle the elusive Knoonk and their strange demand. Reese, the navigator, wasn't much help as she grieved over her fiancée. Pilot Zak Pavlin followed like a zombie. Marc sent two-person search parties to locate those who had left and hunt for supplies. They found neither. The only available food was around this cabin.

As passengers lost hope, who slept with whom became the main distraction, which was what their alien captors demanded. *The perverts.*

Marc refused to give up. He called everyone to the front porch. "We'll find a way home. For now, we've got to follow certain rules."

"We've had enough of you taking charge." The words came from Sorin, another big man destined for construction detail on the Moon. Marc suspected that Wil and Sorin weren't so much chosen for the lunar base as sent there as punishment. With robots and other equipment, they didn't need big men on the Moon. Now, Marc was stuck with the results of that selection process.

He scanned the weary faces around him. "I'm trying to keep us all alive. We're looking for more food. Until then, we need to stretch what we have. At the same time, we can't abandon our values."

"What's the point?" Sorin asked, playing to his audience. "They won't let us leave. Why not enjoy what we have?"

"That's short-term thinking."

"You and your religious values." Sorin wrapped his arm around Reese and pulled her closer. Her flimsy skirt rode high on her hip, revealing red underpants. When he kissed her on the lips, she didn't resist, though she did look miserable.

Marc bristled. He couldn't fight over every provocation. There had to be another way. "We can't give up hope. Pregnancy will worsen our chances. Besides, we have no doctors and no food for more mouths."

As others paired up, Marc took a deep breath. This was much easier in the military. "From this point forward, women get the upstairs, three per room. Men sleep outside. I'll move to the living room. Gather your things."

Zak joined Marc. No one else moved.

"What'll we do?" Zak whispered.

"Wait here." Marc approached Sorin and Reese. "Lieutenant! On your feet."

"She doesn't want to." Sorin pulled her bare legs toward him.

Reese didn't appear to want much of anything except her fiancée. While Marc empathized with her pain, she was part of the crew. She needed to help lead.

Marc felt an unexpected surge of adrenaline, a wave of anger. He didn't like how it clouded his thoughts. Clenching his fists, he saw the same anger in Sorin's face.

Sorin dropped Reese like a moldy banana. He jumped to his feet and stumbled as his body overreacted to the light gravity. He steadied himself and threw the first punch. Marc dodged a glancing blow and brought his fist down hard on his opponent's neck. The surge of satisfaction stunned him. This was getting out of control.

Elena's words rang in his ears: *Show that we're peaceful.*

Red-faced, the big construction worker tumbled to the ground, groaned, and got up again. His next punch connected with Marc's jaw. Marc blocked another blow. "Is this necessary?"

Sorin threw another punch. Marc dodged and threw an uppercut, sending his opponent back down. This time Marc dropped onto the big man and launched three hard blows to the face.

He stopped himself, suddenly feeling ashamed. For an instant, he'd wanted to kill Sorin.

Sorin stayed down. "To hell with you. You're not worth it."

Catching his breath, Marc held out his hand to Sorin. "Sorry, man. We need to stand together against the aliens, not fight among ourselves."

"Whatever." Sorin got to his feet.

Marc turned to the others. "How about if we let the women take the upstairs while men move outside?"

"Why do you get the house?" Wil asked.

Another wave of adrenalin seized Marc. He took a deep breath and headed toward the living room. "I'll be in my office."

While the women moved upstairs, Marc invited Zak and Wil to join him in the living room. Marc knelt. When Zak knelt next to him, he gave thanks aloud. "Thank you, Lord, for sparing us. Please help us in the days to come."

Chilled air swept through the open front door. Shivering, he prayed for help to get home and drew his arms tight to his chest. Zak's breath steamed before him. This wasn't imagination gone wild.

Marc got up and went outside. The overhead lights had dimmed. Snow floated down, large flakes and then a thick veil of snow.

"Okay, men, in the living room."

>====>

Nalon Krok entered the commander's lavish quarters that could have held ten of her own and bowed before Commander Zurbiz and General Gorg. "We've resettled all of the humans except six we couldn't save."

The ridge crest on her forehead eased up as Commander Zurbiz stepped forward. The commander's movements betrayed pain while carrying her bulk. Not only did she have sweeter quarters, she also had a sweeter diet.

"Good, except you should have recycled the old man," Zurbiz said.

Nalon raised her head, making sure her forehead ridge-crest was showing proper respect. "His body was recycled. It was important to maintain the illusion for Dr. Pyetrov."

"Pyetrov is a strong-willed trouble-maker," Gorg said. "She must submit."

"I will distract her and the others until we have what we need."

Gorg waved her hand dismissively. "The girl should be ripe."

"She still has seizures. She is not well." Nalon's attention fell to one of the wall-screens. Her curiosity attracted her superiors. The image showed two human men hitting each other, aided by a remote application of a fight enhancement serum they'd tested on other humans. The serum was having the desired effects.

Gorg turned up the volume. When the fight ended, she spoke to the commander. "We cannot tolerate this military man. Nalon made it clear they must mate. Despite hormonal enhancements, he resists." Gorg smiled and turned to Nalon. "Your experiment has failed; I will deal with them."

The commander's ridge crest wrinkled, letting the others know her disapproval. "Your mission is to catch the traitorous couple on Earth." Zurbiz nodded for everyone to leave.

Gorg dismissed Nalon and turned to Zurbiz. "When Supreme Commander Viv returns—"

"Until then, you will obey! You wasted valuable resources crashing their vessel the way you did."

"No more than you in keeping the old man alive. Drama and terror will teach humans their place."

Nalon quietly slipped out the door before they could acknowledge that she'd overheard their conversation. *Evidently, rumors of a pending change might be true.*

>====>

For days, Elena waited for her sister to return. While she did, Elena figured out how to use the com-link in Network Cave to scan news sites. *Food Riots in Cairo, Beijing, and Delhi. Lunar Transport Lost.* The last post listed the passengers and crew, with condolences from world leaders. *How touching,* Elena thought, given how many opposed her quest.

President Archer closed the lunar base pending further investigation. Even friends spouted nonsense that Elena would want them to suspend the program. She felt betrayed.

Studying the corner of one image, Elena spotted someone who might have understood. A quiet man, Ahmed Amladi had been skeptical. She'd won him over on behalf of his son, who was determined to join the original mission. Ahmed had grilled Elena about mission conditions. Would Anton's food be properly prepared? Would there be separation of men and women? Would she allow him to conduct his prayers? Most important: what was the character of this woman who would lead Ahmed's son? As special agent for the FBI, Ahmed had screened Elena and her team before he bestowed his highest honor—accepting her as his son's leader. With his son safe on the lunar base, would Ahmed still understand?

Distressed by the news, Elena dropped to the floor and performed her daily exercises. After a twenty-minute workout, she returned to Paradise Cave.

Elena looked for Thelma and brought out the harmonica. The girl didn't show. It was dinnertime when Elena located another cave hidden behind a thick growth of ivy. This large gray cave had no garden, no house, not even a loose pebble.

Frustrated that she was getting no closer to Thelma, the Knoonk or to communicating with anyone back home, she returned to Network Cave and tried to bypass the security block so she could send a warning. There were too many layers in an unfamiliar system. The aroma of sweet cooking caught her attention and drew her downstairs. In the kitchen Thelma fixed stir-fried vegetables. Her head bobbed as if to music Elena couldn't hear.

Elena leaned toward Thelma and tried a different approach. "Make stir fry, please the eye, tastes so good it makes you cry."

Thelma fled the house and dove into the tunnel. Elena ran after her. By the time she reached Paradise Cave, Thelma had disappeared. It made no sense. Elena was only trying to make a connection.

By the time she returned to Network Cave, the place reeked of smoke. Elena ran to the kitchen and put out the flames. She'd ruined a wonderful dinner trying to match rhymes with Thelma. By the time she finished cleaning up the mess, lights had dimmed. She gathered vegetables from the garden and ate her dinner raw.

The cave and house lights went out without Thelma's return. Stumbling in the dark, Elena found a bed and collapsed. The coyotes in her head circled around, keeping her uncomfortable company. She needed direct contact with the Knoonk. So far, that wasn't happening and Thelma might hold the key. Elena was already regretting the commitment she'd made to their father to look after Thelma. Maybe if he'd explained the girl's condition and behavior that might have helped.

Half asleep, Elena felt the covers move. She jumped. A slender hand covered her mouth. Thelma was back. Elena threw her arms around her sister and let the tension of the past week release.

Thelma poked her finger into Elena's ribs and began tapping, nervously. Elena removed the hand. Her sister pinched hard, dug her fingernail in, and tapped again. Recognizing the rhythm as Morse code like what she'd used with her father, Elena spelled out on the girl's back: *Again.*

Thelma sobbed as her fingers tapped out "*Never copy me.*"

Elena froze. "*OK.*"

"*We cannot talk. U want to meet Knoonk. I arrange.*"

"*Yes.*"

"*Do not trust.*"

That wasn't encouraging. "*Why?*"

Thelma slipped out of the room.

This was what her father was trying to do with his blinking and reaching for Elena's arm. It must have been horrible to go through life not trusting. Yet Thelma had trusted Elena with Cottage Cave, Network Cave, and her private communication. Maybe that was all the time they had. *What have the Knoonk put you through and what are their intentions?*

TEN

In the morning, Elena couldn't find her sister in Cottage Cave, so she hurried to Paradise Cave to continue looking for other openings and caves.

Across the long garden cave, Marc and Wil banged stones against the walls to explore for exits. Elena sighed. If this were Europa, their probing could bring a flood. Good thing they weren't. Given the shuttle's transit time and local gravitational pull, the only alternative that made sense was Mars. Political interference had left the planet largely unexplored. If they were on Mars, Marc and Wil risked shattering rock and creating a crack through which their oxygen would vanish.

Marc poked and dug as energetically as he did everything else. The work was futile, yet he had brought the crew and passengers together into a team of sorts.

Tara L'Enfant joined Elena. "When I asked to join your mission, this wasn't what I had in mind." She pushed aside ivy and ran her hand across the gray stone, mimicking what Elena was doing.

"Me either. Nothing personal," Elena said. "It was hard to choose. You have a great background."

"Well, it doesn't matter now."

"If it's any consolation, I'm glad you're here, not stuck here, but … I have an idea. Follow me."

Elena crossed the cave and showed Tara the unseen handholds. The two of them climbed up to Network Cave and into Thelma's room with the com-link. "If anyone can figure this out, you can."

"Is this real?" Tara's eyes lit up at the sight of the virtual electronics, since there was no hardware, only a holographic keyboard and screen. She sat down to study the strange symbols that appeared on Thelma's bedroom table.

Tara's face grew somber. "Alien protocols. I'd be guessing."

"Then guess."

Tara tapped at symbols that appeared to be an alphabet of sorts, as different from English as was Chinese. Then the keyboard switched to recognizable English. "Assuming I can get anything, who do you want to contact?"

Elena considered for a moment. The President made sense, though his assistant would intercept her message as a hoax. Under the same circumstances, she would have. It had to be someone she knew. Her mentor and advisor at NASA came to mind. She gave Tara the name.

For several minutes, Tara tapped and tried to navigate the system, clicking on images as well as letters, words, and symbols. "It feels as if I'm wearing handcuffs. Every step I take has heavy security, and the mix of languages doesn't help."

"Can you bypass security?"

Tara laughed. "Unlikely." She glanced under the table and shook her head. "This is completely foreign."

"Alien."

After a few more moments, Tara leaned back. "I'm afraid your father was right about them not wanting us to send a message. Someone is shadowing me. Even if I break through, they can cut me off before I can send anything."

"So it's hopeless?"

Tara grinned. "Mind if I play for a while?"

"It's Thelma's room." Elena sighed. "Go ahead. I'll talk to her." *If I can find her.*

Tara brought up an English feed that led to NewsNet: *Billions In Aid, Too Little, Too Late.* Elena wondered if the Knoonk could help. They certainly had capabilities humans didn't.

One news clip showed FBI agent Ahmed Amladi reunited with his son, who had just returned from the lunar base.

"Let me know what you find," Elena said.

She left Tara and the networked cottage. As she entered the dark tunnel, Elena's coyotes howled and nipped at her heels more urgently than before. *Mom, what was it you tried to tell me about these amazing animals?*

She imagined her grandmother living in a traditional Navajo hogan with no indoor plumbing or lights, living close to nature and communing with the spirits. She would know, but Elena had turned her back on her mother's heritage with an eye on becoming more like her father.

Distracted, Elena slipped when she turned to climb down the wall.

Marc caught her. "Find anything interesting?"

She looked into his eyes. The weariness was still there; the effects of too much caffeine and no sleep had worn off. "It's just another cave, nothing special. You can put me down now."

He eased her to the ground. "Have you considered my offer to jointly lead the group?"

"I need more time with Thelma."

"Where is she?"

Elena hurried toward Cottage Cave and called out over her shoulder. "When I find something useful, I'll let you know."

>====>

Not wanting to use up the little food Marc and the others had, Elena ate dinner alone in Cottage Cave and considered her next move. It was vital that she meet the Knoonk and size them up. When her father had talked about Thelma being special, Elena at first thought that only meant the attacks and strange speech, but Thelma had shown another side that Elena wanted to get close to. Maybe she would have to take moments at a time, but Thelma knew things Elena needed to understand.

After dinner, Elena set out for Paradise Cave. As she scraped her knees along the uneven surface, she pondered what trauma Thelma had endured to be so cautious and how she could get more time with her sister.

Emerging from tunnel darkness into cave darkness backlit by dim starlight up above, Elena almost tumbled into Paradise Cave. She couldn't read the dim display on her wristband, yet her eyes picked out star patterns on the ceiling, including the Big Dipper.

She climbed down to the cave floor and headed toward the stream that divided the cave. Howling echoed in the distance, much as it might have from her New Mexico ranch house. So far, she hadn't found any animals here; she held her breath. The stillness of the air reminded her it was a cave. Perhaps the Knoonk hadn't mastered the subtlety of indoor wind.

Sensing someone watching, Elena played her harmonica. A silvery moon appeared on the ceiling. When the howling resumed, she stopped.

"Elena, that you?" Marc's voice startled her from across the stream. He stood with Ben Mirk, an engineer transferring to the lunar base.

"Why are you working in the dark?" Elena asked. She couldn't see the falls. In fact, she couldn't hear them, either.

"We found an opening. Then your alien friends turned out the lights. I marked the spot. Now we can't find it."

The howling turned into a growl and grew louder, closer. Something crept nearer with a throaty snarl.

Elena froze. At home, she wouldn't have ventured out without a taser. Here she had no such protection. Marc and the other man headed for where the falls should have been. Elena moved toward Cottage Cave.

A grumbling roar startled Elena. She spun and caught sight of something yellow with dark spots sprinting toward Ben. Before he could react, the leopard pounced, knocking him against the rock floor. He didn't move. Marc rushed into the open, tree branch in one hand and a rock in the other. The leopard charged. Elena yelled to divert the animal's attention.

At the last moment, Marc jumped. The leopard slid beneath him. Marc threw the rock and cracked the tree branch over the animal's head. The leopard slumped to the ground. Marc tumbled onto a mossy slope by the stream.

Elena ran toward the path behind the falls. A second leopard swooped from the underbrush toward Marc. He froze. Terrified for him, Elena jumped into the opening and yelled across the stream. "Hey! Over here."

The animal stopped, glared up at her with haunting cat eyes, then at Marc, the closer target.

"Over here," Elena yelled. She ran for the raised tunnel to Cottage Cave.

Looking back, she glimpsed the leopard making a run at the stream. With the benefit of lighter gravity, the animal launched itself across and raced toward her.

Dumb, dumb, dumb.

She sprinted toward the dead end and, in the dark, tried to remember where the tunnel was. Behind her, the animal's paws clacked on rock. Time slowed as she rushed the wall. She would only get one chance.

Elena leapt, drew her feet up, and hit the wall with her left knee. Pain shot up her leg. Reaching up with her right hand, she caught the ledge. She swung, grabbed the ledge with her left hand, and pulled up.

Marc yelled from somewhere behind her. More howls floated in the distance. A cool breeze swept her face as she pulled herself up toward the tunnel opening. Searing pain enveloped her left leg, which hung as dead weight. The beast had her ankle and was pulling her down. Her hands slipped.

Two thin arms grabbed hold of her wrists from above— Thelma. The leopard wouldn't let go and Elena couldn't raise herself. She pushed through stabbing pain, her consciousness slipping. The beast tugged on her ankle. She gripped the ledge. Pain seared into her brain. She slipped.

The animal let go. With Thelma's help, Elena climbed, but her left leg hung beneath her. She groped for a foothold. Her right foot slipped. Teeth clamped onto her good ankle. Thelma's hold slipped and Elena fell.

ELEVEN

Wrapped in nausea, pain nerves firing wildly, Elena opened her eyes. Bright ceiling lights blinded her. As her eyes adjusted, she glanced around for the leopard. Thelma's moist eyes looked back. For the second time since she'd arrived on this rock, someone had spared Elena from certain death. Once again, Thelma had come to help.

Marc clutched her hand. "You okay?" His attempt to look confident couldn't mask the dread on his face.

"Where ... are the animals?"

"Gone."

"And my legs?" she asked.

He forced a smile. "Good as new."

"Don't sugarcoat it."

"Look for yourself."

Sitting up, Elena took in the shades of gray of the small, hexagonal room. She was on an elevated platform, a table with a thin mattress and a pale gray sheet. It didn't feel like a bed, more like an examination table. There were view-screens along one wall and a robotic arm collapsed against another. Nothing looked like any medical equipment she would recognize.

The pain and burning had faded, though not the memories of the leopard mangling her legs. When she lifted her gown, there wasn't a scratch or a scar on her legs, not even the one she'd received during mission training. She wiggled her toes and touched the skin. Not even a bruise. "How is this possible?"

"I don't know," Marc said, "but I wasn't expecting wild animals."

Elena slipped off the bed and steadied herself from sudden dizziness. "What about Ben?"

He stirred on a nearby table and lifted his gown to show he wasn't missing any limbs.

She took Thelma's hand and looked into a set of moist eyes. "Are you okay?"

Other than the tears, her sister's face masked any emotion.

Elena tapped out a soft *OK* on Thelma's palm and let go. Thelma gave a brief nod and moved away.

"What about our hosts?" Elena asked.

"Haven't seen them." Marc pushed on a panel that might have been a door. "We're on their spaceship or something. If we can get to the controls, maybe we can go home, because so far I haven't been able to find a way out."

"You'd leave the others behind?"

Marc sighed. "No. We'll get everyone home."

One of the walls opened as gray panels receded. A slight, pastel-blue-clad Knoonk entered the room with a different crest on her forehead than Nalon had.

Thelma pulled Elena back into the corner and bowed her head; Elena mirrored.

Marc approached the stranger. "Would it be possible to see your ship?"

The stranger pointed a thin tube at Marc's head. He went into convulsions and slumped to the floor. Ben dropped to his knees and placed his hands behind his head. The stranger then glanced at Elena and Thelma.

Marc grabbed the stranger's spindly legs and tackled her to the ground. A yellow-clad alien appeared in the doorway and touched Marc with a long stick. Whimpering, he curled into a ball and gagged.

This was so unlike Marc, who was usually so polite and civil that Elena couldn't fathom what had gotten into him. She wanted to check on him, but Thelma held firm and tapped "*No.*"

After the convulsions stopped, Marc's body twitched for a time. Then he fell still.

The blue-clad Knoonk got up and moved aside. The larger, yellow-clothed one pointed the stick at Marc. Marc got to his knees and drew in his arms. *Don't do it.*

Elena moved to stop him; Thelma tugged back with a desperate grip.

Marc grabbed the alien's stick and turned it on his assailant. The Knoonk's eye slits twitched, the first reaction Elena had seen from them. The slight creature slumped to the floor like a doll. Two yellow-clad stick bearers swept in from the corridor and poked Marc. The veins in his neck bulged. His muscles contracted in spasms. His eyes threatened to pop out. Then he slumped to the gray floor, motionless.

Thelma clung to Elena, tapped out *"Can't help,"* and pulled away.

Elena couldn't imagine anything this girl could have done to warrant knowing this punishment. Perhaps it had something to do with her mother dying, though Thelma had been only five.

The two yellow-clad Knoonk stood at stiff attention on either side of the doorway. Another Knoonk strutted in wearing pale lavender. Bigger than the others with a large ridge-crest on her forehead and presence that filled the room, the new arrival introduced herself. "I am General Gorg." Her face turned up in what looked like a sneer.

So far, all the Knoonk appeared female, at least by human standards, though maybe that was just their physiology. The largest, Gorg, was only five-foot-five, smaller than Elena.

Moving with masculine swagger, General Gorg stepped over Marc's prone body. She stopped. Behind her, Marc's face reddened. His muscled tensed. Without looking back, Gorg aimed a pen-sized stick at Marc's groin. He contracted into the fetal position and passed out.

Elena's knees were ready to buckle. Adrenaline coursed through her veins; fear turned to anger at Marc for acting brash when he was usually cool in tense situations, and at Gorg. All he'd asked for was to see their ship. Thelma's fingernails dug into Elena until she wanted to scream.

Gorg pressed her face into Elena's, daring the scientist to make a move. While Elena had taken self-defense, which she'd had to use one night against an intruder on Earth, she wasn't violent. Besides, that wasn't the way. Taking a deep breath, Elena closed her eyes. The smell of rancid fish oil turned her stomach. As her nose twitched, she prepared for an electric jolt.

When Elena opened her eyes, Gorg stood over Marc, whose face was beet red, his eyes vacant. He stood up and towered over the lead alien. Gorg appeared confident and Marc, for perhaps the first time in his life, hesitated. Gorg tapped the rod against Marc's head. "Bow."

Marc complied.

Gorg touched Marc's substantial bicep. Marc flexed and didn't see the electric shock coming until the jolt sent his arm into spasms. It fell limp at his side. Before he could react, Gorg zapped his other arm. Marc stood like a buffoon. His mouth opened with no words forming.

To divert Gorg's attention from further hurting Marc, Elena stepped forward and bowed. "Why have you brought us here?"

Gorg got into Elena's face again.

Bowing as low as she could, Elena tried not to choke on the rancid odor and wondered if to the Knoonk humans smelled foul.

"Do not waste my time," Gorg said. "You were told to mate." She pointed to Marc. "He's a poor specimen but willing. You must comply."

"Why——?"

Gorg's face moved closer, as if daring Elena to say or do something. Then the general marched out, taking her guards with her.

Elena lifted Marc's arms. They hung like broken tree branches from his shoulders. His eyes bulged, his face reddened, yet he didn't move. She guided him toward the wall so he had something to lean on.

He coughed, choked, and coughed again. "Any lingering illusions about your aliens?"

"What happened," she mouthed.

Marc lifted his shoulders in a half-shrug and stared at his feet. "I don't know. One moment I was thinking how vulnerable they looked. The next, one of them was on the floor and someone electrocuted me. I'm not one for excuses, but it was as if someone had given me a squirt of adrenaline."

Elena nodded. She'd been thinking drug manipulation for some time. She glanced at Thelma. *Don't trust them.*

Marc vanished along with Ben. A faint bluish haze lingered for an instant and then there was no evidence that Marc or Ben had been there. Elena was startled and annoyed by the suddenness of the Knoonk transporting them around. Thelma stood up and relaxed.

The Knoonk hadn't closed the door panel so Elena checked the corridor. Yellow-clad aliens stood on either side of the doorway, ready to zap her. She turned her attention to her recovery room formed by a pattern of hexagonal wall panels in a structure that human engineers had demonstrated as strong and stable. She could discern no medical gadgets, yet somehow the Knoonk had healed her legs as they had injuries from the crash.

Another blue-clad figure appeared in the doorway. "He is too violent." It was Nalon, Elena decided, noticing a cleft in the chin that was absent in the others.

Elena nodded. Thelma stepped forward and bowed her head. Elena did likewise.

"You will be fine," Nalon said without any hint of emotion. "Animals got loose."

"You saved my life again. Thanks." Elena maintained eye contact.

"Hey diddle diddle, the cat and…"

Elena studied her sister. The girl's eyes rolled up as she drew her arms to her chest. Elena hugged the girl, but Thelma pulled away and crawled into the corner.

Nalon approached Thelma, who shrank into a tight knot on the floor. "We could medicate. Put her to sleep for her own good."

"No, please." Elena crawled onto the floor and held her convulsing sister.

Nalon stood over them. "She needs help."

"She's my sister. I'll take care of her."

Thelma tapped on Elena's arm. "*Don't stare.*" Elena observed Nalon from the corner of her eye. *Just tell me the rules.*

Nalon turned to leave.

Elena looked from the alien to Thelma and back. This might be her only chance. "Nalon, I'm a scientist. Can … could you, please, show me around?" Elena stood, head bowed, avoiding eye contact, and wondering what her next cultural blunder would be.

Nalon stared for a moment. "Come."

"Can you show me how you healed me?"

Nalon moved to a table by the wall. Pictographs appeared on the counter like the virtual keyboard in the Network Cave. Elena tried memorizing the symbols Nalon used; there were too many.

A three-dimensional display hovered over the counter displaying Elena's mangled legs. Hunks of flesh and muscle dangled from exposed bones. Blood was everywhere. A scanner moved over the limp body. The body disappeared for several seconds and reappeared. Of course, if they could scan her body to transport it, they could restore it, but how? MIT scientists had proven the whole idea theoretically impossible two years ago.

Elena pointed to the floor. "What happened to all the blood?" She couldn't believe how clinically detached she felt watching her own bloodied body.

"We collect all of the tissue to heal you."

Another question burned. "Why make us mate?"

Nalon stared at Elena for several moments, those eye slits piercing in their vacantness. "You must stay here. It's healthier if you mate."

"Why have us make babies when supplies are always limited?"

Nalon stood in the doorway. "Come."

They entered a hexagonal tube of a corridor whose grayness blended with that of the Knoonk so only their pale yellow, blue, and lavender outfits prevented them from fading into the background. Taking Thelma's hand, Elena followed the alien down a honeycomb of corridors with rooms on both sides. Light emanated from a triangular latticework of ceiling and wall panels.

"*Any more rules*," Elena tapped.

"*Stop*," Thelma replied. Her eyes rolled up as if looking for cameras.

Two yellow-clad Knoonk hurried past, giving no indication that humans were unusual. Elena nodded and got no reaction. They passed small rooms crowded with aliens acting busy.

This was a bustling Knoonk settlement of small spaces and quite a few Knoonk. If her conclusion was correct, it made no sense to give humans large caves while the Knoonk lived in cramped quarters. It made even less sense to create more humans.

Two more Knoonk glided past. In gray robes, they'd have been impossible to see next to the black-haired half-Navajo in yellow chiffon.

"How long have you been here?" Elena asked.

Continuing her hurried pace, Nalon hesitated before answering, perhaps translating. "I was born eighteen years ago."

Elena smiled. "A few years before Thelma."

When Nalon didn't reply, Elena continued, "What about your people? How long have they been here?"

Nalon stopped before a doorway to a large gray room. Hundreds of yellow-clad Knoonk scurried around alien equipment. "How many?" Elena blurted out.

"Two hundred thousand."

Elena's mind raced at the prospect of so many aliens with technology that could take humans millennia beyond where they were, or grind them to dust. Yet they were crowded together like bees in a hive.

She approached the opening to the large hall.

"Hoita!" Nalon said.

Elena froze.

The bustling alien civilization so entranced Elena that she extended her hand toward the opening. An electric jolt threw her against the opposite wall. She crumpled to the gray floor, her brain on fire.

The next thing she noticed was Thelma rocking next to her, eyes rolled up in her head. "*Ask permission*," she tapped in rapid Morse code. Nalon stood dispassionately over them, observing. As her mind cleared, Elena decided "Hoita" must mean stop.

After several moments, the muscle twitching ceased, yet she couldn't focus. With Thelma's help, she got to her feet. Together they followed Nalon down the hexagonal hallway. They entered another gray room the same size and shape as the recovery room, with three elevated seats by a counter.

Elena sat and waited for her blinding headache to ease, while Thelma and Nalon played some form of 3D chess that looked like the one in Thelma's room in Father's Cave. On a virtual matrix of nine by nine by nine, the combinations of moves would be staggering. Thelma seemed to enjoy the game, though Elena gathered by the colors of the pieces that her sister didn't stand a chance.

Thelma stood up and danced across the room. "Lost the game, what a shame, bet you couldn't do the same." She pulled her chair over and plopped down in the corner behind Nalon. Her fingers danced on a virtual keyboard, bringing forth a stream of images too fast for Elena to recognize.

Nalon reset the game. There was something charming, even disarming about Thelma. She hopped, played, and had her attacks without offending the Knoonk. At other times, she acted terrified like a child in a dysfunctional home.

"Can you teach me?" Elena asked.

Nalon explained how the pieces moved and captured in three dimensions. "However, mechanics is not strategy."

"I'd like to try." Elena recalled college tournaments she'd won against more experienced opponents and reminded herself that this game was different.

Nalon trounced her in fifteen seconds.

Humiliated, Elena tried small talk to connect and gather information. "Do your mother and father live here?"

After resetting the game, Nalon stared at Elena for a very long time. "Unlike humans, the community raises Knoonk from earliest childhood."

Like a commune, Elena thought. "Do you have brothers and sisters?"

Nalon commenced play. "Genetic sisters grow up in our communities."

"You don't know your brothers and sisters?"

"Only co-workers."

Sounds lonely. "Can you understand there are people on Earth I want to see?"

"Use com-link. If not on com-link, we can set up cameras."

I bet you can. "Do you have friends?"

"All Knoonk are friends."

"Can you and I be friends?"

Nalon moved toward the portal. "It is best if we are not friends."

"I like you and I believe you like me." Elena approached Nalon, careful to keep her head low and eyes averted. "I need your help."

"You cannot leave."

Elena kept glancing at the eye slits and noticed subtle movement. "Why can't you send the shuttle passengers and crew to the Moon? They pose no threat to you."

"They have seen me. You must settle down." Nalon opened the doorway.

"Wait. I don't understand, and we need supplies. The food is good, but we need more to feed all our people."

Nalon pointed to a screen on which appeared an image of Marc and Sorin. "We could terminate the troublemakers. That would make the food last longer."

Alarmed, Elena leaned against the wall for support. "We can deal with our own, thank you."

"Supplies are limited. You must make do. When we came, we had nothing except what we brought."

"And if we mate?" Elena asked.

"You will have more."

"We'll also have more mouths to feed. Why?"

Thelma rose from her station. She'd been quiet during this exchange. Now she hopped across the room.

Elena wasn't finished. She turned toward Nalon. "Please tell me what happened to the rest of our shipmates."

Elena felt queasy as she transported into another room. She wasn't sure she would ever get used to this mode of movement and was sorry she asked. The stench of week-old dead flesh filled her nostrils. Six chilled bodies lay on long tables, their skin, muscles, and organs pulled away from the bones. It looked like an autopsy, or worse.

Elena couldn't pull her eyes from the horror. "What—"

Thelma tugged on Elena's arm. "*Leave.*"

It's okay, Elena wanted to say. *I know better this time.* Thelma pulled away before she could tap.

"They died," Nalon said, showing no emotion. "Nothing could be done."

"Why cut them up?"

"Nothing can be wasted."

Forcing herself to observe, Elena approached the bodies. Thelma held her back, but Elena persisted. The pain of their deaths etched in their faces and in Elena's mind. Reese's fiancée looked grotesque, with organs missing and lips pulled away. When Elena closed her eyes, the images remained. The Knoonk had dissected her shipmates as humans dissected frogs.

TWELVE

Transported back to Cottage Cave, Elena stared across the kitchen table at Thelma, who rocked to some imaginary beat. Her eyes floated in their sockets.

Marc appeared at the door, his hair a mess. "That was an eye-opener."

Thelma scooted into the corner and glared up at Marc. Elena tried to understand. The only man Thelma would have known was their father. This made no sense.

Elena moved between Marc and Thelma. "I'm as angry as you over what those Knoonk did to you, but you shouldn't have tackled that one."

He cupped his hands over his head and winced. "I haven't been able to clear my head since we got here. One moment I'm as angry as … I don't know, then I feel almost lethargic, as if the energy has drained out of me."

"This place has us all on edge, and you know you can't stand not being in control."

He closed his eyes and sighed. "It's not that. I feel drugged all the time. Do you think this is their doing?"

"You mean as in they wanted you to attack one of their people?"

"I don't know. I didn't want to. I mean, yes I was angry, but…"

Elena had also felt drugged, too calm and detached for one thing.

"It's as if there's someone in my brain," Marc said, "mucking things up."

Thelma left the room. Marc held Elena back and whispered, "I need your help."

"I know; so does Thelma." Plus Elena needed more time with her sister to communicate in Morse code.

"The team needs you."

Elena released his grip and held his hands. "Look, we can learn a lot from the Knoonk, and we need their help. Try to control whatever it is that has you questioning yourself. You're stronger than that."

"I'll try if you'll join us. You can be our liaison to the aliens. You're the most levelheaded person I know. The women are scared. The men fight and—"

"And you want Thelma there?"

"Of course I don't want to put her in danger," he said. "I'll help in any way I can, but you have a knack for getting people to cooperate."

"You want me to whip the girls into line."

"No. I forbid it."

"I bet that went over well." Elena let go and brewed up some coffee.

"No one's happy ... at least there's no alcohol or drugs."

"Anything else?"

"Two more couples snuck off," Marc said, laying out two cups. "They took what little food we had."

"Wait here. Let me talk to Thelma."

She hurried to the back of the cottage. Thelma wasn't in her room. Elena went outside and glanced toward the tunnel entrance. Tara stood there, wearing an uncomfortable micro-skirt and tube top that left little to the imagination.

"Have you seen Thelma?" Elena called out to her.

Tara didn't have to reply. Thelma hovered across the cave like a caged animal ready to flee. Elena approached her sister. "We need to find the couples who ran off. Can you help me find other caves?"

Thelma blinked out a Morse code "Maybe," and climbed up to an elevated tunnel.

Elena let her sister go and joined Tara. "Did you find anything?" she whispered.

"Thelma must be able to use the pictograph aspects of the com-link system. I figured out how to use the viewer to see just about anything, but to do more will require using the underlying code, which is written in those Knoonk symbols."

"Thanks for trying." Elena turned toward the cottage and stopped. "I have another idea."

Marc joined them. "Coffee's ready."

"Drink up," Elena said. "We're going to Paradise Cave to look for the passengers who left."

Elena led the way, followed by Tara and Marc. As soon as they reached the big garden cave, Elena spotted Thelma climbing like a monkey, high on one wall. The girl sat perched on a ledge.

Zak Pavlin joined them. "I'm glad you're back. The fighting hasn't stopped since you left."

While the others tested the wall near the falls and worked their way along one side of the cave, Elena headed across the cave. She examined the angles of the girl's limbs, looking for signs, and worked her way to a spot in line with the girl's pose. Then she ran her hand across the gray cave face, up and down, without finding anything.

Thelma disappeared. Puzzled, Elena moved loose strands of ivy from the wall and worked a pattern away from the initial spot. Her hand disappeared into the void.

"Marc, over here."

Together they descended a dark tunnel into a lower cave. A cool breeze brushed her face when she emerged. This cave contained a pond surrounded by white sand that stretched up to the gray walls. The big construction worker, Wil Benning, was making out with Janet Akers, an ex-marine who had been on the way to the lunar base's security detail. A bottle of whiskey lay nearby. Farther back, passengers Daryl and Joan rolled into the water.

Averting his eyes, Marc approached Janet. "Get dressed, lieutenant!"

Wil rolled off Janet, but didn't get up. "You're not our boss."

Janet looked dazed, as if more than alcohol was clouding her mind.

"That's an order, lieutenant."

"Where did the booze come from?" Elena asked. She picked up a prescription bottle nearby. The label, which bore no patient's name, read "Omega X," Omega Ecstasy.

"And this?" Elena showed the bottle to Marc, who shook his head in disgust.

Zak nudged Marc and Elena. "Hey, guys. What happened to Daryl and Joan?"

The water rippled with no sign of the couple. Zak dove in. Fully clothed, Marc jumped in after him.

Elena handed Janet her clothes. "How many pills did you take?"

"I dunno," Janet managed before slumping onto the thin layer of sand. "It was here."

After Wil pulled on his jeans, Tara helped him up. They both fell and tumbled into the water.

"Nooo!" Elena yelled. Dropping to her knees on the sandy floor, she reached for Tara, who sank with Wil. Elena was alone in the cave with Janet, who had passed out. Pulling off her shoes, Elena prepared to jump in.

Water splashed. Marc burst through the surface with Tara. Gasping for air, he pulled Tara to the edge and pried her fingers from his back. Elena helped a shivering Tara out of the pond. Another splash brought Zak to the surface, struggling with Wil's limp form. Marc pushed them to the side. Together, they pushed and pulled Wil up onto the sand.

Marc and Zak dove in to find the others while Elena dragged Wil away from the edge. She gave him CPR, working on him until he coughed and rolled over.

When he sat up, Elena looked around. Realizing that Marc and Zak had been gone too long, Elena stood over the calm waters. She looked up toward the luminescence above. "Nalon, if you hear me, please help. I fear for Marc, Zak, and the others."

Tara joined her and whispered, "You think she will help?"

A loud disembodied voice thundered off the cave walls. "Kneel before Thor." It didn't sound familiar.

Getting to his feet, Wil looked for the source of the noise.

Again, the voice hammered at them. "Kneel before Thor."

Elena and Tara knelt near the pond. Wil stumbled toward the tunnel. A spark of electricity like a lightning bolt shot down from the ceiling; Wil collapsed onto the sand. Elena crawled over to find his head bleeding and the skin on his cheek burned. She eased him onto his back and examined him. The burn didn't look bad, so she ripped his tee shirt and wrapped a makeshift bandage around his head.

Marc and Zak returned to the surface, both shivering. Marc shook his head. "It's too deep."

Elena crawled across the sand to the edge and helped them out. Marc and Zak slumped onto the sand, catching their breath.

"They want us to kneel." Elena pointed to Wil, holding his head and the blood-splattered bandage.

Marc and Zak knelt next to Elena and Tara. A blue haze flashed before them as Daryl and Joan materialized, fully clothed. Despite their bluish skin, they appeared to be alive. Knoonk medicine healed so easily that Elena couldn't understand why they couldn't have saved Reese's fiancée. *There must be limits.*

Marc stood up.

"Kneel and praise your new lord," the alien voice said.

Marc looked for the source. Elena pulled him to a kneeling position. "Don't alienate them."

Grumbling, Marc knelt. "What's this nonsense?"

"Praise Knoonk, for they hold key to your survival," the voice echoed.

"Hold 'the' key," Marc corrected the speaker.

From above came an electric jolt. Marc slumped to his side. Elena leaned over to check his pulse—racing. She held him until his body relaxed.

"Praise the Knoonk so they will be merciful," the voice said.

Elena looked up and didn't like how first contact was going. This wasn't how she'd envisioned it, but she wasn't ready to give up hope.

THIRTEEN

"We praise ye oh merciful Knoonk," Elena said to forestall more punishment. Then she repeated it with Tara and Zak.

As she helped Janet to her feet, Elena hoped Thelma wasn't watching.

Tara took Elena aside and whispered, "If there's a God, how can he or she permit these aliens to pretend to be God?"

While Marc helped the others to their feet, Elena pondered that. "I don't know, but we can't give up."

"Let's go," Marc said, his confidence wearing thin.

Elena led the way to Paradise Cave. When they emerged, Thelma sat perched on her ledge. Elena couldn't help wondering if her sister had known about the drugs and alcohol before she'd given clues that led to the pool cave. Hoping that her sister might indicate other caves, Elena left Janet by the stream with the others and took Tara toward the far wall. She moved carefully so she didn't give the Knoonk the impression Thelma was guiding them.

Tara moved ivy and ran her hand over the wall behind. "I don't like these surges of hormones or whatever is making me feel like a teenager again," she said. "I know the others have experienced the same thing. That's the farthest thing from my mind." Tara looked directly at Elena. "Every now and then it's as if someone turns off my cognitive thoughts like a light switch."

"Marc said something similar."

"You think the Knoonk are manipulating us?" Tara shook her head. "Are we nothing but lab specimens to them?"

"I'm not sure," Elena said, thinking of the three dead bodies being autopsied and probably worse. "I hope not." She didn't think it would help to share that image.

She kept checking Thelma and adjusted her search pattern. "Marc wants me to return to the group."

Tara's eyes lit up. "That would be a big help."

"I'm not sure." Elena pushed ivy aside and slid her palm across another patch of gray wall. "Thelma needs help. In time I can reach her, but not if I'm weighted down with other problems."

"I'd be happy to help. Anything's better than the fighting. I'm afraid some of the guys … you know."

Elena cut her hand on a hidden outcrop of rock. She licked the wound. "Do you think they'd leave Thelma alone?"

"I don't know. There's talk she's epileptic or retarded."

"She's not retarded and she hasn't hurt anyone, except when Marc was trying to force me to return. I'm worried they'll hurt her." Elena's hand located an opening masked by holographic ivy. "Marc, over here."

Marc hurried over. "Another cave?"

He insisted on going first. Elena followed, joined by Zak, Tara, and the others from Pool Cave. They emerged into a cave that looked like a western ghost town in the center of which stood Burdon's Tavern and Strong's General Store. Marc headed for the tavern and bumped into an invisible barrier that gave a thrumming sound as it bounced him back.

On a terrace that overlooked the street stood the first couple to leave the group, Dan Burdon and Sally Strong.

Dan raised his mug in cheer. Then he leapt over the railing, landing catlike on the dusty street. "Great to see you guys." He approached the barrier. "Glad you found us."

Elena was amazed at voice clarity as if no barrier existed. She held her hand out and felt tingling—a force shield.

Returning to the barrier, Marc eyed Dan and gently touched the invisible wall. "What happened?"

"Great digs, don't you think?" Dan fanned out his leather-jacketed arm to show off the town. "General store has anything you can imagine. Tavern has all you can eat."

"Are there others with you?" Elena asked.

Dan shook his head. "It's just me and my wife. You heard it. We got married."

Wearing navy slacks and a taupe pullover, Sally joined him.

Elena pushed against the barrier, which pushed back. "And who conducted the ceremony?"

"Since we're alone, we married ourselves, said our vows up there." Dan pointed to the terrace.

"There's a combination fridge-cooker," Sally said. "Once we figured it out, it provides anything we want, hot or cold."

"Can you invite us in?" Marc asked.

Dan shrugged, his wiry arms hugging his slender body. "All you've got to do is mate." He slipped his arm around Sally and gave her a squeeze.

Marc removed his shoe and pounded it on the barrier, which didn't give.

"We couldn't stand the fighting," Sally said. "After we got here, the aliens transformed this cave for us."

"When are you due?" Elena asked.

Sally looked embarrassed. "Dan says I've been glowing all day."

"And you're okay with that?" Elena wondered if they were slaves or lab animals.

"This is better than the dump I had on Earth." Sally had volunteered as a laborer on the lunar base for pay and benefits. She looked at Dan. "Besides, we'd have gotten married and had a family anyhow."

"Don't you wonder why they insist on that?"

"Come on," Dan said. "Look at this place. It's not Earth, but we have everything we need."

Zak, Tara, and the two couples from Pool Cave joined them at the barrier.

"So all we need is a partner and they'll set us up like this?" Daryl asked.

"You can pick the Bahamas or anything you want," Dan said.

"No!" Marc turned to the others. "Listen to yourselves. Can't you see they're dividing us?"

Sidling next to Daryl, Joan spoke up. "We have no food. You can't do anything, but the Knoonk can."

"And you think pills and Scotch will help," Marc said. "The only way home is to stick together and avoid pregnancy." Marc glared at Dan. "Have you considered what the aliens plan for your child?"

"So far they've been helpful," Dan said. "As long as we're stuck here, why not make the best of it. We'd love some company. If anyone wants to join us, say the word."

"It's a trap." Marc stood between the others and the barrier. "They don't care about us. There's no free meal. They'll want something in return."

Daryl slipped his arm around Joan. "What do you say babe? Shall we?"

"Don't do this. Zak, Wil, Elena, help me out here."

Elena studied Daryl and Joan. The offer was tempting: all the food and supplies they needed. That was more than many had on Earth. Back home, they wouldn't have hesitated to hook up. On the other hand, here they were being coerced.

"Marc's right," Elena said. "We should stick together."

"I choose to join Dan and Sally," Joan said.

Daryl kissed her. "So do I."

The couple disappeared in a blue flash and reappeared beyond the barrier. At first, they seemed disoriented. Then they shook hands with Dan and Sally. All four headed into the tavern.

The good news was that Marc and the others would have two less mouths to feed. Yet Elena couldn't help seeing them as caged in a zoo.

>===>

Elena returned to Father's Cave with Marc and the others. Entering her father's house, she saw gaunt-faced women dressed in micro-skirts, and lustful looks from several men sharing bottles of whisky and vodka. The Knoonk had spared nothing to wear down their resistance.

Looking years older, Reese approached Elena. "We aren't going home, are we?"

Others gathered around. After listening to Marc for more than a week, they flocked to Elena for insight she didn't have.

The engineer, Ben Mirk, limped over, wincing with each step. "You've met the aliens. What are they telling you?"

"Tell us," several people said in chorus.

While Elena didn't want to give them false hope or add to their despair, she had to be mindful that the Knoonk heard everything. "I've met our hosts. They're an advanced race, likely peaceful or they'd have destroyed us already."

"You've seen their weapons?" Wil asked.

She nodded. "We need to show them we can live together in peace, that we're not a threat to them."

"Why not join Dan and the others?" Janet asked.

Elena studied their thin faces and, through the window, the trampled garden outside. The Knoonk had destroyed their food to get them to hook up. "I can't tell you what to do. However, if you join Dan, you give up the struggle to be free."

Marc stepped forward. "I believe we can get home. I don't know how and it won't be easy. I ask you to stick with us."

Wil pushed his way forward. "I say if we're stuck here, why not choose plenty over starvation? Will any of you lovely ladies take me over wasting away?"

"Don't do it!" Marc said, scanning the faces of the women. "Wil, think about what you're doing."

Desperation filled their faces. With eleven women and seven men, choices would diminish quickly for women who waited. Three stepped forward. Elena was horrified that in the matter of weeks they'd regressed to this.

"Take me," a petite brunette said.

A redhead pushed her out of the way. "No, me."

"Enough!" Elena said. "This is demeaning."

"Speak for yourself," a young blonde said.

Wil wrapped his arm around the blonde and drew her near.

Marc grabbed Zak and headed to block the exit. "No one else leaves. We stick together."

Wil smiled at the blonde. "Marry me."

With no enthusiasm, she nodded.

Elena approached the woman. "We don't know each other, but this is wrong."

"Get your own man," the blonde said.

Wil dropped to his knees, pulling the blonde down with him. "Oh merciful Knoonk. Take us."

Marc ran toward them. "This is lunacy. This won't get us home."

Wil and the blonde vanished.

Sorin stepped forward. "Any of you cuties want to come with me?"

"This isn't an auction," Elena said. "There has to be another way. The Knoonk I've met appear to be all women. They can't be without compassion. I don't believe they plan to starve us. I, for one, won't get hitched for a bowl of rice."

"Thanks, Elena," Marc said. "If we remain calm, we stand a better chance."

Elena scanned the faces of the other women for signs they were listening. "I'll ask our hosts for food."

"They've made it clear what we have to do," Sorin said, looking around. "I'll take two honeys off your hands."

She approached him. "Are you a puppet or a man?"

Sorin took Reese's hand. "Why don't we pick up where we left off?"

Reese looked to Elena who shook her head.

Behind Sorin, Ben Mirk and the brunette knelt. Before Elena could stop them, the couple vanished.

"Has everyone lost their minds?" Marc said.

"We're all scared," Elena said, "but this isn't the way. In the past five minutes, we've given up a hundred years of social advancement. I never thought I'd live to see us sink so low."

Tara squeezed Elena's hand. "We don't need to lose our minds here. I'm with you."

"Come on, girls," Sorin said. "Don't be a bunch of losers. These Knookers will starve you. Come with me. Reese, what do you say?"

No one stepped forward. His eyes burned with anger as he pushed his way past Marc and Zak. "You losers haven't heard the last of me." He charged out of the house and ran out of the cave.

Worried for Thelma, Elena ran after him, which must have given the others the wrong idea. At the exit, she turned to see Reese and Carl disappear. She left to find Thelma.

>====>

Marc couldn't believe he'd witnessed the crew and passengers acting like animals. At least he still had Zak, though the man was scared witless. Reese wasn't a surprise. She'd been in a trance since losing her fiancée. He'd expected better from the ex-marine, Janet.

Of the others, Sorin was itching for a fight. Shell-shocked Barry wasn't reliable. Other than Elena, the only other passenger of note was Tara. He was tempted to abandon the group for Elena, but she still hadn't forgiven him for accepting Senator Jorgensen's offer. He hadn't cared about the reasons, only the opportunity to join Elena. Now, he didn't even have that.

"We need to explore for food and tools," Marc announced, "in two-person teams. We'll post guards to keep animals away. Distribution will be equal, with no preference for crew or officers."

Nine pairs of weary eyes stared at Marc. "Sleeping arrangements have been simplified," he said. "Women have the upstairs, two per room. Men move to the living room. If we work together we will survive."

His first dilemma came in assigning explorer teams. A coed team risked losing another couple. Sending two women left them vulnerable to Sorin. If Marc and Zak left, he had no confidence in Barry. Therefore, either Zak or Marc had to stay behind.

Zak and Barry took the first mission, leaving Marc with seven women. One by one, they approached him in the study, displaying midriff and plunging necklines. With each invitation, he closed his eyes. His heart was set on Elena. He sent them away.

Tara L'Enfant approached last. She was attractive, intelligent, and a whiz with electronics. "I need to know if you meant what you said," she announced.

"About what?" Marc stared at the chessboard and noticed Elena's queen had moved.

"Not choosing partners."

"Are you asking if I'm interested?" Marc made a counter-move on the board.

"I want to know if you'll stick around." Tara nervously ran her fingers through her hair. "These people put their faith in you and Elena. Don't screw it up."

Marc looked up. "Thanks for helping today."

Tara nodded, and lingered. Something inside him stirred as if spreading its wings. The reasoning part of his brain shut down. Longing for Elena only made it worse.

"You'd better go," Marc said, his heart pounding. "We don't need gossip."

Marc stared at the game. He couldn't focus. When she didn't move, he shuffled toward the door.

"Am I unattractive?" Tara asked, breathless.

His hands trembled; his eyes watered. When he reached the door, she vanished. Then queasiness enveloped Marc. He materialized in a tight, gray cube, naked and panting like a dog. His knees and hands rested on cold stone. A dark ceiling chilled his bare back. There wasn't room to stand or to stretch.

Illumination appeared up ahead. A smorgasbord of mouth-watering aromas filled the faintly chlorinated air. Starvation urged him forward. A different hunger throbbed in his gut. The Knoonk had drugged him; he was convinced of that. He'd never felt this out of control. He struggled to think or to pray. He was salivating, slobbering on his hands.

An opening just wide enough to crawl through led away from his cell. He scrambled forward, following the scent of food until the path ended in a T. To his left was Tara, to his right a buffet. He followed the barbecued ribs.

The passage turned and twisted, growing smaller and tighter until he couldn't move forward. Up ahead, barbecue spices enticed him, as did a table steaming with tantalizing dishes. Unable to reach it, Marc inched backward until he found a new opening that led to Tara and beyond her to another table that brimmed with meats, vegetables, and fruits.

Marc fought this growing urge inside with every shred of conscious thought. He tried to remember Elena. His prayers vanished. This had to be Omega Ecstasy or something worse. Knowing didn't help.

The aroma of chicken and pasta sauce washed over him. The drug's pull grew stronger. The aliens had seen to everything. Like a rat in a maze, if he didn't grab the cheese, he would starve.

FOURTEEN

Not finding her sister in Paradise Cave, Cottage Cave or Network Cave, Elena returned to Father's Cave.

Looking frantic, Zak greeted her on the path before she reached the house. "Marc and Tara disappeared. They just vanished."

That news came as a punch to the gut. Despite having turned Marc down on several occasions, Elena felt pangs of jealousy. Pairing up had to be a tempting alternative to starvation, but Elena believed his pitch that they should resist. She hadn't thought him capable of caving in so easily.

"Sorin threatened to return," Zak said. "Without Marc ... It's not safe. I could really use your help."

"I have to find Thelma." Elena scanned the faces of the women seated on the porch and read their despair, yet she couldn't leave Thelma all alone with Sorin out there.

She hurried out of Father's Cave, through Paradise Cave to Network Cave, where she found Thelma seated at her table speeding through online pages like an image junkie. Elena was relieved to find her sister.

"Can you slow down so I can read?" She pulled up a chair next to Thelma.

Before she could sit, Elena felt a queasy tumbling deep in her gut. When she got her bearings, she was sitting in a gray hexagonal cell, the one where Thelma and Nalon had played 3D chess.

Nalon sat across from Elena with the game set up. "Ready to play?"

From the corner of her eye, Elena glimpsed Thelma at another screen flipping images, her head swaying. At least she was safe here. Elena nodded.

Over the next week, while keeping an eye on Thelma, Elena got better at 3D chess. She couldn't get Nalon to talk, however. Whenever she mentioned the lack of food or asked about the Knoonk, Nalon pointed to the virtual game. "Play."

After days of near silence except for game instructions, Elena couldn't take it. "You've saved our lives. Why don't you give us food? That makes no sense."

Nalon moved her regent down five levels, attacking the heart of Elena's defenses. "When you are with child, you will have food."

Elena countered with one of her guards, but she'd already lost the game. "I don't want to have a child. Don't you have choices?"

"We obey. So must you. Commander Zurbiz is wise in all things."

"I respect your leader's wisdom, but I don't wish to mate. As a woman you should understand."

"We don't mate as you do." Nalon moved a scout down to support her regent.

Careful not to stare, Elena studied Nalon's face and noticed subtle variations. The eye slits showed movement like dark eyeballs. Facial lines appeared different when Nalon pondered her moves. Elena pushed her guardian to protect her commander. "I guess if you're all female, you'd have to find another way. How does it work?"

Nalon's face grew rigid. "The commander decides." She activated a spy behind Elena's lines and captured Elena's commander. "Game over." Nalon hadn't corrected the all-female comment.

"Can I meet your wise Commander Zurbiz?"

"The commander will not meet humans." Nalon reset the game. She seemed to enjoy beating the prisoner.

Elena tensed at the sight of Thelma frantically swaying in her chair. Then her sister dropped to the floor beneath the counter. The girl needed professional help, help the Knoonk could provide, though Elena wasn't sure what else they'd do to her. At least her sister hadn't had a seizure in a while.

Thelma banged something and held up her thumb, which was bleeding, a thin line like a paper cut. Nalon turned away, as if the

Knoonk was squeamish around blood. Elena got up to see to her sister.

"Sit and play," Nalon said.

Thelma studied the wound with detachment, licked it, and swayed while she hummed. Then she climbed back into her seat to gaze at flashing images. She seemed okay so Elena returned her attention to Nalon.

Tired of sitting and playing games with few answers, Elena got up to stretch. "Can you show me the rest of your home as a goodwill gesture?" Maybe she could learn what the Knoonk were really doing.

"Sit. Game is ready." The creases in Nalon's ridge crest tightened.

"I need a break. My head's busting from learning your difficult game. Can't you show me other caves you've built?"

Thelma rocked in her seat, growing erratic.

Elena paid attention and smiled. "I don't mean to impose. I enjoy the game but I want to learn more."

Nalon hesitated. Elena couldn't tell if her opponent was thinking, communicating with someone using a hidden microphone, or using telepathy.

"Follow me," Nalon said.

As the gray panels slid open, Elena caught her reflection in the door. Even she appeared gray and sickly. She wasn't eating or sleeping well. The garden was fine, though it had a limited selection. Refrigerator contents once used didn't replenish. The full English breakfast had become a hard roll. Yet, Thelma seemed well fed.

In the corridor, yellow-robed Knoonk hurried past, barely acknowledging each other. Elena fine-tuned her observations for subtle cues, an almost undetectable head nod and the flick of the eye slit. She gathered from these encounters that Nalon had status.

Nalon stopped at a room similar to where Elena had recovered from the leopard attack. Elena's muscles twitched in remembrance. Two yellow-clad Knoonk stopped working over a table. Their forehead ridge crests tightened. They argued with Nalon in a rapid-fire singsong language, punctuated with beeping sounds. With some sounds so high-pitched that she could barely hear them, she couldn't help wondering if part of their speech went beyond human auditory ability. Thelma curled up in the corner on the floor under a counter and rocked in silence.

Elena approached her sister and then a table in the middle of the room. On a slab lay Barb, a construction worker headed for the lunar base. She'd paired up and disappeared from the group. Back then, she was a tough, attractive woman. Now she'd sustained deep burns over her entire body. Charred flesh looked as if cooked on a spit. Elena felt her breakfast roll coming up.

Thelma approached, grabbed Elena's arm, and pulled her toward the floor by the wall. "*Must leave,*" she tapped out.

Elena yanked free and stood; her legs buckled. She braced herself against a wall panel and then moved closer to the table. Thelma went into convulsions.

The two lab workers backed away. Nalon moved aside. Thelma yelled and kicked at Elena's ankles.

Elena scanned the hardened Knoonk faces. "What's the meaning of this?"

They showed no fear of her.

Bowing, Elena turned to Nalon. "What happened?"

"Kitchen fire," Nalon said. "Grease."

"Why bring me here?" Elena stared into those elusive Knoonk eyes.

"You asked to see repairs." Nalon nodded at the lab workers.

One of the technicians passed a thin rod over the body. The body vanished in a brief bluish haze and then reappeared. Rags fell away. The woman's naked flesh had regained pink tones. Her brown hair had returned.

Elena stared at Nalon, then at the body. Apparently, they were experimenting, allowing drowning and burns to test their restorative technology on humans. Their medicines couldn't restore the psychological wounds, however. Elena still felt burning where the leopard had ripped into her legs and had to wonder how they'd experimented on Thelma.

One of the yellow-clad Knoonk approached Nalon, arguing. Thelma pulled Elena toward the exit. "*Go,*" she tapped.

Nalon stood her ground. The other Knoonk grabbed her frail-looking arm. Nalon expressed harsh words. Then she backed up toward the door and left the room.

While she followed her guide down the narrow corridor, Elena whispered, "Why were they angry?"

"I should not have taken you."

Agreed, Elena thought. Nalon could have described the procedure or shown videos. "Why did you?"

"So you could see what our medical tools can do."

"And what they can't do," Elena added. "Why did you burn that woman?"

Nalon hurried through a honeycomb of corridors. The entire structure appeared to be a cluster of hexagonal rooms. That arrangement provided a hive-like appearance, with Knoonk scurrying to support their community. Elena half expected to hear bees buzz.

Other Knoonk rushed by in the corridor on thin, almost insect-like legs. Most wore yellow tights and nodded in deference to Nalon. Pint-sized robots like the one in Network Cave buzzed by. Nalon's pace picked up.

Elena had to jog to keep up. "What's going on?"

"Commander Zurbiz will see you."

>===>

Nalon approached a wide door panel and waited. Thelma clutched Elena's hand and tapped, *"Careful."*

Elena identified no eye scanners, palm readers or other devices that had to be checking her identity. The doorway's size and the wide hallway before it hinted at importance.

Trembling, Thelma held tight to Elena's hand. Before Elena could tap out a reply that she understood, the massive gray panels parted. Nalon led them into a large chamber, mostly gray with pastel displays, charts, and pictures. Impressionistic, in 3D, the subdued-color images gave the sense of order and structure amidst chaos. On an elevated platform stood a half-dozen pale-blue-clad Knoonk. Thelma moved to the wall, and curled up on the floor. The Knoonk seemed to pay her no notice.

Elena had expected someone as important as Commander Zurbiz to be six feet tall. Instead, as the blue-clad group parted, a compact Knoonk stepped forward, five-seven and rotund, wearing pale violet. She was taller than most of her people with a pose that hinted at charisma. Her head was larger, with a prominent crest over the forehead and more creases than Gorg, which might have been a sign of distinction or age.

While Nalon presented her, Elena bowed in deference and waited for Zurbiz to speak. When the commander spoke in their language, Elena heard a tonal speech like Chinese, which would be tough to pick up without lessons.

Zurbiz approached Elena. "You're interesting specimen."

Elena bristled at being called a specimen, but reminded herself of Thelma's warning. She noted that the Knoonk tended not to use the articles "a" and "the" and didn't always use plural nouns or even the verb "to be" when appropriate. That implied something about the structure of their language. As to specimen, Elena imagined the joy of dissecting the rotund commander with her thin spindly legs and arms. She brushed that thought away.

"You have many fascinating technologies," Elena said.

The commander moved closer, violating Elena's space. Zurbiz' nose twitched as she took in the scent of this human specimen. "Do you believe we have much to learn from each other?"

Looking eyeball to eye slit with Zurbiz was intimidating. Elena inched backward. "My friends want to return to Earth where they'll no longer burden you."

"And you?"

Elena imagined herself sparring with a master. "I want to learn about your culture and see how we can work together."

The corners of the commander's mouth twisted upward. "You wish to work with us?"

"The better we understand each other, the better we can find common ground."

The stocky General Gorg emerged from behind the commander, her rough leathery face expressionless, with hard lines near the eye slits and mouth.

Averting her eyes, Elena bowed deeper.

"You seek enlightenment?" Gorg asked. There was economy in the general's walk and minimal facial movement. "You presume to find common ground?"

Gorg tilted her head in deference toward the commander. "Give me this one and the girl."

Zurbiz had harsh words with the general. Then she placed her hand on Elena's shoulder and led the way into a smaller room, decorated with pastel images. Gorg joined them and closed the panels. Elena studied the images on the walls without raising her head. They pictured other worlds, dark and full of mysterious grayscale imagery and shadows. It was amazing how much could be conveyed in shades of a single color.

The general glared at Elena with dark, haunting eye slits. "I watch. You think you are clever. You're mere human. You live or die by our rules."

After an awkward silence, Elena felt compelled to reply. "I understand."

"Do you? It's time you and your sister have children."

Eyes burning, Elena glared at the general. She raised her hand to make a point that cultures could learn from each other.

The electric shock caught Elena by surprise. Pain shot out to the tips of her fingers and toes and reverberated like cymbals in her brain, ending with a migraine. She slumped to the floor, recalling Thelma's convulsions.

As her mind cleared, Elena glanced up at Gorg and the commander. Gorg's thin lips turned up in what appeared as a smile; Elena couldn't be sure.

"Now you understand," the general said.

Unable to move her mouth, Elena nodded. Zurbiz lifted her with one thin arm. Averting her eyes, Elena stood.

"This boy," Gorg said. The wall filled with the image of a boy, sixteen or seventeen, in a wooded cave. The rugged boy had his arm around Thelma. Her head bobbed, showing no fear until the boy kissed her. Then she fell into an attack.

"She's too young," Elena protested.

"She's ripe. He's ready."

"Why is this so important?"

"Can you not guess?" Gorg grinned.

"Slaves?"

"Point for human. All great people have slaves for menial work."

"Thelma's only a child," Elena said.

"Will you take her place?"

Elena swallowed hard. She wasn't going to breed for the Knoonk. She turned to Zurbiz. "You're a woman. How can you force this on other women?"

Gorg moved closer. "You breed dog."

"We're not dogs."

"Mere human." Gorg's ridge-crest flexed forward. Her knobby nose turned up.

Commander Zurbiz spoke to Gorg and the general left the room.

"General Gorg is zealous," Zurbiz said, "good general, not

good diplomat." The lights dimmed. "She believes humans too barbaric for common ground."

"We have many fine qualities and skills," Elena said, and hated how she was apologizing for the human race.

The wall displayed Marc and Sorin beating on each other. Sorin went down and Marc stood over him.

"That's not fair," Elena said. "I believe you drugged them to make them aggressive. Most of us don't fight." She detected a moment of acknowledgement or something in the commander's eye slits.

The next grainy picture showed four humans, semi-nude on the beach. They snorted powder, popped pills, and washed it down with whisky.

"You drugged them as well," Elena said. "This isn't our behavior. It's your experiment. Is that all we are to you, one large experiment?"

"Human species acts violent," Zurbiz said, pointing to a picture of Marc zapping a Knoonk.

"That wasn't fair," Elena said. "He was punished for not knowing he should bow."

"How did you know?"

Elena felt Zurbiz setting a trap. "It seemed the right thing to do."

"Do you bow at home?"

"In some of our cultures it's expected. I did so out of respect."

The commander smiled. "You like our technology. What can humans offer?"

Elena's mind froze trying to come up with what they could offer a technologically advanced species. "We're an energetic people." The image on the wall changed to violent street demonstrations. "We have wonderful art." The picture switched to pornography. "That isn't art."

"And that?" The picture changed to Michelangelo's nude statue of David.

"Yes. The artist carved a piece of marble into something exquisite. We may have problems, but when we rise above them, we're capable of great things."

Zurbiz offered an enigmatic smile. "What about your Sisterhood of Nile?"

Elena wondered if the commander could read her thoughts.

The Sisterhood of the Nile was a secret society of professional women from around the world dedicated to the proposition that women held the key to taking society to the next level. Since the Sisterhood had no public discussion, no web page, and no media, the commander should not have heard of this group.

"Secrets do not build trust," Zurbiz said.

"Then perhaps you can tell me where in the universe we are."

"You already know. Now tell me about the Sisterhood."

"Are we on Mars?" Elena asked. "We certainly aren't on Europa."

Commander Zurbiz raised her hand as if to make a point and then snorted what might have been a laugh. "You are clever. Okay, you get credit for that. Tell me about the Sisterhood."

"I don't know what you're talking about," Elena said, wondering how Thelma was doing in the other room.

"Do not insult me again. You joined on July fifteen of your twenty-first year."

The penalty for divulging Sisterhood secrets was banishment or worse. Elena closed her eyes. "Who gave you this information?"

"Better but evasive." Zurbiz moved within inches of Elena's face as if to better smell the fear. "You are natural leader. It would be a shame to give you to General Gorg."

"What do you want with me?"

The panels slid open. Gorg entered, chattering staccato in their language. Elena studied the language's tempo for clues. Then Zurbiz followed Gorg out. "Duty calls."

Nalon rushed in and hustled Elena and Thelma from the commander's quarters.

"What's the emergency?" Elena asked as they hurried down the corridor.

"No emergency. Just a visitor."

FIFTEEN

The revelations troubled Elena; there were few secrets from the Knoonk. The immediate concern was Thelma and the boy. Their father had said they were alone in these caves. The boy's appearance begged the question of how many others were down there.

Transported to Cottage Cave, Elena cornered Thelma in her room. The girl looked ready for another attack.

Elena held Thelma's arms. "I know you're scared. We need to talk now." She clasped her hand over the girl's mouth before her sister could say anything or flee. "I know about you and the boy."

Thelma's eyes bulged as she struggled to break free. Her body convulsed on the bed. Holding tight, Elena absorbed blow after blow as the girl thrashed about and hummed as loud as she could.

"Stay away from that boy, from all boys. Do you hear?" Elena yelled, trying to drill her point into the girl's head.

Thelma's eyes rolled up. Her muscles fell limp.

Elena didn't let go. "How many others haven't you told me about?" Elena couldn't feel the girl breathing. Removing her hand from the girl's mouth, she placed her cheek nearby and felt no breath. She placed her mouth over the girl's and breathed for her, pushing down on the girl's chest to exhale. "Please come back." Elena continued with CPR.

Thelma choked and curled into the fetal position, coughing. At least she was alive. Elena stroked the girl's hair. Thelma was more fragile than Elena had thought. How could those monsters consider forcing a child on her? Elena sat with her sister for a long time. When Thelma fell asleep, Elena went downstairs.

Greeting her in the kitchen was the ex-marine, Janet Akers, looking emaciated, and Reese, who appeared as if she'd crawled through hell and back.

"What happened?" Elena hugged Reese.

Janet helped Reese to a chair at the table and dropped into a seat next to her. "There's no food. No one expects Marc to return. Barry is worthless. Sorin took over."

Through the window, Elena watched the tunnel. "Does he know you're here?"

"He's too busy having his way," Janet said. "When Zak tried to stop him, Sorin almost killed him. We're not waiting to see what happens next."

"He's only one man," Elena said.

"He's as big as two and he eats for four. He was a professional wrestler before he signed on. We have no weapons."

"Tie him up while he sleeps."

"I swear he sleeps with one eye open," Janet said. "He bloodied two women who tried. We don't know what else to do."

"Not much protection here," Elena said, "but you're welcome to what we have. What about the others?"

"They're waiting for Marc."

"How about you, Reese?" Elena studied the rag-doll slumped next to Janet.

"Things didn't work out with Carl. He chased other girls, got into fights. Now he's with Sorin and I'm having morning sickness."

Elena patted Reese's arm. "I'm so sorry. You deserve better."

Reese's eyes brightened. "Thanks for not saying 'I told you so.'"

"We girls need to stick together." Part of Elena's Sisterhood pledge.

Thelma danced into the kitchen and opened the refrigerator, now stocked, as it had been their first day. Thelma showed no surprise at their guests as she pulled out eggs and steak. The bounty would be short-lived if Elena didn't cave in to the Knoonk's demands.

While Thelma cooked the steak, Elena wondered how long she could protect the girl from the Knoonk's horrible plan.

>===>

After feasting, Marc and Tara transported, fully clothed, to a dingy gray cave with a hut and a stocked refrigerator.

They wouldn't starve, but he didn't feel like a man. He'd failed to lead the group or to live up to his own ideals. Never before had he faced an opponent like the Knoonk. He'd failed in everything that defined him as a man.

He curled up in a corner of the kitchen and considered sticking his head in the oven. It was electric. He considered ending things with a dull knife from the nearby drawer. He couldn't do that to Tara. She deserved better.

She sat with him for hours, making him more uncomfortable. "Do you want to talk?" "You need to eat." "Let me fix you something." "You can't just lie here."

He felt paralyzed.

She slapped his face. "Snap out of this. I won't be stuck with a corpse."

Her strength made him feel smaller.

"Sit up and eat!" She pushed him into a sitting position and forced a spoonful of soup into his mouth. "I'm going crazy here. Don't you dare check out on me."

Peering into her concerned eyes, he let her feed him like a baby. "I can't go on."

"Stop feeling sorry for yourself. We need to get back to the others. I've gone over every inch of this cave and can't find an exit."

Marc nodded. She was right, yet he couldn't move.

Tara knelt beside him. "Oh merciful masters, return us to the others."

"Stop it! They aren't gods."

"We can't stay here," Tara said. "Pray so our hosts will set us free."

Marc closed his eyes and knelt. They prayed to the Knoonk. Then he embraced the queasiness, for it meant leaving Hut Cave.

He and Tara materialized by the waterfall in Paradise Cave. Leaving her, Marc hurried to Father's Cave. Halfway up the path to the house, he stopped.

The garden had turned to dust. The picket fence lay in ruins. Window glass had scattered all about. The front door lay on its side. He stalked into the house.

Someone had trashed the downstairs. The sofa leaned against the wall. Tables were smashed, pictures torn down. Tara screamed outside.

Marc ran to her side. Over the back porch, microbiologist Barry hung by the neck. "Jesus!"

Tara threw her arms around Marc's neck.

He pulled away, trying to muster his strength. "Where's everyone else?"

He ran upstairs to beds on their side, dressers turned over, broken mirrors, and no other bodies. "Elena! Reese! Zak! Janet!"

Downstairs, blood covered the kitchen counters and floor. Heart pounding, he shoved the table against the wall. Groaning came from under the sink. Opening the cupboard doors, he saw Zak's head scrunched up behind the pipes. He was covered in blood.

"What the hell happened?" Marc stared into the dazed, swollen eyes of the pilot.

Marc helped Zak out from under the sink one limb at a time and stretched him out on the floor. Tara brought water to Zak's lips.

"They came early morning," Zak whispered.

Footsteps sounded on the porch.

"The lord and master returns," Sorin said from the front hall.

Marc confronted the big man and his sidekick, Carl, in the disheveled living room. "You sons of bitches."

Sorin's fist grazed Marc's jaw, sending him backward into the kitchen.

"Stop it!" Tara called out. "We have an injured man here."

Marc got to his feet. "Outside then."

"Gladly." Sorin patted Tara on the head. "I'll be back, sweetie."

Tara moved to let him pass.

Outside, Sorin tackled Marc to the ground. Marc broke free and jumped to his feet. He eyed Carl, who stood back, watching.

Feeling a surge of adrenaline, Marc swung. "Why'd you do it?"

Sorin caught his fist. Marc kneed the bigger man in the groin and slammed the palm of his other hand into the man's nose. Sorin fell to the ground, holding his face. "I didn't trash this place," he said.

"Where are the women?"

Scrambling to his feet, Sorin looked dazed. "I told you I didn't do this."

"Then who did?"

Tara stood by the kitchen door. "Marc, you've got to hear this."

He joined Tara in the kitchen.

"There's a gang here," Tara said. "They raided this morning. Six huge men. They took the women and killed Barry. Zak survived by crawling under the sink. There's no more food."

Marc glared at Sorin, who wiped blood from his mouth. "Look, man, no one messes with our clan. I say we find those bastards and ice them."

"All six of them?" Marc asked.

Sorin headed for the porch. "They've taken our food. I say we get them before we starve."

"I'm in," Carl said.

Marc stared at the pair, itching for a fight. "Okay, but we come up with a plan first. Agreed?"

Sorin hesitated, and then nodded. Carl followed his lead.

>===>

After breakfast, while Elena tried to comfort Reese, Thelma slipped out of the cottage and the cave. Reese curled up on the sofa and went to sleep.

"She's not handling any of this well," Janet said. "At least I had training for survival."

"We need to create a safe haven here," Elena said. "But I have no idea how to do that."

"Let me ponder that. You want to check on Thelma. Go. I'll stand watch."

Elena smiled and left Cottage Cave to look for Thelma and try for more communication time. Her father and sister had neglected to mention there were other humans. She couldn't let that boy lay a hand on Thelma.

Thelma obviously knew more than she'd let on, and Elena needed to make sense of the Knoonk mating demands. If they wanted slaves, they could kidnap them, as many humans as they wanted. It made no sense to take eighteen years to raise slaves from infancy. The Knoonk were too efficient and resource-strapped for that.

From the tunnel's ledge, Elena scanned Paradise Cave before

descending. At the far end, by the entrance to the first cave, Thelma and that boy held hands. It was criminal what the Knoonk demanded of her. Elena had to stop this.

She dropped to the ground and stalked across the cave. As she drew near, the boy, several years older than Thelma, embraced the girl. Thelma struggled to get free. The boy wouldn't let go. Thelma convulsed, her body jerking and contorting.

"Let her go," Elena called out as she ran into the clearing.

Startled, the boy let go. Thelma slumped to the pebbled ground in one of her attacks. Standing back, the boy grabbed a stick and prepared to fight.

Elena held her sister. "Stay away." She absorbed the rhythm of muscle spasms.

"*He's OK*," Thelma tapped out.

Elena shook her head. "You're too young for boys."

Hearing noises, Elena looked up. The boy and three bearded men dressed in western attire surrounded her. Elena stood over Thelma. "Leave us alone!"

A hand clasped her from behind. Another covered her mouth. She twisted and kicked to no avail. Strong hands held her and carried her. More hands grabbed her feet. Then they entered a dark tunnel.

SIXTEEN

Marc returned to the kitchen and saw that Zak's right leg had swollen to twice its normal size. With no medical supplies, he didn't know what to do.

"I'll go look for help," Marc said. "Don't move." He glared at Sorin and Carl. Was it asking too much for them to watch over Zak?

"Yeah, yeah," Sorin said with a shrug. "We're all screwed unless we work together. I get it. We'll keep watch and see if the bastards left anything useful."

Marc hurried into the tunnel leading to Paradise Cave. Tara followed. Though her presence made him uncomfortable, he couldn't leave her with Sorin. Keeping his distance, Marc searched Paradise Cave, finding no trace of Elena, her sister, or the others.

In Cottage Cave, the garden was intact and the house undisturbed. He hurried inside. Reese and Janet sat at the kitchen table. Reese looked as if on her deathbed. "Is Elena around?" he asked.

"She left to hunt for her sister," Janet said, getting him a cup of coffee.

While Marc told them about the attack, Reese slumped in her seat.

Red-faced, Janet stood and confronted him. "If you two hadn't run off…"

"We didn't," Tara said. "The aliens kidnapped us for one of their experiments."

Marc slumped against the wall, the wind knocked out of him, with his own sense of impotence. "It wouldn't have mattered. Six men attacked without warning. At least you two are safe."

Tara hugged Janet and sat next to Reese.

"Do you have any medical supplies?" Marc asked. "Zak's in a bad way."

Janet patted a medical pouch on her belt and headed for the door. "Let's go."

"Give me the kit," Marc said. "It could get rough out there."

"I'm going and that's final. You girls stay out of sight until we return." Janet led the way.

She had a toughness Marc admired. Now that he was away from Tara, maybe he could concentrate on what they had to do.

Back in Father's Cave, Marc helped Sorin and Carl pull apart fence posts to sharpen as weapons while Janet helped Zak.

"Now that we know what we're up against, we'll be ready," Sorin said.

Marc doubted that. "We haven't been ready for anything yet." Returning to the house, he wished he had his sidearm. He settled for making weapons out of refrigerator shelving and lampshade wire. They might have the element of surprise since their attackers believed they'd killed or captured everyone.

In the kitchen, he found Janet on her knees, praying. "Oh merciful ones, pray heal this man."

"For God's sake, Janet."

"I can't help him." Janet returned to prayer.

Marc stared at Zak. Blood oozed from his cheek, and his leg had turned the colors of the rainbow. Marc knelt, folded his hands and prayed to the Knoonk.

"Thor is a merciful god." The voice resonated through the cave. "Your prayers have been answered."

Zak's tortured body vanished, down to the last drop of blood on the tile.

Marc helped Janet to her feet. "You did all you could." He was disgusted at having prayed to the Knoonk, yet if that kept Zak alive, he would for now.

The pilot reappeared in a flash. The bruises and cuts were gone and his leg had resumed its usual shape and color. Still, his face showed the strain of what he'd experienced. "I failed you," Zak said.

"You couldn't have known," Marc said. "Can you stand?"

Zak stared past Marc to Sorin.

"It's okay," Marc said. "He's agreed to help."

"Gonna teach those scumbags to mess on our turf," Sorin said.

Marc winced at the bravado. "Zak. We're going after the bastards who did this. You and Janet hang back. We have no idea what to expect."

"Then you need every soldier." Zak got to his feet. "I did a tour—"

"You should rest here."

"I'll be fine. Give me a moment."

Janet helped steady Zak. "I'm in, too."

Marc shook his head. "I appreciate your valor, but—"

"Don't make me kick your ass." Janet grabbed a wooden chair, smashed it against the table, and pulled free two legs as weapons. "I'm not waiting for some cave crawler to get me in my sleep."

Zak took a few uneasy steps toward the door.

Marc grabbed his arm. "We do this my way. You wait until your strength returns."

"I want to catch those bastards," Zak said.

Taking Zak and Marc's hands, Janet motioned for the others to stand in a circle. When they did, she led a prayer. "Oh merciful Thor, pray favor us with surprise and victory against our enemies."

>====>

The frontiersmen carried Elena into a cave containing six log cabins surrounding a bonfire around which sat young girls and women in full-length, eighteenth-century dresses. The men wore something out of a cheap western, without six-shooters. She expected outlaws to shoot the place up, at least for show.

Thelma danced off after the boy, leaving Elena with the three bearded men who set her down near the campfire. All eyes were on her as she stood up. She felt just a twinge of self-consciousness in her micro-skirt, which would have been scandalous in such an eighteenth-century community.

Young girls, the oldest maybe twelve, swarmed around, gawking at her. Except for the boy with Thelma, she saw no other boys. Women with swollen bellies approached out of curiosity. Elena counted three men and sixteen women. More women emerged from the cabins.

One of the bearded men undressed her with his eyes. She

backed away. A cluster of young girls blocked her escape.

A brown-haired woman in a checkered dress approached. "Where did you find her?"

"She's attached to the girl," said the man who had dibs on Elena.

Cornered, Elena turned to the woman who had spoken. "Thelma is my sister."

"The girl has no sister," the woman said.

A freckled woman approached. "We don't need more mouths to feed." That sounded strange, given that she was expecting.

Others crowded around, suffocating Elena with their closeness. A man's hand grabbed her shoulder and drew her to him. She closed her eyes and clenched her fists. Alone, she'd have gone down fighting, but she had to think of Thelma.

Thelma's boy pushed through the sea of women and girls, who backed away, giving him space. Standing before Elena, he placed his arm around Thelma's waist. Elena couldn't read her sister's blank expression, a poker face if ever she'd seen one.

The teenage boy reached for Elena's hand. "This is the girl's sister."

Elena accepted a handshake and pulled free of the man behind her. Joey knelt on one knee. "My name is Joey Rugger. I'm in love with your sister. Will you permit me to court her?"

Before Elena could respond, Thelma ran toward the back of the cave, causing the women around them to move away. Elena hurried after her sister. The girl leapt, slammed into the wall, and clung to holds only she seemed to see. She scrambled higher.

"Thelma, hon, please come down." Elena brushed her hand over the wall and couldn't find a single crevice for climbing.

Joey joined her. "No one will harm you, Thelma. You have a very pretty name."

Elena glared at Joey who looked older up close. "She's only thirteen. I beg you. Leave her alone."

"I can't," Joey said. "There are clans down here. Thelma can't be on her own."

"She isn't. She's with me."

"With respect, she's often on her own. I've been watching over her."

"I bet you have," Elena said. "Why haven't I seen you before?"

"It's best to stay out of sight."

"Why?" Elena motioned for her sister to come down.

Joey did likewise. "I was raised by a clan that would hurt Thelma."

"This isn't your group?"

Joey shook his head. "There are tunnels and networks of caves. One day I found this place and met Thelma." He shrugged and stared at the ground. "Two days ago my clan followed me. They destroyed your cave, killed the men, and carried off the women. That's what they do."

"Your people did that?"

"They kidnapped me when I was young. I had no choice. This clan agreed to take Thelma and me. I want her safe."

Elena glanced at the multitudes watching from the campfire. "How long have these people been here?"

"Five years," Joey said. "The Knoonk kidnapped them from a small town in western Montana. They seem to take people from remote locations where they don't leave anyone who could report what happened. These people arrived in this cave a few days ago."

That explained why they hadn't crossed paths. "And your clan?"

"Captain Rick's clan has been here nine years. They've absorbed many others during that time. He's mean, very mean. He'd kill you for looking the wrong way."

"Where are the men from this clan?" Elena looked around.

"They died in clan wars. These survived and kept moving."

"What happens if your clan finds these people?"

"Pray to Thor they don't. They kill males and take the others. Women and children please the Knoonk. For them, our hosts provide food, clothing, and shelter, whatever they need. Kids are like gold down here."

Clans had been the basis of human society from ancient prehistory up to the current era, surviving in places like Afghanistan, the Middle East, Africa, and the Balkans. Modern governments crossed clan lines, yet when crises arose, clans stuck together. It sickened Elena to think humans had tumbled so far in these caves.

She gazed up at Thelma and at imagined cameras. *Zurbiz, what's your game?*

The girl's grip slipped. She dropped into Elena's arms. While adjusting Thelma's weight, she glanced into that peaceful face. "You and I need to talk."

The look Thelma returned said *No, we don't.* She twisted out of Elena's arms. Elena pulled her sister back and hugged her, tapping her finger into Thelma's side. *"Talk."*

Thelma smiled, spun free, and ran toward the exit, but didn't leave. She circled around, keeping her distance. Rather than give chase before all these people, Elena approached the campfire. Nearby stood a shrine. It held small, carved images of Knoonk prayer idols, no doubt for protection from the other clans.

SEVENTEEN

Marc, Carl, and Sorin hid in the bushes of Paradise Cave while Zak and Janet sat by the stream. Marc had no illusions about their chances of success. He'd faced tough challenges before, but never with so little situational intelligence.

Lights dimmed—evening. Marc's stomach growled. They had no food unless they raided limited supplies in Cottage Cave. He couldn't do that to Elena, Reese or Tara.

The ground rumbled like an earthquake. After the shaking stopped, it grew eerily quiet. Marc held his breath and squinted in the false-moonlight, wishing he had his military infrared.

Two huge, muscular giants emerged from beneath thick hedges along one wall and replaced the bushes to conceal their tunnel. Clad in animal skins, the bearded men scouted the cave and spotted Zak with Janet. The men moved catlike toward their prey, a redhead from the front and a black-haired giant who circled around behind without so much as snapping a twig. *You're good, too good*, Marc thought.

Red entered the clearing. Zak stood uneasily. Janet jumped to her feet. Red dove for Zak, crashing him into a yew, which broke his fall. Janet spun, jumped, and rammed her foot into Red's thick neck. The big man fell away. His partner laughed. Marc sprung up and drove a wooden stake into Black-hair's back.

Black-hair thrashed, reaching behind with huge hands for Marc and the weapon before he dropped to his knees. Nearby, Sorin

121

jumped Red and smashed a rock into the giant's head. Carl brought a fence post down on Black-hair's head. The huge man brushed Carl away and stood. Marc charged his giant again, driving a second stake into the giant's neck. Black-hair fell forward and hit his head on the rocky ground, now covered with his blood.

Red flung Sorin to the ground. Janet managed a kick to Red's stomach. Red caught her foot and tossed her into the stream. Marc jabbed a stake into Red's neck as Sorin tackled him to the ground. Red pinned Sorin. Carl drove a splintered fence post into Red's lower back. Something snapped. Red groaned and lurched, his legs twitching.

"Get him off," Sorin yelled.

Marc and Carl pulled on one of Red's arms. Red choked Sorin with the other. Zak and Janet pried Red's other arm loose. His legs appeared paralyzed, but he thrashed with his arms while they rolled him. His strength was immense. Carl cracked a stone onto the giant's head.

With great effort, they rolled Red onto his back and pinned his arms.

Marc crouched over the huge man. "You want to live or die?"

"Die. And so will you."

"How many are in your group?"

Red grinned, showing huge cat-like incisors. "Grrrrrr." He pulled his right arm free.

"You need help?" a deep, cavernous voice asked from behind them. This brown-haired giant tossed Janet back into the stream, grabbed Zak by the neck and threw him like a rag doll after her.

Red wrapped his free arm around Marc's throat. Marc couldn't believe the strength of this monster.

From behind Brown-hair came a war cry. Brown-hair looked startled. Then he fell onto his face. A teenage boy withdrew a dagger from the man's neck and charged Red.

"Joey!" Red released his grip on Marc and reached out for the boy.

Marc grabbed Red's arm.

Joey landed on the giant's chest and drove a blade deep beneath the big man's ribs. "This is for killing my family."

Red's face carried a look of betrayal as he gasped his last breath.

Marc pulled away from the giant and rubbed his neck. "I owe you my life, son."

Arms bulged beneath Joey's tee shirt as he grabbed Brown-hair's arm. "Best hide them or it won't be worth much." He dragged the big man down the path.

Thanks to the lighter gravity, Marc and the others dragged Red and Black-hair to the first cave. Then Marc dropped onto the gray rock to catch his breath. "Tell me, son, where did you learn to fight?"

"We have to go before others look for them."

"He knew your name, Joey?" Marc wasn't moving until he got answers.

"Your women are vulnerable."

"Why?"

"These men raided your camp. Others will come."

Marc thought of Reese, Tara, and Elena. "Why help us?"

"These are bad," Joey said. "Will you help fight them?"

Marc stared at the boy. They didn't stand a chance against a clan of giants. He nodded.

"I can get you in," Joey said. "It won't be a fair fight."

"How many?"

"Six more animals like these," Joey said. "Six other big guys, all mean."

"Twelve against three." Marc nodded toward Sorin and Carl. Even with the element of surprise, they didn't stand a chance. Still, he refused to wait for them to attack, or to die of starvation.

Janet joined them. Before she could speak, Joey interrupted. "It'll be a fight to the death."

"I'm in," Janet said. "They murdered one of our scientists."

"Are you prepared to see women and children killed?" Joey asked.

Janet stared at the boy, then at Marc. "As I see it, we don't have a choice. We have no food."

Marc shook his head. "I can't let you risk your life."

"If we don't stop them, I won't have a life," Janet said. "I'd rather go down fighting."

"She's right," Joey said. "They've conquered every clan they've met. I'm sorry about your friends."

From a canvas bag, Joey supplied each with weapons: long nails, sharpened sticks, and a makeshift hammer. Then he scaled the gray rock-face and disappeared into the wall above them. A few moments later, he unraveled a rope. One by one, the others scrambled up. Then Zak pulled up the rope, leaving no indication of the exit.

The tunnel was pitch-black until Joey lit a torch. Then the walls shimmered gray. This passage rose, fell, and meandered back and forth, becoming narrow in places with a low ceiling that forced Marc to duck. Here and there, they passed metallic posts, perhaps installed for structural integrity.

After what seemed like hours, Joey stopped and extinguished his torch, enveloping them in darkness except for a faint glow up ahead. They moved in silence to a ledge beneath ceiling lights. The cave below had no buildings, dwellings, or other signs of civilization beyond primitive men, Neanderthal or Cro-Magnon. Marc couldn't keep them straight.

Two giants stood guard by the cave entrance below. Two slept on slabs of rock nearby. In an alcove to the left, another giant lay with a woman. A sixth ambled across the cave. To the right, the cave fanned open with alcoves along both walls. Men and their consorts occupied two nearby. In the middle stood a ceremonial mound with carvings, and what Marc imagined were human sacrifices.

He spotted three of the female passengers, bound, awaiting their fate. Farther back in the cave was a nursery with dozens of small bundles lined up in rows. Two men guarded a dozen or so women. They'd been busy.

Marc counted the men once more and came up two short. Across the cave was a tent, presumably for their leader, Captain Rick.

Overhead lights flickered as the false-moon shifted position toward the back of the cave. Marc swallowed hard. This was a suicide mission, but he refused to wait for these bastards to attack. He took a deep breath and looked for Joey, but the boy was gone. *Thanks for the help.*

In the faint light, Marc signaled for the others to take up positions along the ledge and anchor several ropes Joey had supplied. If they didn't silence the six giants, nothing else mattered.

Joey appeared at the cave entrance. The two giants let him in. Then he pointed up toward Marc. *Bastard.*

He'd lured Marc and his team into a trap. Even so, with no food, Marc didn't see a better option. These people weren't the negotiating type.

He dropped his rope and climbed down before he realized something was messing with his judgment and training again. He hadn't thought this through. Adrenaline kicked in at such a high level all he felt was rage. The rest of his team stared down in disbelief. One of the door guards ambled his way, taking his time. Marc looked up. He needed to climb out of this mess, except he couldn't think clearly. He felt anxious and angry. Rage kicked in.

Joey ran up behind the giant, jumped, and drove his knife into the big man's neck. Marc dropped to the ground. The rest of his team began their descent.

The other giant by the entrance stood with a stunned look on his face. Then he fell face first to the ground. From behind him, three men wearing wild-west outfits sprinted toward the first of two giants asleep on a ledge to the left.

Marc, Sorin, and Carl ran to the alcove on the right. This giant looked up, angered at the interruption and swatted Marc away. Sorin stabbed the giant's neck. Nearby, a woman screamed.

The three cowboys reached the first alcove as screams pierced the air. That giant reared up. Two cowboys rammed spikes into his skull before he could defend himself. He fell on top of his bed-partner, who didn't utter a cry.

So far it had gone well, but they'd lost the element of surprise. Shrieks filled the air, a general alarm.

EIGHTEEN

Elena had enough of Thelma running off. After Joey kissed her goodbye, on the lips, no less, Thelma followed him to the exit of Frontier Cave.

Elena grabbed her sister's hand, tied one of the cowboys' ropes around Thelma's waist, and wrapped the other end around her own arm. "I don't want you seeing him again."

Thelma gazed at Elena as if to say, "Don't worry," which got young girls into trouble. *Not this time.*

"Why didn't you warn me about the clans?" Elena asked.

Thelma acted almost apologetic, as if she didn't mind Elena scolding her, either that or Elena was making too much of the pensive stare. While holding her sister, Elena watched the men of Frontier Cave leave and the women return to their campfire or inside their buildings, leaving Elena alone with her sister.

Thelma tried to wiggle free. Elena held tight. "I love you, kiddo. I don't want you hurt."

Thelma's body convulsed, limbs struck out in all directions. Elena picked up her sister and tried to comfort her. Thelma pulled free and tugged on the rope to get away. Elena followed her sister into the tunnel leading to Paradise Cave and pulled back on the rope until the other end fell into her hands. Thelma had untied the knot.

Hearing a wisp of stirring above her, Elena reached up and grabbed hold of a foot. She heard a yelp and the girl fell on top of her. Thelma struggled to break free. Elena pulled the girl's leg and fastened the rope tighter around Thelma's waist.

"Not so fast young lady. Where are you going?"

Thelma struggled and had another attack. Elena refused to let go.

"Lives are in danger, young lady. Now talk."

Thelma tapped out Morse code on Elena's back. *"Not now."*

Elena held Thelma close and rocked her. *"When?"*

"Danger. Must go."

Beneath a moonlit ceiling, Elena dragged Thelma across Paradise Cave and up to Cottage Cave. Reese and Tara sat at the kitchen table, looking worn and battered. Janet was gone.

As Tara described what had happened in Father's Cave, the ground shook, rattling dishes. Elena led her friends outside. The quakes ceased as quickly as they'd begun. Thelma darted for the exit. Elena pulled on the rope to find the end untied. She sprinted after her sister. Thelma dove into the opening. Elena followed, scraping her bare knees on the rock floor.

Thelma had to know Elena would catch her if she went to Paradise Cave. Therefore, halfway into the tunnel, Elena reached up and found another opening. In the dark, she climbed and caught the girl's foot. Unable to pull Thelma backward, Elena slipped a noose around the girl's leg, pulled it taut, and climbed up. The tunnel they entered ran perpendicular to the one below and was tall enough to stand in. Unable to see, Elena clasped the rope and embraced her sister. She tapped out, *"I'm coming."*

Thelma must have figured taking Elena was better than being delayed. She stopped struggling and hurried along the path, which weaved up and down in pitch darkness. After a long time, they approached lights and heard commotion ahead. Thelma sped up, struggling with the rope. They reached an opening overlooking a huge cave that reeked of sweat and fear, with fighting throughout. The ceiling lights had turned on as during daytime.

Amid screams and chaos, Elena saw bodies. Blood covered the gray rock floor. Ropes hung over the ledge from where she stood. She held Thelma and tried to pull her away from the carnage. *"We must go,"* Elena tapped out.

"Must help," Thelma replied.

Yells came from below and one voice in particular. "Janet, behind you."

Along the side of the cave, Marc fought a giant of a man. Janet spun and nailed a kick to a man attacking her. Elena spotted the reason for Thelma's concern. Joey fought a muscular man bigger than Sorin, who was fighting alongside Marc. It made no sense.

As much as she detested fighting, Elena scooted over the ledge and shimmied down the rope. These were her friends and this clan had murdered members of her group.

Marc fought hard and bravely, the quintessential marine. Losing wasn't an option. Janet took several punishing blows from a muscle man and returned each. Elena jumped the big man who attacked Janet. Janet spun and nailed him in the groin. The man pushed Elena off. As he did, Janet nailed another kick to his jaw. He went down. Janet plunged a sharpened fencepost through his chest.

"Here," Janet threw another stake to Elena. "Make it count."

Elena stared at the stick. She wanted to negotiate, not fight.

The giant Marc fought flicked him away like a speck of dust and turned on Sorin, who got in three punches before the giant head-bashed him against the wall. The huge man picked Sorin up and rammed his head, snapping Sorin's neck. The heavyweight wrestler fell limp to the gray floor. *This isn't a negotiation.*

When the giant rose up, a war cry screeched from their left. Before the giant could respond, Joey spun through the air and jabbed a spike into the giant's shoulder. Dazed, the giant thrashed about to remove the weapon.

Six big men dressed in caveman skins approached from the back of the cave with heavy clubs, longer than the weapons Marc and Joey had. One, covered in scars, appeared to be their leader, Captain Rick. The cavemen swung their clubs, driving the rest of them toward the last remaining giant. The giant picked up a frontiersman, the one who had leered at Elena, and flung him toward the cavemen, who clubbed him until he stopped twitching.

Elena and her friends were pinned between the giant and six cavemen. Sorin was dead. Marc and Carl looked beaten. Zak barely held on. Covered in welts, Janet and the two remaining frontiersmen were reeling from seeing their friend killed. Elena threw a rock at a caveman to distract him and swung her stick when he turned her way. Their weapons were no match for the big man's club.

Thelma dropped from the ridge above and noosed a rope around the last giant's neck. She clung to the loop of rope, pulling the knot tight. It wasn't enough to strangle the giant, though it did stun him. He fell backward. As he did, the rope tightened against the ridge above. The rope held. His neck stretched by the rope, the giant choked and struggled to get up

Marc flung his body at the giant's massive chest. The giant punched and missed. Marc jumped up and landed on the giant's neck. The huge man gasped and fell limp.

The six cavemen appeared shocked to see their last giant die. Captain Rick rallied his men. "I want the girl. Kill the men and take your rewards."

Thelma hugged Joey. Six cavemen closed in, swinging their clubs. When one on the left swung at Joey, Thelma spun into a cartwheel, slamming both feet into the man's head. Joey grabbed the club while Janet followed through with a flying kick to the nose. The caveman's head snapped backward as he fell to the ground.

Two cavemen rushed in to save their friend. Fighting turned chaotic. Behind the cavemen, women gathered. None raised any weapons to help.

Marc wrestled a club from a second caveman. The caveman hit Marc until Zak rammed a fencepost into the man's neck. A third caveman clubbed Carl. The two frontiersmen attacked that caveman, jabbing stakes into his neck and back. A fourth caveman attacked Janet. Elena jumped in, ducked a swinging club and kicked the man's knee. Joey leapt onto his back and stabbed a knife into the base of his skull.

Captain Rick shoved Joey toward another caveman and faced Elena with a huge grin. "You girlies want to play rough. That's not how it's done."

"Then why don't you surrender," Elena said, steadying her breathing. "Let's work together." She lifted the club she'd acquired and found it unwieldy to swing.

The only other caveman standing stood back-to-back to Captain Rick, as the frontiersmen circled behind.

Captain Rick lunged at Elena. "I'll start with you."

Elena tried to swing the club. Thelma spun into a cartwheel. Captain Rick brushed her away. Joey leapt in. Rick spun away and knocked the boy down. Marc jumped in with a club. Captain Rick batted him away. Zak and Carl sparred from the side. The captain wasn't a giant, yet he had better moves. They couldn't get behind him.

The two frontiersmen attacked the other caveman. Janet joined in. Despite her marine training, she was no match for the cave fighter. Joey leapt in, scored another hit, and landed between them. Captain Rick turned to finish the boy off. Thelma dropped from above and noosed a rope around the captain's neck, pulling it taut as she clung to the loop between the man's neck and the ledge above.

Groaning, Captain Rick grappled with the rope with one hand while swinging the club with the other. His partner turned. In that instant, Joey cut the man's belly from side to side. "That's for killing my mom."

"Will you yield?" Elena asked, facing Captain Rick.

"Never!" The captain reached for Elena.

Marc swept his legs. Losing his balance, Captain Rick fell against the rope. His neck snapped.

Joey cut Captain Rick's throat. "And that's for what you did to my sister."

Marc took Elena in his arms. "You shouldn't have come. I'm glad you're okay."

Closing her eyes, Elena savored the warmth of his embrace and memories of long walks by the lake back on Earth.

She pulled away to examined the carnage. Sorin was dead. Carl was injured. The frontiersmen had lost one man and one injured. Was the fate of humankind to act no better than cavemen, or was this another Knoonk test? At least they'd stopped the ones who had attacked her friends.

Thelma danced around Joey without letting him get close. When he approached, she ran and danced at a distance. Elena saw the girl wanted him, yet she seemed afraid. Elena didn't want her to lose that fear. Yet, she couldn't deny that her sister had shown remarkable courage in attacking a giant and Captain Rick. Elena needed more time alone with her to understand what this meant.

Turning toward dozens of women who gathered around, Marc announced, "The war's over. We haven't come to conquer but to stop these bullies. You're free to stay or come with us."

A tall pregnant redhead approached, wearing loose tan cloth. "You killed our men. Now you must provide. That's the way."

Elena stepped forward. "You're free to stay and form your own society, join a frontier society with these folk, or join us. Either way, let's try to live in peace."

The redhead stepped closer to Elena. "Let me explain how this works. The war is never over. Only strong clans survive. If you leave, we'll have nothing but death and misery."

"Then let's work together for mutual defense."

The redhead moved closer. "Who will lead us to victories and safety with the giants gone?"

Elena turned to Marc. "That's your specialty. You want the job?"

Marc looked to the frontiersmen, who gave no indication they'd follow.

Joey stepped forward. "I yield to Captain Marc."

The frontiersmen chimed in that they would as well.

With that settled, Marc addressed the women. "I pledge to keep us victorious and safe."

Elena counted over sixty women, most showing signs of pregnancy. This would be a huge challenge, and they had few resources.

With effort, the redhead knelt. The other women followed and gazed up at Marc, who didn't know what to do.

Joey tugged his arm and whispered, "We must kneel. It's expected."

Marc did, and a chorus rang out. "Praise to Thor and the Knoonk. We ask your blessings for this night and tomorrow."

Elena felt ill. The Knoonk weren't gods. They just had fancy toys.

A voice resonated throughout the cave, waking infants in the back. "Thor is merciful to her children. Praise Thor."

"Amen."

"Praise Thor."

"Amen."

"Praise Thor!"

NINETEEN

The air in Big Cave hung thick with man-sweat, rage, and fear. Stirrings of primal anger gripped Elena as she gazed over the sea of swollen bellies—slaves, for that was what they'd become. They'd abandoned their Earthly beliefs to worship the Knoonk in order to survive. They'd erased thousands of years of progress in a matter of years or weeks. She couldn't believe they'd fallen so low and so quickly.

While Janet released all of their captive passengers, all eyes focused on Marc. Elena stepped forward to say something. He blocked her and babbled on about leading by example. He still believed they could go home. His enthusiasm was infectious, or maybe these women simply were relieved that he would stay.

Marc slipped his arm around Elena. She felt primitive stirrings for this warrior chief who had vanquished their mortal enemies. He was their hero, the alpha male, and he wanted her. She wasn't convinced. He'd mentioned something clouding his judgment and she felt it too, another Knoonk manipulation.

Elena stepped forward. "Excuse me. How can you forsake hundreds of years of progress?"

"Keep your ideals to yourself," the tall redhead said. The others deferred to her. "Here we do what we have to in order to survive."

"Are we but rats in a maze?"

"Unless you've got another brilliant idea, this is our reality." The redhead pushed past Elena to stand next to Marc. She held up his arm in a victory salute.

Marc acted confused.

"Stop this," Elena said, appealing to the other women.

"How? With empty stomachs?" The redhead approached Elena.

When Elena backed up, the redhead advanced. Elena faced the other women. "Stop breeding for the Knoonk. Don't give them more lives to play with."

The redhead got into Elena's face. "You still don't get it. The Knoonk provide triple rations when we conceive. If we refuse, they punish us. Many have died with their pride. Have you ever been in these caves when they turn out all the lights, drop the temperature below freezing, deprive you of water and food for days, and drop in ravenous beasts to cut down your friends? The Knoonk control everything, including the air we breathe."

Elena turned away. There was no point arguing. Knoonk did make the rules, including manipulating their moods. These women didn't care what Marc said as long as he stayed, fought, and provided.

It still made no sense for the Knoonk to breed humans to test and study their behavior. They could do that through the com-link and social media on Earth.

When Marc resumed talking, Thelma joined Joey across the cave. She was playing a dangerous game of flirt and reject. She liked Joey yet was afraid, which was good unless she frustrated him until he did something rash. Still, Elena preferred Joey to the men. Elena crossed the cave and gave Thelma a hug. "You were very brave."

She started tapping out a message, but Thelma moved away. Elena looked around. They were too visible. She would have to be more patient.

"I won't let anyone hurt her," Joey said.

"She's too young and too fragile."

Joey smiled. "I told her to stay away. She wouldn't."

Elena sighed. "She obviously cares about you. Don't hurt her."

Joey nodded and joined Thelma in an alcove. Elena watched from a distance and considered her sister's behavior. Thelma had jumped into the fight to save Joey yet wouldn't let Elena use their Morse code. She felt twinges of jealousy that her sister might be sharing messages with Joey and not her. She needed to get Thelma alone, but could they ever be alone with all of the Knoonk cameras?

While Marc droned on about responsibility and his hopes for

saving them, the women listened patiently, too patiently.

"Resources are scarce," he said. "We will pool and share everything."

"Amen."

"No more pregnancies. We have enough young mouths to feed."

"Amen."

Not everyone was impressed. Abandoning their fallen companion, the two frontiersmen peeled away from the group with their reward: two young women who didn't resist. Elena moved toward them. A hand on her shoulder drew her back.

"Crazy, isn't it." Marc slipped his arm around Elena and held her tight. "I didn't think we'd make it, almost didn't. I did this for you and the others. I hope you know that."

She did. Closing her eyes, Elena released tension that reminded her of how scared she'd been during the fight. He kissed her and she kissed him back, following a powerful urge she didn't trust. She glanced up at the ledge. *Are you drugging us?*

She lowered her head and whispered, "This isn't real, Marc. We're rats in a maze, expected to perform."

"I'm sorry." Marc brushed her hair over her ears. "I do love you, always have."

Elena pulled away. "We're being watched, manipulated."

Marc embraced Elena. Even his sweat smelled deliciously musky. She broke it off and found her sister and Joey in an alcove, making out. She stood over them. Thelma glanced up and cocked her head as if trying to say something.

"We're going home," Elena said.

Thelma's face flashed a dozen mixed emotions, indicating intelligence behind the nonsense before it turned into her poker face. Then she blinked out, "*No.*"

"Did you hear me? We're going home."

When Thelma didn't budge, Joey sat up. "Can I come?"

"The idea is for you to respect that she's too young."

"I'll be good to Thelma, but you need to understand. There are other clans."

Elena stared at the boy. She wasn't sure she could trust him or anyone, though perhaps having Joey wouldn't be so bad. "As long as you behave you can stay with us."

Joey took Thelma's hand and helped her up. It would be crowded at the cottage, but Elena felt safer there than here. She refused to believe these women had regressed so swiftly to the primitive for a few scraps of bread. On the other hand, she hadn't been there for years.

While she followed Joey to the exit, Carl and Zak each snuck off with women. The pregnant ones returned to the back of the cave where infants slept, unaware of the dangers they faced. Peace had returned for them though not for Elena.

Perched on a ledge, Marc watched her. His eyes pleaded for her to stay. For Thelma's sake, she had to leave.

>===>

The return to Cottage Cave seemed to take forever along the dark tunnel. At several points, Elena lost Thelma and Joey. Each time, Thelma returned for her.

When they emerged into the bright cave, Elena filled with apprehension. She had so focused on the cave war and protecting Thelma that she hadn't considered that other clans might attack here. It was too quiet.

Elena ran into the cottage to find it empty with no sign of Reese or Tara. Thelma took Joey to her room and closed the door. Elena opened it to Thelma playing loud music.

"Me-o, see-o, rhee-o, tee-o." Thelma's voice blended into the music. It rose, fell or quivered with each pair of sounds. Joey joined in. "Wan-see, ban-see, tan-see, fan-see."

Before Elena could turn off the ear-splitting music, Reese and Tara emerged into the hallway. Elena closed the door and gave the two weary women a hug.

"I thought they'd taken you," Elena said, her voice breaking.

"We hid in the attic until we heard Thelma's music," Tara said.

Elena led them to the quieter kitchen where she described the cave war and Marc becoming their new leader. Reese poured herself a mug of coffee and slumped into a chair.

"Should we join the others?" Tara asked, brewing some more. "For safety's sake?"

"I'm not sure anywhere is safe," Elena said. "Other clans might attack."

"Why?"

"Down here clans fight over limited resources, and babies bring wealth. You starve if you can't or won't have kids."

"Why?" Tara asked.

Elena shook her head. "No idea."

"How barbaric. How many women and children?"

"Around forty pregnant women," Elena said. "Twenty others I couldn't be sure, and seventy children, plus five of our group."

"And the men?"

"The cave men are all dead. So is Sorin."

"I can't say I'll miss him," Tara said. "What am I saying?" She filled three cups with fresh coffee.

"I know," Elena said. "This place plays with our emotions. Marc, Zak, and Carl survived, as did two men from another clan that helped us. They left afterwards."

"So most of the men were killed in these wars?"

Elena nodded.

"How many women died?"

Elena thought and shook her head. "None."

"Isn't that unusual?"

Unable to think through the noise, Elena went to Thelma's room and opened the door. Holding on to Joey, her sister danced to the music and sang her rhymes. Elena turned off the music and barred the door. Thelma continued to dance, rhyme, and hold Joey.

"Joey, I need to speak with Thelma."

Joey removed Thelma's grip and moved toward the door.

Eyes wide, Thelma faked left and right, testing Elena's resolve.

Elena stood firm. "You and I will share this room. Joey sleeps on the sofa. Reese and Tara get the other bedroom."

Thelma seemed okay with Elena's announcement, though she grew anxious when Joey reached the door.

"Tell me about the other clans," Elena said. "Lives depend on it."

Thelma dropped onto the bed into another attack. Joey reached her before Elena did and stroked her hair. Elena sat next to him and held her sister's hand. She tried to find a way to use Morse code, but they were too visible. After a few minutes, the girl's body relaxed.

Elena motioned Joey away and turned to her sister. "I don't mean to upset you. I need to know what we're up against."

"Let me help," Joey said. "What do you want to know?"

Elena studied the boy, wondering how much to trust him. Reese and Tara crowded into the room. "Start with how you got here," Elena said to him.

"Five years ago we were camping in the Rockies. Dad and my sister went to scout a trail. Next thing I knew, mom and I were looking at Earth from space. Then we were all transported to these caves. Others arrived, mostly women and girls. I guess they made a mistake with me." Joey combed his fingers through his long dark hair.

"After a week," Joey said, his voice breaking, "Rick's clan captured us. Mom defied him so he grabbed my sister. Mom and Dad fought back. Rick tortured them until Mom submitted. Dad committed suicide. His last words were to survive at any cost. When I resisted, they starved me to make me fight for them."

"What about your mom?" Elena asked.

"They…" Joey paused.

"It's okay."

"No, it isn't." His face took on hardened determination. "After Rick hurt her, the Knoonk took her away. I haven't seen her since. That's the penalty for resisting."

"Where would they take her?" Elena asked.

Joey took a moment, his face sagging. "There are rumors of special colonies."

"Colonies?" Elena glanced at Thelma sitting on the bed.

"Clans cut off by some force field."

Like the couples that left, Elena thought. "How many other clans are there?"

Joey shrugged. "Every time I think I know, more show up. I've seen six big clans who didn't know the tunnel system. They only reached some of the caves. I thought when I joined the frontier clan with Louis and Thaddeus that I'd gotten far enough away from Rick."

"How big is this place?" Elena fanned out her arms.

"No one knows."

"What about weapons?" Tara asked. "How can we defend ourselves?"

"Each clan that submits to the Knoonk gets its own tools. Rick's clan got giants, which gave them the advantage."

"Where did the giants come from?" Elena asked.

"They just showed up one day."

"Does Thelma talk to you?"

Joey shook his head. "Just nonsense rhymes. Sometimes I see such sweetness in her eyes and at others uncontrolled craziness."

Elena got to her question. "What's your interest?"

"I really care for Thelma," he began, then sighed. "My little sister and I used to fight all the time. That ended when we got here. I see some of her in Thelma."

"So you care for Thelma like a sister?"

"At first, but … you saw her tonight."

"That worries me," Elena said.

"I won't hurt her. I promise."

>===>

Marc gathered Janet, Carl, and Zak together in the quietest part of the big cave. "I don't know what we've gotten ourselves into, but we need weapons, a defense alert, and food if we're going to survive."

"We could go back to the house," Zak said. "At least they had running water."

"And no food," Marc reminded him. "There's nothing to go back to and these people need our help."

"I don't see a stockpile of anything," Janet said, looking around. "If they have food storage other than baby food. We need Maggie," she said, referring to the redhead who seemed to be in charge.

"Then get her. If she wants to be in charge, let her."

"You'd trust her over one of us?" Carl asked.

As Janet headed off to find Maggie, Marc eyed the guy who had been Sorin's right hand man not long ago. "Do you want to play nursemaid to a cave full of children?"

"No."

"Well, then." Marc looked up as Janet returned with Maggie.

"I've been summoned?" Maggie asked.

"Nothing like that," Marc said. "We're new here."

"Obviously."

"If we're going to be working together, we need your help understanding how we get food and other resources."

"I've already told you," Maggie said. "Submit to the Knoonk and they supply."

"Could you be a tiny bit more specific?"

"Okay, off the Desert Cave just outside that exit," she pointed toward the tunnel, "there are caves with gardens, water, and other supplies. If we submit, we have access to those caves. If not, then all we get is the desert."

"So you have no reserves of food?"

"Only for the babies and children. Don't plan on digging into those supplies for yourselves. That comes with stiff penalties from the Knoonk. If you plan to lead, you need to protect our foraging parties in case other clans show up. I'm guessing that won't be easy with only three men." Maggie looked Zak over and shook her head. "Unless you come up with a really unique defense plan."

"I can fight," Janet said.

"You shouldn't," Maggie said. "Women don't die in clan wars unless they refuse to submit. The Knoonk won't allow it. Now, do you plan to defend our clan?"

"To the best of my ability," Marc said.

"Then you have work to do."

>===>

In the crowded Cottage Cave, Joey acted the perfect gentleman. He frustrated Thelma by leaving the bedroom door open except when she played her music.

At night, Elena insisted that Thelma sleep with her, a chance to use Morse code. *"Tell me about hosts,"* Elena tapped.

"Can't let them suspect."

"OK."

"Stay alive," Thelma tapped. *"Joey OK."*

"No. Don't."

"You don't understand. Must go."

Elena wanted to hold her sister back, but she didn't want the Knoonk to suspect.

Over the next few days, Elena turned for answers to Joey while Thelma lingered nearby, watching, as did the Knoonk, through their cameras. "Wars explain the shortage of men," Elena said, "But why no teens except for you and Thelma?"

Joey shrugged. "Other boys arrived. If you can't fight, you don't survive."

"You did."

"At school, I was small for my age and had to learn to defend myself."

"What about teen girls?"

Joey stood at the bedroom window, staring out at gray cave walls. "When girls come of age, they become pregnant or disappear."

Elena glanced toward her sister who hid in the hallway. "What about Thelma?"

"I don't know."

"She's too young."

"Other girls her age were taken. Thelma's different. Maybe they don't like different."

Elena pondered what Thelma might understand. She knew the tunnels, anticipated trouble, and knew how to fight. If the Knoonk didn't take different, perhaps Elena could help. "I'm afraid there's insanity in our family. I don't want her harmed."

From the window, Elena spotted Janet by the cave entrance, which meant one thing. Elena hurried to the kitchen to find Marc standing over Reese. Eyes closed, the navigator drew her arms to her chest.

"No more splinter groups!" Marc announced. "We're stronger if we come together as one group. We explore the other caves and we eliminate threats."

"Wonderful." Elena stood between Marc and Reese. "We go from victims to bullies."

"That's better than staying victims." Avoiding eye contact, Marc approached Elena. "If we work together, we can improve things. What do you say?"

"No matter how safe you think you are, it won't matter unless we can find a way to work with the Knoonk."

"I'm trying to hold everyone together." Marc looked at Elena and then looked away. "It would help if you, Reese, Tara, and the rest of our group supported me."

"I take it the cowboys didn't return."

Marc shook his head. "They came looking for the boy and took four more women."

Joey entered the kitchen. "They were allies only to kill the giants. They'll fight you for dominance."

"Why can't we work together?" Elena asked.

"That's not the law of the caves," Joey said. "They want their own clan. They had more people than you did. They'll raid and fight until they have it all, or die trying."

"We can't let that happen," Elena said. "The Knoonk want us

warring among ourselves. Wouldn't it be better if we worked together? What about other clans?"

Joey sat across from Reese. "When they appear, we have alliances and betrayals."

"So we fight like rats over crumbs for our jailer's entertainment?"

"It's always been that way," Joey said.

"What are your allegiances?" Marc asked.

Joey glanced at Elena. "I'm here for Thelma. When the time is right, I plan to marry her."

"And where is she?" Marc asked, looking around.

The moment Marc spotted Thelma, she ran into her bedroom.

Marc turned to Reese. "I need you and Janet to watch over the women and make sure they aren't hurt or anything. We found a cave off the main one that we can use as a refuge."

"Can't your redhead help?" Elena asked.

Marc shook his head. "Maggie is okay with having more children so the Knoonk continue to provide food. We have eighty infants under the age of five. I haven't a clue how to care for another forty in the next few months. We're running a day-care facility."

That haunted Elena. When humans needed rats for lab experiments, they bred them by the thousands. Why breed humans though?

"Please come with me, Elena."

"I can't." Elena left to look for her sister. Thelma wasn't in her room, so Elena sat on the girl's bed.

Marc entered and closed the door. "I hoped we'd get a few moments alone."

"Marc, the Knoonk watch everything."

Marc hesitated. "Everything?"

"They orchestrated your fight. They even turned on the lights in the middle of it all. Rick's clan must have offended the Knoonk, so they favored you. Don't for a minute think you were that good."

"If we're going to work with the other clans, Elena, we can only negotiate from strength. I need you. Not only because of your ideas." He hesitated. "I want us back together."

"Together we're vulnerable."

"I can't do this without you."

"Thelma is my first concern," Elena said. "She's not

comfortable around you or the clan. Until I understand why, I can't go."

"I can't protect you here."

"My mind's made up." Elena would take her coyotes of doom over constant bickering and cave warfare. Perhaps with Joey, she might get Thelma to stay long enough to learn something useful about the Knoonk. *Maybe.*

Elena tried to talk Reese out of joining Marc. In the end, Reese followed Marc and Janet out of Cottage Cave.

After the threesome had gone, Tara joined Elena in the kitchen. "What did Marc want?"

"To pressure me into joining him." Elena was glad Tara stayed. At least she'd have someone to talk to when Thelma disappeared.

"I'm glad you didn't give in," Tara said.

She seemed to want to explain her reasons, but clammed up. Elena didn't press.

After Joey left to find Thelma, Elena took Tara to Network Cave in the hope she could break through security to send a message.

Com-link news from Earth was discouraging. The Europa expedition had become a punch line in the battle against space expenditures. The government closed the space station and lab. Satellites that had faced space turned inward to address problems of food, water, and fuel shortages. Riots spread worldwide. Senator Jorgensen stood at the center of the anti-space movement. Many touted her as the next president.

She didn't have Elena's vote.

TWENTY

Despite the changes brought on by the clan wars, Elena transported each morning for chess with Nalon. It struck her as absurd to play a game in the comfort of Nalon's room, while the rest of her people suffered.

Nalon set up a new game and made the first move.

"Why do you promote clan warfare?" Elena asked.

"Play."

Elena struggled to transition between daily survival and the strategic game of 3D chess. Nearby, Thelma sat in the corner with her head bobbing as if to imaginary music while she flashed images before her eyes. Elena understood Nalon bringing her for an easy win, but not Thelma. She didn't ask or push the point because she didn't want her sister left with the clans.

Elena made her move. "Who is Thor?"

Nalon gave what Elena interpreted as a nervous smile. "He is one of your gods." She moved a ranger.

"Is he Knoonk?"

"Not Knoonk. Primitives respond to the god of thunder. Now play or leave."

As the days wore on, Elena improved at 3D chess, which meant Nalon took a half hour to destroy her. Whenever Elena thought she'd figured out game strategy, she confronted another nuance like spies and traitors that popped out of nowhere. She tried to get Nalon to talk.

"Do you want me to return you and your sister to the caves?" Nalon asked.

"No, ma'am." Instead, Elena took the tack of explaining human history and culture. Nalon showed particular interest in early American history.

"With better technology, Europeans took the land from the Indians," Nalon said as she set up another game.

Elena took a deep breath. "That's a dark spot on American history, not one of our proudest moments." She braced for another humiliating game.

"If Europeans had not taken over, there would be no America. Are you not proud of America?"

"I'm proud of America and upset at the ignorance of those who hurt the native peoples. If I'd lived back then, I would have fought to save Navajo lands."

"Strong people migrate and take from the weak," Nalon said. "Germanic tribes took Rome. Angles and Saxons took Briton. English and Spanish took America. Viking, Turk, Hun, Mongol, Greek. They all took land from weaker tribes."

"Like the clan wars you promote here," Elena said. "And where exactly is here?"

"Play or I'll send you away." The tone was abrupt and staccato, heavily accented.

To spare Thelma from the caves, Elena moved her ranger and took a deep breath.

She couldn't leave this alone. "I beg your pardon; do the Knoonk plan to invade Earth?"

Nalon leaned toward Elena and whispered. "It is treason to defy the commander."

Stunned, Elena pondered her opponent's words, and that Nalon had risked speaking them. The Knoonk did plan to invade Earth and there might be dissent. Elena couldn't decide if Nalon was falsely raising her hopes or offering to help. Why risk anything for a mere human? "Does Commander Zurbiz have a superior?"

Nalon focused on the game until she had the upper hand. "While Supreme Commander Viv was away, Commander Dod rose to challenge. Commander Zurbiz terminated her."

Elena was shocked and intrigued. Zurbiz had eliminated a rival. A rival to what? Elena couldn't focus and the game quickly deteriorated. "Has that happened before?"

"Never. Now Dod's troops belong to Commander Zurbiz."

"What are they planning?"

Thelma grew agitated; Elena was pushing things. She took a moment and asked what she was dying to know: "Are all Knoonk female?"

"Yes." Nalon fell silent and focused on the game.

Elena didn't press. She was amazed that Nalon had shared anything, though humans evidently didn't pose any threat. Still, after four games, which Elena stretched into three hours, Nalon hadn't ended their encounter.

Even though she was tired of losing, Elena welcomed a fifth game over life in the caves. "We have Democrats, Republicans, Independents, and Socialists," she said. "Do you have political parties?"

Nalon destroyed Elena's game in two minutes. If Elena didn't improve, Nalon might stop these visits.

After she'd set up a sixth game, Nalon looked up. "Our people are like your Puritans. We escaped persecution and seek new home."

"In America, we accommodate many people fleeing persecution. I'm sure we can work something out."

"We must be strong or enemies will destroy."

"How can we work together to help you escape persecution?" Elena sensed Nalon's discomfort, perhaps over a mere human presuming to help this superior race.

"Knoonk traitors on Earth must be caught."

Elena tried not to act surprised. "How can I help?"

"You cannot."

Yet Elena imagined purpose in these revelations. "What about the Sisterhood of the Nile? Commander Zurbiz acted very interested."

Nalon hesitated. "We are matriarchy. Sisterhood seeks matriarchy on Earth."

"We don't advocate a particular society except one that respects and protects women," Elena said. "Perhaps through the Sisterhood I can help you."

Gray panels slid open. General Gorg barged in with a sadistic grin across her leathery face. Nalon stepped back. Elena did likewise. Gorg smacked Nalon across the head, sending her victim like a doll against the far wall. "Tell human nothing. Leave."

Nalon scurried out of the room. Thelma curled up on the floor under the table, muscles twitching. Gorg grabbed Thelma by the neck and lifted her off the floor. Cringing, Thelma withdrew her limbs into the fetal position.

Elena prepared to pounce; she hesitated. She had no idea how strong this Knoonk was, though strong enough to lift Thelma with one hand, and there could be guards in the corridor. Fighting the rage building inside, Elena searched for anything to use as a weapon.

Gorg pushed Thelma against a wall panel and sniffed at her.

"Stop it, you're hurting her!" Elena lunged.

Still holding Thelma with one arm, the general spun and slammed her hardened foot into Elena's stomach. Doubled over in pain, Elena slumped to the floor. Her guts heaved. Gasping for air, she got onto all fours.

"Girl is ripe," Gorg said. "If not, we will recycle."

"Take me instead," Elena said instinctively.

Holding the girl's limp body, Gorg injected something into Thelma's arm. "This will fix her."

Thelma convulsed. Her face turned red, then purple. She frothed at the mouth. Her limbs flailed from her frail frame. Gorg turned away in disgust.

"Please stop, you're killing her." Elena's stomach hurt too much to let her stand. She doubled over in pain.

Gorg dropped Thelma to the floor like a squashed bug. Thelma thrashed about. Her skin turned purple.

"What did you give her?" Elena crawled to her sister.

"We shall see."

The attack consumed the girl in violent convulsions. Muscle spasms caused her limbs to move chaotically. Thelma's eyes rolled up until Elena feared they'd inverted. She held tight to keep the girl from banging her head against the floor.

"Stop before you kill her," Elena said.

"The human body is fascinating but weak."

Thelma threw her head back. Blood spurted from her mouth. She vomited. The poor girl wet her pants. The odor filled Elena's nostrils. Her own stomach wanted to heave. "Stop it!"

Setting Thelma's rigid body on the gray floor, Elena rose and approached Gorg. Wanting to lash out, she clenched her fists.

"A touching connection you share with the girl." Gorg's eye

slits narrowed to a line. "Take your best shot. She will never recover."

"I beg you. Release her." Elena tried to steady her breathing and push back this rage that was consuming her inside.

"Kneel."

Elena dropped to her knees and studied the Knoonk's intricate knee mechanism, a tempting target.

"You are little people. After we capture traitors, humans will become slaves."

Gorg didn't move a muscle yet Thelma vanished. Moments later, the girl reappeared, looking terrified. The muscle spasms had ceased. Elena took the girl in her arms.

Thelma's eyes glazed over, showing no sign of life. Her body hung like a rag in Elena's arms. At least she was breathing.

Gorg must have tired of the game, for she transported them to Cottage Cave and Thelma's bed. Elena held her sister for a long time before she sensed any stirring.

Thelma pressed her finger into Elena's side and fell limp. Then she clung to Elena and tapped, *"Love U."*

Elena broke down and wept.

>===>

Marc hadn't asked to lead the bigger clan, yet he couldn't turn his back on these people, either. At least his new responsibilities took his mind off having humiliated himself with Tara, though not the fact that he couldn't fix things with Elena.

He took it as his mission to prevent more pregnancies until they could sort out supplies. He set up High Cave, ten feet above the main floor, and asked Janet and Reese to stand guard over the women he could convince to go there. Carl and Zak found excuses to visit, and others protested that these women weren't doing their share of childcare. Marc couldn't win.

That night, Louis and Thaddeus from the Frontier clan snuck in. While the pair picked out women who had stayed below, Marc, Zak, and Janet dropped out of High Cave.

Marc approached Louis, the leader. "Either join us or leave."

"You're starving these women with your BS." Louis swung a club at Marc.

Marc ducked. "Why must we do this the hard way?"

The bigger man, Thaddeus, grabbed Marc from behind.

Women gathered around, interested in the fate of their clan.

Carl slugged Thaddeus, catching the big man by surprise. When Louis swung his club, Marc dodged and tackled the Frontiersman onto a rocky ledge. Zak grabbed the club and wrestled it free.

"Will you yield?" Marc asked.

"Not a chance." Louis caught his breath, grunted, and rolled on top of Marc.

Behind him, Thaddeus boxed Carl like a professional. Janet jumped and rammed her foot into the big man's neck. Thaddeus went down.

Louis looked up. "You make women to do your fighting."

"Ex-Marine," Janet said while she deflected a punch with a swift kick.

Marc rammed his fist into Louis' face.

Louis gurgled, rolled off, and got up. Marc stood, spun around, and landed his fist into the Frontiersman's Adam's apple. Choking, Louis swung his fists wildly. Marc landed a kick into Louis' stomach and the man went down.

Marc got him into a chokehold. "Will you submit?"

Louis eyed his partner on the ground and nodded.

Marc stood over the Frontiersmen. "Now that's settled, I have a new plan. We combine clans, find tools, and find out what's behind this rock."

Louis nodded. Marc led the men, plus Janet, to High Cave, a simple gray cave with no buildings. "Let's find out what's above those ceiling lights. Maybe the wiring will lead us to our hosts."

Most of the women hurried out of their confinement in High Cave. A tough-looking brunette approached Marc. "If you're going to dig, we'd like to help."

Two other women joined her.

"Very well." Marc pointed to a corner where the ground rose and the ceiling appeared closer. "Thad, Carl, why don't you start there. Let's find out what's hidden behind the screen."

Now that he'd had a look around, Louis headed for the exit. Marc stopped him. "Are we combining forces or do we have to keep fighting?"

Louis nodded. "We'll try it your way for now."

"Then let's bring your clan here."

Marc took Louis, along with Zak and Janet to retrieve the frontier clan. Once he'd settled everyone in Big Cave, Marc took Louis to High Cave.

While Janet watched over Big Cave, the five men and three women worked all day using tools formed from refrigerator shelves and lampshade metal. Digging crevices into the rock wall, they climbed and worked on the ledge by the ceiling.

With crude tools, digging went slowly. Beneath the gray veneer of the frame around the ceiling light was brown, crystalline rock. At first, they were careful not to damage the crystalline ceiling, but when Carl cracked a piece with no ill effects, they decided it was fair game to chip away at the overhead lights.

>====>

In the morning, when the overhead lights turned on, redheaded Maggie called on Marc as soon as he dropped into Big Cave. "Our food rations have been cut."

"See," Marc said, "we can't feed the people we have."

"You defied our hosts."

A young woman returned from Garden Cave where they'd been getting fresh vegetables. A vicious rash covered her entire body. She could barely walk.

Janet touched the woman's forehead. "She's burning up."

"The tomatoes are poison," the woman said. "Thor told me."

Maggie confronted Marc. "Thanks to you, we no longer have favor with the Knoonk. They'll bring plagues upon us, and other warrior clans. We must submit."

"Submit how?" Marc knew they couldn't feed all these people without Garden Cave.

Maggie closed her eyes. "It pains me to say, but the girls are prepared to bear children to bring back the food."

Marc took Maggie away from the others. "We're starting to dig. If we work together, we can find out what's behind all this. We don't need more mouths to feed."

"I've been here four years. Back then, I had lofty ideals. If we don't obey, the Knoonk will starve us. Dig, but allow us to eat."

Marc lowered his voice. "I say we abstain for a while."

"Then we're doomed."

Shaking his head, Marc joined the men in High Cave along with the three women diggers. One, Darla, approached Marc. "I'm ready to do my duty."

"Thanks, maybe we'll get lucky today."

"No, I mean to have a child. I've talked to the others. It's okay."

"We can't submit. They aren't gods."

"You dare defy mighty Thor?" The voice thundered off the walls of High Cave.

The others stopped working. Marc climbed to a ledge and hammered on the crystalline ceiling.

"You will obey." The cave shook as if from a mighty earthquake.

Marc steadied himself and resumed scraping. A crystal panel broke loose. Water dripped onto his face. He wiped it. Ice-cold water trickled down his neck. He stopped. A steady flow of cold water poured onto his shoulder, stabbing at him like a bed of nails. He moved aside. "Damn."

"What the hell?" Carl called out.

Water poured down from the ceiling rim on all sides, even from where they hadn't dug.

"Get to the other cave." Marc dropped into six inches of ice water with more pouring over him. Cold stabbed at every part of his body.

"I can't find the exit," Zak yelled. "The water isn't leaving."

"Keep looking." With water approaching a foot, Marc waded toward where the exit should have been.

The others joined him as water cascaded down the walls. He felt for the exit and couldn't find it.

Water rose quickly. Two feet, three feet, as if the ceiling had cracked open and an ocean was spilling into the cave.

"Get to the ledge!" Marc yelled.

"How?" Carl asked. "The water's coming too fast."

"What do we climb on?" Zak asked, pointing to water cascading over the walls.

"How dare you defy your god? Kneel before Thor!"

Marc's feet grew numb. The temperature in the cave plunged as icy water poured in. Four feet. Thad and Louis knelt, as did the women, Zak, and Carl. They submerged beneath the frigid water.

Marc's body felt numb; his head still ached. A million needles jabbed at him. Kneel or die. Kneel or die. He knelt.

TWENTY-ONE

Back in Cottage Cave, Elena and Tara listened to Joey's adventures with various clans, while Elena waited for a chance to message with her sister. From Joey's tales, Elena gathered that the cave system was extensive with untold numbers of humans in small groups. If the Knoonk's only requirement was that they have children, which still made no sense, it made even less sense for them to encourage clan warfare or for the clans to fight. In all his time here, Joey had never met a Knoonk.

That night, while Joey stood watch, Elena slept alone. Thelma had vanished again, depriving Elena of a chance to learn more. The only thing that made any sense was that, after helping Elena in other ways, Thelma didn't want the Knoonk to see her and Elena grow close. Thelma was protecting Elena, but from what?

The next morning's visit with Nalon began late. Thelma curled up in the corner under a table, facing the wall. When Elena approached to see how her sister was doing, Thelma babbled and shook.

Nalon pushed Elena to her seat and commenced play as if yesterday's confrontation hadn't happened.

Elena couldn't concentrate. "I'm sorry I got you into trouble. I need to know what Gorg did to her."

"Thelma is sick. General Gorg gave her medicine."

"No, the general gave her poison. She's getting worse."

Nalon sat expressionless. "It's your turn. She will be better in a day or two. I could medicate."

"No more drugs." Elena watched her sister twitching in the corner. "How can I get her back?"

"Move."

Inside, Elena wept. Her mission had been to discover. That no longer mattered. Now she wanted to take Thelma to Earth, get her medical attention, and make her better.

"Play!" Nalon said.

"You can't treat her that way."

"Play or I return you to the caves."

Elena couldn't see the virtual pieces through moist eyes. *Focus.* If she lost her connection with Nalon, who knows how much worse things could get. Elena moved a scout. "Did Gorg punish you?"

"We speak as one." Nalon rushed her move, as if she, too, were distracted.

Choosing an aggressive strategy, Elena matched Nalon's game. "You have your own mind. Teamwork is great, but when bad things happen, we must stand up."

"Dissent leads to death, permanent death."

"You mean no rebirth?" Elena was guessing something like what the Knoonk had done to revive passengers.

Nalon nodded, keeping her eye-slits on the game.

"You tell me things I can't use. Why?"

Nalon advanced a scout. "Your move."

"Is your transporter powerful enough to reach your home planet?"

"Move!"

Rattled, Elena arranged her guards to stop Nalon's advance. "You can't, can you? That's why you needed a ship. Can you transport to Earth from here?"

Nalon moved her troops to support her scout. "Too many questions lead to dissent and disaster."

The answer appeared to be not at that distance, which explained why they'd transported Joey and others via spaceships.

Elena activated her spy, which put her opponent at a disadvantage. "Why do you encourage clan warfare?"

Nalon stared at Elena who peered back into those eye-slits. On the wall behind Nalon, an image appeared showing a cave filling with water. Humans screamed in agony. Marc splashed frantically. The cave shouldn't have filled above the exit. Elena moved her regent and approached the screen for a closer look.

"You lose," Nalon said.

"What is this?" Elena asked.

The screen went blank.

"You're drowning my friends," Elena said. "I beg you to stop."

Nalon froze, as if awaiting instructions.

Nausea gripped Elena. Before she could protest, Elena reappeared in Big Cave with Thelma. The girl ran. Joey chased after her and caught up. Closing her eyes, Thelma clung to him.

While Elena pondered the meaning of Thelma's actions, eight soaked bodies appeared on the ceremonial platform. Elena hurried to Marc. Other women approached. Knotted into the fetal position, Marc shivered so hard she thought he was having convulsions. Ice crystals clung to his cotton top and jeans. "Get blankets," Elena yelled. "Quickly."

Janet and Reese joined her, as did Maggie. Elena covered Marc with a blanket and huddled next to him, offering her warmth.

"Hurry," Maggie said. "More blankets. We need volunteers to warm them. Start a fire. Gather round. Remove wet clothes and dry them." The redhead was their real leader and could have been matriarch if she'd wanted.

While Maggie ran the show, Elena massaged warmth into Marc's body, willing him to recover. "Come back to me."

Marc looked up. "I refuse to give up," he whispered, "but I don't know what else we can do. They almost drowned us."

"I know," Elena said. "Rest. I want to check something."

She headed for High Cave. Entering the tunnel from Big Cave, she crept along the rocky path until she hit a dead end. A metallic door blocked the entrance to High Cave. With all this technology, was she kidding herself to think humans and Knoonk could live together in peace?

On Earth, technological disparities led to wars and dominance by those with superior tools. That spelled doom for humans, and left Elena with three problems. She needed to understand the Knoonk's capabilities and objectives and Nalon wasn't sharing much. She had to find their weakness, which would be tough without understanding their technology. Then, she had to find a way to warn people on Earth before it was too late.

Elena returned to the others. Marc approached, shivering under three thick blankets. "Thanks." He looked devastated. "I've let pride get the best of me," he said. "We can't defeat the Knoonk. They have all the toys. All we have are fists, which don't count for much down here. Hell, I'd settle for five minutes in the ring with one of them."

"Careful," Elena said. "They're strong for their size."

"A fair fight. That's all I ask. Man to man."

"I'm afraid they're all female."

Marc's jaw went slack. He averted his eyes. "I know I've done crazy things. I've made far too many mistakes."

Elena closed her eyes. "Marc, I appreciate all you've tried to do. I can't join you. My focus has to be on Thelma. Besides, I haven't given up hope of getting home."

"I thought you weren't in a hurry to leave," Marc said.

"I'm not, but I haven't resigned myself to staying, either."

Marc stalked away, deep disappointment etched in his face. Though his needs tugged at her, she located Thelma and took her and Joey to Cottage Cave.

>===>

Despite Joey's security precautions at Cottage Cave, Elena barely slept that night. Coyotes howled and drew near, as if trying to tell her something she'd missed. She believed to her core what she'd told Marc about getting home, yet when she analyzed every scenario in gory detail, none got her out of this cave system. Even if they'd been in caves on Earth, that wouldn't help. Besides, the gravity was too light.

The coyotes howled louder as she went into labor, producing guinea pigs for Knoonk experiments. After interminable hours, Elena gave birth to a beautiful thirteen-year-old girl, which the Knoonk tore from her arms to produce more. With no time to recover, she entered labor again. When the Knoonk took this child, she resigned to die. The Knoonk restored her body for an eternity of producing for their pleasure, an eighth level of Dante's Inferno.

Elena woke from the nightmare. It was still middle of the night. She went to the kitchen to write in her electronic journal in the hope that would bring to her a solution. Her notes took the form of dialogues with Dad, a continuation of their discussions on first contact. She fixed a pot of coffee and set it aside.

After she finished an entry on Knoonk physique and another on their decor, Elena glanced up from the kitchen table to see Tara in the doorway. "Care to sit?" Elena poured two mugs of coffee.

Tara reached for a mug and let her arm drop. "How do you do it?"

"Do what?"

Tara's face creased, adding years to her appearance. "Keep a journal when there's no chance of getting home."

"I don't doubt we'll get home." Yet Elena was filled with doubts.

"The Knoonk won't let us go. Even if we could dig our way out, we're not on Earth. The lack of atmosphere would kill us. We might as well be dead." Dark clouds filled Tara's otherwise beautiful blue eyes.

Elena put her hand on Tara's arm and pushed the mug of coffee closer. "Why don't you tell me what's troubling you?"

Tara looked away. "Is Thelma around?"

"She disappears at night. Come, sit."

Tara sat across from her and cradled the mug. "I don't know how to say this."

"We're both professionals."

Shuddering, Tara steadied the coffee mug with both hands. "I'm sure you've heard about Marc and me."

"You did it?" Elena couldn't believe she'd blurted it out. She knew Marc and Tara had disappeared, and that she had no right to claim him after turning him down, yet she'd pushed the conclusion into the recesses of her mind.

Tara's forehead wrinkled. "That's the thing." She twisted blonde curls between her fingers. "I'm pregnant."

Elena felt the wind kicked out of her and tried hard not to show it.

"I'm having morning sickness." Tara struggled with the words. "At first I thought they were transporting me again. When that didn't happen and the feeling got worse, I realized I could be expecting."

"I guess congratulations are in order." Elena struggled to breathe.

"I shouldn't have said anything."

"Please continue." Elena's voice broke. "What happened?"

"You don't understand. Nothing happened."

"What?"

"The Knoonk put us in a maze," Tara said. "We couldn't eat unless we did it."

Elena placed her hand on Tara's arm. "I'm sorry."

Tara lowered her voice. "Marc didn't want to. He kept talking about you. They drugged us. We were both scared. He couldn't perform."

"Accidents happen."

"I know about accidents. This wasn't one."

"Are you sure?" Elena asked.

"It isn't Marc's and I haven't been with anyone else. So whose is it?"

Elena stared at Tara for a long time. If anyone else had said this, she wouldn't have believed it. Tara was a meticulous, levelheaded engineer who missed nothing. If she said she couldn't be pregnant, what did it mean? Whose baby indeed? "Have you told Marc?"

"He avoids me like the plague. Besides what could he say?"

"Have you told anyone else?"

Tara shook her head. "I didn't want to tell you. I had to tell someone. You're the only one who thinks clearly."

"Don't be so sure."

"You still care about him, don't you?"

Elena nodded.

"I shouldn't have dumped this on you." Tara tugged at clumps of hair. "I didn't know what else to do."

"Don't tell anyone else."

"What does it means?"

Elena stood and paced. "It's another Knoonk experiment."

"If they can make me pregnant like this, why make such a fuss about mating?"

When Elena placed her hand on Tara's shoulder, it struck her like a bolt of lightning. "If you know the child isn't yours, can you care for it as much?"

Tara picked up her mug and set it back down. "We've been acting as if they're here to experiment and learn about us. The cost of space travel is prohibitive and consumes huge amounts of energy that has to come from somewhere. There has to be a stronger justification for their being here."

Settling on Earth, Elena kept to herself.

Coyotes circled ever closer. That was when Elena remembered that Coyote was the trickster. Her mind hadn't been playing games, but rather warning her.

TWENTY-TWO

At the morning's chess match, Elena played recklessly to see how her opponent responded to a no-mercy approach.

Thelma resumed flashing images in the corner, seeming oblivious to what the Knoonk had in store for her. Or was she? Thelma wouldn't let Elena get close enough to find out. Joey wasn't much help, either. He knew the caves, but he'd never visited the alien lair.

Elena funneled her frustrations into the game. "Why make us have children?"

"You were told," Nalon said.

"Nice fantasy. What's your real plan?"

"Babies ensure good families," Nalon said. Then she made an ill-advised move, the first indication the Knoonk could be rattled.

"Come on, Nalon. You don't see families. Where are the fathers?"

"They died in war."

"Why do you encourage wars?"

Nalon moved a virtual chess piece. "Humans are violent."

"Gorg is violent."

"No! General Gorg is a great leader."

"Okay, a violent leader." Elena moved her regent. "I've answered your questions about humans. Why not tell me about your people? I thought we were friends, chess friends at least. Besides, who could I tell?" Elena smiled as she activated her spy deep in Nalon's territory.

Nalon sacrificed her regent to blunt Elena's move and stared across the game. "Are we friends? Then why distract me during the game?"

Inwardly, Elena smiled. "Just making conversation. You need something from us. Why not ask?" She folded her arms.

Nalon motioned for Elena to take her turn. When Elena didn't move, Nalon's face grew intense. "We tell you to settle down and have children."

"In other words, you can't ask an inferior species." Elena leaned away from the game. "When you ask, we have the opportunity to work together."

The alien's face tightened. "Very well. Knoonk need human help to adapt to Earth."

"Wonderful," Elena said. "How can we help?"

Nalon stood up. "I must go."

Elena gently touched Nalon's arm. The skin had a tough, leathery texture over tight tendons and stringy muscles.

Nalon faced Elena, annoyed as if buzzed by a mosquito.

Removing her hand, Elena bowed. "Sorry, that's how humans show affection."

Nalon appeared confused and agitated.

Elena looked away. "I understand you're not permitted to discuss these things." Elena backed up to remove any perceived threat. "So please take me to Commander Zurbiz."

"I cannot." Nalon's hand clutched her zapper.

"Tell the commander I wish to speak with her."

"It's not wise to make demands."

"Wisdom comes with age, and I'm young." Elena looked up.

Nalon's eye slits narrowed. "Do not anger the commander."

"You are wiser than I, but I need to speak with her."

Nalon hesitated as if getting instructions telepathically or through a microscopic earpiece. "Very well." Nalon opened the panel to the corridor.

In her haste, Elena took the lead.

"Wait!" Nalon dragged Thelma by the arm and hurried to keep up.

Passing rooms full of yellow-clad aliens, Elena imagined their busied activity as an ant colony with no one idle. Yet, unlike Earth's slave history, humans here lived at leisure with the exception of clan wars and the need to care for children. It didn't add up.

"Wait," Nalon said. "Wrong path."

Elena entered a narrow corridor and followed the pungent odor of rotting flesh. It reminded her of decomposing animals in the desert, only stronger. Nalon grabbed her arm with an iron grip. Elena yanked free and entered a room.

None of her nightmares prepared her for this. Hanging from ceiling hooks were the bodies of the six giants, upside down, minus their heads. Blood drained into pans. Elena felt nauseous.

Thelma buried her head into Elena's chest and tapped *"Leave."*

Nalon reached for her zapper. Elena grabbed Thelma's hand and ran out into the corridor. She collapsed to the floor, her stomach in knots. Thelma crumpled on top of her, rolled away, and went into convulsions.

Nalon stood over them. "Stand! Commander Zurbiz will not see you."

Fighting back the nausea, Elena stood. "I think she will."

Nalon pointed the zapper at Elena's head.

Standing, Elena yanked the weapon from Nalon's hand and placed it on the floor. "I wish to see your commander. I won't make trouble." Elena bowed and stepped back.

Arriving with two yellow-clad guards, Gorg croaked something to Nalon. The junior alien scrambled to pick up her weapon and get out of the way. Gorg pointed hers at Elena, who braced for the shock. The general turned and zapped Thelma, who convulsed on the floor.

Gorg grinned. "You offend, I zap her. How much more can she take?"

Thelma's eyes rolled up to show the whites. Elena knelt to help.

"Rise or I zap again."

Glancing up at Gorg, Elena had no doubt the sadistic alien feasted on human flesh. She stood up. "Thelma is innocent."

"You're not. March!"

Nalon led Elena down the corridor. As final humiliation, Gorg dragged Thelma by the hair with the girl's body still twitching. Elena couldn't think how to help her sister without making things worse. She couldn't escape the image of naked humans hanging from meat hooks. Were they breeding humans as food, a delicacy?

When they entered the commander's quarters, Gorg clobbered Elena with something hard, sending her sprawling onto the hard gray floor. When she got up, Thelma still hung by the hair from Gorg's left hand.

"You wish to see me?" Zurbiz pressed her round, leathery face into Elena's, close enough to smell Elena's fear.

Elena inhaled the strong fish odor of the Knoonk commander. "Yes, your highness. First, would you ask General Gorg to release Thelma?"

Gorg dropped the girl, bouncing her head against the floor. Elena closed her eyes. Poor Thelma was paying for Elena's obstinacy.

"Thank you." Elena wanted to ask about the meat locker; she stuck to the main issue. "I'm confused by your need to make human babies."

Gorg stood over Thelma, pointing the pen-sized tube at the girl's head. Elena swallowed hard. Even with eyes open, she saw her coyotes circling—beware.

"Tara." Zurbiz moved away and up a step, which allowed her to appear taller than Elena. "She gave good performance."

"Whose child is she carrying?" Elena watched Thelma crawl toward the wall.

"Are you demanding?"

When Gorg pointed her weapon at Thelma, Zurbiz raised her hand.

"A request," Elena said. "Who are the mother and father?"

"Mixed DNA," Zurbiz said. She straightened up to look even taller. "Mostly Marc and Tara."

"Why are you doing this?"

Gorg zapped Thelma. The girl's body knotted into a tight ball.

Hot tears burned Elena's eyes. "Please stop."

"Don't waste my time." Zurbiz' ridge crest folded forward like an angry fist. "Or I will have you both destroyed."

"You mean recycled, like the giants from last week's war."

Zurbiz raised her hand to stop Gorg. "It would be a shame to cause more brain damage. The girl is almost useless."

"You haven't answered my question," Elena said.

"Watch yourself." Zurbiz shifted her weight.

"If you wanted me terminated, you'd have done so already."

Zurbiz smiled. The lines in her face relaxed as her ridge crest returned to neutral. "Lucky for you I find you amusing." She moved to a screen on the wall. "It won't matter. You can't tell humans on Earth and even if you did, they can't stop us. Besides, if you cause trouble, Thelma and your friends will suffer."

Elena bowed until she could barely see them. "Why mate humans?"

"So we can study you," Zurbiz said.

"For what purpose?"

Zurbiz acted amused. "To see if it can help us."

"Help how?"

"You tread on thin ground."

Elena stared in silence. That often worked since people couldn't stand quiet. Zurbiz was no ordinary opponent, though. The commander glared, her narrow eye slits a mystery. Elena took a deep breath. Humans couldn't defeat this technologically superior race, so she would have to find another way. She would have to find common ground. She waited. She had the rest of her short life.

The commander's mouth stretched into a smile. "You are fascinating. Very well, a terrible war consumed our world. We need a new home."

"Now we're getting somewhere," Elena said. "You wish to settle among us."

Zurbiz let out a high-pitched wail that shot up beyond Elena's ability to hear. "I thought you were smarter than that. We will take Earth."

"I wanted to hear you admit it."

The commander glared as if contemplating punishments. Then she let out another rolling laugh.

"I'm glad I amuse you," Elena said. "We should be able to find you some land to resettle."

"We will take Eurasia, Africa, and the Americas."

"How about Bermuda? How many Knoonk are there?"

"You think you're clever?" Zurbiz said. "It won't matter."

"It does. If you have a million Knoonk, we have many options."

Zurbiz shook her head. "Humans feel threatened. They will make war and lose. Knoonk will conquer. Enough silly questions. Leave."

Nalon headed for the exit. Gorg lifted Thelma by the hair and dragged her toward the door like a sack of garbage.

Elena lifted her sister in her arms. "I'll carry her."

Gorg smacked Elena's head, knocking her toward the doorway. Sharp pains transformed into a headache. Elena kept her balance for Thelma's sake and hurried after Nalon. There was no negotiating with Gorg. The general had a pathological hatred of humans. Elena's only hope was that she could somehow reason with Zurbiz because there was no way humans could overcome Knoonk technology.

While struggling to balance Thelma's weight, Elena caught up with Nalon.

Nalon whispered, "I warned you."

"I'm learning, but you know it's wrong."

"Is it wrong for the Knoonk to survive?" Nalon picked up speed.

"There are options. You don't have to conquer Earth. Let's work together."

"I cannot help."

"You're the only one I can talk to." Elena struggled to keep up, her arms growing weaker with each step. "It's wrong to conquer."

Nalon slowed and nodded to an approaching blue-clad colleague. "I obey."

Elena stopped and laid Thelma against a triangular wall panel. When she brushed the girl's hair from her eyes, Elena caught a flicker of awareness and with it the terror that had gripped her sister.

"You know our history." Elena held Thelma close. "In the twentieth century we fought many wars. We learned that each individual must choose to do right even if ordered to do wrong."

"The Knoonk fought wars. We learned that when individuals take their own paths, it leads to death and destruction."

"You're an individual, Nalon. You can think for yourself."

"I am part of a community that depends on me."

The queasiness of transport interrupted Elena's thoughts. She hadn't gotten the answers she wanted, yet something in Nalon's manner indicated there might be dissidents. Elena wondered how many and what influence they might have. Her only hope was that her actions hadn't killed her chess matches.

>===>

Nalon returned to the commander's office. Zurbiz whispered something to General Gorg and then motioned for Nalon to join them.

"We are behind schedule," Commander Zurbiz announced. "You will need to distract the humans so they don't interfere."

"I say we kill the sisters," Gorg said. "The younger one is defective and the older one is asking too many questions." She turned to Nalon. "You must not tell her anything."

"I am keeping her away from the others so she doesn't stir up trouble," Nalon said. "Her attachment to her sister is useful."

"Nonetheless, tell her nothing."

"For now, we keep the sisters alive," Zurbiz said. "The Supreme Commander has plans for them." She turned to Nalon. "How will you distract the humans?"

"I will let Elena believe she is making progress by learning things she cannot use."

"Give them all-out clan wars," Gorg said. "That will keep them busy. Then they will beg for our mercy and submit."

Zurbiz nodded. "Nalon, make it happen."

Nalon hurried out, thankful to avoid further reprimand.

TWENTY-THREE

The exchange with Zurbiz and Gorg rebelled against everything Elena believed. According to games she played with her father, first contact should have been to share culture and exchange ideas, not conquest and enslavement. Nalon hinted at being friends. Zurbiz kept humans as pets or lab rats. Gorg brimmed with hatred. She wouldn't hesitate to pull arms off a young girl.

The Knoonk planned to conquer Earth and there didn't seem to be anything Elena could do. Yet her stubbornness wouldn't allow her to give up.

While Thelma slept on her bed, another nightmare invaded Elena's thoughts. The Knoonk could implant an embryo without her knowing. It might or might not have her DNA, and she had no equipment to test it. Could she love such a child?

She gazed into Thelma's placid face and shed a tear. Elena wasn't violent, but she wanted to strangle Gorg and Zurbiz for abusing this poor child. *I will protect you until my last breath.*

Thelma opened her eyes and gazed up. Elena stroked the girl's brown hair, careful not to irritate the roots. Thelma made no attempt to run. Her eyes seemed less alert. Gorg had fried her precious mind.

Elena kissed the girl's forehead. A strange protectiveness grew inside like a lioness protecting her young. While Thelma wasn't her child, Elena felt maternal.

"Feeling better?" Elena asked.

Thelma slumped on her bed, muscles relaxed, and eyes vacant.

"Hon, I need you to listen. This is important." Elena almost wished Thelma would run, to show she was whole. "It's vital for you not to have sex with Joey or anyone else. You know what that is, don't you?"

Thelma nodded so slightly that Elena couldn't be sure.

"I could tell you many reasons not to. The most important is your body isn't ready. At your age, carrying a child would be difficult and might kill you. Promise you won't."

Elena found her sister's pulse normal. She brushed hair from the girl's face and kissed her. "You're a good girl, Thelma."

Not sure if Thelma would ever recover, Elena fought back tears. "I'm so sorry they zapped you. It's my fault. I never meant for them to harm you."

Thelma wiped tears from Elena's cheeks and pasted them on her own.

>====>

Elena left her sister to rest and fixed herself a salad. When she looked out the window, Thelma was heading for the tunnel entrance. Elena put the salad makings in the refrigerator and followed her sister to Big Cave.

Thelma and Joey embraced, leaving Elena to wonder if anything she'd said had sunk in. Thelma broke away and ran across the cave.

Joey approached Elena and sat on a nearby rock. "They hurt her pretty bad, didn't they?"

She stared at him. "She told you?"

"I see it in her eyes. What happened?" He acted much older, which raised Elena's concerns for her sister, who returned and hovered just out of reach.

"It's my fault," Elena said. "I wanted answers and they took it out on her."

"General Gorg's behind the experiments," Joey said, "bringing giants, mutants, and drugs."

"Drugs?"

"That's how the giants get so big. Growth hormones and steroids, I'm guessing. They created cat-men, horse-men and other aberrations. Rick's clan destroyed them all. Now he's gone."

"You sound disappointed," Elena said.

"Most times he was okay, but after battles, he had blood lust."

Thelma ran up and tagged Joey, teasing him to chase her. When he stood up, she bolted. It gave Elena some comfort that her sister might be getting better, though Thelma didn't understand the consequences of teasing Joey.

In the back of Big Cave, Maggie acted as den mother to pastel-gowned women who sought advice and supplies. Nearby in the nursery, dozens of babies gurgled and cooed. Others cried, demanding attention. The redhead appeared worn out by the burden yet kept her cool.

Elena joined Maggie. "Can I help?"

She was surprised that such a primitive cave held a sink, a small tub with running water, and shelves stocked with supplies. The infants wanted for nothing.

Maggie hung a towel on a rack nearby. "Come back at feeding time." She held out her long beige gown and eased herself onto a nearby rock.

"I couldn't help notice that everyone looks up to you." Elena sat on a ledge across from Maggie. "Why don't you lead this clan?"

Maggie smiled; her face suddenly appeared youthful and vibrant. "Years ago I asked the same question."

"Everyone listens to you. Marc can't run things without you."

"Before they dragged me down here, I was a palimony attorney. Now I help women have babies so we can eat. Ironic, eh?"

"What if you refuse?" Elena asked.

"You saw what happened at High Cave. The Knoonk control everything."

"How could female Knoonk do this to women?"

Maggie shrugged and picked up a fussy baby. "We're animals to them."

"Why not lead instead of depending on men?"

Maggie shifted weight, rubbed her belly, and placed the infant on her shoulder. "In war, the losing clan's leader is killed. Too many people depend on me." She burped the baby and put it into the crib.

Commotion drew Elena's attention to the cave entrance. Marc returned with Carl and Thad. "We're under attack," Marc announced.

When Elena got up, Maggie took her hand. "Sit and watch. Don't challenge anyone."

"These are our people."

"That's not the way." Maggie led Elena to an alcove behind the nursery. "If we fight and win, great. If we don't, losing warriors face punishment and death."

"If we don't fight, we become the property of strangers. I'd prefer death." As Elena said this, her hands trembled. They couldn't put up much of a fight without weapons.

"We don't know how strong the attackers are." Maggie sat where she could watch. "If you submit, they won't harm you. I've watched brave women skinned alive, their body parts put on display. As a result, women haven't fought for years and they don't die in battle or after. That's how we survive, unless you have a fabulous new plan."

Twelve hairy attackers burst through the cave entrance, dressed in tattered rags and wielding clubs. Maggie was wise in her way, though it made more sense to engage everyone, as when they'd defeated Rick's clan. Elena couldn't see Thelma or Joey and hoped they'd escaped.

Spotting ropes along one wall, half the brutish attackers headed that way. Others fanned out through the cave and headed toward the back where Elena sat with Maggie.

Shaking, Elena faced a dilemma. She wouldn't submit to these barbarians, which meant death. It had to be better to fight when she might affect the outcome. She glanced around for anyone willing to help, and saw only pregnant women and children.

Tara joined Elena and Maggie. "This looks bad. Have you seen these guys?"

While they moved like men, their hairy bodies and long arms seemed apelike. An attacker with a scruffy golden beard lifted a first trimester blonde off the ground and examined her. He handed her to his companion and approached Elena. She reached behind and grabbed a loose rock the size of her fist and another slightly larger.

Maggie cast a frightened look and moved away. Tara scooted back. Elena was on her own.

Gold-beard singled out Elena as his prize and reached out to touch her hair. With all her might, Elena rammed a rock up between his legs. Stunned, the man slouched as if to vomit. Stepping aside, she slammed the other rock into his face like a huge fist and the first into the back of his head, like crashing cymbals. His nose gushed blood. He swung his arms to grab her and she brought a stone down on his head. He fell to his knees.

His partner picked up Elena and threw her against the wall. Pain shot out like a lightning bolt from her left shoulder to the tips of her fingers and down her spine. She slumped to the ground. This second attacker jumped on top of her, pinning her against the rock slab. She couldn't breathe, couldn't move. *What was I thinking?*

The man grimaced and rolled off. Elena gasped for air as Maggie and Tara beat him with clubs. Blood oozed from his nose, cheek, and the back of his head. He flailed his arms and went limp. Maggie helped Elena to her feet. "You'd better pray we win."

From the top of the rope-lined wall to the right, Janet and Reese fired arrows. Below them, two men hung onto ropes with arrows in their chests. They struggled to keep from falling. Two others lay on the ground below with spears protruding from their torsos. Janet and Reese reloaded and fired again.

In the center of the cave, Marc, Carl, and Thad fought three attackers, trading blows with clubs and sticks. A fourth circled behind. He fell to his knees when an arrow penetrated his neck. Nearby, another attacker lay on the ground. By the opposite wall, a hairy beast attacked Zak, pushing him up against the wall. Elena picked up a club and raced over to help.

Maggie joined her. When she did, the other women picked up whatever they could use as weapons. Janet dropped to the ground to help. Elena reached the hairy attacker before the other women did. "Will you surrender?"

The man swung his club in a circle. Though surrounded, he refused to yield. When he faced Zak, she threw one of her stones at the attacker's head. Stunned for a moment, the man spun toward her and Zak clobbered him. Janet rammed a spike through the man's heart. He fell face first onto the now red stone floor.

Feeling a rush of adrenalin, Elena broke out of that group to help Marc. One attacker was down with an arrow in his back and several women were clubbing him. A second swung his club to keep the women away. They pelted him with stones. Marc, Louis, and Carl surrounded another attacker. Thad was on the ground bleeding. He dragged himself behind one attacker and tripped him.

By the time Elena reached them, the man was dead. By cave rules, all attackers had to die. She pushed through a mob of angry women to the last man standing. He no longer was. The bloody pulp of what had been his head lay in a pool of congealing blood.

Elena glanced up in time to see one of their attackers with an arrow in his chest limp out of the cave. Nearby, Thad struggled to his feet.

Marc rushed to Elena. "You okay?"

"No thanks to you."

"We had things under control. You should have played by the rules. You almost got yourself killed."

"You might have told me." Elena pointed toward the exit and the fleeing attacker.

"Hate me later." Marc headed after the man. "We can't let him escape."

Carl and Louis joined him to pursue the injured attacker.

Before Elena could follow Marc and the others, Maggie grabbed her arm. "Remember what I said. Today we were lucky. If you fight and lose…"

"I know," Elena said, "but I can't just sit here."

Elena met Janet at the cave entrance. Covered in blood, the ex-marine looked weary yet determined. "Ugly business," she said.

Janet led the way through the tunnel. "Marc asked me to hang back to warn the others if necessary."

When they reached Desert Cave, the large central cave for this part of the underground network, Elena pulled Janet aside. "If we're going to survive these caves, we have to find a way to negotiate instead of fighting. Fighting doesn't bring more resources. It only kills off our men."

"That would take a miracle. Did you look at those guys? Something out of pre-history."

"The women fought well today."

"They followed Maggie," Janet said, "that's all."

"At least we defended ourselves. I'm tired of others telling me what I can and can't do."

They stalked behind tall cactus following a trail of blood to a cave opening. The three men pursued their attacker with clubs. As much as this primal behavior disgusted her, Elena needed Marc to vanquish their foes. Still, there had to be another way.

>====>

Elena followed the men into a new cave while Janet stayed behind. Large adobe tenement buildings filled the space. They towered over narrow gray streets and rose almost to the lighted ceiling. Balconies brimmed with pregnant women surrounded by children watching the commotion below.

"Stand and fight," Marc said. He approached the last attacker who dragged himself toward one of the buildings.

The hairy man turned and raised a stick. Louis brought a club down on his head. Carl swung, hit the arrow in the man's chest, and drove it through. The hairy man looked down with surprise and slumped to the ground without a fight.

Elena was stunned that none of the women offered to help this man as he gasped his last breath. *How sad.*

The women on the balconies neither cried nor cheered as they watched.

Marc looked up at the crowded balconies and shook his head. "Let's go," he whispered.

Their victory seemed empty. Marc eyed Elena for some confirmation of what he'd done. Unable to give him any, she headed for the nearest adobe building.

"Elena?" Marc said. "Let's go home."

She stepped into what looked like a hotel lobby to the left and to the right a nursery with fifty-some babies in neat rows of cribs in front of windows looking on the scene outside. The woman by the desk appeared older and grayer than the other women. Beneath a loose tan gown, she looked pregnant. Her weary eyes followed Elena as she approached.

"Are you in charge?" Elena asked.

"Some think so." The woman's voice sounded tired.

"I … No one's upset over what happened out there."

"What happened?" The old woman stroked her belly.

"You know very well." Elena cursed the inhumanity of not mourning their dead.

"Brothers, fathers, husbands, boyfriends, and sons are dead. Why mourn now?"

"What about the man who died?"

The gray-haired woman shrugged. "This community has been in these caves for ten years. Those men showed up last week and did what they do. It was time for them to leave." She spoke with only the ghost of emotions long ago spent.

Elena glanced at the front desk and a thick registry. "This is a community of women?"

The gray-haired woman nodded. "When all of a clan's men die, women and children come here."

"How many?"

"Two thousand women. Six thousand infants. That's a full time job."

Elena's knees buckled. She leaned against the counter to steady herself as she contemplated the enormity of the Knoonk plan. This wasn't dozens or hundreds, but thousands and tens of thousands. She looked around at dozens of haggard faces. "How many humans live down here altogether?"

The woman shook her head. "Our clan keeps growing. Every time a war kills off the men, the women and children transport here."

Elena thought of Maggie and the others. If Marc hadn't stayed, they could have ended up in a facility like this. Like quicksand, the cramped gray quarters had sucked eight thousand souls into one cave. "What happens when the children grow up?"

The woman sighed. "Boys rarely survive. Girls join the women when they reach maturity."

It shouldn't have, but the news stunned Elena. "When?"

"At the beginning of maturity."

"How can you do that to young girls?" Elena asked.

"The Knoonk demand it or force starvation. We run a safe community and punish abusers. We have plenty of food and medicine."

"And you accept this?"

"On Earth, I lived in a dump, trying to feed two infants," the woman said, rubbing her back. "We didn't have food. Plumbing didn't work. This is like heaven, and we have no disease."

"No disease?"

"None. We play by the rules and the Knoonk take care of us. Why return to my Earthly dump? We don't get sunlight, but I rarely saw any on Earth."

Elena took a deep breath. "You're running a—"

"House of ill repute?" The old woman laughed, which gave her face renewed youthful beauty. "The men pay for nothing. If we meet the Knoonk's sixty percent quota and pray to them, we get what we need. It beats the heck out of scratching a living back home."

"Mind if I talk to some of your girls?"

"Be my guest. You got a name?"

"Dr. Elena Pyetrov." She wasn't sure why she added the title except she was tired of people talking down to her.

"I'm Chrissie. A doctor no less."

"Not that kind."

"Figures," Chrissie said. "Pyetrov, eh? A Pyetrov lived here years ago."

Elena got excited. "Did you meet him?"

"No. There were stories of an astronaut by that name who arrived eighteen years ago. How are you related?"

"Daughter."

The woman stood with effort. "Hmm. He has another daughter, doesn't he?"

"You know her?"

"Come." With an air of mystery, the old woman lifted her dusty tan gown and led the way. As she did, she appeared much younger.

Chrissie was suddenly all talk. "What do you think of the pictures lining the hallway and stairs? These are my children now, my charges." She introduced each like her only child.

Along the well-lit gray hallways were dozens of photos of girls. Elena noticed how beautiful the younger ones were. Such a travesty they were bred for the Knoonk.

Chrissie knocked at a plain plastic door, one of two dozen on this floor. A girl in her mid-teens answered, blonde, attractive, worldly, and beneath loose beige pants and yellow top, pregnant. Two little girls played on the vinyl floor behind her.

"Vanda, I have a guest for you." Chrissie entered the tiny apartment with a sofa, a couple of chairs and a small kitchen. "Dr. Elena Pyetrov."

Vanda's face turned pale. "Do you ... have you met Thelma?"

Elena nodded. "Do you know her?"

Vanda slumped onto her pale blue sofa, her weathered face clouded with sadness. "We used to play together. The Knoonk took me four years ago for this. How is she?"

"She's okay, but she only talks nonsense rhymes."

Vanda lifted one of her girls and balanced the plump infant on her knee. "When they took Thelma's mother, it hit her very hard. Then her father became ill."

"Her mother died in an accident."

Vanda shook her head.

"Mother's dead, knocked in head, lay on ground until she bled."

Elena spun around, "Thelma! You scared me."

Thelma's eyes were wide with fright.

Arms out, Vanda approached Thelma, who fled. Elena ran after her sister. By the time she reached the street, Thelma was gone. Elena ran through the tunnel into Desert Cave and came face to face with three bearded men resembling drifters she'd seen in New Mexico. One was bald. She didn't get a good look at the others. Not seeing Thelma, Elena ran back into Tenement Cave.

When she reached the narrow street, one man grabbed her from behind. "Not so fast, pretty lady. We've come to sample the wares."

Elena stomped on the man's instep, slammed her foot into his knee, and broke free. She ran into the tenement on the right hoping to find Chrissie. The woman wasn't there. Before she could reach the stairs, a second man with an eagle tattoo on his forehead grabbed her arm. She spun to kick. A third man with a scar on his cheek grabbed her leg.

Baldy joined in. Elena screamed. Tattoo pulled on her flimsy blue top. Scar forced his lips on hers. *This isn't happening.* She couldn't even scream. Elena lashed out, confronting too many arms and legs.

Chrissie entered. "We'll have none of that, mister."

Baldy backed away to deal with the intruder. Other women joined Chrissie, carrying an assortment of frying pans and kitchen utensils. The men dropped Elena on the hard floor.

She was thankful for the lighter gravity, but before she could get away, Scar fell on top of her.

"Get off," Elena screamed. She pushed the man's face away to avoid his horrid breath.

Scar tried to get up. There were too many bodies and the incessant sound of metal against bone. Scar's body lifted away and vanished behind the women.

Chrissie helped Elena to her feet and the crowd of women parted. Lying on the floor were Baldy and Tattoo, covered in blood.

"Are they…?" Elena asked.

"The penalty for abuse," Chrissie said.

"Thanks."

"Is this one of yours?" Chrissie pointed to Marc, who had Scar in a chokehold.

Elena nodded.

When Marc let go, Scar slumped to the floor.

Marc approached and took Elena in his arms. "I never should have left."

Elena threw her arms around his neck, hugged him, and wept. *This fighting has to end.*

TWENTY-FOUR

The more Elena discovered the more determined she became to stop the Knoonk.

Vanda left her daughters with Chrissie and led the way down a dark gray tunnel lit by her slender flashlight beam. Elena followed. Marc insisted on joining. Elena sensed her sister nearby. The girl had a knack of lingering in the shadows.

Vanda's nervousness heightened Elena's fears. The narrow, dark tunnel closing in around them didn't help. She couldn't stop thinking how helpless she'd felt when those men attacked.

She took Marc's hand and wondered why cave law dictated killing when the Knoonk focus was on children. She reminded herself that if those men had lived, they would have come back for revenge.

Vanda made a sharp right and stopped at a flat, gray wall, the maze's dead-end. "There used to be an opening," she whispered.

Elena ran her hand across the smooth, metallic surface and noticed a thin seam around the edges: a door. "When were you last here?"

"Four years ago, just before they took me."

"What's behind this wall?" Elena placed her arm around the frightened girl to comfort her, and to keep her from bolting and leaving them stranded.

"Tunnels that lead to where they took Mrs. Pyetrov."

"You've seen her mother?"

175

Vanda shook her head. "Girls come from all over and tell stories."

Marc tugged Elena's arm. "I don't like this. We should go."

Her gut told her he was right, but she couldn't leave. "Is there another way?"

"I don't know," Vanda said. "Tunnels meander. The trick is not getting lost."

Elena examined the door. "This must be how they flooded High Cave."

Marc drew near. "We'll only find what the Knoonk want us to. Let's go while we can." That didn't sound like Marc the adventurer.

"They took my mother, too," Vanda said. "And my older sister."

The ground vibrated. The gray door slid up. Unlike the panels in the alien lair, this one consisted of a thick rectangular sheet.

Marc held Elena back. "If we go, we might not be able to return."

"I need to know."

"What about Thelma?"

Elena took a deep breath. When she looked behind them, she couldn't see her sister, but sensed her sister's presence. Elena took the tiny lamp from Vanda and led the way. Vanda attached her clammy hand to Elena's elbow. For a long time they hiked up and down an uneven path with the light illuminating only a few feet ahead.

They reached a split in the passageway and Elena stopped. "Which way?"

Marc took her hand and looked around, probably trying to form a mental picture of the tunnels. *Good luck with that*, she thought.

"Are you sure you want to do this?" he asked.

"Keep your antenna up. I need to know." While Elena's hands trembled at the risks they were taking, her anger at not getting answers from Nalon or Zurbiz drove her forward. "Which way?"

The frightened girl pointed to the left. Elena led the way with Marc at her side, while Vanda tagged along. Lights shone up ahead.

Elena turned out her lamp and approached the ceiling ridge of a wide cave. Along the sides were dozens of alcoves. Rows of beds lined the huge room. Women lay down, sat in groups watching old TV shows, or shuffled about. They all looked exhausted and dazed, possibly drugged. There were no children.

"What is this place?" Elena whispered. She counted beds.

"Hell." Vanda's cheeks streamed with tears. "The Knoonk send those who disobey here."

There were over fifty women. "They sent you?" Elena asked.

Vanda nodded. "They plant babies and harvest them. Many girls die." She sobbed. "They bring the girls back alive for more."

Elena slumped against the wall. This was her recurring nightmare, what her coyotes were warning her.

"I say nuke 'em," Marc said.

She shoved him. "Do you even know where the Knoonk are?"

"You know what I mean."

"Keep your epiphanies to yourself." Elena clenched her fists and stared into the cave. "Vanda, how do we get down there?"

"You can't be serious," Marc said.

"Don't go," Vanda said. "If they catch you, they'll keep you." She turned to Marc. "I don't know what they'll do to a man."

Elena did—the meat locker. Pulling away from Marc, Elena hurried along until she located an opening. She followed a winding path that led down to the tunnel into the cave.

When she emerged into the light, Elena froze. Thelma stood by a haggard woman in white rags who looked old enough to be her grandmother yet bore a striking family resemblance to Thelma. The girl dragged her mother into an alcove.

Elena caught up with them. "Natalie Pyetrov? I'm Elena."

The old woman sat in a drugged stupor. Thelma caressed her mother's face and then smacked her own. She repeated this until Natalie clutched her daughter's hands in her lap.

Natalie looked up, her eyes vacant. "Thelma's a good girl. Alexander talked about you."

Elena placed her hand on the woman's wrinkled arm. "I want to help Thelma. Tell me what happened to her."

Natalie forced a smile; her face wrinkled in pain. She spoke in short bursts between shallow breaths. "Alexander lost legs. Knoonk wouldn't help. I loved him ... very much. After Thelma ... they demanded more. I refused. They brought me here. Every three months ... another fetus. I die. They bring me back."

Three months wasn't full term, which meant they were harvesting fetuses.

Elena leaned closer and whispered. "Where are the Knoonk?"

"Never see. Take Thelma. I can't help."

"You know what they want for her."

Natalie nodded. "I love her … so much." She hugged her daughter, yet no tears flowed.

"She only talks nonsense," Elena said.

"Likes fairy tales. Take her before they come."

"Come with us, for Thelma's sake."

"Can't," Natalie said.

Thelma pulled her mom's arm.

"Think what it would mean to her," Elena said.

"Chip in brain. If I go … they catch you. Leave."

Elena pried her sister from her mom and held her. Thelma struggled. Desperate not to draw attention, Elena tapped out on Thelma's back. *"Can't help."*

Thelma calmed and reached for her mom.

"Act like the others so we don't draw attention," Elena whispered.

She took Thelma's hand and pulled her away. Near the exit, another haggard woman in a worn beige robe grabbed Elena's arm. "You don't belong here."

Thelma disappeared into the tunnel, still holding Elena's hand. Elena tried to let go, to let her sister escape. The grip grew tighter. Another hand grabbed her wrist, Marc. He pulled her into darkness and lifted her to the higher tunnel as others entered the passage below. Holding her breath, she listened to the women acting agitated about Elena's visit.

A Knoonk guard spoke. "Get back or you go to other place."

Elena couldn't imagine what could be worse. When the voices died away, she reached for Thelma. The girl had gone.

Vanda led the way down the ceiling passage. By the time they reached the steel door, it had sealed again.

"I told you they wouldn't let us return," Marc said.

"That isn't helping," Elena said. "Vanda, if we keep moving down this passage, where does it lead?"

"I don't know."

"We're about to find out." Elena led the way, hoping they'd find another crossing to Big Cave.

For an hour, they followed the tunnel until they reached an opening above another cave. Below, dozens of men ankle deep in murky water dug reddish-orange rock with pick-axes. One looked like a defender at Big Cave who had died, unless the Knoonk had cloned him. Nearby were the three dead men from Tenement Cave. *Death isn't the end.*

Vanda screamed. Elena turned to see the girl on the ground, twitching. A blue-clad Knoonk aimed a zapper at Elena's head. She dodged; a flash hit the wall inches from her face. Marc took her hand and they ran the way they'd come. She wanted to help Vanda, but it was too late.

The tunnel dead-ended at another door. Elena turned in time to get whacked in the head. Dazed, she stumbled and couldn't get up.

TWENTY-FIVE

Shivering, with nausea in the pit of her stomach, Elena forced her eyes open. She and Vanda lay in several inches of cold water, surrounded by reddish rock and men with pick-axes. Nearby, the three men who had assaulted Elena encircled Marc. He had no weapons this time. Other men from various clans approached Elena and Vanda.

Elena knelt. "Oh merciful—"

A high-pitched noise reverberated off the walls.

Elena covered her ears, as rhyming grew louder and more intense, a pulsing harmonic. Nearby, two men fell to their knees. Marc crawled to Elena, his face bloodied, his mouth cut. Other men dropped to their knees. Fighting the pain in her ears, she grabbed Vanda's hand and stumbled through the icy water looking for a tunnel out. A man grabbed Elena and then fell backward into the water, as the screeching grew louder.

Letting go of Vanda, Elena covered both ears. Even so, her head pounded. The noise seemed to be coming from the wall now. She led Vanda toward the sound and located an opening. The noise stopped as they entered. Inside the tunnel, Marc pushed Elena up to a higher passage and they both helped Vanda.

When they reached the ceiling passage, Thelma led them down the narrow corridor in the dark. Elena's guts churned over what the Knoonk were doing to them. Even if she found their lair, resistance brought untold miseries. They couldn't even defy the

Knoonk through death.

>===>

As soon as they reached Big Cave, Elena and Thelma transported to Nalon's room. Elena was in no mood to play chess, yet it gave Thelma a break from the barbarism and allowed contact with Nalon.

Nalon made her first move. She appeared different, worried, if Elena read her opponent correctly. She must have seen the incident at Slave Cave. If Nalon had helped them behind the scenes, she could be a secret ally, or their tormentor.

Thelma sat on the floor, staring at the gray wall. Finding her mother had been a shock. She needed to talk but couldn't.

Elena pushed her luck with risky chess moves, though she couldn't concentrate. "What you've done to Thelma and her mother can't be justified."

Nalon glanced up. "Play!"

"Is that all you can say?"

"You do not understand. Survival depends on discipline. Natalie disobeyed."

Using every bit of her chess knowledge, Elena played aggressively. "Will no one stand up and do the right thing?"

"Play and lower your voice."

Elena puzzled over Nalon's interest in spending time with the humans. She couldn't decide if Nalon was a zookeeper or genuinely interested. "You're a good person, Nalon. You've been fair with me." Not wanting to offend, Elena slacked off her chess attack. "Why is Gorg so angry?"

"General Gorg lost her sister on Earth. When her ship crashed, humans dissected her like an animal." Nalon's telling resonated with disgust. "Essence gone. No resurrection. No more life."

Elena was shocked. That meant that at least some humans knew about the Knoonk, but she'd heard nothing in the news. She closed her eyes. There would be no quelling Gorg's fury. "I'm sorry. It was a savage thing to do."

Nalon studied Elena. "We should not treat you like animals."

Leaning against the chess grid, Elena whispered, "Are there others?"

Nalon didn't answer; Elena sensed there were. Humans couldn't hope to halt the Knoonk on their own. They needed allies, which meant she had to find a way to make contact without compromising her friends.

From the corner of her eye, Elena caught Thelma at the keyboard scanning images again.

TWENTY-SIX

Strapped to a bed with an enormous stomach, Elena plunged into labor. She'd lost track of how many she'd delivered. Exhausted and drenched in sweat, she delivered a full-grown Knoonk, Gorg's sister, who turned her venom into strangling Elena.

The Knoonk resurrected Elena for another round. Convulsions came in waves until she prayed for death and lost consciousness.

The aliens returned her to the delivery room. She pushed forth a full-grown hairy beast that reached down, tore her heart out, and devoured it.

Elena bolted upright and pressed her stomach, still flat from daily exercise. *For how long?*

She looked around the cottage to find Joey and Thelma missing. Reese was in the kitchen cradling a mug of coffee. "Tara went with Joey to look for Thelma."

Elena shook her head. For days, she'd tried to get Thelma alone so they could message each other. "I'm going to the other big cave. You shouldn't be here alone. Why don't you come?"

Reese dumped the coffee in the sink and grabbed a small bag. "I think I'm ready."

She didn't look ready, but Elena kept that to herself. Taking a small backpack with rope and other supplies, she led the way along the upper tunnels using a thin flashlight she had found in Thelma's room. When they reached Big Cave, Elena took Reese to Maggie. "I need to go," Elena said. She turned to Maggie. "Could you look after Reese? She lost her fiancée and…"

"I'll be fine," Reese said. "I know he's not coming back." She turned to Maggie. "How can I help?"

Unwilling to wait for what the Knoonk had planned for her, Elena decided she had to get back to the tunnels to explore. She found Janet with a group of six women. "I need to do some exploring and would love your help," she whispered.

"I'd love to join you," Janet said, "but I'm needed here to help protect foraging parties." She led the women out to gather food.

Marc joined Elena. "Sorry, I overheard. You can't go out. It's too risky. What if you get stuck?"

"I'll take Joey. He knows the caves."

"I'm coming with you."

"You can't," Elena said. "You have responsibilities. You need to keep these people safe."

That brought a hint of a smile to his face that he was useful. It didn't last. "I don't want to lose you."

She kissed his cheek and he kissed her lips. She felt a surge of desire she was sure was Knoonk interference, their way of bringing the couple together. She saw the same in his eyes and pulled away. "Not here. Not like this. I trained to explore; I have to do this."

She headed toward an alcove where Joey was sitting with Thelma. Marc crossed his arms, shook his head, and watched.

Tara intercepted Elena. "Get me away from the gossip, please," she whispered.

Elena brushed aside her image of Tara with Marc in that maze and nodded. It wasn't fair that her friend had to carry a child that wasn't hers. "Very well, but it will be dangerous."

Tara nodded. "So is staying here."

Elena headed toward where Thelma was now making out with Joey. The pain of finding her mother must have torn her apart, but this wouldn't help. Elena pulled Joey away from Thelma. "You promised to protect her."

Joey shielded his face with his hands. "I love her. I wouldn't hurt her."

"Don't go near her for a while. Promise me. She just saw her mother and must be devastated."

Thelma kicked Elena's shin. Wincing, Elena grabbed her sister's arm.

"You need help?" Tara asked.

"No, I've got this."

Thelma wrenched her arm free. Elena pinned the girl against the cave wall and fastened a rope around her waist.

Joey stepped back. "Go with your sister."

Thelma scowled at Joey and worked on the rope knot.

Elena pulled the knot behind her sister. "We're going to explore and I need you with me."

Thelma twisted; Elena held tight.

Massaging her stomach, Vanda joined them. "I've missed you bunches," she said to Thelma.

Ignoring her friend, Thelma tugged at the rope and moved as far from Vanda as she could, which puzzled Elena.

"I'm sorry about your mom," Vanda said.

Thelma covered her ears and chanted.

Vanda shrugged. "It's okay. We're all a little crazy. I should return to my girls."

Elena gave Vanda a hug. "Thanks for helping yesterday."

As Vanda left, Thelma gyrated a dance for Joey. Elena slapped her sister's hand. "Never do that! Don't tempt boys."

She sensed Thelma itching to say something.

Elena glared at Joey, who stood beyond her reach, and brushed hair from her sister's face. Thelma pushed the hand away.

"I'll remove the rope if you both promise nothing will happen," Elena said.

"I want what's best for Thelma," Joey said.

"She's too young. Now I need a guide, someone who knows his way around. Do you mind?"

Joey grinned.

Elena removed the rope and then she, Tara, and Joey headed out of Big Cave with Thelma tagging along. Their first stop was Tenement Cave to speak with Chrissie. When they entered, Vanda sat in the midst of a large gray cell devoid of tenements and people. "They've taken my babies."

Shocked, Elena held the girl. The Knoonk had removed every trace of the Tenements as if preparing for another clan.

Thelma sat next to her old friend, but when Vanda went to hug her, Thelma left the cave. Joey ran after her.

"Where did they take my girls?" Vanda sobbed.

"We'll find them," Elena said, reminding herself she shouldn't make promises she couldn't keep. "I'll take you to Big Cave."

"I don't want to be with strangers. Please."

"Can she come with us?" Tara asked. "Joey seems preoccupied."

Elena closed her eyes and nodded. "Can you watch out for her?"

Tara took Vanda's hand and the girl smiled.

When the three of them emerged into Desert Cave, Elena couldn't find Joey or Thelma, so she led the group into the tunnel and up to the higher passage. Conventional wisdom held that when navigating a maze, mark your position at each turn and follow consistently to the right or left and you'll either find an exit or return to your original position.

That didn't apply to tunnels where doors could appear and disappear, and where paths moved up and down and crossed each other. Any passageway might therefore lead anywhere. They would have to travel by their wits and hope the Knoonk didn't trap them again.

For hours, they walked narrow passages, guided by Elena's flashlight. Any moment they could run into a Knoonk sentry or another living hell.

"Are we about done?" Vanda complained. "My legs are killing me."

"I'm sorry, sweetie. I was sure we'd find something by now." Elena's coyotes floated among the shadows, warning of danger, or was the trickster teasing her to look deeper. *Things aren't as they appear.* She thought back to her first encounter with the time distortion and holographic images.

"Let's take a break," Elena said. "I'm turning out the light to save batteries." She waited until Tara and Vanda sat against the wall. Then she looked back along the passage to see if Joey and Thelma were behind them. Seeing only shadows, she switched off the light.

Leaning against the wall in the dark, Elena spotted ghost images from very faint lighting up ahead. She heard whispers of the Knoonk singsong language.

A hand grabbed Elena's arm that she recognized as Thelma. *"Turn back,"* the girl tapped on Elena's shoulder. Then she tugged on Elena's arm.

"Joey?" Elena whispered.

"Shhh." The boy's face appeared in dim light from up ahead and then his profile as he moved toward the light.

Elena pulled free of her sister and hurried after Joey. He tiptoed up a stone path to a softly lit corner, held up his hand, and peered around. He waved them on.

Tugging on Thelma's reluctant hand, Elena moved cautiously. The penalty for being caught could mean the incubation ward, no more chess with Nalon, no contact with potential allies, no hope for warning Earth, and the defeat of Earth by the bloodthirsty Gorg. So far, Elena hadn't identified anything she could use to stop the general or warn Earth. Maybe there was something up ahead.

They crossed a corridor and hurried to the next junction. Elena stopped when she reached open gray panels to her left. Inside worked a dozen Knoonk in pale, lime-green tights. All appeared to be pregnant. That meant they weren't just breeding humans.

She slipped past the opening and passed several similar rooms.

In her undergraduate studies of migrations, she'd learned about population politics, the use of expanding populations to allow one people to overwhelm another. The Germanic tribes used it against the Romans, the Europeans against her Native American ancestors. If this was the Knoonk plan, then breeding humans made no sense.

They reached a chamber where Knoonk in protective white suits worked. Harsh voices rang out from down the corridor. Joey ducked into a dark room. As voices approached, Elena pulled Thelma under a table and held her breath.

Thelma tapped on Elena's back, *"Must B with Joey."*

Elena responded, *"Wait,"* though time was running out. *"Is this K home?"*

"Nearby. Danger."

Lights flashed on. Voices chattered their singsong. Pale green gowns entered. Knoonk bellies bulged over spindly legs. Two Knoonk stood over Elena and Thelma, working at a table. It dawned on Elena that the Knoonk seemed to prefer subdued colors. In fact, even Commander Zurbiz had decorated her otherwise spacious office in pale colors. Yet, the human women had brightly colored, though skimpy, clothes. She didn't see how that could be of use to her, but she filed it away.

The Knoonk workers were so close Elena smelled a dense fish odor. Pregnancy must have brought out a heavier dose of oil-based hormones. She prayed they couldn't smell the humans.

A sneeze tickled Elena's nose. She pinched until her nose hurt. As they worked, the two aliens shifted their weight from foot to foot. She studied feet with hardened soles that didn't require shoes. She couldn't see Joey behind the aliens. Tara shielded Vanda in the other corner, too exposed. Elena's hand in Thelma's grip had gone numb, yet the girl hadn't made a sound.

"What are they doing here?" Elena tapped on her sister's back. It was taking too long to get her questions out.

"Experiments on humans," Thelma replied.

"How can we stop their plans?"

The green-clad Knoonk put a container into a cabinet and left.

Joey checked the corridor. Elena stood, opened the cabinet, and saw a glass incubator with a human fetus, three months old. The image brought a headache behind her right eye. As the lights dimmed, she closed the cabinet and spotted a view-screen where a window might have been. She touched a symbol below the screen and the wall lit up, or maybe became transparent. Beyond the window was a huge warehouse.

Joey whispered. "Let's go before they return."

Elena stared at dozens of rows of shelves of containers like the one in the cabinet, each attached to apparatus.

"Let's go." Joey pulled on Elena's arm.

She pointed to the warehouse. "They're mass-producing us."

Joey took Thelma's hand and entered the corridor. Vanda followed. Tara tugged Elena's arm, tearing her from the horror. Knoonk voices approached outside.

Elena removed her shoes and ran after the others up the corridor to the last junction. A green-clad Knoonk turned the corner in front of her. Puckering her petite nose, the alien opened her mouth. Joey grabbed her by the neck in a chokehold and dragged her toward the dark tunnels.

Despite what the Knoonk had done to her friends, Elena couldn't allow Joey to hurt the alien. Any one might represent an opposition resource that could help her. She caught up with them by the shadows. "Let her go. We don't kill."

Joey maintained his grip. "She won't be so merciful."

"We aren't murderers," Elena said.

She grabbed hold of Joey's arm, loosened his grip, and took hold of the alien, finding the Knoonk's skin tough yet pliable.

"Do you understand what we're saying?" she asked the Knoonk.

To Elena's surprise, the alien nodded and rubbed her belly.

"We don't abuse women."

The Knoonk stood still, her ridge crest twisted forward.

"If we let you go, will you help us?" Elena asked.

"Eeeeeeeeee," the Knoonk screeched, her voice modulating higher into the range humans couldn't hear.

Elena covered her ears. The Knoonk ran. Joey gave chase and grabbed the alien's arm. She flung him across the corridor. Thelma ran to Joey. Vanda fainted; Tara eased her to the rocky floor.

Breaking into a sprint, Elena jumped the Knoonk, crashing with her to the stone floor. She almost pinned the Knoonk. Then the alien flipped Elena backward toward the darkness. The green-clad Knoonk got to her feet and began to scream.

A lavender-clad Knoonk turned the corner. For a moment, Elena thought it was Gorg. She had the general's fierce ridge-crest, though without the creases down the side of the face, and she was shorter.

The newcomer spoke to the first Knoonk in their language and brought out her zapper. Thelma and Joey retreated into darkness. Vanda lay in the open with Tara trying to revive her.

Elena stood and bowed.

Zapper ready, the green-clad Knoonk approached.

Elena closed her eyes. "We mean you no harm."

She heard a faint electrical discharge and braced for the jolt. When it didn't come, she glanced up and saw the lavender-clad Knoonk standing over the other. Electricity flowed into the alien, sending arcs of lightning. Maroon blood oozed from the eye slits, nose knob, and small ears. Gray skin turned charcoal as the alien twitched and stopped.

"I'm Major Narn," the lavender-clad Knoonk said. "Go before we're noticed."

"Can you help us?" Elena asked.

Narn paused, then handed Elena the green-clad's zapper. "Be careful. We'll meet again." She slung the first alien like baggage over her shoulder and hurried away.

Elena slipped the zapper under her skirt and joined the others running down the dark tunnel. She couldn't decide if Major Narn had risked herself to save them or whether there had been another purpose. Elena hated being a puppet on a string. Now she risked becoming a pawn in the Knoonk's political intrigues without knowing if any side was good.

TWENTY-SEVEN

When she reached Big Cave, Elena was shocked by the same barrenness she'd seen in Chrissie's Tenement Cave. The alcoves were empty; the cribs were gone. So were the people. At first, she thought an attack was under way. Joey left to find Thelma. Vanda clung to Tara.

Elena ran to the back of the cave where the sink basins had been, along with food and supplies for the children. It had all vanished.

Marc sat on a ledge, defeat etched across his face.

"What happened?" Elena asked, standing over him.

Marc didn't attempt to get up. "They've taken all of the pregnant women. They also took Reese and Janet and all of the children."

"Chrissie's people are gone as well. What's going on?"

"Thor upped the quota to seventy percent."

"That's insane."

Marc's eyes darted to the entrance. "I've visited other caves. The Knoonk emptied them all of people. Now they're full of new arrivals, and something else."

"What?"

"Mutants. They slaughter men and … they're cannibals." Marc hung his head in his hands. As a marine, he was used to having to fight against long odds, though not when the rules kept changing.

Elena checked the zapper in her waistband. "What about Maggie?"

Marc shook his head. "She gave birth this morning. They took her baby and left her behind. For food and supplies, we have to go beyond Desert Cave and risk a fight every time we venture out. We've fought two skirmishes while you were gone."

Elena shook her head. "Casualties?"

"My wits. I don't know how to help anymore." He looked up; his eyes had sunk deep into his brow.

"Marc, you've done a great job. I mean it."

"I've made a mess."

"No one appreciates what you're up against," Elena said. "Let's talk with Maggie and figure this out."

"Your confidence amazes me."

"Quitting isn't an option," Elena said.

"Then I won't quit either."

While Tara calmed Vanda over losing her daughters, Elena took Marc and Maggie to an alcove to talk about strategy. She eased herself onto a ledge so as not to expose the zapper.

"We need to get the clans to cooperate instead of fighting," Elena said. "That's the only way we can survive."

"How do you propose to do that?" Marc asked, sitting across from her. He kept eyeing the entrance.

"With the Knoonk manipulating supplies," Maggie said, "each clan looks out for itself."

Elena shifted the zapper from digging into her thigh. "We'll have to change that. If we stop fighting among ourselves, we stand a better chance." A better chance of working with the resistance, she wanted to add. If humans had any advantages, she hadn't identified them. Everything favored the Knoonk, even surprise, yet they hadn't attacked Earth.

Returning from water patrol, Zak yelled, "We're under attack." His voice echoed throughout Big Cave.

Marc leapt to his feet. "Battle stations."

The few people in Big Cave moved into position. Several women poked their heads out of the ceiling ridge with bows. Others poked their heads out of High Cave. Marc joined Zak by the now-barren ceremonial platform with Carl and the Frontiersmen, Thad and Louis. Maggie called together the remaining women in the back of the cave.

Elena tapped Maggie's shoulder. "How can you sit while we're under attack?"

Into the cave jogged three huge men, the mutants Marc had described, wearing animal skins. Their heads were huge and their bodies like muscle-builders on steroids. They moved with fluid swaggers, their arms long and apelike, wielding clubs. The largest stopped and scanned the cave. "In the name of Thor we defeat you. Surrender or die."

Marc and Louis faced off against one intruder, who flung them both to the ground. Thad and Carl took on a second. Their leader ignored those fights and headed around the ceremonial mound as if he'd already won. Smiling with huge incisors, he glided toward Elena.

Bowing, she observed his over-muscled form. In a primitive society, he would have been the one all the women would flock to for protection.

"Get back," Marc yelled.

"Don't listen to your ex-leader," the lead mutant said. He held out his hand.

"Listen to me." Elena glared up at the towering figure.

The leader moved closer.

Elena stood her ground. "We aren't the enemy. The Knoonk are."

"Smart broad." He stared her down.

"Together we can stand up to them."

"This one's got brass." He inched closer. "You ever see a Knoonk?"

"This morning. If we kill each other, we lose. If we work together we can win."

"All I got to do is get you pregnant and I eat. Sounds like a better plan." He grabbed for Elena.

She fell. Marc broke off his fight and ran to help. The leader swatted him away like a mosquito. The intruder reached for Elena. She planted the zapper between his legs and activated. His body lifted off the ground and fell backward. Elena tucked the stick under her skirt and leapt on top of him, pushing the point a knitting needle into his temple.

"Listen or die," she said.

Stunned, the leader nodded. "How'd you do that?"

"Just listen. Together we bring peace. No more killing."

"I get you as my bride."

Elena pressed the needle harder. "I belong to no man."

"So, you're the leader?"

She hesitated. Part of her itched to say yes, as a way to change things. She pointed to Marc. "He leads. I support."

The mutant leader pushed her off and stood up. When Marc approached, the big man swung. Marc ducked.

Elena stepped between them. "Enough, you two. No more fights. Marc leads the combined clan. You can be military commander."

The big man studied Elena for a long time. "You sure you're not the leader?" He laughed. "Very well. They call me Spartacus."

"You two shake on it," Elena said.

Marc glared at her. This violated cave law. The men expected to duke it out to the end, but Marc didn't stand a chance against their newfound friend. He shook his opponent's hand.

"Good. Our first peace treaty," Elena said. "Tell me about your clan."

Spartacus grinned and moved closer. "Ten men and three women. The Knoonk took the rest. We're looking for partners."

"Around here you can woo, but no intimidation or abuse."

Spartacus placed his arm around Elena's shoulders. "Why don't we go make some plans? I can protect you better than anyone."

She twisted free. "The answer remains no." Behind him, she spotted Marc, fuming. She found his jealousy touching, but she couldn't allow him to sacrifice himself for her. "First of all, you can't provide for me, the Knoonk do. As to protecting, it seems you need me."

Spartacus burst out laughing. "You're quite a woman." His face turned somber. "No one defies me."

"Yet you kneel before your superiors."

He looked around. "I see no superiors."

"The Knoonk," Elena said. "If they don't defy you it's because you ask too little of them."

Spartacus grabbed her and pressed his body against hers. "I will have you."

With difficulty, Elena twisted away and got the zapper out. She activated it, which sent Spartacus sprawling onto his back. She had to scramble to conceal her weapon. "Kneel and beg forgiveness or I'll put you to death."

Holding his stomach, Spartacus got to his knees. "Don't do that again."

"Will you submit?"

He nodded.

With any luck, Elena had cemented her first alliance. "Pledge to fight alongside us against all others and bring your clan here. You may court women under our rules, which means no force and only with the woman's consent."

"I swear it." Spartacus stood and motioned for his two partners to join him as he left the cave.

Marc took Elena to a quiet alcove. "What just happened, and what are you doing?"

Elena produced a knitting needle. She wasn't sure Marc bought it, but she couldn't let him know.

"We should have killed them when we had the chance," Marc said. "They'll be back, itching to take over."

"You have arrows; make preparations. We can't spend all our efforts fighting each other."

"You've invited them in," Marc said.

"Are you jealous?" Elena rubbed his shoulder.

Marc blushed. "It's time you and I got together."

She gazed up at him. "Tempting, but not under these conditions."

"You know the rules. The Knoonk won't let up."

"That's the most romantic proposal I've received all day. You used to charm my pants off. What's happened?"

Marc closed his eyes. "This place. It messes with our minds. One moment I'm trying to sort things out. The next, I'm so enraged I'd…"

"You and Tara?"

Marc hung his head and turned away. "The Knoonk stuck us in this maze and drugged us." He glanced at her with pleading eyes and sighed. "You know, don't you?"

She nodded.

"Then you know nothing happened, not really."

"It's not a picture I want, but I don't blame you," Elena said. "Still, I won't put on a show for the Knoonk."

"I hope you know what you're doing."

So did Elena.

>===>

General Gorg marched into Commander Zurbiz' quarters without saluting, which itself could be cause for disciplinary action. Not only that, she made no attempt to conceal her anger in the tilt of her ridge-crest.

"What's the meaning of this?" Zurbiz demanded as she fumbled for her weapon. "Can't you see I'm busy?"

"Too busy to notice that the astronaut is stirring up trouble. I warned you about her. Give her to me and I'll make her produce for us. I'll squeeze every bit of that defiant temperament from her."

"She might yet prove useful. If nothing else, she's helping to distract the humans. For now, the Supreme Commander wants the scientist alive. Have you caught the traitors?"

"Don't change the subject," Gorg said, courting disaster. She was beyond caring about the nuances of chain of command. She was not going to let things unravel because of an incompetent commander.

Zurbiz held the trigger to her office defense. "Leave voluntarily or involuntarily. Your choice."

"You take care of that trouble-maker or I will," Gorg said. She backed out of the commander's office aware of the two guards who now stood by the door, weapons drawn.

>====>

The next morning, when Elena transported to Nalon's room, the chess grid hadn't been set up, Thelma wasn't there, and Nalon seemed agitated.

"What's going on?" Elena whispered.

Nalon opened the panels and slipped into the corridor. Elena followed and observed those they passed in the tight hallway, looking for hints of resistance in eye contact, or hand movements. Though if she could tell, so could Gorg.

They entered the commander's office. Zurbiz sat in a large chair behind a massive table facing two smaller guest chairs. Elena was surprised not to see Gorg. Nalon backed out of the large hexagonal room and closed the panels, leaving Elena alone with Zurbiz. Elena looked around to be sure and found the subdued colors depressing.

"I asked to see you alone," Commander Zurbiz said. "Please sit."

The courtesies seemed out of place. Elena expected cuffs to clamp her arms as she squeezed her hips between the narrow armrests of the guest chair. The seatback forced her to lean forward. She brimmed with questions but waited to learn the purpose of this meeting.

"General Gorg is zealous," the commander said. She attempted a smile.

Elena avoided staring. "Why treat us like lab animals?"

"You want to work with us?"

"Yes. What's the catch?"

"Fine. We were not always a matriarchy. When we escaped tyranny, we were male soldiers. In order to survive, we decided to become all female to maximize having offspring."

It took all of Elena's self-control to keep her jaw from dropping. It certainly explained a lot. "How do you reproduce?"

"That's personal, but I'll answer," Zurbiz said. "Lab fertilization and cloning bring new life."

"With the essence of those who died?"

Zurbiz smiled and studied Elena. "I offer you matriarchy over the humans."

"What?" A chill shot up Elena's spine.

"I make you the leader over all humans."

"Why?"

"You act as loner, but you are leader. You could have killed Spartacus. You spared him."

Zurbiz had watched the fight and could have guessed about the zapper. Elena grew cautious. "I did what I thought right. The barbarism you see is not who we choose to be. No more killing."

"You want the power to change. I make you commander over all human clans."

Are you afraid of my alliance? "I don't want power."

"You are natural leader. They follow."

"They follow without your blessing." Elena tightened her grip on the armrests.

"Not if we punish your resistance."

Elena sighed. That was the hook. She could lead if she promoted the Knoonk plan. "What are you asking of me?"

"No more resistance."

"So I get this job if I do what you ask?"

Zurbiz nodded.

"And if I refuse?"

"Thor's wrath."

Elena didn't like the arrangement. "In exchange for my help, there will be no more cave wars."

"That is up to you."

"I get access to all humans?"

Zurbiz nodded.

"No more unwanted pregnancies."

"Not acceptable."

"Then I can't agree," Elena said.

"I will exempt you."

She glanced at the commander. Zurbiz was trading on her fears. "And Thelma."

"You can take her place."

Elena clenched the armrest. She couldn't let them continue to abuse Thelma. She wasn't prepared to take her sister's place, either. "Why push this when Earth is already overpopulated?"

"You or Thelma. Choose!"

"Exempt us both or no deal."

"Only one exemption," Zurbiz said. "Do not take too long to decide."

Nalon entered and Zurbiz waved for them to leave. Nalon hurried Elena out of the commander's office before she could ask more questions.

Opportunity or curse, Elena couldn't decide. Zurbiz offered leadership with more power than Marc or Spartacus, but only at an unacceptable price. On the other hand, maybe this could help her connect with the resistance.

TWENTY-EIGHT

Transported to Big Cave, Elena confronted all the reasons she didn't covet leadership. She didn't mind helping, but she didn't want the responsibility for making life and death decisions for others.

Maggie dragged Elena to an alcove. "We desperately need food and supplies. Tomorrow when they take you, can you plead with them?" She rattled off a list and left.

Zak hurried over. "Elena, would it be possible to appeal to our hosts for better weapons?"

"What happened?"

"Another clan of mutants showed up. Spartacus and his men defeated them. Two of his men died."

"Any survivors from the attackers?"

Zak shook his head. "Spartacus insisted."

"I'll see what I can do."

Zak left and Spartacus swaggered over. "It's good to see my queen home, safe and sound." He sat next to her.

"Did you bring the women from the defeated clan?" Elena asked, keeping her distance.

"Two dozen, though none as enticing as you."

"I'm sure you can find desirable women among the combined clans." She wondered if he wanted her or the power she seemed to wield. "If you have no other business, I do."

After Spartacus moved on, Tara sat next to Elena.

"Has he been behaving?" Elena asked.

"I suppose," Tara said. "Could you get our hosts to provide ointment to prevent stretch marks? And a gallon of chocolate peppermint ice cream?"

Elena laughed. "I'll ask."

Tara left and Marc shuffled over. She patted the ledge beside her.

"How are our friendly jailers?" Marc forced a smile and reached for her hand. "I was hoping we could go for a walk."

"There's nowhere to go," Elena said.

"I need you." He acted tentative as he had the first time he'd asked her out in college. Back then, she'd found it sexy.

She scooted closer and lowered her voice. "I know, but not here." She squeezed his hand. "I don't pretend to understand all this. It'll take all my attention to try to help these people."

"Let me know how I can help."

Marc joined Spartacus and the other men. It would have been so easy not to refuse him. If he'd known how easy, he might not have left. Maybe he did know. In any case, she couldn't be sure if what she felt for him was real or Knoonk drugs administered like their transporter.

She left in search of Thelma, concerned that it might already be too late.

>====>

Elena found her sister in Cottage Cave, washing dishes with Joey, and acting too much as a couple for Elena's comfort. Thelma gave Elena a bear hug and pulled away. A flash of terror crossed her face. The girl must have recognized the zapper beneath Elena's skirt.

"It's okay, hon," Elena whispered. "I only want to protect you."

Thelma's eyes flashed that she didn't think she needed protection. She did. Her eyes blinked out *"Ditch it."* Then she darted through the door with Joey in pursuit. Elena followed, losing them in the tunnel.

Head aching, Elena returned to the cabin and her bed, where she curled up. Everyone was pressuring her: the Knoonk wanted her to manage their plan, the women expected miracles, and Spartacus and Marc wanted her. She didn't want to cave in to Knoonk demands and couldn't be sure her sister hadn't already, making Elena's sacrifice count for nothing. Besides, the Knoonk could change the rules.

Cold sweat trickled down her back; muscles cramped.

Someone lifted her head and slipped a pillow beneath her—Marc. He rolled her onto her stomach and massaged her legs until they relaxed and stretched out. Realizing that Marc was getting close to the zapper, Elena rolled away and crashed onto the floor.

The zapper slipped from her makeshift garter and slid under the bed.

"You okay?" Marc lifted her up onto the bed.

"As much as I can be under these circumstances."

"I've waited a long time to be alone with you."

"Then wait longer, please." Elena moved to the other side of the bed.

He sat next to her and held her in his arms. "I'm sorry for everything I've done wrong, including not believing in your mission."

A flood of desire washed over her. "This isn't real," she said.

"It could be."

"Not with them watching." Yet her body wanted him. The Knoonk were thorough, she granted them that.

He caressed her cheek and kissed her. "Forgive me. I can't fight this anymore." Marc rolled her on top of him.

"Not like this." Elena pushed his arms away. She had to get him to leave before she lost her will to resist.

Marc pressed his lips to hers. The kiss felt warm, inviting, and insistent. It reminded her of feverish evenings they'd enjoyed on Earth after they'd been apart for weeks on end.

Breathing hard, Elena shoved him and moved to her side. "Please. Not here."

"I love you. I always have." Marc ran his fingers through her hair, kissed her, and guided his hand down the curve of her neck.

"It's their drugs, Marc."

"Whatever it is, I can't resist any longer." He pulled her on top of him and tugged at her top.

She twisted, wedged her feet against the wall, and shoved him away. Thelma stood in the doorway with a fight-or-flight look.

Elena pushed again and fell onto the floor. "Thelma's here."

As if he hadn't heard, Marc dropped on top of Elena. He'd

become an animal possessed of one motivation. Thelma looked puzzled.

"Go on, hon, get out of here," Elena said, looking right at her. "I'm okay."

Elena tapped on Marc's back the distress Morse code: three short taps, three long, and three short (SOS). He seemed confused for a moment and then lifted her onto the bed. Then he dropped down beside her, kissed her, and tugged at her top. She repeated the distress signal and pulled free.

When she looked up, Thelma was gone. Elena focused on Marc's erratic behavior. He tugged at her top as if he'd never seen one before and had no idea how to lift it off. Detached, she watched him try to sort out what to do with her arms and the sleeves. This wasn't the man she'd fallen in and out of love with. He'd become a puppet for the Knoonk.

"Stop!" she yelled.

That stunned him. He pulled away with a flash of clarity. His face showed the struggle between obeying her wishes and the drug that was overwhelming her as well. She couldn't escape the realization that if she kept resisting, she couldn't protect Thelma.

Marc fell onto his back, clenched his fists, and groaned. Elena leaned into him. "I'm not angry with you, but..."

He caressed her stomach. Miles away, her mind rattled off all the reasons to stop. She couldn't. He rose up and fumbled to pull off his shirt, as if he'd forgotten how to unfasten buttons.

"We should stop," she protested.

"I know," he said, giving up on his shirt. "I love you so much, Elena. Help me."

She clutched his hands to give him strength and kissed his lips. She felt on fire inside.

"If I closed the door we'd be alone," he said, leaning over her.

"You're forgetting the Knoonk."

Zak entered the room. "What the ... Elena, you okay?"

Tara joined Zak. Behind her, Thelma stood by the doorway, her head cocked to the side.

Marc rolled off the bed onto the floor and hurried to the door. "I'm so sorry, Elena." He ran out.

Tara motioned for Zak to leave and closed the door. "I'm not judging. Are you all right?"

"Not really." Elena's hands trembled as she straightened her skirt. "I'm tired of the Knoonk manipulating every aspect of our lives. Don't blame Marc. He didn't do anything."

Tara sat on the bed. "We were passing through Paradise Cave. From the tunnel entrance, Thelma waved insistently for us to follow her. She was frantic. We thought it was another clan attack. We never imagined."

Elena looked up. "Nothing happened. The Knoonk pumped us with drugs and we fought it."

Tara glanced at Elena. Then she got up and paced. "The girls have been talking. They want you to lead. They're tired of Marc, Spartacus, the attacks, and all. This seals things."

"It wasn't Marc's fault."

"It doesn't matter. We want you."

"What do they think I can do?" Elena straightened her lemon yellow top and stood up.

"You brought peace with Spartacus."

"The Knoonk won't budge on having babies, Tara. How can I lead?"

"We don't expect you to have all the answers," Tara said, "but we'd rather follow you than anyone else."

"Why can't Maggie lead?" Elena slipped into her pumps and ran her fingers through her hair.

"Maggie's okay dealing with ordinary problems. The clan needs a leader."

Elena gazed at Tara. This was what Zurbiz wanted. How ironic that for years she'd shunned leadership, only to have both humans and Knoonk thrust it on her. "What if I mess up?"

"You've done well so far. How about it?" Tara offered her hand.

"If you don't expect too much, I'll give it a try." Elena shook.

"Great. Maybe you could see about better accommodations."

Elena laughed. "Don't press your luck."

>====>

Elena reached Big Cave, escorted by Zak and Tara, with Thelma and Joey trailing behind. The entire community gathered to greet her, including hundreds from the Tenement clan and all of the members of Big Cave. They had all returned and gazed on her as if she'd become a celebrity. Her legs felt like jelly; she had little to offer, yet they all looked to her like some savior.

Maggie gave Elena a big hug and glanced at Tara, who nodded. Maggie raised Elena's arm. "Hail to our queen."

"How about president?" Elena looked for Marc, hoping he'd be there so she could vent and read his eyes. He wasn't.

"How about commander?" Maggie offered.

Elena felt manipulated. The Knoonk had orchestrated everything. They wanted her leading and would do anything to get what they wanted. Well, maybe they'd get more than they bargained for. "Don't get your expectations up. We're still prisoners."

She felt humbled and terrified that so many now depended on her. She motioned for Zak, Spartacus, and Joey to join her. "I appeal to everyone to join in bringing dignity to all humans. Let's show the Knoonk that we can be better than what they've seen so far."

"You know Knoonk law," Spartacus said, standing before her.

"I do, but from now on, we'll show them human decency. There will be no sex without consent. We know the dilemma the Knoonk have placed on us. Romance, not brutality will be our response."

Spartacus smiled. Elena feared his desire more than Marc's. She knew Marc better than he knew himself. He was incapable of hurting her and in the end, he hadn't.

Elena smiled at Thelma and nodded her thanks. The girl gave a quizzical look and Elena detected a hint of a nod. They'd reached an understanding that forbade dialogue.

Gazing out over the crowded cave reminded Elena of her pledge to the Sisterhood: protect women wherever oppressed. Somehow, she had to lead these people to freedom.

TWENTY-NINE

Millions of women pawed and poked their messiah with unceasing demands, while she had to produce an endless litter herself. After hours of labor, Elena's body ripped open to deliver twins. The Knoonk healed her body, left her memories to stew, and returned her to deliver triplets, quads, quintuplets, and then sextuplets. She no longer saw what she gave birth to as if all that mattered was giving the Knoonk more babies.

Bolting upright, Elena was drenched in sweat. Maggie dabbed her forehead with a cool cloth.

Tara held Elena's hand. "Another nightmare?"

Throat too dry to answer, Elena nodded. "How long?" she croaked.

"Just rest," Maggie said.

When closing her eyes returned the visions, Elena stared at the gray ceiling ridge around the lighted dome. She was too weary to make them stop fussing over her. After three days of listening to petitions, Elena was ready to flee, yet she couldn't abandon her friends.

Days passed as a blur, with Maggie acting as mother to the clans. Tara organized and kept track of supplies. Spartacus acted as military commander, though not a single battle took place. He also made excuses to discuss defense plans with Elena while trying to win her affections.

It surprised the others, although not Elena, when the women and infants who'd disappeared earlier returned. That miracle confirmed her leadership status. Looking healthy, Janet and Reese were back. Janet rejoined their defense team and Elena put her in charge of armaments, primarily making arrows she hoped they wouldn't need. Even the lost couples joined Elena's Clan, the biggest anyone could remember.

Every day brought more grievances. A woman's two children didn't get their milk allotment. Another complained that someone took too much space for her three girls. Everyone hated the depressing gray to the point Elena talked Nalon into supplying paint and assigned the complainers the task of painting.

With the steady stream of visitors, Elena didn't have time to think. The Knoonk were keeping her busy to silence her and stop her from exploring. She considered resigning, but as leader, she might find ways to lessen the burden on her friends.

A big-boned woman pushed to the front of the line with a baby on her hip. "Seventy percent means once a year." She stated the obvious with anger and spite. "We weren't meant for this. Look at this place. It's overcrowded. Why bring more lives?"

"I'll fight for you," Elena said, "but all depends on the Knoonk."

"Not good enough," the woman said. "We're humans, not guinea pigs. I say resist."

"We've tried," Elena said. "King, Gandhi, and Chang fought societies that believed in the rule of law. The Knoonk don't subscribe to the Geneva Convention. Resistance leads to famine, attacks, and special wards where they drug us into submission. I'll appeal to the Knoonk. For now, we can only choose with whom." Elena didn't add that it didn't matter since the Knoonk chose the DNA.

"That's not acceptable," the woman repeated, shifting her weight.

"What do you propose?"

"We find our leathery jailers and convince them to stop."

Several women behind her yelled out, "Stop them. Stop them."

Elena tapped the zapper she'd moved to her waistband and hoped she wouldn't have to use it. "They watch everything we do. We can't surprise them. They have superior weapons. It would be slaughter."

"I won't submit." The woman turned to the crowd. "No more. No more." The women chanted until the cave echoed.

Elena stood and raised her hands. When the crowd quieted down, she scanned hundreds of expectant faces. "I'll fight for you. I'll carry this to the Knoonk. Give me a day to come up with a plan. If you have any ideas, bring them to this woman and I'll meet with her in the morning."

Most of the women drifted away in small groups, grumbling. Frustrated, Elena asked Maggie to take her place while she talked with Tara. She led Tara to the cave's exit.

"I can't do this," Elena confessed when they were alone.

"You're doing fine," Tara said as they paced off the dark tunnel. "Everyone loves you."

"That woman wanted to lynch me."

"At least you listen. Marc just told everyone to bear up."

Emerging into Desert Cave, Elena felt overwhelmed. This once deserted cave brimmed with life. Clusters of mothers hovered over young girls, dressed in upscale chic with lively yellows and greens. Zurbiz had rewarded Elena's acceptance of clan leadership by rewarding the clan. Their hosts could just as easily punish them if she resisted.

Chrissie ran up and threw her arms around Elena. "I don't know how you did it. They've enlarged our quarters. We have medical supplies, a real clinic with a pediatrician, and an obstetrician. Bless you."

"I don't know what to say." Elena saw among the women and young girls many new faces.

Chrissie looked healthier and more alive, as did the cave, with murals on the gray walls. Elena felt like Dorothy crossing into the Land of Oz, only her wicked witch planned to invade Earth. Lavish attention on humans while Knoonk lived with austerity made no sense. Still, if this kept the clans from rebelling until she learned more, so be it.

Vanda ran up and hugged Elena. "Thank you so much." Two young girls held onto their mother's long dress.

"You've given us hope," Chrissie said.

Children flocked to Elena as if she were Mother Teresa. Inching her way toward the wall, she pulled Tara with her. Elena had a sick feeling in her stomach. "What's going on?"

Chrissie shielded them from the crowd and whispered, "Rumors have circulated that we have a savior, a woman who made peace with the Knoonk and can speak for us."

"I'm no savior."

"Thor said if we followed you, our lives would improve and they have." Chrissie bowed and those around her followed, including the youngest.

Zurbiz had been thorough. Elena was a miracle worker as long as humans bore children at a murderous rate. She noticed something else. Until recently, she'd seen mostly whites. Now, to her left stood a clan of Oriental women; to her right blacks; behind them Native Americans, Hispanics, and other groups. Desert Cave had become majority non-white and they all showed reverence toward her.

As Elena pushed her way through the crowd, brightly clothed mothers touched her. She hadn't seen such joy since they'd crashed. Maybe their elation was misplaced, but they had precious hope. False hope had to be better than none.

Spartacus pushed everyone out of the way to join Elena. "You okay?"

She gazed into his warm brown eyes. He was intelligent and sensitive despite his brutish physique. She smiled. "We need to tend to all these people. I need you to help keep the peace." She scanned the diverse groups. "Among all the people."

"Whatever you say." Spartacus kissed the top of her head, which must have proffered official status since people made a path as he left.

"Chrissie, I can't lead without help," Elena said. "I need you to remain in charge of your people and find out who's in charge of these other groups."

Chrissie nodded and squeezed her way through the crowd.

Elena turned to Tara. "Can you help me find Thelma? I need to see her."

Vanda raised her hand. "I'll find her, your highness. Let me."

"Find Thelma. Find Thelma." The cry floated over the cave like a human wave, becoming louder as it crashed the walls.

Elena covered her ears and the chorus quieted. Across the cave, Thelma's head emerged from an invisible ledge high up a painted wall. She peered at the crowd with a sense of wonder. Elena pushed her way through the various groups to the wall and sought the crevices Thelma used for climbing. Elena ascended one hold after another until she almost reached the ledge.

Glancing down made her lightheaded. People poured into the

cave to view their unwilling savior. From above, Thelma reached down to help. Distracted by the audience, Elena missed a handhold and clung to the rock wall by one hand.

Gasps rang out from below. "Oh, blessed Thor, spare our queen."

A thought crossed Elena's mind. If she fell and died, her ordeal would end. Then she gazed into her sister's eyes.

Elena located another handhold and worked her way up to the ledge, where Thelma helped her into the tunnel. Elena hugged her sister for a long time. "I love you, hon. Thanks for being there." She couldn't see Thelma in the darkness, yet heard the girl's heavy breathing.

Elena had one chore before she could tend to her sister. She poked her head out of the tunnel and waved to the crowd.

"It's a miracle," they chanted. "Miracle. Miracle."

Unable to take her celebrity status, Elena withdrew into the tunnel. At the other end, she reached a small cave with a wooden hut and no vegetation. Joey stood by the front door with Thelma. They'd set up house away from the others.

"Thanks for your help, Joey," Elena said, catching her breath. "I need to be alone with my sister."

"Ms. Pyetrov, we haven't done anything," Joey said. "I do want to marry your sister."

"Why? Does she talk to you?"

Joey shook his head. "She's a wonderful companion. She lets me tell her stories and we work well together."

"Not good enough."

"She needs me and I need her."

Thelma glanced back and forth as if reading lips or faces. Wheels of intellect ground away behind that stolid face. Knowing that the Knoonk listened, Thelma denied them a window to her mind.

"I only want her happiness," Elena said, trying to catch Thelma's reaction.

"I love her and would do anything for her."

"Then don't make her pregnant."

"I don't want her taken away," Joey said.

"I'm working on a way so they won't." Elena had said too much. She saw a flicker of understanding in Thelma's eyes, a cross between relief and caution: You can't trust the Knoonk. *I know,* Elena thought, *but if I can save you, I will.*

Elena waited until Joey disappeared into the tunnel. Then she took Thelma by the hand and led her into the sparsely furnished hut to a tiny wooden table in the kitchen.

"I want to make things better for you," Elena said.

Getting no response, she continued. "I like Joey. I just don't want you two doing anything until you're much older." Elena detected that Thelma wanted to talk, despite her head bobbing from side to side in a nonchalant manner.

"The worst thing anyone can do is make you carry a child you don't want," Elena said. She detected fleeting anger in Thelma's eyes. "Dad wanted you. I saw it in his eyes. He may have talked about me, but he wanted you in his life."

Thelma seemed confused, as if wrestling her own demons.

"I want to take you to Earth, Thelma, and show you oceans farther than the eye can see, mountains so huge few humans have climbed, and buildings so tall they touch clouds you've never seen. I want you to see the bustling city and the calm New Mexico desert, not a desert cave, the real thing, and to know people who aren't focused every moment on survival. I want you to see a world in which humans are not slaves." Elena's eyes welled with tears. Thelma hadn't known a world without Knoonk masters.

Thelma danced around the kitchen as if moving to her own music.

"Right now, Thelma, I need your help. There are so many children. The oldest appear to be thirteen and their mothers are weary. I know it's asking a lot. Joey can help, too. Look after them and keep them safe."

>====>

While she waited for some acknowledgement from her sister, Elena transported to the gray chess room. Nalon wasn't there and neither was Thelma.

Grinning, Gorg stood by the doorway twirling her zapper. "The commander is soft on humans. You have new clothes while we wear old. You have space when we squeeze into tight quarters."

"She asked me to be their leader." Elena bowed.

The general pointed her zapper. "Did I give permission to open your sewage hole?"

Elena withdrew into Thelma's corner.

"Better. You are royal manure among humans. Here you serve me."

Elena studied the leathery creases in Gorg's neck. She knew right where she'd put pressure given the chance. Instead, she raised her hand. Gorg brought a long stick down before Elena could pull away. Her knuckles stung from the blow. She studied the stick and Gorg's stun weapon, inches away. A surge of adrenaline had her wanting to grab it, which would doom her, Thelma, and any chance to stop the Knoonk.

"May I speak?" Elena steadied her voice.

"Only to pledge compliance."

"Seventy percent is unreasonable. Their bodies can't handle it."

"That's a human weakness," Gorg said.

"I beg you to make it sixty."

"We cannot meet our schedule."

"What schedule?" Elena asked.

"Comply or I return misery."

"You want healthy babies. This is hard on our organs. Your best result would be sixty percent so they can recover."

"Perhaps the commander underestimated you. I will not."

"The commander wants healthy children. I'll keep production at sixty percent."

"Sixty-five percent and after each birth I will restore organ and tissue function."

Elena considered the despicable offer. Knoonk were breeding them like cattle. However, Gorg did offer something interesting, restoration of organ function. At least her friends would get health until she could find a better solution. Elena nodded.

Then she handed Gorg a list of supply needs. "To help with production and care."

THIRTY

As punishment for failing to live up to his own values and beliefs, and most of all for failing Elena, Marc dragged himself up to a high ledge over Paradise Cave. He knew this wasn't the right answer and that it would condemn him for an eternity. He saw no other choice. Closing his eyes, he jumped and relived his failures on the way to meet his doom on the gray rock below. Not only couldn't he protect Elena, he'd become what she needed protection from.

Because of the lighter gravity, it took longer than he expected. He landed on his right leg, which shattered. Pain shot out like nothing he'd experience before. Semi-conscious, with nerves firing in all directions, he transported to a hard metallic table with too thin of a mattress. Knoonk poked him like a frog in biology class. When they finished, they returned him to the ledge.

On the second try, Marc's skull cracked open like a melon. Every pain center fired at once. Still, no amount of punishment could atone for his sins.

Returned after his fourth attempt, Marc stared down at Paradise Cave. Had the Knoonk learned enough or did they plan to keep him in his own Purgatory? He decided against another jump. *Why bother?*

Marc hurried toward Big Cave to see Elena. Inside the tunnel leading out of Paradise Cave, he hit a wall. While groping in the dark, all he found were dead-ends, including the passage he'd taken from Paradise Cave. The Knoonk had locked him into darkness. He welcomed death, not this.

He found an opening that led up. He climbed until he rolled out into blinding light and fell to the floor of Paradise Cave.

From the piercing pain in his back and legs, Marc must have crushed his spine. While on the operating table, surrounded by blue-clad Knoonk, the horror replayed. His tormentors were getting their money's worth. He couldn't fight back due to straps holding him down. The Knoonk cut at him and repaired the damage without anesthetic.

Healed again, Marc reappeared on the ledge above Paradise Cave and rolled off. Closing his eyes, he dashed his head against the floor.

>====>

Elena emerged into Desert Cave. Women mobbed her, shielding her from something.

Tara came over. "Marc was here. Now everyone's worried for you."

A barrier of tall women blocked Elena's view. "Where is he?" She pushed her way through and climbed up to a ledge overlooking the cave. She didn't want him turned away for something he couldn't control.

"It's not safe," a tall black woman said, climbing up next to her.

Elena held up her hands and waited until the people around her quieted down. "Listen to me. I said no more attacks and that includes on Marc."

They listened in awed silence. "The Knoonk drugged Marc," Elena said. "He did not hurt me. I've known him for many years and this is not who he is. Let's show the Knoonk that we aren't barbarians. I'd like to see all of the clan leaders in an hour. Bring your issues to them."

She climbed off the ledge and made her way toward a cluster of cacti that reminded her of her home in New Mexico.

The big-boned woman who had collected complaints earlier stopped her. "These women treat you like the second coming. You're not."

"I know," Elena said.

"Since I wasn't invited to the clan meeting, here's my list." The woman shoved a piece of paper at Elena.

"You're invited. It's just I can't deal with everyone and do justice to anyone. I don't have answers and I don't want this job."

The woman grimaced, forced a smile, and walked away.

While she waited for the clan leaders, Elena headed toward a cactus patch away from the others for a moment's respite. On the way, she stopped to talk to a group of women and listen to their stories. One had disappeared from her farm in France along with her husband and three daughters. The husband died in a clan fight. Another woman vanished outside a bar in Seattle along with two friends.

In all cases, they left behind no credible witnesses, and none of the women had seen a Knoonk unless they needed medical attention. For all they knew, these could have been caves on Earth.

Leaving the women, Elena joined a reserved brunette girl in a simple yellow frock, standing alone by the cluster of cacti. With sadness in her eyes, the brunette watched other girls play and mingle. With a young woman's figure, the girl appeared to be slightly older than Thelma. The girl didn't acknowledge Elena.

"This must be baffling," Elena said in a soothing voice.

When the girl didn't respond, an exhausted, thirtyish woman approached. "Two of her friends disappeared. She's afraid she's next."

"Disappeared? When?" Elena asked.

"Yesterday, while they worked in Garden Cave."

"Other clans?" Elena asked.

The woman shook her head. "The Knoonk."

An unspoken assumption after the return of Chrissie's group and the others was the end of kidnappings. Elena felt betrayed; the Knoonk kept changing the rules. "I didn't know. I'll do what I can." Then something struck her. "Forgive me for asking. Has she entered puberty?"

The woman glared at Elena. "She's only seven."

"Are you sure?" Elena stared at the girl's developed teenage figure.

"I know my own daughter. Her friends were also seven."

Stunned, Elena nodded. "I'll look into this."

Elena excused herself and found Chrissie with a teacher and a dozen girls maybe eight or nine. At least they were getting educated. Elena pulled Chrissie aside. "Who's the oldest girl born here?"

Chrissie pointed toward the cactus. "The one you were talking to. Jenny is seven."

"She looks like a teenager."

Chrissie nodded. "It could be the nutrient-rich air or the food the Knoonk supply." She shrugged.

"And these girls you're teaching?"

"Four."

Elena shook her head and recalled the time lapse on the shuttle. There she'd been convinced only one day had lapsed for two on the clock. This appeared to be the reverse. "You must be using a bad calendar."

"Several women had watches with dates. We've kept very careful track of time."

"Thelma is thirteen."

"Could be. She was here when I arrived." Chrissie hugged a bright-eyed girl who seemed to crave the attention.

"Have you noticed anything else unusual about the children born here?"

"Other than rapid maturity, we've had no disease, except when the Knoonk punish us."

The twelve girls with the teacher used some mobile network ports to scan for information. "Do they learn faster?" Elena asked.

"Now that you mention it, they walk at four months. It's a blessing when we have to move."

Elena studied the twelve girls with their teacher. If they were growing and learning at twice the normal pace, that meant they would mature in eight or nine years. The Knoonk must have modified DNA to get brighter, healthier humans. Why?

A loud male voice echoed across the cave, contrasting with the cacophony of female cadence. "Elena! Elena Pyetrov? Elena!" Marc stood by the cave entrance that led to Paradise Cave.

Two archers took aim.

Elena approached him. "Don't shoot." She ran and took his hand. Something stirred inside, her bargain to spare Thelma.

"I have no excuse," Marc said. "I behaved atrociously. I want to come home." He'd developed a tic by his right eye and a head tremor, as if he'd aged decades since she'd seen him.

Elena squeezed his hand. "As long as you understand that things have changed."

"I don't expect anything except to work for my keep." Marc glanced past her. "Where did all these people come from?"

She lowered her voice. "The Knoonk want me to lead. In exchange, they've released all these groups. With all my responsibilities, you can't be coming around expecting us to get back together, not here."

Marc stared at the ground. "I understand."

"Spartacus supervises defense. You'll report to him."

She felt sorry for Marc as he shuffled off with Spartacus. He'd become a ghost of the man she'd known for so many years. Still, she was glad he'd come back.

>====>

While Elena didn't regret following her father's quest, she wished she'd learned more of her mother's Navajo traditions. Her mother's family disowned her for marrying her father. Then her mother tried to blend into the life Alexander Pyetrov offered.

Somewhere in that lost heritage, among the four sacred mountains were the healing, harmony, and balance that Elena longed for. If only she could tap into that, it might clear her head so she could figure out how to defeat the Knoonk. Unfortunately, leading the clans was absorbing all of her time and attention.

Unable to sleep, Elena strolled through Desert Cave beneath the star-lit ceiling. The calm shattered with the howl of her coyotes. A thought nagged at her, though she couldn't quite grasp it.

The attack came without warning. Eleven animal-skin men swarmed into Desert Cave. The night watch didn't respond.

At the top of her lungs Elena yelled, "Raid!"

The sound distorted and reverberated through the cave as "Rape!"

Startled by the thunderous echo, the eleven men froze.

Elena rushed forward beneath false starlight, swung her zapper free, and stunned the closest man. Spartacus entered from Big Cave with several of his men and rushed the intruders. Arrows rained down from ledges above Desert Cave. The intruders huddled around the bodies of three fallen comrades.

Elena zapped another intruder. The others organized around a big grizzly man and faced off against Spartacus and his men.

One of the animal-skins with a bushy black beard grabbed Elena. When she tried to zap him, he grabbed her weapon and jolted one of Spartacus' men. She kicked the man in the groin. He groaned and turned the zapper on her. Marc leapt at Black-beard and tackled him to the ground. The zapper bounced on the gravelly rock. Elena dove for it. A red-bearded animal-skin tackled her. She wedged the zapper into his ribcage and paralyzed him.

Elena got to her feet and spun around. Another intruder swung a blade at her. She ducked in time and counted two other animal-skins standing. The three backed up to each other in a defensive triangle, each brandishing a blade.

Arrows rained down on them from above. One intruder fell. Elena leaped at a second animal-skin and zapped him. Marc and Spartacus grabbed the last intruder and ran a blade through his chest.

Elena took a moment to catch her breath. She walked by each of the intruders. They faced the meat locker or resurrection as slave labor. The fights were supposed to have ended. The attack meant the Knoonk were impatient for their quota. It was a warning.

>===>

Anticipating her daily chess match with Nalon, Elena waited in her alcove. She didn't want to draw attention to the time she spent with their hosts. Her people wouldn't appreciate her playing chess while they bred for the Knoonk.

Never sure what to expect, Elena bowed at the first twinge of nausea.

After transport, Thelma sat at her display. A barrage of images absorbed her attention. Nalon paced next to the virtual chess display. Elena had questions she needed answered. She studied Nalon to gauge her reception.

Nalon seemed distracted as she pointed to the game. "Play!"

Elena moved a champion. "Why do the children grow so fast?"

Thelma stopped flashing images and stared at a blank screen. Nalon moved her commander. Elena took her turn and looked over toward Thelma. Unable to see her sister, Elena stood.

"Sit!" Nalon demanded.

Elena sat and tried to glimpse her sister behind Nalon.

The ground shook. Elena held the tabletop to keep from tumbling off her seat. Lights went out, plunging them into darkness.

"Do not move," Nalon said. "We have little time."

"Thelma?"

"She is fine. I will tell you what I can. Narn is resistance. The plan is to enslave all humans and take over Earth."

"When?" Elena asked, holding tight to her seat.

"First Gorg must capture the Royal Couple on Earth. She calls them traitors and seeks to use them for political power."

"Other groups?"

Nalon spoke quickly. "The Knoonk tried to impose their way. They lost our civil war and escaped here. They seek to start over on Earth. The resistance believes taking Earth is wrong."

"Bless you."

"Time is short. Resources are devoted to improving a gate worm-hole."

"What's that?" Elena asked.

"Today, we can only transport short range. With the gate, millions could come to colonize Earth."

"What about the children?" Elena asked. "Why do they grow so fast?"

Beeping resonated from the corridor.

"No time." Nalon grabbed Elena's arm and pushed her toward the door. "They will punish me with the incubator ward. My sister died there."

"Sister? I thought—"

With a gentle whoosh, the door panels slid open. Nalon held Elena back.

"How did you know where I was?" Elena asked, unable to see.

"Infrared vision."

"That's how you see in the tunnels."

"Shhhh."

Nalon's small, leathery hand gripped Elena's arm and tugged her down the corridor. Thelma trailed behind. They jogged in darkness until they spotted lights. Other Knoonk hurried ahead of them. Elena lowered her head as much as she could without stumbling. Thelma ran beside her. In the narrow passageway, Elena kept bumping into the hexagonal wall panels.

Knoonk ahead of them ducked into doorways. Elena tripped. Nalon dragged her for several feet before Elena regained her footing. Elena couldn't get used to how strong the Knoonk were. When they stopped, she glanced into a room and couldn't believe what she saw. Several human girls Thelma's age sat at virtual displays.

Before Elena could absorb that, Nalon dragged her down the corridor. Out of breath, Elena struggled to keep up with her alien friend. They reached what Elena presumed was their destination. Nalon pushed Elena and Thelma into another gray cell.

Bowing, Elena turned to Nalon. "What about—" She felt

nauseous and reappeared in her private alcove within Big Cave.

Thelma lay on a nearby ledge, crying. She must have recognized one of the girls.

A terrible thought gripped Elena. If those girls weren't human, then maybe the cave children weren't, either. The idea seemed too monstrous. The Knoonk could be using humans as incubators to breed human-looking Knoonk. These Terran-adapted Knoonk (TK) would be difficult, if not impossible, to identify. That would explain why Gorg couldn't find the couple on Earth. TK could take Earth and no one would know until it was too late.

You can't trust the Knoonk, and you can't even recognize them.

THIRTY-ONE

Elena strolled through Desert Cave, studying girls playing tag or jump rope amidst clusters of women. Chrissie pulled her to a quiet corner. "Every day we find new caves and more clans."

While Elena listened, her focus was on the girls. They looked like healthy humans, except they grew faster and learned quicker.

"I thought we had them all," Chrissie said. "Then more show up. Are you even listening?"

"Un-huh."

"This morning's census had over twenty thousand. Elena? What if there are millions?"

"Then we'll care for them as best we can." When Elena had heard news of disappearances in the months before her mission, she'd dismissed them as child custody disputes. If only people knew.

Leaving Chrissie, Elena spotted Jenny alone by the cacti again. The brunette appeared not to have slept in days. She had to be confused by changes to her body and what had happened to her friends. *Are you a Terran-adapted Knoonk, a TK?* The idea was too grotesque.

She appeared human from the petite nose to the beautiful head of light brown hair and delicate ears. There had to be another explanation. *I'm just being paranoid.*

Elena sat on a ledge near the girl. "Sometimes it helps to talk."

"Why? You wouldn't understand," the girl said, without looking up. "I don't."

"Try me." Elena lifted the girl's chin. "My parents were taken from me when I was young. Most of my life has been confused."

Jenny grimaced. "I can't sleep." She took a moment to compose her thoughts. "I have nightmares."

Elena squeezed the girl's hand and smiled. "So do I. Tell me about yours."

Jenny looked away. "You'll say I'm crazy."

"Not after what I've lived through."

Jenny's sad eyes studied Elena for a long time before she continued. "I feel someone else in my head. I remember things I've never seen, places I haven't been. I see creatures like none I've known. They're an angry people. They want to impose their will on me."

"Do they look like the Knoonk?"

The girl shrugged. "I've never seen our hosts, but the creatures in my nightmares are how other people have described them."

"When did these dreams start?"

"Right after my friends disappeared. They had nightmares, too. I thought they'd made it up." Jenny wept.

Refusing to believe this could be a genetically altered Knoonk, Elena leaned the girl's head against her shoulder. Nearby, the girl's mother looked concerned yet weary from watching her other children. Closing her eyes, Elena tried to make sense of it. Her coyotes circled, howling until they drowned out conversations nearby. A gentle whiff of fish oil filled her nostrils.

Elena froze.

She inhaled again. It wasn't the strong rancid odor of the Knoonk, though it was distinct. These Terran-adapted Knoonk might look human, but they still had a hint of that aroma.

Elena glanced at hundreds of children in Desert Cave. They were all TK. That was what her coyotes were warning her. Their hosts were producing Knoonk children to colonize Earth. They had schedules to meet. That was the meaning of the quotas.

She took a deep breath. If they wanted humans raising their young, maybe Elena could socialize them to love humans so they could live side by side.

Coyotes howled louder. The Knoonk had the technology to take Earth at any time, yet they hesitated. She continued to hold Jenny even after the girl stopped crying.

The air. When they'd first arrived, Elena had noticed its thick texture. It must have had nutrients the Knoonk needed that Earth's atmosphere lacked. TK wouldn't have that problem. Moreover, they'd be resistant to Earth's diseases. The Knoonk had tested all this on their human hostages. They'd engineered a superior species of Knoonk adapted to Earth.

That didn't explain why they had humans raise their children. The Knoonk even promoted this by getting women to believe the children were theirs. Mothers had grown accustomed to their children's smell. So why weren't the Knoonk worried about socialization?

Jenny's nightmares.

The implications stunned Elena into holding her breath. The girls gained Knoonk awareness when ... when they went through puberty. That had to be the trigger. That was why they removed the girls at that point.

Their captors didn't care if Elena socialized their young. When they reached puberty, they would assume their Knoonk identity and the regeneration would be complete. Those weren't humans in the alien lair; they were TK and Thelma had recognized them.

Trembling at the possibility that Thelma could be TK, Elena clung to Jenny. She refused to believe her special sister was one of them, but all evidence pointed that way.

Jenny wiggled free and ran to her mother. When the transformation took place, would this child turn on her own mom? Did their seven years together count for nothing?

Elena would have preferred a disease they could have fought. This was far worse. These children were ticking time bombs, ready to blend in on Earth, on university campuses, and in cities. Worse, Elena had become a leader of this conspiracy. She had to do something. Yet she couldn't tell anyone without the Knoonk overhearing.

>====>

Leaving Tara and Reese in charge, Elena waited in her alcove for her daily chess match.

Anger filled her from aching feet to bloodshot eyes, but rage could get her killed or worse. With or without resistance help, it was time to act. The cycle from birth to Knoonk adulthood had to be eight years or so. Given the oldest kids' ages and the fact that many had already disappeared, the Knoonk could soon be ready for invasion.

As nausea faded, Elena was relieved to see Thelma at her display, flashing images as if nothing had happened. Elena looked for any indication that her sister could be TK. That made no sense with Gorg torturing her. Besides, their father had said she was thirteen. She didn't fit the pattern.

"Play!" Nalon insisted.

Elena moved her regent. "You know you've treated humans badly. Don't the Knoonk have morals?"

"We are very moral."

"Then why permit terrible acts?" Elena played aggressively.

"We must obey."

"If there's a way for us to live together, shouldn't we try?"

Nalon focused on the game.

"Why can't you help me?" Elena whispered. Aware she'd gained the upper hand in the game, she played recklessly. She didn't want to embarrass her host.

"We cannot disagree with our community."

"Why?"

"Years ago, after a terrible war, people demanded change. The new order decided the community was everything and individuals should serve."

"What if the community is wrong?" Elena didn't exploit an opportunity to neutralize Nalon's spy and gain advantage. She'd noticed that while Knoonk chess was much more complicated than human chess, its spy had a weakness. It couldn't operate alone, something fundamentally Knoonk.

"Our community is not wrong. It supports survival."

"You've studied human history. In the twentieth century, we fought terrible wars and decided that when the community did wrong, the individual had an obligation to oppose."

"That is your history. This is ours."

"You seek to destroy us. I see it in Gorg's eyes," Elena added.

"I cannot oppose our community."

"We could do so much working together. I couldn't help noticing that you've let human women work alongside Knoonk. As the human leader, I request a visit."

Nalon raised her zapper. Elena stepped away from the game, and braced herself for the jolt.

Nausea gripped her.

THIRTY-TWO

Elena touched an inflamed lump on her head. Fog clouded her thoughts as when she woke up in the morning. She was in a backlit cell, five feet in diameter, lying in the fetal position.

She rubbed her scalp and stared at triangular gray panels. Nalon's response to her question confirmed suspicions. If she couldn't see the humans in the alien lair, they must be TK, and the Knoonk would know how to tell them apart, perhaps by smell.

The cell rotated, bouncing Elena from side to side. When it stopped, the cell went dark. A panel opened, bringing a strong whiff of fish oil. She couldn't see, but the Knoonk could with their infrared vision. Elena rotated into a sitting position.

"Nanobots will repair any head injury." It sounded like Major Narn. "We need to maintain the illusion of animosity."

"What illusion?"

"We have little time. The commander and the general are under pressure."

"Why would the resistance help us if it hurts the Knoonk?" Elena asked.

"We can go home, but the Supreme Commander seeks power and social purity here. She wants to start a new colony."

"Why have the Knoonk taken human form?"

"Our home planet has strong gravity," Major Narn said. "Our atmosphere gives nutrients and protection from solar radiation. We don't find those on Earth."

"Sunburn?"

"Worse. Listen. If the commander finds the Royal Couple, she will hold power here and back home. If she harms the couple, she faces a terrible war."

"That's why Gorg can't just destroy all humans." Elena strained to make out the Knoonk's features in the negligible light.

"She needs the couple alive, which makes capturing them harder."

"Why are they so important?"

"They are the last royal offspring," Narn said. "They can bring unity for our people. The commander wants to control them. Gorg would kill all humans. Your technology is inferior. I fear we hold no respect for other species."

"What's the plan?"

"Capture the couple. Replace key humans with Terran-adapted Knoonk. Then incubate and displace all humans."

"What if Gorg can't capture the couple?" Elena asked.

"Then the commander will continue to place more of our people on Earth until we do. She cannot commence the invasion until we control the couple."

"What about the worm-hole?" Elena asked.

"After the supreme commander secures Earth and the gate is completed, they will transport more loyal Knoonk and anyone willing to convert and serve."

"Is there any plan to allow humans to live?"

"Perhaps in special preserves for study and observation or as slaves," Narn said. "Many of our people oppose this but it's futile to challenge the community."

"How much time do we have?"

"Children mature in eight years. Many approach that now."

"How can I help?" Elena asked.

"You will know when the time is right. Do not hesitate. You will not get second chance."

"How can I get to Earth?"

"Must go," Narn said.

The panel slid closed and the cell rolled, bouncing Elena head over heels and banging her arms, legs, and head.

No one communicated much here, not the Knoonk, not Thelma, and not the resistance. Except she now knew their plans. A lot of good that did stuck in this cave system most likely on Mars.

When the cell stopped rolling, Elena sat up, tucked her knees under her chin, and waited for what came next.

>===>

Elena transported to a large gray conference room. The nausea lingered along with disorientation that had her mind fogged. Surrounded by Knoonk, she lowered her head.

Gorg approached with a zapper in hand. Elena no longer had hers. She bit her lip. That would have been too simple of a plan.

Elena backed away until she bumped into a triangular wall panel. Blue-clad, Major Narn stood by the doorway. Smaller than the other Knoonk, she looked surprised to see Elena, or annoyed. Nalon sat at a table talking with several others. Thirteen Knoonk stood around the room.

Zurbiz stepped forward wearing a tight smile. "You do well with the humans."

"To serve you," Elena said.

"Then serve by keeping up production." Zurbiz grabbed the general's weapon and Gorg stepped aside, mumbling something in their language. Evidently, all wasn't well with their search for the couple. That gave Elena an idea, perhaps the window of opportunity Major Narn mentioned.

"I know you run missions on Earth," Elena said, keeping her head low. "Wouldn't it be better to employ human guides knowledgeable of Earth and aware of your power and mercy?" Elena spread it on thick.

"We need no stinking humans." Gorg moved beyond the commander's reach.

"I'm guessing missions failed because of pilot error and Knoonk were captured."

Gorg lunged at Elena and threw a leathery fist. Elena dodged sideways and fell onto the gray floor. It took three guards to restrain the general.

Elena thought it interesting that they even bothered for a mere human. Rubbing her jaw, Elena stood and bowed.

"What do you propose?" Zurbiz placed her hand on Elena's shoulder.

How charming, just like a politician. "If I were permitted to join your team, I could help with your missions." The historical irony wasn't lost on her of her Navajo ancestors helping the Europeans.

"You cannot consider this," Gorg said.

"We listen," Zurbiz said. She smiled at Elena. "You would do this in exchange for what?"

A trade? Elena had their interest. "Thelma comes with me."

"No."

Elena sighed. They would hold her sister hostage in case Elena decided to flee. She couldn't condemn Thelma, yet she owed it to billions of humans to try to stop the Knoonk. "No one touches her until she's at least eighteen."

"You will take her place?" Zurbiz asked.

"Not while I'm helping with missions. It would slow me down." Elena watched the commander weigh this.

"We do not need humans," Gorg said.

"You have failed to capture the traitors," Zurbiz said. "Perhaps this one can help."

"Humans have nothing to offer."

"Perhaps."

Zurbiz raised her hand to silence the general.

Apparently, the commander didn't have Gorg's loyalty or a free hand to make this decision. This was a community culture and Zurbiz was using political capital to humor Elena in the hope of gaining an advantage.

Elena didn't have time for political intrigue. She had to challenge the source before she lost her chance. "I suggest a chess match to determine whether I have anything to offer."

"We do not play trite human games," Gorg said, her ridge crest taut as a fist.

"3D chess. Knoonk rules." Elena had everyone's attention. While their disdain for humans made her uncomfortable, she couldn't turn back. She glanced at Major Narn. The major gave no indication of knowing her.

"Stop wasting our time." Gorg scowled at the commander.

"Are you afraid of losing to a mere human?" Elena studied Gorg's face. The anger and disgust was priceless. She stepped aside in case she misjudged.

"I fear nothing."

"Then play me."

Gorg glared at Elena, and then scanned the room. If humans hadn't been the prime enemy before, they'd just moved up.

Elena judged Gorg as competitive to a fault. The general talked like a man, acted like a man, even swaggered like a man. All win and no compromise. Gorg had lost a sister for eternity. That would make any woman vengeful.

>===>

While Nalon instructed the chess grid to set up, Elena sat across from Gorg. The general glared in silence. Elena felt the daggers aimed her way. She'd dishonored the general among her people. If Elena won, there'd be hell to pay. If she lost, there'd be no end to what pain Gorg could inflict.

Gorg opened aggressively. Elena hesitated before engaging. She'd gotten used to playing Nalon; she knew nothing about how Gorg played, and she wasn't sure she knew all of the intricacies of their game.

In the early game, the general thrust deep into Elena's territory with scouts and guardians, followed by her regent and commander. Elena could have used her spy to blunt the advance. She left the piece dangling by a thread.

Gorg attempted to hold the purest of poker faces, yet she couldn't conceal her contempt from the wrinkled ridge-crest. Elena could learn much from how someone played. That was how she knew her father loved her, and what gave her confidence to believe in Nalon when coyotes warned not to.

Clenching her teeth, Elena sweated attack after attack by Gorg's forces, blunting them at the last moment at heavy cost. She couldn't keep this up.

Taking advantage of Elena's deteriorating position, General Gorg threw in her commander and regent, which sent Elena reeling for cover. Barely dodging defeat, Elena activated a traitor and a champion to make a run at the general. Her opponent counter-attacked, bringing all her forces to bear.

"Game over," Gorg announced as she made her next move.

All was lost. Elena couldn't see a path to victory, couldn't think enough moves ahead to change the outcome, yet she refused to concede. Then she recognized something from the many games she'd played in her head. Even after she activated her spy, her opponent acted as if moving in for the kill. Elena double-checked every position, every option.

Gorg cheated. She moved her spy when it wasn't her turn. Several Knoonk saw it, too. Elena read it in their otherwise blank faces. It didn't seem wise to bring this up.

Swallowing hard, Elena moved her commander and prayed she

wouldn't fall into Gorg's trap. Gorg responded, but having moved her spy worked against her. Elena neutralized her traitor before Gorg could use it.

Gorg swatted the grid, sending the image away. She rose to zap Elena and hesitated. The other Knoonk must have recognized bad sportsmanship. Gorg rushed the door, zapping panels when they didn't part fast enough. The odor of singed materials filled the air along with heavy fish oil. Elena lowered her head.

Zurbiz cleared the room, approached Elena, and sniffed. "The general has underestimated you. I will not. You help find the traitors. I will show gratitude."

Thus, the commander had to sniff to be sure Elena wasn't TK. That was encouraging. "Do I have your promise Thelma will be protected and won't be made pregnant?"

Zurbiz nodded. "Bring me the couple. If you fail, Thelma goes to incubation."

Elena struggled to breathe. She'd hoped to take Thelma with her. Now she had to weigh Thelma against saving humanity. "I understand."

"If you fail, we will recycle Marc and Spartacus."

"That's not fair."

"Then don't fail me."

Elena hung her head. "What are we looking for?"

"Do we understand each other?"

Elena nodded and felt the weight of responsibility for the fate of family, friends, and billions on Earth.

>===>

Elena stayed in her alcove in Big Cave, mulling her commitment. The Knoonk couple's only crime was having royal blood. Chances were the kids didn't understand. Making matters worse, she couldn't decide who if any were the good guys.

Gorg wanted revenge for her sister and didn't mind taking out ten billion people. Zurbiz acted fair to a point. However, if the resistance sided with Gorg, Zurbiz might be all that stood in their way. Finding the couple might remove Gorg's restraint. Elena could be condemning the human race either way.

She called together the clan leaders in Theater Cave. She invited Spartacus, Marc, Reese, and Tara. It was hard to leave her friends and tougher to decide who should lead in her absence.

"I have to go away for a while," Elena began. "It's a mission to Earth for the Knoonk."

Exclamations of dismay echoed off the walls. Thelma darted off. Elena recalled her father abandoning her for his mission. She was doing the same to Thelma.

Glancing at dozens of clan leaders, Elena walked to center stage. "If I'm successful, I believe I can make things better for everyone."

"What kind of mission?" Marc asked.

"When will you return?" Maggie asked.

"Who will be in charge?" another asked.

Elena held up her hands. "Please, one at a time. I hope this mission will bring goodwill between the Knoonk and us. It could take days or weeks. I'd like to ask Tara to be in charge with help from Chrissie and Reese. Spartacus will remain in charge of defense. We haven't had a single casualty since we joined together."

Everyone nodded agreement.

"I beg you to continue working together," she said. "I ask everyone to accept Marc as I do, as a valued member of our community." She stole glances his way.

After fielding the usual questions, Elena ended the meeting and pulled Marc to a bench at the back of the cave.

He acted subdued, as he had on their first date after he realized she hadn't come out to watch him practice but rather to measure the physics of the game.

"I've waited days for a chance to tell you how sorry I am," he said.

"I know." Elena patted his arm. "I've known you half my life. You like to play tough guy, but you couldn't hurt me unless someone forced you."

Marc gazed into her eyes. "I'm crazy about you. You know that. I couldn't bear you leaving and hating me."

"I don't hate you, Marc. If we'd stayed on Earth, who knows how things might have turned out. I've thought long and hard about my need for this mission. I'm not sorry. I got to see Dad and I met Thelma. I just wish I hadn't gotten you and the others into this."

"You were meant to find the Knoonk."

Elena smiled. "I can't imagine what for."

"Someone had to."

"Marc, I want you to continue supporting the community for me and in particular to watch over Thelma. The Knoonk promised not to force her if I helped. I wanted to tell her. She probably won't come near you so work with Reese and Tara. I'm worried sick. I'll never forgive myself if anything happens to her."

"We'll be fine. Just be careful."

THIRTY-THREE

Elena sat in a briefing room on a gray Knoonk cruiser in Earth orbit, wishing she could see an image of her home planet. They would be there soon enough. She focused on how to escape her TK tracker once they reached Earth. She could blend into crowds, make her way to freedom, warn Senator Jorgensen, and head for New Mexico in search of her mother's people. Then Thelma would face unfathomable horrors, as would the others. Elena couldn't live with that. Yet if she didn't act, humans didn't stand a chance. Besides, if Thelma turned out to be a TK spy, returning for her would be in vain.

General Gorg entered the room and everyone gathered around. Elena stood behind her tracker. Lieutenant Debra Telet was tall, blonde, athletic, and dressed like Elena in green Dura-pants and Kordo-top, the latest fashion for young women seeking to look fab with low maintenance.

The faintest whiff of fish oil from Telet wafted into Elena's nostrils. Unfortunately, Elena had to get vulnerably close to smell it. She wondered how many TK had already assimilated on Earth. Telet was the only one in the room.

Gorg briefed the other Knoonk in their language while Telet lingered behind two Knoonk Elena took to be guards. Then, without ceremony, Elena felt the trademark queasiness of pending teleportation.

Appearing in a field of tall grass, Elena sucked in fresh air and looked at her first sunrise in ages. She felt lightheaded in the thinner atmosphere and weighted down by heavier gravity.

"Let's go," Lieutenant Telet ordered and marched north.

Taking deep breaths, Elena followed the tracker. Telet had a bodybuilder's figure. She swaggered like a man and swung her arms wide. She reminded Elena of Gorg, with the air of a superior species.

Before the briefing, Zurbiz had warned Elena that TK brain capacity was double that of humans. Elena glanced over her shoulder, wondering if other TK or Gorg was stalking them. Gorg would stand out and couldn't handle the sunlight or the air.

Telet set a determined pace. After months in light gravity, Elena had difficulty keeping up. Her footfalls fell hard; she adjusted.

She recognized the Minneapolis skyline from when she'd visited her Uncle Donald. Although it had been eighteen years since she'd seen them, Elena hoped they might accept Thelma and news of her father better than when they'd taken Elena after her mom's death.

Glancing back from time to time to make sure that Elena didn't escape, Telet treated her like the family dog, giving her everything she needed except the couple's names, how to recognize them, and what assets Telet had. "Keep up, you're slowing me down." The lieutenant moved as if she could win an Olympic marathon.

Elena slowed. "Why don't we get a car?"

Telet returned, grabbed Elena's arm, and dragged her on a forced march toward Minneapolis. "Humans are weak and mealy-mouthed. You don't deserve this bountiful planet." Telet tugged Elena to make her point of how superior the TK was.

Elena expected the tracker to steal a car. Instead, Telet entered Foley's Premium New Vehicles.

Elena looked for an escape. The tracker stayed close and likely could outrun any human. Along one side of the dealership were scattered commercial buildings. The other side was a residential neighborhood of clean lawns, neat homes, and few people mulling about.

Time wasn't on Elena's side. If she escaped, other trackers would hunt her down. If she couldn't distance herself, she'd face a life sentence producing TK or worse, with no chance to warn anyone.

When they entered the showroom, a rotund man in his forties approached with a phony salesman's smile.

"I want a Bunko," Telet announced. She glared at Elena.

The man stared for a long time, as if this should have made sense. Then his face lit up. "Ah, you mean our new Bronco All-Terrain?"

Telet's nose curled and her arms tensed as if ready to squash his bald melon head.

Elena stepped forward. "What kind of deal can you make us?"

"We have all-leather interior."

"That one!" Telet said. "How much?"

The rotund man waddled over to a red Bronco parked in the showroom. "Sixty-two-thousand-four-hundred-eight-three. Now—"

Telet opened her side satchel and slapped onto the counter a roll of coins with gold rims encased in clear plastic. "I'll take it."

Telet didn't care about the money. When TK took over, gold would be worthless.

Rejecting dealer prep, Telet signed without reading the documents and nearly drove the Bronco through the showroom window as the plump salesman scrambled to open the doors.

"I need to use the restroom," Elena said.

Telet slammed the brakes, missing the salesman by inches. "Make it quick."

Elena had hoped to find an exit and run for it, but Telet's fish-oil aroma followed her into the restroom, whereupon the TK checked the stalls before she let Elena go.

They returned to the Bronco with Telet behind the wheel. "No more distractions." She placed a device on the console and tuned it to pick up the police band.

Glancing out the side mirror, Elena saw no evidence of other trackers.

On the way into town, Telet parked by a convenience store. Elena scanned other stores and the streets for escape routes. Few people were out, which would make her too easy to track. Before she could make a move, Telet grabbed Elena's arm, pushed her into the store, and approached an elderly woman behind the counter.

"You had a burglary?" Telet said, holding onto Elena as if with cuffs.

The old woman cringed at some memory. "The police were here. Are you the detective?"

Elena couldn't loosen the tracker's grip.

"Young couple?" Telet asked.

The old woman nodded.

"How old?"

"Teens."

"Can you describe?" The tracker used an economy of words and motion, efficiency with little emotion. Yet the Tracker appeared agitated while the old woman gave a generic description that could have fit millions of teens.

Telet herded Elena outside. Inside the Bronco, Elena asked, "What was that all about?"

Telet turned on the police radio. Elena turned it off. "I can't help if you don't tell me what's going on. I know Minneapolis."

The tracker reached for the radio. Elena palmed it.

Telet slipped into morning traffic. "There were five burglaries in the past few days by a young couple."

"The couple?"

"Traitors. Now give me the receiver."

Elena placed the radio on the dash and listened.

For the rest of the day, they followed up on one burglary after another with Telet dragging Elena along to interrogate witnesses. Each involved a young couple with witnesses giving inconsistent descriptions. Telet also showed interest in news of homeless couples, loiterers, and indigents. Now and then, she called someone, using the Knoonk language. Elena picked up speech patterns, but without context, she couldn't translate.

At the Chancellor Hotel, Telet handed the lobby clerk two crisp hundred-dollar bills, probably counterfeit, and dragged Elena to their room. Telet made a call, which became an intense argument Elena couldn't follow.

When Telet turned her back, Elena slipped out of the room. She got ten paces before Telet caught up and delivered an electric shock. Elena felt as if she'd jumped ten feet into the air before crumbling to the carpeted hallway floor.

Telet dragged her into the room like a sack of trash and cuffed her to exposed pipes under the bathroom sink. "Another attempt and you won't move for a day."

"I wanted to check out the pool."

Telet cast a harsh don't-take-me-for-a-fool look.

So much for escape. Besides, with no money, she'd have to beg or steal to survive. With no idea who might listen in, she couldn't contact anyone by phone and would have to get close in order to know who was a TK. She rattled the cuffs against the pipe, yet couldn't pull free.

Elena spent the night chained to the bathroom sink, having to ask permission to use the toilet, which Telet didn't use. Whenever she closed her eyes, Elena's coyotes howled until she woke, covered in sweat.

The morning brought a repeat of the prior afternoon with visits to three retailers who described that, yes, it was a young couple and the girl had brown hair, blonde hair, red hair, and various combinations in between. The boy had long hair, short hair, or wore a hat.

"Could be different couples," Elena said.

"Same couple, different disguises," Telet said.

Then the radio broadcast a disturbing incident: "Attractive blonde found dead in Meacham Park."

Telet pulled over and fumbled with her communicator. She brought up the image of a muscular blonde who could have been Telet's twin splayed on the grass. In a bluish haze, the body vanished.

"Did you know her?" Elena asked.

Telet's eyes teared up and turned red. "We worked together." Her voice scratched with venom. "If you weren't here, she'd still be alive."

"I'm sorry. Didn't she have a partner?"

"Me!"

"You think the couple did this?"

"They're heading east," Telet announced, as she pulled into traffic. "I'll get them."

"I believe they're heading south," Elena said. "The park's in south St. Paul. My guess is Mall of America." The refurbished mall was a hangout for teen lovers. She wondered if TK could experience love or if they were bred as worker ants.

"Why?" Telet sped up.

"They can get lost there." So could Elena if she played her cards right.

Telet smiled.

"Aside from fuzzy descriptions," Elena said, "what can you tell me about them?"

"Fifteen."

"You mean fully grown?"

"Only in the last ten years have genetics permitted rapid growth." Telet headed south. "They will look their Earth age. As you've heard, we have no reliable descriptions."

"So we have a billion possibilities. That shouldn't take long. How will we know when we find them?"

Telet didn't say. After she identified a couple with the fish oil scent, she had only to compare them to the list of known TK and seize anyone not on the list.

Elena considered the couple. They stole to survive, which meant they were on the run from human authorities as well. Already Elena liked these underdogs, though they were sloppy, leaving too many clues.

When they reached Mall of America, Elena looked for escape routes from the huge parking garage.

Taking the police monitor, Telet grabbed Elena's arm and pushed her toward the mall entrance. "You were right."

"What happened?"

"Store burglarized with no reliable descriptions."

"Mind manipulation?" Elena wondered what other advantages the TK had.

Dragging Elena with her, Telet ran toward the mall entrance. Keeping up was easier than the day before. "Then what?" Elena asked.

"Not mind manipulation." Telet wasn't even breathing hard. "They outsmart humans."

Letting go of Elena's hand, Telet burst through the revolving doors. Elena stopped. Before she could make her break, Telet returned. She was fast as well as smart and strong. Her kind could swarm Earth and displace humans.

Inside the mall, Elena followed Telet past throngs of shoppers and mall rats. Pretending to catch her breath, Elena searched for opportunity. She would only get one chance.

"Don't slow me down." Telet yanked her along. "You know what happens if you fail."

Elena didn't need reminding.

Telet stopped at a teen accessories store and dragged Elena over to a pretty girl in the latest bright-color fashion, who had just finished talking to the police. "Excuse me," Telet said. "I know you've already done this. Could you describe the couple who robbed you?"

"It was two girls," the brunette said.

"I saw two guys," another girl said.

"No, it was a redhead and a blond guy," a slender boy added.

Telet pulled Elena into a corner and called on her cell. It spooked Elena that she had no idea how many assets Telet had. The tracker adjusted her ear bud, tucked the police scanner into her satchel, and pulled Elena from store to store, listening for more activity.

They were chasing a puff of air. The couple was toying with them. Then it hit her; the couple had no use for things while they were running. What they'd most prize would be cash and food, not clothing.

Pulling free, Elena ran toward the food court. Telet caught up and grabbed her arm. Elena yanked free. "Either you want to catch them or you want to play jailer."

Telet backed into a big man sporting a cowboy hat and boots. He caught her and held on a moment too long. She spun, slammed her fist into his face, and knocked him into the middle of a crowd. People moved away.

Elena used the commotion to run down the concourse. She stopped at the railing over the food court to catch her breath and scanned the people below.

Young couples mulled arm-in-arm reminding Elena of Thelma and Joey. Elena swept that thought from her mind and tried to focus. She either escaped or caught the couple. With so many couples, she couldn't possibly sniff out "the" couple in this crowd before Telet arrived.

Intelligent selection, she reminded herself. Able to choose genetics, they'd take the best. The couple would be attractive, though not to the point of standing out.

Telet sprinted toward her, swatting people out of the way like mosquitoes. Elena waved and rescanned the food court. *Escape or catch the couple?* Neither seemed promising, yet if she didn't act, she wouldn't get another chance.

She leapt over the railing, crashed down on a metal table, and hit harder than she expected. *Damn Earth's gravity.* She bruised her hip and rolled through to a sitting position on the ground.

Above, Telet stood at the railing, red-faced. She might have superior genes, but she opted for a safer way down.

Elena sprung to her feet. The exit was to her right. She turned and spotted a teen couple nervously eyeing her by Holloway's Roast Beef. Elena sprinted toward them. They sprung to their feet and fled.

The girl had short-cropped blonde hair, a yellow halter, and faded jeans. The boy was taller with a tuft of brown hair. Elena chased the girl.

Dodging tables and teens, she sprinted as fast as she could. The girl made tracks toward the arcade. Elena followed, unable to gain on her.

Elena slowed. So did the girl, who turned and made the fatal mistake of entering the game arcade. There wasn't a back exit, as Elena had learned years ago when playing with her cousins.

Inside the arcade, Elena scanned row by row, checking each set of reality games. When she reached the back, the blonde stood there, trapped.

"Don't do this. You're not one of them." The blonde's eyes were alert, her body ready to spring into action.

"Not one of whom?"

"You're not a tracker. You're good. Don't take us back."

Stunned, Elena hesitated. Her mind jammed up with questions. If she failed to bring them in, Thelma and the others would be punished. She couldn't help thinking this couple could hold the key to stopping the Knoonk. Once they had the couple, Gorg would be free to kill humans.

"How much do you know?" Elena asked.

"Plenty, but we haven't time. I beg you."

Elena could no more turn in this girl than she could Thelma. "Will you be okay?"

"Go before she finds you," the blonde said.

Elena told the girl how to sneak out of the mall. "Be careful."

"Bless you," the girl said.

Reaching the arcade entrance, Elena looked across the courtyard toward an exit. Not seeing Telet, she ran. The tracker grabbed her from behind. Covering her head, Elena dropped to the ground and screamed. At least she could distract the tracker until the girl escaped.

THIRTY-FOUR

Shocks of pain radiated out and back like an ocean tsunami, hitting every cell of Elena's body until her brain rebelled. Her soul screamed to die. Death brought resurrection and renewed vigor to withstand another attack. Discordant pictures morphed into foul screams, dissonant smells, ugly taste, and the jab of a million needles.

Another jolt left Elena void. She had nothing left to give. General Gorg grinned on a screen that covered the wall and ceiling. With each attack, Elena prayed for the end. She must have died a dozen times, only to revive for another assault.

"This is for Major Burb." Gorg's voice stabbed Elena's ears. "Killed in Minneapolis."

On another screen, Thelma cowered next to a scruffy giant. She was no match for the DNA-enhanced beast. She crouched, ready to spring in any direction, as she ran her hands along a gray wall searching for openings. She worked her way around the cave, without finding crevices to climb or objects to throw. There would be no mercy. Elena had failed them both.

"Please stop," her voice croaked. Elena wept, though her dry eyes produced no tears.

Gorg remotely adjusted the headrest, forcing Elena to see. "You failed because you are human. You're not so smart now."

The giant reached for Thelma. The girl slipped away and ran at the far wall. She found no holds to grasp and fell onto the gray floor. The giant ambled toward her.

"For mercy's sake," Elena muttered. "Don't do this."

"You let the traitors go."

"Spare Thelma." The words scratched Elena's throat. Blinking was like sandpaper across bone-dry eyes. "The couple was fast, smart. I needed help."

"You had help. You ran off."

The brute grabbed Thelma. She couldn't break free.

"Save Thelma, please." Elena reached toward the screen. Her arm slumped at her side.

The giant flung her sister onto the ground. Thelma lay there, not moving.

"Hurt me, not her," Elena said. "She never hurt you."

Muscles twitched in waves of spasms. Elena's eyes squeezed shut and burned.

>===>

Elena floated in a sensory-deprived void. She wasn't sure how long she'd blanked out. When she next became aware, Thelma was alone, frightened, and curled in the fetal position in the middle of a barren cave. Elena lost consciousness.

When she revived again, she lay on her back staring at gray ceiling panels.

Zurbiz glanced down at her and whispered, "Recover now. General Gorg is gone."

"Thelma?" Elena blinked her eyes, now moist. Even her throat no longer felt parched.

"She is fine."

Elena tried to move her arms; she was strapped down. Although Knoonk medicine had repaired the physical damage, every muscle replayed the terror. "Did that beast hurt her?"

"No, but you failed me. I gave you a chance. Now we must punish Thelma and all humans as you agreed."

Failed her? They weren't on the same side. It appeared the commander had used her against Gorg. "Please, I came close. I can catch them next time."

"How? Even you admit the traitors are too smart and fast."

Elena forced clarity into her overloaded brain, hoping their meds could restore her mind. Major Narn had said to seize the opportunity, or something. It all blurred. Elena needed another chance. "I need someone fast, who could win the couple's trust."

"You have Lieutenant Telet."

"They're wise to the trackers. Thelma could reach them. She's the right age. She can get close without making them suspicious. They'd take pity on her and I could catch them. With Thelma's help we can catch them."

Zurbiz moved away from Elena's table/bed. Elena strained to watch the commander pace. "This couple, what have they done?" she asked.

The commander moved within view and grinned. "How will you control Thelma and stop her attacks? We cannot allow her to run off."

"If she's with me—"

"She runs from you."

"I've learned to keep her from running," Elena said. "Besides, you'll have several trackers, won't you?"

Zurbiz grinned. "I need the traitors in three days."

"I got close once. With Thelma's help I can catch them."

"It's not that simple."

Elena was afraid of that. Zurbiz had lost face. Gorg's position had improved.

"General Gorg doesn't like humans," Elena said. "How can I help you?"

Zurbiz gave Elena a spiteful look. She'd insulted the commander by implying a human could help. These Knoonk exhibited more macho behavior than any man Elena had encountered. She'd expected a female culture to be more humane, less confrontational, and more cooperative. Zurbiz once said they'd been all male during their civil war. Years of DNA manipulation and inbreeding hadn't helped. Again, her fate rested in the hands of those who despised her.

>===>

Transported to a Knoonk conference room, Elena couldn't believe she'd survived Gorg's torture only to have the general goad her into fighting in their special arena. Elena hadn't seen another choice. Her self-defense training didn't qualify her as a fighter, but if she didn't fight, Thelma faced life in the incubation ward, while Elena would be at Gorg's lack of mercy. At least in the arena, Elena could fight back.

A smug grin on her thin lips, General Gorg raised a mug of some brownish concoction toward Elena. "May you die a thousand deaths."

241

Elena felt like a cat clinging to its last life. The Knoonk had repaired the body damage. Nothing could remove the scathing attack on her nerves. Every muscle twitched and burned in remembrance.

She hung her head. Misfiring muscles told her she hadn't the nerve to fight Gorg's passionate hatred.

"Now that we've settled on a fight," Commander Zurbiz said. "The question is who you will fight."

The room grew still.

Gorg's ridge crest tightened. "I will fight the human insect."

"Save your anger for the mission," Zurbiz said. "We shall have Traitor Narn fight the human."

Elena was shocked to hear they'd caught her supposed ally.

The general barged out of the room. "I will have my vengeance."

Elena didn't want to hurt one of the few Knoonk who'd shown mercy, but it was a fight to the death. Elena needed to live or all humans were doomed, including Thelma.

After an exchange in the Knoonk language, Nalon escorted Elena down a long gray corridor to a barren gray cell with what looked like a locker. "You should not have angered General Gorg. This will not go well."

Elena sat on a narrow bench across from Nalon. "What happens now?"

Nalon pulled a pale yellow material out of the locker and held it up—a bodysuit of some kind. "I will not vote. I have no confidence you can defeat Major Narn."

"Thanks for the encouragement." On the screen two Knoonk resistance members fought in a state of weightlessness.

"This is not about feeling. It's about tactical advantage. Remove your clothes and I will help you put this on."

Elena hesitated. "I can dress myself."

"No doubt. You need help with this. Quick, do not offend the commander by being late."

While she removed her thin blouse and micro-skirt cave outfit, Elena watched in horror as the two Knoonk resistance members tore at each other. It was awkward in zero gravity and bloody. "I understand fight to the death. What happens to the winner?"

Nalon stretched the bodysuit over Elena's feet. "The survivor gets to serve."

That didn't sound promising, though wrestling Narn sounded better than facing Gorg. On the screen she studied the contest in a sealed chamber. It looked complicated like Knoonk 3D chess.

Nalon tugged the yellow bodysuit up over Elena's hips with great effort.

"Don't you have a suit in my size?" Elena asked.

"The suit flows like skin." Nalon pulled the fabric over Elena's breasts and stuffed her arms into the holes.

"I can't move." The suit covered everything from neck to toe, like a second skin, leaving only hands and head exposed.

On screen, the Knoonk traitors floated around each other. They attacked, scooted away, and repositioned for another attack, like choreographed wrestling, only more deadly.

Nalon smoothed wrinkles in the bodysuit. "Do not let her get behind you."

"I wasn't planning to." Elena studied as much technique as she could from the blur of motion on screen. The fighters were well matched.

"Do not underestimate our strength. Our planet has high gravity. The Knoonk developed greater strength to mass than humans."

"With help from genetic engineering."

"Careful," Nalon said. "There will be no gravity to stabilize. Get a feel for your space before the fight."

"Why are you helping me?" Elena watched one attacker close in.

"A poor showing reflects badly on me as your guide."

"That shows distinct signs of individuality."

"Why insult me?" Nalon asked.

Elena smiled. "I can't insult you unless you're an individual. What are my chances?"

Nalon stared at Elena for several moments. "A thousand to one."

"Can I bet on me?"

"With your life."

"How can I win?" Elena asked.

"With no gravity, do not get caught floating in the center. Use the walls to position yourself. If she gets you in a choke hold, beg for mercy."

"Will that end the fight?"

"If she offers you a swift death it will."

That sounded ominous. Don't let Narn get behind and don't get stuck in the middle. That didn't sound hard. What wasn't Nalon saying?

A wave of muscle spasms shattered Elena's thoughts.

THIRTY-FIVE

A buzzer sounded. Elena transported into a gray sphere with no exit. She floated to the jeers of a crowd she couldn't see. Her muscles twitched from Gorg's shock therapy. Across the expanse of seven meters floated her opponent, gray body in gray attire, blending into the gray background. Elena had to strain to see her. In contrast, olive-skinned Elena wore yellow.

Thousand to one, eh. Her muscles tightened.

Six inches shorter than Elena, Narn looked frail. She showed no sign of recognition, or wanting to. It must have been the ultimate insult to have to fight a human. With rail thin arms and legs, the Major looked no match for Elena, yet this was zero gravity and the Knoonk were stronger than they looked.

Elena stretched her limbs. Her movements were fluid but recalled memories of her torture. One by one, she thrust out her arms and legs and was dismayed that despite her physics training and space preparation, the action-reaction didn't come naturally. A thrust of a leg sent her spinning backward. She swung her twitching arms to the amusement of hidden spectators.

Narn floated toward her. Unable to sidestep, Elena tried to orient herself not to let Narn get behind, which turned out to be tougher than she'd imagined. Narn bowed and Elena did likewise.

Closing in, Narn thrust out her arm and adjusted her body so she didn't spin. Elena blocked a blow and spun backward. To keep her opponent from getting behind, Elena kicked to get away. There was nothing to kick against.

The Major grabbed Elena's leg and pulled herself around behind. Before Elena could act, Narn had her by the neck. Elena reached behind to stop her opponent from connecting a chokehold. Too late. The alien located the pressure point to cut off oxygen.

In a matter of seconds, Elena would pass out and all would be lost. Her mind resisted focusing on anything but Gorg's torture.

Reaching behind with her legs, Elena found nothing to push against and no sign of her opponent. She felt behind with her hands. Narn had curled into a tight ball and clung to Elena's neck. As the audience cheered, Elena swung her legs back and forth and began to spin.

As her nostrils filled with fish odor, Elena felt consciousness slipping away. *Thelma!*

Sensing the wall beneath her feet, Elena drew her legs up and thrust out, hurling the fighters across the sphere. Throwing her arms out, she caused a spin so that when they crashed against the opposite wall, the full impact of her mass compressed against the alien's chest.

The grip on Elena's neck loosened. Grabbing a thin, steely arm, she wrenched it loose and pried the other limb from her neck. She propelled off another wall and was free.

The crowd jeered. Well, Elena planned to disappoint them again. She hoped Gorg had everything bet on this match.

Narn wasted no time in attacking again. "Kill me or I will kill you," Narn whispered as she pushed off one wall, then another to get position on Elena.

Elena couldn't tell if this was a friendly warning or bravado to unsettle her. It had the latter effect. If Narn smelled fear, she was right.

Swallowing hard, Elena coordinated arm and leg movements to block Narn, yet ended up floating in the middle. Narn hit her hard in the stomach. The blow and its companion knocked the air from Elena's lungs. Gasping, she blocked the next blow. Each action had an opposite reaction altering her orientation. It wasn't fair that her opponent was experienced in zero gravity. It didn't matter. *It's time to learn fast.*

Doubled over in pain, Elena floated backward. She was unnerved at having to wait for her opponent to act, yet she didn't have the hang of maneuvering to mount her own attack. Her position was tenuous. Narn had strength, agility, and experience. All Elena had was size, which offered little benefit in this weightless environment.

With the calmness of experience, Narn drifted to the wall below and pushed off toward Elena. Approaching another wall, Elena kicked and twisted her body to keep her opponent in view. Narn still got behind her. Elena rammed both elbows into the alien's stomach.

Narn gasped, fell away, and grabbed Elena's right leg. Elena kicked with her left. Narn caught that leg and held both in a vise grip. Unable to move from the waist down, Elena bent over to reach Narn. She couldn't bend far enough. Tingling like spiders swarmed over her, her muscles fired at random.

Narn climbed up Elena's body from behind, aiming for the vulnerable neck. Elena twisted, kicked, and turned. She couldn't get any advantage. Narn drew her body into the smallest target to stay out of reach. She was far more agile and stronger than her thin limbs suggested.

Major Narn wrapped her arms around Elena's waist. Elena grabbed one steely arm, twisted in vain, and beat on the hands. Nothing helped. Narn let go for a second. Elena tucked her knees under her chin and threw her arms and legs out in star formation. She got hold of Narn's arm and for an instant got behind her opponent. The alien spun away.

Approaching a wall, Elena pushed off and maneuvered to face Narn. The alien got behind her. Elena rotated. Narn landed on Elena's head and scrambled to get her arms around the neck.

Sensing a wall beneath her, Elena pushed off and rammed her head into the alien's chest against the next wall. Narn let out a ghastly groan and let go. Elena grabbed Narn in a headlock and maneuvered so the alien couldn't use the wall. Then she wrapped her legs around the alien's spindly legs, pinning her opponent.

Narn reached for Elena's neck. Unable to get hold, she grabbed Elena's arms; her fingers clawed at flesh. Elena couldn't hold her grip for long. She was no match for the genetically enhanced Knoonk. She couldn't win this as a test of strength.

Elena let go of Narn's legs and pushed off a wall as hard as she could, propelling them across the open space. Releasing the chokehold, Elena pressed both hands on Narn's neck as they collided with the far wall. The neck snapped with a loud crack.

Elena bounced backward across the sphere.

Narn floated away from the wall, unable to move her limbs. In her language, she grunted something. Then she shouted in English, "Long live our royalty." Then she gasped and floated with her mouth hung open.

Elena felt sad for Narn and angry with Zurbiz and Gorg for forcing this. She tried to console herself that they would only have tortured Narn. She was better off dead, though as a traitor, she wouldn't receive regeneration.

The crowd jeered. Elena imagined a barrage of rotten tomatoes. She was thankful the enclosed space protected her from the mob, and wondered what to do now that her opponent floated lifeless across the sphere. She wanted to honor Narn, to thank her for helping, but associating with this traitor might ruin Elena's last chance.

Gravity returned with a jolt, tossing Elena on top of Narn's lifeless body. The body vanished. Elena glanced up to see Zurbiz on a virtual screen.

"You did well," the commander said.

Despite wobbly legs, Elena stood.

"You are the first non-Knoonk to win in ten years."

"What happened then?" Elena asked, careful not to assume too much.

"We castrated the eunuch and put him into service. You get a second chance."

>====>

Exhausted from torture and fighting, Elena reappeared on a cot in her alcove in Big Cave. She marveled at vibrant murals painted across the walls showing gardens, sunsets, and pleasant memories from Earth.

Tara hurried over. "See what the women have done in your honor." Tara knelt by the cot. "With the supplies you obtained."

Sitting up with difficulty, Elena took delight in the aura of pride and hope in the faces of childcare providers gathered around with their well-fed charges.

"It looks wonderful," Elena said. *And terrible*, since they couldn't leave these caves and were carrying the seeds of human destruction in their TK children. She decided it wouldn't help to destroy their illusions.

Maggie and Reese joined Tara by the cot, making Elena

uncomfortable with their misplaced reverence.

"We're glad you're back," Tara said. "It's been a terrible strain trying to keep the peace."

Head aching, Elena tried to stand. Her muscles had lost their ability to coordinate. Tara and Reese caught her and eased her onto the cot. Elena pulled free and moved uneasily toward a crowd that had assembled nearby. She wanted to tell them about the Knoonk plans and the delicate mission she was embarking on, but she had to keep it simple.

She cleared her throat and leaned on Tara. "I'm grateful for the efforts you've made working together. No one can lead unless others follow. Please continue to maintain our community in peace and dignity." Elena nodded to indicate she was finished.

From across the cave, Thelma ran to Elena, tears flowing down her young cheeks. Elena caught her sister and together they tumbled to the ground. Would Thelma even like Earth? Closing her eyes and dreading the possibility, Elena inhaled. For a moment, she noticed a whiff of fish oil. Then the sweet aroma of lilacs filled her. She inhaled again to be sure, sighed, and took another whiff. Thelma wasn't like the other children.

With Thelma clinging to her arm, Elena got to her feet. "I would like to see the clan leaders and Tara's staff in Theater Cave."

Unsteadily, Elena led the way. Thelma's body swayed as it often did, her head bobbing. She held tight to Elena's hand.

Elena hated that her plans would have consequences for Tara, Marc, and the others, yet their chances were poor if she didn't succeed. This time the Knoonk would watch her even closer. There wouldn't be a third chance.

As clan leaders assembled, Marc watched Elena from the back of the cave. He wanted to apologize again; she saw that in his eyes. It was unnecessary, though his empathy and concern were part of what she loved about him. She'd felt a primal tug when he'd shown up on her loading dock looking as handsome as when they'd dated at school. He did look fabulous in a uniform.

She hadn't rejected him, but rather the responsibility for the children he wanted. She couldn't after she'd failed her brother. Yet she'd taken responsibility for Thelma, all these people, and the fate of humankind. Leaving would jeopardize Marc's life as well.

Thelma leaned her head against her sister's shoulder. She said nothing, not a single rhyme, as if she'd lost her ability to speak.

Although it wasn't cold, the girl shivered, and tapped on Elena's side. "*Thanks for returning.*"

Choking back tears, Elena held her sister and spoke to the clan leaders. "I can't give details, but my mission failed. I have to return to complete my obligations to the Knoonk."

Thelma dug her fingers into Elena's forearm.

Wincing, Elena carried on, without removing her sister's grip. "I wish I didn't have to go. This is important. Given the nature of the mission, I'll be taking Thelma."

Thelma released her grip, buried her face behind Elena's arm, and sobbed. "*Be careful.*"

Elena hoped she could control her sister enough to do what she had to without saying much.

"Why does the girl get to go?" Chrissie asked.

"Yeah, why not one of us?" another clan leader added.

"Tell us about the mission," a third one said.

"Whoa." Elena thrust up her hands. "I can't discuss the mission except to say if I succeed, it will improve our situation with the Knoonk."

"And if you fail?"

"We can do this."

When the barrage of voices grew so deafening that Elena had to cover her ears, Maggie stood in front of Elena. "Silence. All of you."

She waited like a stern grandmother until the din quieted down. "Have you forgotten all that Elena has done for you? I trust her to do the right thing. You should as well. After all, see how much better our lives have become since she took over. I trust her choice of Tara to lead us in her absence. Tara has done a great job. I will continue to support her. Now return to your people and tell them nothing has changed, for nothing has. We will await word when Elena returns. Now go."

Elena was amazed to watch the clan leaders oblige and make their way to the exit. "Thanks, Maggie. I needed that."

"You look like the Knoonk put you through a meat grinder. Let's get you somewhere to rest."

"Thanks, but I need to talk to Tara."

Marc lingered by the tunnel. Elena wanted a chance to say goodbye without subjecting Thelma to more anguish. The girl couldn't understand without knowing their history.

When Elena took Tara to the back of Theater Cave, Thelma tagged along.

"I wish you weren't going," Tara said. "The clan leaders don't listen to me like they do for you."

"I have to go." Elena hugged Thelma.

"I'll try to hold things together until you return then."

Tara looked exhausted. Elena hoped Chrissie, Maggie, and Reese could help enough. Leading here was a thankless job.

"What else is troubling you?" Elena asked.

"We can't meet quotas. Some girls refuse. I'm afraid the Knoonk will retaliate."

While Elena applauded their resistance, it was futile and she couldn't share why. "I know you're walking a fine line. Tell your Knoonk contact to be patient until I return. I'll make things right."

Smiling through her weariness, Tara nodded.

"How have the men behaved?"

"Marc's been wonderful. I thought you said he couldn't work for a woman. I took him on as my assistant and he's been a great help; and I do mean work assistant."

"I figured." Elena looked over at Marc patiently waiting by the exit.

"He watches over Thelma and Joey as much as anyone can. I'm sure you two have a lot to discuss." Tara left.

Elena glanced at Marc and at Thelma.

Suddenly, Thelma let go, smiled at Elena, and hurried to Joey who had joined Marc. *Of course, you need to say your goodbyes.*

>===>

Elena's reunion with Marc in Network Cave left her exhausted yet satisfied. She hadn't been sure she could let herself be with him under the watchful eyes of the Knoonk. For a moment, she forgot about Gorg and Narn, and focused on why she'd fallen in love with Marc so many years ago.

While lying in Marc's arms beneath thin gray sheets, Elena tapped out Morse code on his back. When he rubbed hers, she pinched him and signed again, beginning with "*SOS*." This time he paid attention, though he didn't seem to follow. She wiped the slate and tried again.

"*K watch everything.*" Elena had so much to say, but using code was too slow and she didn't want the Knoonk to catch on.

"*I warned U.*"

"U were right."

Marc kissed her lips. *"I luv U."*

Elena pushed him away. There were things to say. *"I may not return."*

Marc held her so tight their bodies seemed almost as one. *"Do what U must. R lives matter little if U fail."*

"I forgive U. I love U."

Tears filled her eyes as she drew him to her. It was a bittersweet, final goodbye.

THIRTY-SIX

At the briefing in a small gray room aboard a Knoonk cruiser, Elena clutched Thelma's hand. Next to her was Telet, the only tracker in the room.

Zurbiz' plump figure floated before them. "You have one day. We tracked the couple to Chicago, an incident at Gurnee Mills Mall. They were sloppy, like humans."

Elena detected disgust in Telet's face that she hadn't caught these amateurs. Unlike their previous visit to Earth, this wouldn't be a leisurely search. The Knoonk would bring in all available trackers.

"May I speak?" Elena hung her head.

General Gorg glared from a corner seat, no doubt looking forward to the next confrontation. Her ridge crest pinched forward as if ready to launch weapons.

"Speak," Zurbiz said.

"I'm certain they'll head to Great America's amusement park," Elena said, "across the highway from Gurnee. It's a teen hangout."

"Another joke?" Zurbiz said. "Great America."

"She's right," Telet said. "It's a logical choice."

Moreover, it had great places to hide.

With a wave of Zurbiz' hand, nausea engulfed Elena. As queasiness faded, she located Thelma seated in tall grass. The girl stared up at the broad sky and rosy sunrise. She was experiencing Earth for the first time. While Telet got her bearings, Elena had hers. She wasn't proud of her youthful indiscretions. As poor students, she and Marc had snuck into the park without paying.

Telet pointed toward a twelve-foot wall that surrounded the park, covered with barbed wire intended to keep out non-payers. "Move."

At her side hovered something new, a foot-tall robot that looked like a harmless toy. It probably contained sophisticated tracking equipment.

"You missed the drop site by fifteen feet." Elena took Thelma by the hand and tapped out, *"Don't run off."*

Telet moved toward part of the wall hidden by a cluster of maples. "It's important we aren't seen. Hurry."

They could have paid. The Knoonk had plenty of money that would be worthless after they took over. Elena convinced them they needed to scout the park before it opened. She needed time to find an escape.

Telet covered an obvious camera, climbed the wall, and threw a fibrous sheet over the barbed wire. The robot levitated on its own, hovering close to the lieutenant. Elena led her sister toward the park's wall.

Pulling back, Thelma took in the wide expanse, reaching out with her hands as if she could touch the walls and ceiling with painted sky, trees, and buildings. She saw more in the blink of an eye than she had in her entire life.

"Come on, hon," Elena whispered. "We can sightsee later."

Thelma didn't budge. Telet looked back, her face a scowl of impatience.

Elena ran toward the wall. Thelma hurried to her side but refused Elena's hand. *This isn't the time for stubbornness.* Elena climbed a rope Telet had flung over the wall.

Looping near this part of the wall was one branch of the Black Hole, an enclosed roller coaster. If you had any twinge of claustrophobia, which she did, or fear of darkness, this wasn't your ride. Elena had tried it once with Marc.

From atop the wall, Elena checked the layout. Rides and activities had changed, though paths and buildings remained as she remembered. At seven in the morning, the park was deserted except for maintenance crews for the old Beast.

When associates arrived, Elena, Thelma, and Telet, dressed in park uniforms, would blend in. Until then they needed to scout the park and find a place near the entrance where they could watch incoming visitors. Since Elena had seen the couple, she could identify them. Thelma would tag along to gain their confidence. After they caught the pair, they would beam out, no longer caring who saw.

They climbed off the wall. Inside the park, Thelma clung to Elena's arm and looked wide-eyed at each activity, store, and ride while Elena explained what she was looking at. Basketball and carnival activities were still there, but rides had become riskier as the park competed for teen dollars. Their theme became "if it thrills and isn't illegal, you can find it at Great America."

"No time to waste," Telet said.

"It's important for Thelma to be comfortable in order to help. You go ahead. We'll catch up."

"Don't get any ideas. You're here for one reason. Fail this time, and no one will save you or your friends."

Elena's muscles twitched in remembrance. With her knees wobbly, she braced for a fall. Thankfully, the Knoonk had restored her physical strength.

Telet nudged Elena. "Move!"

The watch Maggie had given Elena showed opening wasn't for another forty-five minutes. She smiled at Telet and continued to show Thelma around. At one point, her sister stopped and stared up at the enormity of a sky beyond reach and at structures hundreds of feet higher than anything she would have seen in the caves.

"That's a roller coaster," Elena said, pointing to the Super Nova. "It rides up and down and makes you feel weightless."

Thelma cast a puzzled look and skipped off. *Not again.*

She returned, wind blowing through her hair. Elena had no idea how Thelma's brain was processing the bright colors, the rustle of leaves, and the breeze on her face.

"Wind," Elena said and blew into Thelma's face.

The girl skipped off down the path. Telet acted alarmed. Elena ran after her sister and grabbed the girl's arm. "You can't run off or they'll send us back." Elena saw a glimmer of recognition in the girl's eyes before Thelma danced around Telet, Elena, and the robot.

Not only couldn't Elena keep her sister under control, worrying about the girl distracted her from the couple and from finding an escape.

"Enough play," Telet said. "If you can't control her—"

"She's getting a feel for the place. You want her blending in so she can get close to them."

Associates floated toward nearby activities. Telet glanced around. "How far is the entrance?"

Elena pointed, hoping the tracker would leave. Telet stayed, her face drawn tight.

Studying the gray robot, a ball above a cylindrical base, Elena figured it had sensing devices, and like the Knoonk, was small but deadly. When she ran to catch her sister, it kept up.

While Thelma listened and gaped with the wonder of a child, Elena searched for hiding places, escape routes, and the other trackers that had to be there. They could have been any or, more frightening, all of the hundreds of associates. They would stop at nothing to win. If the couple reached the amusement park, they'd be trapped and Elena would return to the caves forever.

Elena grabbed her sister's hand and sprinted around the merry-go-round, a two-story antique that framed one end of the entrance area. She had moments before the robot and tracker caught up. "Listen," Elena whispered. "Stay by me. We're going to escape."

Thelma pulled away and skipped off along the reflecting pool toward the entrance gates. The gray robot chased after Thelma, catching up halfway to the entryway. Telet pulled out a thin device Elena took to be a controller or a weapon.

Elena grabbed Telet's muscular arm. "Please. She's only a child. Things will work out. She's excited. Where can she go? She has no money. I need time to settle her down."

"Be quick. It's opening time. If she gets in the way, I will terminate her."

Elena ran after her sister. Hovering at the girl's waist, the gray metallic robot drew attention from associates who viewed it as another new gimmick to fascinate their young guests. After all, the park had brought in numerous virtual reality games and other technological toys.

"Stay by my side!" Elena said when she reached her sister.

Thelma danced away without a care in the world.

Elena caught up, grabbed her sister's hand, and sat with her by the pool facing the entrance. "*Stay,*" she tapped. Telet and the robot joined them before Elena could message more.

Once the gates opened, they needed to appear to be doing something official, like greeter, to maintain their cover. She'd wanted to use the crowd as a cover for their escape, but the Knoonk could transport her out before she got free. She couldn't rely on police. Coyotes lurked in the corners of her vision, taunting her with their sad howl.

Nearby, a male associate in uniform had character shaped balloons. Elena approached him. "Don't get me into trouble. I have to watch my little sister today. Would you mind letting her hold a few of the balloons.

The guy parted with a half-dozen and Elena handed one to Thelma. "When I point, I want you to—"

Thelma let go of the balloon and watched it float. She grabbed for it, too late, and opened her mouth to say something. Her face turned into the first pout Elena had seen on her.

Elena held out another balloon. "Hold tight. They're helium filled. They fall up."

"Humans are ridiculous," Telet said, scanning the area.

Thelma bounced the second balloon, getting the hang of the novelty.

"We're looking for a boy and girl around fifteen," Elena explained. "When we see them, go up and give them a balloon."

>===>

Head swaying from side to side, Thelma played with the multicolored animal balloons.

A few patrons trickled in. Then the entranceway filled with teens dressed in anything from blue jeans and tie-dyed tops to fluorescent tights and military surplus outfits. Five scantily clad girls younger than Thelma strutted in front of some boys, drawing their attention.

Scanning every face, Elena sought that image of innocence and vitality she'd seen in the female half of the couple. She tried to recall the brief glimpse of the boyfriend.

Thelma played with the balloons, deriving joy from the pretend animals. She lost another balloon and still they waited.

After an hour sitting by the park entrance, Elena feared the worst: that the couple wouldn't show. She needed a viable escape plan and to get Thelma to cooperate, sneak away from Telet and her robot, and elude other trackers until they got out of the park.

Then, with no money, she would have to find shelter and help until she could reach someone who would listen, hoping they weren't TK. *Where are you?*

Thelma stood and danced around her balloon. "Boys and girls, have to twirl if you seek to find a pearl." She followed with more nonsense rhymes.

"Shut her up before she draws unwanted attention," the tracker said.

Elena took her sister's hand. The girl's head bobbed back and forth on her shoulders. At first, Elena thought Thelma had lost it again, yet these were Thelma's first words since they'd arrived. She hadn't been quiet that long before. Elena looked around.

The royal girl stood by the merry-go-round in a bright yellow halter. A slender boy stood next to her wearing a bright orange top. *What are you playing at?*

Elena couldn't yell for them to run without giving them away to other trackers, and condemning herself and her friends.

"What is it?" Telet spun around.

"Not sure." Elena glanced at the tracker and down toward the merry-go-round. The couple had vanished. Narn had said don't hesitate. "I think I see them." She took Thelma's hand and ran toward where the couple had been.

"Where?" the tracker demanded.

"Stay with me," Elena said to her sister as they ran.

The yellow halter darted from behind the merry-go-round and headed left. Elena couldn't see the boy. The tracker was twenty yards behind and catching up. The robot closed rapidly.

"I need you to memorize a number," Elena whispered. "It's my cousin. Tell her you're family. She'll help. The best way out of the park is to the left of the Beast we saw earlier."

The robot caught up by the merry-go-round. Telet was two yards behind. Elena's head ached with the realization they couldn't outrun either.

Heading left, Elena kept running. She needed time to think and a lucky break. The tracker stuck to her.

"What did you see?" Telet demanded, not even winded.

To avoid answering, Elena darted right. Not used to fighting Earth's gravity, Thelma was tiring. Spotting a burger shop, Elena headed inside and held tight to her sister's hand. The girl was panting.

Thelma struggled to get free. Elena held on. "You can't run off. Not this time."

Thelma pointed to a bottle of water and pretended to drink. Then she pointed to her groin.

"Bathroom?"

Thelma nodded.

"I'll come with you."

Thelma shook her head almost imperceptibly and pointed to the food counter.

"I don't know what you want."

Thelma danced out of the burger shop and toward the bathrooms. Telet pulled out a screen on which she tracked the girl's movements. "I thought you could control her."

"Don't you ever get hungry or need to pee?" Elena placed bottled water on the counter.

Telet shrugged. Taking no chances, she sent the robot to stand guard outside the bathroom.

Also in the burger shop was an older couple sharing a milkshake and two young couples. They were all doomed if Elena couldn't escape.

"Humans obsess with body functions," Telet whispered. "You're wasting time."

"She needs nourishment."

Elena ordered two chicken sandwiches. Telet got nothing for herself and dropped two bills on the counter. Elena sat watching a colorful collection of people mull by and planned her next move. Halfway through her sandwich, she realized her sister had been gone too long. She tried not to appear concerned.

Telet puzzled over her screen. Elena hoped her sister hadn't run off. Panic welled up inside her. She'd been confident she could catch the couple and find an escape, but unless they got away from Telet and the robot, and removed whatever tracking device they'd applied, it wouldn't matter.

Thelma emerged from the bathroom, her head and body swaying to unheard music. Telet got up. "Time to go."

"Let her eat." Elena pulled out Thelma's seat.

The girl stood beside the chair and took a bite of her sandwich. Telet grabbed the rest and threw it in the garbage. "Enough delay," Telet said. "You're letting the traitors escape again."

Elena glared at her jailer. The Knoonk were always several steps ahead. Even so, she'd beaten the all-powerful Gorg at a Knoonk pastime. They weren't invincible, but now they were playing chess with real lives. She couldn't afford to lose. "I believe I saw them at the merry-go-round. I didn't get a good look."

"Tell me your plan," Telet insisted.

"Like you share plans with me?" Elena studied several groups of teens walking up the path. "When they appear, Thelma distracts them while we capture them."

"You can train a monkey easier than that girl."

"Monkey, punkey, clunky."

Elena scanned the crowd for any sense of what had caught her sister's attention. She didn't see anything striking. Thelma tugged Elena's arm and pulled her toward the ring toss across the way. When Elena pulled back, Thelma let go and went to the counter with the rings.

Telet pushed Thelma away from the game. "She's a mistake. We aren't here for the child's amusement."

I am, partly. "Please," Elena whispered. "You've had her confined for so long I can't imagine what this is like for her. Thelma's role is to distract the couple. She'll do that once we find them."

Telet started speaking in her language into a mobile device.

"Please, wait," Elena said. "I saw the girl before she disappeared. They know we're following them. They're avoiding you and your tracker friends. Perhaps we should split up."

"Enough! This isn't a game. You have no idea what's at stake."

"Then enlighten me."

"You've got one hour." Telet moved away and focused on her mobile screen.

Elena led Thelma away. The robot followed close behind. They ducked into one booth after another, unable to shake the tracker or her electronic companion. With escape doubtful, she considered sacrificing the couple.

Thelma tugged Elena toward a face-painting booth with all sorts of animal art displayed.

"You're courting disaster," Telet reminded her. "Forty minutes."

"Let me rest a moment. You watch."

"What's your pleasure?" a tattooed redhead said from inside the booth.

"She doesn't talk," Elena said. "How about flowers?"

Thelma took the redhead's hand, followed her into her booth, and pointed out something.

"Can I see?" Elena asked.

Thelma closed the curtain.

Fine, Elena thought. *We're all going to fry. You might as well get your last wish.* She sat outside the booth scanning crowds for the couple. Telet studied the faces of everyone in the area. Her robot hovered near Elena. Inside, Thelma hummed.

"Why is it so important to catch this couple?" Elena asked to distract her tracker.

Telet continued watching people. "If you don't, you'll face annihilation. What do they look like?"

"I see the girl from time to time in the distance. Perhaps we could coordinate with the other trackers." Elena was fishing.

"Either you help or you can't," Telet said.

"How many trackers can we count on?"

"Not important."

"I can better help if you let me know our resources," Elena said. "You didn't tell me in Minneapolis, yet I found the girl. I was right about them coming here."

"We have six trackers."

"In pairs or alone?"

Telet stood over Elena. "We work in pairs and move alone."

"How do you communicate?"

"Enough questions. What are they wearing?"

"I didn't get a look at the boy," Elena said. "The girl is blonde with an innocent face."

"Not innocent."

"It's a look. She's shorter than me."

"That tells me nothing," Telet said. "There are hundreds like that. Thirty minutes."

Thelma emerged from the booth. Elena gasped. Her sister wore Native American war paint across her face.

"Wipe it off!" Elena said. "How dare you?"

Her sister's eyes were more determined than Elena had ever seen. Thelma grabbed Elena's arm and skipped down the path.

Telet followed with her hovering robot.

Around the bend, Elena had to fight the urge to act surprised, and do a double take. The "traitor" girl darted in to the shadows, also dressed in an associate's uniform with identical face paint. Elena looked to see if the tracker had noticed, but Telet was staring at her mobile device.

Thelma pulled away and danced across the walkway. *You sly thing. What are you up to?* Thelma glared at Elena; then danced in circles, spinning toward the courtyard with the carnival games. She twirled and danced at an ever-faster pace.

"Get control of her!" Telet demanded.

Elena ran after her sister and grabbed the girl's hand. Thelma pulled away, acting as jittery as a hummingbird. She ran with arms outstretched, letting the breeze wash through her hair. Elena couldn't keep up. Telet kept pace until Thelma disappeared into an arcade. The tracker pursued the girl, leaving the robot with Elena.

Elena spotted another painted face on the boy as he darted from the building. Down the path, she saw a third painted face, the girl. The tracker now chased the boy. Thelma ran toward the theater and disappeared. Elena broke into a sprint, her companion robot floating at her side. She couldn't shake it.

When Elena reached the theater, the tracker stood outside, arguing with a beefy male attendant. Telet pushed past. He grabbed, lifted her off the ground, and set her outside. The tracker cursed, but waited. When the attendant opened the gate, everyone crowded in, including Elena.

After her eyes adjusted to dim lights in the theater, Elena looked for Thelma, Telet, and the couple. The robot hovered next to her, where Thelma should have been. People pushed and shoved their way into the auditorium.

The robot scooted down a corridor to the right. Elena followed. At the end of the hall, the hovering machine hung in front of a closed door. Elena waited to see how the robot dealt with this barrier. She didn't have to wait long. The robot vanished, which meant her sister had to be inside.

Finding the door locked, Elena threw her weight into it. The door didn't budge. She ran at the door, hitting it with her shoulder. Something popped. She hoped it was the door. Suddenly the door opened and she was inside a dimly lit storage room with cleaning supplies. The door slammed shut behind her.

>====>

Elena ducked as something flew against the far wall. In the pale light, Telet's head lay on the floor. Thelma crouched in the corner over the robot, which lay in pieces. Nearby stood the couple, dressed as associates, covered in war paint, with headdresses covering their hair. He was slightly taller than she was and together with Thelma, they looked like triplets.

Recovering from shock, Elena stepped around Telet's lifeless body and pointed. "Who did this?"

"Doesn't matter," the boy said. "Let me introduce myself. I'm Daniel Rykner, this is Rosemary Beloit, and you must be Dr. Elena Pyctrov."

Elena nodded. "It does matter."

"Not now," Daniel said. "We haven't much time. We've disabled the robot and the tracker's communicator, but they'll close in on this location."

"Thelma?" Elena asked, watching her sister's head bob while she fingered a tiny piece of electronics.

"It was the tracker or us," Daniel said, reaching for the doorknob. "I wasn't sure they'd let you return to Earth. We had to get pretty sloppy so the trackers wouldn't lose the trail."

"They almost didn't let us come," Elena said, trying to process all this.

"We can swap histories later," Rosemary said. "In a minute, trackers will swarm this place. Let's go."

Elena stepped away from Telet's bloody head and held out her hand to her sister. "They have tracking devices on us. Can you remove them so we can escape?"

"Not in time," Rosemary said.

Elena crouched in the corner and reached for Thelma's hand. "Remove the face paint and uniforms and let's get out of here."

Daniel and Rosemary removed their associate tops and used them to wipe off their war paint. Despite the mockery, they did look a fearsome tribe. Elena crawled toward Thelma who moved deeper into the dark corner behind a cabinet.

"What is it, hon?" Elena asked. She turned in time to see Daniel and Rosemary disappear. She reached for Thelma. Her sister vanished.

Nausea hinted at transport.

THIRTY-SEVEN

Dread and panic gripped Elena. She'd failed. Muscles twitched in anticipation of Gorg's torture room. Coyotes pranced around her watery eyes.

The gray chamber she landed in brimmed with electronics lining a table and ledge along two angled walls. It must have been a different part of the space cruiser, judging by the contour of the room and the starry sky appearing at one end. Two yellow-clad Knoonk held Elena's arms in vice-gripped hands. She couldn't budge as they strapped her to a post by a wall opposite the electronics. The thicker atmosphere reeked of fish oil and chlorine.

At the sight of Gorg, Elena's dread transformed into fury. Thelma and the couple didn't deserve whatever the general planned for them.

Gorg's nose constricted at the sight of Elena. "Separate them."

Slender Daniel struggled with two yellow-clads controlling his arms and another gripping him in a chokehold. The two on his arms tied him with gray straps against the cabin wall to Elena's right.

Held by another two yellow-uniformed Knoonk, Rosemary reached out to her partner. "Don't you dare treat royalty this way." Her two Knoonk guards strapped her to the wall to Daniel's right.

Gorg glared at Elena. "You think you're smart because you won at Knoonk chess. No, you were lucky." Gorg's grin added further insult. "In the end I win."

"In the end, we're all dead," Elena said. "Even the Knoonk."

Gorg reached for Elena's neck.

Zurbiz stood in the doorway. "Leave her." The commander turned to Elena. "I commend your help in capturing the traitors."

"They're innocent kids," Elena protested.

"We shall see." Satisfied that the three prisoners were secured, Zurbiz motioned for the yellow-clad guards to wait outside. Then she approached Elena. "As a reward, you and your pathetic sister can live to serve and watch."

As the guards left, Thelma curled up under the equipment table on the opposite wall and rocked. She appeared unharmed; she couldn't handle more torture.

Gorg sniffed at Elena and sneered. "Your idea to use the girl worked, just not as you planned."

The image on the view-screen to the left of the electronics shifted, allowing Elena to see Earth, that beautiful blue and green home to ten billion imperiled humans. Elena glanced at Thelma, who rocked to music in her head and seemed to disappear into the shadows under the table.

Elena slammed her head forward, butting the leathery crest on the general's head. It had a mushy, muscular feel to it. She did it for Thelma and for what Gorg had in store for them all. The resulting pain bordered on a migraine, and hinted at a pending welt.

Gorg withdrew and grinned. "You think you can take me? You didn't defeat Narn. She let you win."

Zurbiz sang something in their language.

The general bowed and turned to Elena. "You failed. Narn is dead. Nalon is next. Humans will go to the incubation ward." She looked at the couple. "Which of you killed Lieutenant Telet?"

"All the kings' horses and all the kings' men…"

"Shut up." Gorg kicked Thelma's leg and pulled out her zapper.

Cringing, the girl curled tighter into a ball under the electronics table. Elena strained to break free. The straps on her arms tightened as she struggled.

"I'm not afraid of you," Daniel said.

"You should be," Gorg said. "There's no need for you. We'll use Rosemary for incubation. The child will pick her brain clean."

Zurbiz barked at Gorg and then added, "We have clearance. Set the plan in motion."

Gorg holstered her zapper, sat at the electronics table, and kicked Thelma aside.

Outside, a United Nations satellite approached.

Hurray for the humans, Elena thought. The satellite vaporized. Humans had no defense against that.

Thelma scrunched up under the electronics table. She'd acted so alive on Earth, so full of wonder and potential. Now she'd retreated into her shell. Through the fog of a growing headache, Elena pondered their situation.

"You have your victory. Now what?" she asked.

"Pray tell," Daniel said. "You've won. What can it hurt?" He turned to Elena. "I suppose they've led you to believe all our people are Knoonk. We're not. The Knoonk are a religious minority that tried to impose their views on all of the Tracanor people."

"Shut him up," Gorg demanded from her seat at the electronics table.

Zurbiz paced between them. "Daniel is partly right. Knoonk are not the entire people. We were persecuted for our beliefs."

"With good reason," Daniel said.

Zurbiz sniffed at Daniel. "That no longer matters." She barked something out to Gorg and then turned to Rosemary. "Now that we have you, nothing can stop us."

Gorg grunted, banged at the countertop, and sped up whatever she was doing.

"How did you know I'd be on that shuttle?" Elena asked.

"I arranged it." The voice was familiar and human.

Senator Christabelle Jorgensen entered the gray chamber, dressed in her exquisite gray and navy blue Senate uniform. Commander Zurbiz shielded her eyes, bowed, and left the room. That was when Elena recalled that fishy smell in the senate chambers, another of her coyotes' warnings. She clenched her fists, willing blood into her brain. "You?"

Jorgensen stroked Elena's hair. "I missed you, too." She pulled the hair taut.

Gasping, Elena drew back on her restraints.

Jorgensen grinned. "As I planned, the daughter of Indians has removed the final barrier to our victory. How touching that your sister would don Indian war paint for the occasion."

"You will not defeat us," Elena said.

"Proud words. I asked Commander Zurbiz and General Gorg to spare you so that you could be the voice of our victory."

"I won't help you."

"Ah, but you will. The surviving humans will see your miraculous recovery as a miracle. Your voice will get them to submit or die."

"You're Supreme Commander Viv?" Elena asked.

Senator Christabelle Jorgensen nodded.

"If you only perfected your human adaptation with DNA enhancements twelve years ago, how did you get into the Senate?"

Jorgensen petted Elena's head like a cat. "We recruited the real Christabelle Jorgensen into the Sisterhood and guided her political career until I could replace her."

"Then you killed Senator Spentworth?"

Jorgensen laughed. "He posed a threat and had to be removed. You and Rosemary will be coming with me. Daniel, I'm afraid, is expendable."

"No," Rosemary said. "I won't cooperate under those circumstances."

Elena watched Gorg still working at the electronics counter. Fumbling for anything to help their situation, Elena tried diplomacy. "Why can't we work together? Share the Earth?"

"Earth is overpopulated. Sharing won't work." Jorgensen turned to the general. "Are you ready yet?"

"Just a minute," Gorg said, not looking up.

"Target the fireworks display to celebrate our victory." Jorgensen approached Elena. "Cities will be destroyed once our people reach the countryside."

"Give us a chance to work with you," Elena said.

Jorgensen shook her head.

"How can you live with yourselves exterminating a whole race?" Elena looked past the senator to watch Thelma cower in the corner beside Gorg.

"If we permit you to live, you'll demand independence. That ends now."

"Why?" Elena asked. "With the Royal Couple, you can return to your home planet and play politics there."

"To have our society, we must begin from scratch. That's why we need Earth. The Royal Couple ensures non-interference by the Tracanor."

Gorg rose from the console and grinned, her thin mouth stretched. "Everything is set. Countdown is ten minutes. It's time to take the couple and go. We no longer need these humans."

"I am keeping Elena," Jorgensen said. "You secure the couple."

Elena pulled on her hand restraints and scanned the faces in the room. *Think chess*, Elena told herself, except Supreme Commander Viv held all the pieces. Daniel, Rosemary, and Elena were bound hands and feet, unable to act, though that could change when they were moved, except the Knoonk would bring in the other guards.

"You can't win," Elena said. "No matter how many lives you destroy, others will rise up. You'll have a guerilla war on your hands."

"Take Rosemary and the boy," Jorgensen said to Gorg. "I'll handle the defiant one." She stroked Elena's cheek.

Elena jerked away; she couldn't move far. "As a woman, how can you do this to other women?" Her skin crawled as she recalled the first time she'd noticed that fish odor.

Jorgensen slapped Elena's cheek and her face lit up. "Because, my dear, before we decided to become all female, I was male. Since taking human form, I've grown to enjoy what your females offer."

So far, Elena had been appealing to the wrong instincts, hoping the Knoonk had limits. *There has to be another move.*

She had no pieces to play, or did she? Thelma was still free though she'd withdrawn into her own world. She wasn't a champion, guardian, regent or trooper. She wasn't a scout. That would have been Telet for the other side. *Thelma, what are you?*

"Little Miss Muffet..." Thelma swayed on the floor where the general had been working.

Gorg kicked the girl's foot. "Don't for a moment think I'm not wise to you. I saw through your babble a long time ago. Get up."

THIRTY-EIGHT

Elena recoiled and tugged against her restraints. Coyotes nipped at the corner of her thoughts. Thelma went into a convulsive fit. The girl's body froze, a vacant stare etched into her innocent face. Elena had to do something before Gorg destroyed the girl.

Something bubbled up inside Elena that should have registered sooner. Thelma was more than a court jester. Elena took a deep breath.

"You haven't won," she said. "Not by a long shot. You have no idea what forces you're up against."

Gorg reached for her throat. "I could squish you with my bare hands."

Jorgensen said something in their language and Gorg backed away.

Elena mumbled.

Jorgensen moved closer. "Speak up!"

Barely audible, "You've overlooked one minor detail."

Jorgensen leaned in, her nose turned up in disgust.

It was time to activate the spy. Elena butted her head into Jorgensen as hard as she could. The senator's nose crunched as it drove into Elena's tender forehead, sending out sharp stabs of pain.

Jorgensen reeled backward, blood spewing from her nose. "Grab the autistic one."

Gorg covered her eyes at the sight of vibrant red blood, as Elena had begun to suspect from Nalon's aversion to blood. The

269

general spun around, arms out, searching for Thelma.

In swift, fluid motion, a painted warrior leapt to her feet. In her right hand, Thelma swung a table support brace shaped like a "J" with a thin metal edge as its inner rib. The blade caught Gorg's armpit and sliced off her right arm. In Thelma's left hand, a second blade rose and separated Gorg's left arm. Thelma spun and hooked the first blade around Gorg's neck, slicing it like a laser to ice. The head rolled onto the floor. The body stood for one defiant instant. Then the mightiest of Knoonk warriors slumped to the floor.

Jorgensen reached for Elena's neck. Elena drew back, prepared to thrust her sole remaining weapon at her attacker. Wiping blood from her upper lip, the senator jerked away. A bloodcurdling war cry filled the gray chamber as Thelma's blade sliced through Jorgensen's neck. A moment of stark terror froze on the senator's face as her head rolled to the ground.

Elena stared at her special sister. This had to be what her trickster coyote had been trying to tell her. "Where did you learn that?" She had no doubt this not so innocent girl had killed Telet. After all, she'd shown clever fight strategies facing Marc and in the cave wars.

Thelma rushed to Daniel and sliced the straps that bound his arms and legs using precision movements. Thelma dropped the sharp braces and slid into the seat by the controls without saying a word.

"Thelma? Can't you free your own sister?" Elena watched Daniel cut Rosemary's bindings. "Okay. How does Thelma know you?"

Putting his finger to his lips, Daniel hurried to free Elena. "We're being monitored."

On screen, two sets of numbers counted down: 5:02 and 6:00. "What happens in five minutes?" Elena asked.

"The Earth destruct sequence Gorg set." Daniel released Elena's leg bindings.

"And the other?"

Rosemary picked up Gorg's weapons. "Self-destruct."

Freed, Elena headed for the doorway. "We've got to get off this ship."

Daniel took the stun weapons from Gorg. "Wait! She can do this."

Elena glared at Daniel. He motioned that they couldn't talk yet.

She approached her sister, whose fingers attacked the virtual keyboard, as she had in Nalon's chambers, in the alien language no less. "Shouldn't we find a shuttle or something in case she can't stop both countdowns?"

Thelma pointed to another display. Zurbiz and a blue-clad in pressurized gear stepped over bodies of Knoonk guards.

"Thelma removed the air outside this room," Daniel said, "killing the guards to buy us time. Commander Zurbiz is getting away."

"Can we stop her?" Elena asked.

Both displays showed the steady progression of time. Earth destruct in 4:10. Self-destruct in 5:08. Another screen showed Zurbiz's shuttle accelerate out of the docking bay.

"We can't let her get away," Elena said.

A flash filled the screen, followed by starlight. Zurbiz and her shuttle vaporized like the U.N. craft. As Thelma worked the controls, Elena stared in awe at this young woman of whom she knew so little.

"Does that mean the struggle is over?" Elena asked.

"Hardly." Daniel watched the screens. "They have friends and we still have to stop their attack."

Glancing at the screen where moments before the shuttle had been, Elena knew they needed to save this cruiser to give humans a chance. The Knoonk would have other ships.

Earth destruct in 3:30. Self-destruct in 4:28.

Elena's mind raced. She felt responsible for Thelma, who wouldn't leave without using every precious second to save Earth and the four of them. Saving Thelma and losing Earth wasn't an option.

Elena glanced at Daniel, Rosemary, and then at Thelma. They were bound in ways Elena didn't understand. "Daniel, Rosemary, get to a shuttle and off this vessel while there's time."

"We can't let Earth be destroyed or the Knoonk win," Daniel said.

"Only Thelma can stop their plan. She won't leave unless you're safe."

Daniel took Rosemary's hand and hurried toward the door.

Kneeling next to Thelma, Elena watched her hands dance at lightning speed. This couldn't be her sister and yet Elena felt closer to Thelma than to anyone she'd ever known. The eyes were intense and knowing like her father's and yet...

Earth destruct in 2:30. Self-destruct in 3:28.

"If self-destruct happens first, wouldn't that save Earth?" Elena asked.

While Thelma worked the console, Elena wished there were something she could do. Somehow, she had faith in her special sister for things she couldn't understand.

The couple reached a shuttle. Elena could have joined them and saved herself, but she couldn't leave her sister to die here alone. If there'd been a way, she'd have taken Thelma's place.

Earth destruct in 1:40. Self-destruct in 2:38.

Thelma worked feverishly. The times continued to march down. Earth appeared on the front screen. Billions of people had no idea they were minutes from annihilation. The shuttle accelerated away from the ship. The couple might have a chance, depending on the extent of the blast.

Elena recalled moments when she'd seen sparks behind Thelma's stoic face trying to deceive the Knoonk from early childhood. As alone as Elena had felt much of her life, she couldn't fathom the loneliness of Thelma having to hide in full view. What incredible strength of will. It hurt knowing her sister had chosen to free Daniel first.

Earth destruct in 1:00. Self-destruct in 1:58.

The big blue and green ball loomed beneath them. With the shuttle moving away, Elena was tempted to grab Thelma and make a break for it. Instead, she stayed and imagined their hellish death. Would it be quick? At least Thelma wouldn't die alone. Saving lives was all that mattered. Yet, without knowledge of the Knoonk, humans didn't stand a chance. Somehow, she had to survive to warn leaders of the Knoonk threat. The shuttle faded into the starlit background.

Earth destruct in 0:30. Self-destruct in 1:28.

Desperate, Elena offered a sacrifice. "If you speed up the self-destruct, we can save Earth." Her mind burned with anticipation of a fiery death.

Earth destruct in 0:15.

Elena slipped her arms around Thelma's waist. The girl's fingers moved faster. They couldn't let Earth be destroyed. There was no point in defeating Jorgensen, Gorg, and Zurbiz if their scheme succeeded.

Earth destruct in 5:06. Self-destruct in 1:01.

"You've done it!" Elena hugged Thelma tight. "Let's go."

Thelma yanked Elena's hands from her waist and returned to the console. They'd saved Earth, but they had less than a minute.

"I'm sorry, Thelma." Elena moved away.

Her sister had worked feverishly to save them and Elena had cost her precious seconds.

Twenty-one seconds. She couldn't watch.

Moving toward the door, Elena counted in her head. Anticipating the blast, she pushed on the door. It wouldn't budge. Twelve ... eleven ... ten ...

Thelma's arms wrapped around Elena's waist. Three ... two ... one ...

THIRTY-NINE

A fortunate world should have been grateful for being spared the calamity of billions of deaths, though the only evidence of danger was a brilliant flash of light like a starburst in the heavens over Central America. Fighters scrambled. Western militaries went on full alert. Nearby satellites malfunctioned. A few sky-watchers, drawn to two earlier flashes, claimed they saw a UFO moments before the explosion. The Web filled with chatter, blaming one group or another, but no official word.

>===>

As nausea faded, Elena's mind cleared. Her headache faded. In the dim twilight, wheat stalks stood at attention surrounding a matted-down circle fifteen feet in diameter. Daniel and Rosemary embraced nearby. Thelma clung tight to Elena's waist from behind. Elena removed the girl's arms and faced the painted warrior.

Clutching Elena's hands, Thelma peered into her sister's eyes. "Don't abandon me, please. I'm still your sister and this world scares me." Tears streamed down her cheeks and glistened in the twilight.

"She talks." Elena studied Thelma for a long time, trying to process new information about the girl she'd known for months as her special sister. Pain and fear filled the girl's eyes mingling with that precious girl Elena had come to love. Elena hugged her sister. "You're one brave girl. I can't imagine what you've been through." She held Thelma at arm's length. "Who are you?"

"I couldn't speak earlier and couldn't afford to let them know about our secret messaging. They wanted to take me away. If you hadn't offered to watch over me, they would have. You're the brave one, never quitting on me."

"I don't feel brave."

"Don't be modest," Thelma said. "You got me on the ship with Gorg, Zurbiz, and the Supreme Commander. Then you distracted them so I could—"

"How do you know Daniel and Rosemary?"

"Don't hate me. I am your sister, your flesh and blood. I'm also Tracanor."

Swallowing hard, Elena tried to steady herself. "You're not like the other girls."

"No, I'm not."

Daniel approached. "What Thelma's trying to say is we're Terran-adapted Tracanor. We're human, with a few genetic enhancements to give us strength and endurance. The only things not human are the memories of another life. Genetically adapted Knoonk, like the trackers, grow faster with enhanced minds and bodies. Once they reach seven, their Knoonk persona takes over their new bodies. They've resurrected many warriors that way."

"You remember your home planet?" Elena asked.

"It's far more confusing than that. We recall this whole other world and home as memories of a past life. TK experience their human youth as memories of a past life, knowledge to be used by their Knoonk personas."

Rosemary grabbed Daniel's arm. "We should go before someone spots the crop circle." Her eyes betrayed intelligence far beyond her years.

"Is this what happens with your transporter?" Elena pointed to the matted crops.

Thelma chuckled. "No, but you wouldn't want wheat stuck up your nose, would you?"

Laughing at the image, Elena was surprised at how much tension her body released. "Are all crop circles made in this way?"

Rosemary knitted her fingers into Daniels. "Most are made by human pranksters. Some allowed the Knoonk to communicate with their moles and trackers."

Thelma led them eastward through the wheat field into the

growing twilight. "I picked Minneapolis, since you're familiar with the area."

"How did you get your weapons on the spacecraft?" Elena asked, following alongside her sister.

"We didn't. Those were the braces holding the electronics counter in place. To break them free, I needed Gorg to give me an extra push and a distraction for the noise."

"You wanted her to kick you?"

"It was necessary," Thelma said.

"The brace is how you cut yourself in Nalon's room, isn't it?"

"And I showed you the Knoonk aversion to blood, to rich colors actually. It's a byproduct of their genetic engineering."

"How did you three coordinate war paint?" Elena asked as the sky darkened. "And why?"

"We met when I went to the bathroom," Thelma said. "It was the only time I could be out of sight of the tracker and her robot."

"I'm sorry if we offended you," Rosemary said. "We wanted to look interchangeable to confuse the tracker and to get everyone to that room in the theater."

Elena took Thelma's hand to connect and because she could barely see in the dark and Thelma didn't seem to have that shortcoming. "What's your real name?"

"Thelma Pyetrov, and I'm proud of my name." She sighed and stopped. "In my other life they called me Commander Weglew. When the Knoonk attacked and overwhelmed my command, the resistance needed a place to hide me. Your father consented to have a child. He was a wonderful man despite how terribly we'd treated him."

"Did he know?"

Thelma nodded. "He did and he tried to tell you. That's why they killed him. I'm sorry to say this, but it was probably for the best. He wanted to tell you everything, which would have exposed me."

Elena's eyes welled up. "That was why he was reaching for my arm, why he was blinking. He wanted to send coded messages as you and I did."

"I wanted to tell you more, but I couldn't risk the time it would have taken to share code. I also wasn't sure how you would react to partial information."

"Probably not well. You frustrated the daylights out of me."

"I truly am sorry," Thelma said. "The resistance kept our father alive to protect me. It was hard to keep the warring clans away without exposing ourselves, but we managed."

"I can't believe you pulled it off."

"I almost didn't. My Tracanor memories were safe until I turned eleven. Then nightmares of this other life showed up. At first, I didn't know what it meant. I couldn't tell anyone, especially our father. Earlier, when Mom disappeared, they thought I went crazy and they left me alone. As the nightmares got stronger, I pretended to have mental problems in order to protect myself. That's why I couldn't allow us to get close, or let my guard down."

"I can't imagine how you survived so long without being able to talk to people. It must have been very lonely."

"Indeed." Thelma pressed her painted face against Elena's Great America uniform. "Father was great. He cared for me without asking anything in return. The resistance kept him alive until you came. I had you brought to the caves. Can you forgive me?"

"I don't know," Elena said. "You put me through hell." She ran her fingers through her sister's silken hair. "Of course I forgive you. I got to see Dad again and I met a terrific sister."

"Thanks." Thelma resumed walking. "Because of when I was born, Gorg assumed I was human. I didn't wish to enlighten her. In the chaos, Zurbiz and Gorg consolidated their command. I feared Gorg would impregnate me with of one of her faithful who could have probed me from inside."

"I'm so sorry."

"It wasn't your fault."

Elena pulled her sister back, removed her amusement park top, and wiped off the war paint. Behind that fearsome mask, Elena saw in the moonlight the innocence that had captured her heart. Elena smiled. "Thanks for saving us up there."

"It was the least I could do after you showed me Earth."

"Can't they track us?"

Thelma smiled. "I removed the implants when I beamed us. That's why it took so long."

"Let's keep moving," Daniel said. "We need to reach your cousin's place by daybreak."

"By the way," Thelma said. "They wanted you to think your shuttle crashed into Europa. It didn't."

"Mars," Elena said.

"You knew?"

"The gravity."

Thelma took Elena's hand and followed Daniel. "Gorg created the illusion so that you'd accept captivity. I'm glad you didn't."

>====>

By sunup, the four travelers reached Eden Prairie. Elena led them to her cousin's neighborhood. Thelma stopped them two blocks away. Across the street was a tall blonde who looked like Telet, lean and focused, too much so for six in the morning. Five blocks away a similar figure waited outside the uncle's home.

"I don't understand," Elena said, huddling behind bushes. "We watched Zurbiz's shuttle being destroyed."

"Her trackers figured we'd stop here," Thelma said. "There are still hardcore Knoonk who will try to grab power. We should keep moving."

As much as she wanted the comfort of family, Elena yielded to Thelma's wisdom, something she figured she would have to get used to.

Keeping to side streets, Elena led them around the southern suburbs until they reached a small used-car dealership. Daniel paid cash for a beat-up sedan, and they headed east.

Over the next two days, while Daniel and Rosemary took turns driving to the nation's capitol, Elena listened for hours as Thelma released a pent-up dam of words. "Nalon brought me to her room to allow me to connect with our culture, using chess with our father as a ruse. I had to be careful not to seem to understand."

"Is that how you learned the Knoonk, Tracanor language?"

Thelma shook her head. "That came from Commander Weglew, though I had to practice language skills to loud music."

"Nalon took a huge risk to show me things."

"In the hope you could help, I asked her to show you what you were up against. My mission, the Tracanor mission, was as benefactors to Earth. Over many centuries, we intervened twelve times to avoid nuclear and other catastrophes. Interventions were easier before rapid communication and cameras. Roswell was a wakeup call to be more careful. When civil war engulfed Tracanor, the royal family was killed."

"Then who are Daniel and Rosemary?" Elena asked.

"We saved the essence of the prince and princess and brought them to this outpost for regeneration. When we learned the Knoonk were heading our way, we hid the couple on Earth. Because of cultural arrogance, Viv, Zurbiz, and Gorg didn't suspect at first. Arriving in force, they overwhelmed our defenses and embarked on their plans to take over Earth as their new refuge."

Elena wondered what she'd fallen into. Thelma, Daniel, and Rosemary treated her as one of them, but she wasn't. She was human: half Navajo, half Russian-American, dating back several generations. Yet she was like a teen again, facing a new world filled with wonders and fears about her place in the new order. Her father had known Thelma was different and tried to protect her, protect Commander Weglew.

Elena's three companions were aliens, yet not much different from her. One thing was clear. Humans couldn't win this alone. Only with cooperation could they hope to survive.

A new form of nausea gripped Elena, so they had to stop often along the way. Her stomach rebelled from the stress of living on edge and yet she hungered for Belgian waffles with blueberries and whipped cream, juicy hamburgers with Portobello mushrooms and cheddar cheese, and banana mint milk shakes.

Again, she read a letter Marc had slipped to her before she'd left. *I can't apologize enough. Nothing can forgive my behavior*, but she had. She'd known his strength and gentleness enough to know that moment wasn't him. In the end, he couldn't hurt her. She considered the irony that she was here on Earth and he was up there. She ached to hold him in her arms.

Once more, I pledge my life and love to you, he wrote. She'd given up too many good years they could have spent together when he was only a phone call away. Now that she couldn't reach him, she wanted him most.

Don't worry about me. Memories you've given me will carry me through whatever the Knoonk might do. Fly. She had, though tethers bound her to the caves. Deep in her psyche, she'd sensed her father still alive, and that had pulled her across the solar system.

"I miss Joey," Thelma said. "It hurts more than I imagined."

Elena held Thelma and brushed hair from her eyes. "I know, hon. I know."

"I'm afraid he won't like me when he learns what I am."

"He fell in love with crazy you. He'll get over it."

"You really think so?" Thelma gave Elena a quizzical look. "You want Marc, don't you?"

Elena nodded. "There's much you don't know about him."

"There's no need to explain, unless you want to."

FORTY

Shading her eyes from the brilliant sun, Elena watched Thelma and the couple splashing in the Gulf of Mexico. Bobbing in the waves, Thelma drank it all in after a lifelong confinement in caves.

The trip to Washington had revealed the truth of the Supreme Commander's boast: TK were everywhere. The four split up. Elena and Thelma checked out Congress, approached agents at the FBI, and scouted the CIA. Senator Montrose and FBI agent Ahmed Amladi told Elena to lie low until they could decide what to do. Meanwhile, the couple checked out the White House and other government agencies. Elena even looked up contacts within the Sisterhood of the Nile. Many had died. Others turned out to be TK. Washington reeked of dead fish, something Thelma and the couple did not.

"I told you," Daniel had said on the trip west. "We're mostly human. They're not."

"Are there others like you?"

"None we know of."

Elena still puzzled over the connection between the three. "Why do I get the impression you were able to communicate with Thelma before she came to Earth?"

Daniel smiled. "Some trackers work for us. When Telet's partner caught one of our friends in Minneapolis, Major Burb had to be terminated."

"Killed," Elena said. "Let's call it what it was."

"Very well. Killed."

Imbibing the salty fragrance of sea and kelp, Elena glanced up and down the deserted sand beach. Gulls glided overhead. The breaking waves frothed over clear water as a cool breeze eased the sun's rays. This was paradise, not the caves.

Elena unfolded Marc's tattered letter. She couldn't let go. Here she could enjoy this wonderful beach while he suffered an unknown fate out in space.

Looking out at the breaking waves, she had difficulty picturing the couple leading a nation or Thelma as commander of armies. It had been equally hard to imagine the Knoonk. She couldn't help feeling cautious. The Knoonk had underestimated them once. They wouldn't repeat that mistake and they had trackers everywhere. Still, being on the run beat confinement, and she could now share this with Thelma.

Lifting her sunglasses, Elena glanced up toward the rocks behind her. A tall man with olive complexion and flowing white robes approached.

"Ahmed!"

Elena turned to greet him, amazed at how he could stand the heat while fully clothed with his head covered. When he averted his eyes from her bikini-clad figure, she grabbed her flowered cotton wrap, pulled it around her, and hurried his way. "Sorry."

The undercover FBI agent gazed out toward the three figures playing in the water. "Everyone wants to talk with you and them."

"I'm sure they do. Did you take the precautious we talked about?" Elena glanced up and down the beach.

"Sounded fishy to me, excuse the pun. Don't worry. I followed to the letter."

"How's Anton?" Elena asked.

"He was upset by your disappearance; he had his heart set on this mission. I praise Allah that he was not on your transport."

"Me, too," Elena said. "What we found was more amazing and horrifying than anything I could have imagined."

While watching Thelma and the others splash in the water, Elena gave Ahmed a quick rundown.

He sat against sandy rocks and sighed. "Some would say you've lost your mind."

Elena sat beside him. "Wasn't NASA able to track our shuttle at incredible speeds past the Moon?"

"Technical problems cut satellite communications."

"Nice coincidence. How can I prove this to you?"

"I don't doubt what you think you saw, Elena. You're asking me to fight the entire U.S. government on this."

"Listen, Ahmed. I have nothing against the Tracanor, but the Knoonk seek to destroy us and take over our world. Will you help?"

"You're also challenging my faith."

"Ahmed, the Knoonk will kill off the men. They don't need them. Less than five percent of the males in the caves survived."

"Have you anything tangible, any evidence of this alien race?"

"We tried to save one of their ships. We couldn't stop the self-destruct." Frustrated, Elena waved for the others to join her and was amazed at how quickly they moved.

After she made introductions, Elena laid it out. "Ahmed can help, but he needs something more than words in order to believe."

Daniel produced a zapper, probably Gorg's, which he pointed at Ahmed. "Shall I give a demonstration?"

Elena pushed the weapon away. "Not at my friend." She turned to Ahmed. "It produces an intense electric shock."

"We have stun guns, too," Ahmed said, shaking his head.

"Not like these." Daniel aimed at a palm tree thirty feet inland and vaporized it.

Elena was shocked. She'd figured the weapons were short range. They must have had multiple settings.

"I'll buy you have an interesting toy," Ahmed said. "Can I borrow it for testing?"

"We need it," Daniel said.

"Then how do I convince people?"

"First, Ahmed, do you believe?" Elena asked.

Ahmed closed his eyes and nodded. "I believe in you, Elena."

"Then take this," Elena handed him a data cube. "It contains everything we know about the Knoonk, including history, language, technology, and intentions. Show it only to those you trust, and only after they pass the smell test. We need a plan to defend ourselves."

"I'll do what I can."

"Do more, Ahmed. We can't compromise with the Knoonk.

They want it all and they have the technology to take it unless we find a way to stop them. Right now, they depend on their human-looking offspring to execute their plans. We need to round them up. I hate to say this, but every member of the Sisterhood of the Nile and every member of the federal government needs to be investigated."

Ahmed slipped the cube under his robe. "Then we'll find a way."

"The entire human race is counting on it."

He reminded her of Marc in the purity of his convictions and his single-minded pursuit of what he believed.

As her sister and the couple returned to the water, Ahmed waved toward the bushes behind them. "I have a surprise for you."

Glancing toward the dunes, Elena spotted a short weathered man with a rounded face heading their way. She didn't recognize him yet felt that she should. She studied his dark complexion and deep facial creases and tried to imagine him younger.

The man spoke to Elena in what she recognized as Navajo. Then, in accented English, "I am your mother's brother, Eagle-foot. There was much anger when your mother married. We felt she betrayed our people."

"I'm sure you have much to catch up on," Ahmed said, and headed away from the beach.

"Thanks for everything," Elena said as he left. Returning her gaze to her uncle, Elena felt ashamed for ignoring her Navajo heritage and excited at the prospect of what he could teach her. "Did Ahmed tell you what we found?"

"The Knoonk?" Eagle-foot smiled. "There were ancient stories of a tribe from far away. Perhaps you found them."

She pointed to the three playing in the waves. Thelma might be a commander, but she was also a teen, bursting to know what this world had to offer. Elena needed to get to know her sister and the couple better before they risked what would be required to stop the Knoonk. In the meantime, she wanted her heritage back.

"Ahmed tells me you need refuge," Eagle-foot said. "You have shelter with us amidst the four sacred mountains."

Elena hugged him. "Thanks." She took in the salt air and gazed at the horizon, which stretched forever. Her ears savored the rhythmic beat of the waves.

Thelma ran from the water and grabbed Elena's hand. "It's far more wonderful than I imagined."

It was, though they would have to fight hard to preserve it. Elena wiped a tear from her eyes. "Thelma, this is my uncle, my mother's brother, Eagle-foot, and this, uncle, is my very precious sister, Thelma."

Thelma peppered him with questions, soaking up new experiences like a sponge. Then she added, "I wish we never had to leave."

"I know, sweetie. Don't you miss Joey?" Elena asked.

Thelma nodded, and then frowned. "Part of me hungers to enjoy a simple life. Another urges leadership, duty, and responsibility. I'm not sure Joey can deal with that."

"I'm sure he'd be very proud of you."

Elena shared her sister's ambivalence. Ever since Leo's suicide, she'd shunned responsibility. Her mind said her brother's death wasn't her fault. Her heart couldn't forget. Then she met Thelma, who made her care again.

"Soon will be time for duty," Elena said. "For now, enjoy and remember this when times get tough." In the end, the quest hadn't been what mattered but rather the bonds she'd formed.

The Royal Couple emerged from the water and joined them. Thelma ran uphill, away from the beach. On the bluff above stood three figures: a blonde who could have been Telet's twin, Marc, and Joey. Elena could barely control her legs as she scrambled up the sandy path. Marc ran toward her and she leapt into his arms, knocking him to the ground. She hugged and kissed him. After she came up for air, she had to know. "What happened? How did you get here?"

"You're a huge hero to all on Europa," Marc said.

"It wasn't Europa."

"Huh?"

"Long story," Elena said. "Tell me about the caves."

"When the resistance heard that Gorg was dead, they took over. Gorg is dead, isn't she?"

Elena nodded. "Thelma did the honors."

Thelma held both of Joey's hands and glared at Marc. "Treat my sister right or you'll find out how." She winked at Elena.

"You…" Joey couldn't find the words.

"A ruse to protect against the Knoonk," Thelma said. "You know what they did to girls."

Joey nodded and gave her a hug. "I knew it."

Elena kissed Marc and pulled away. "Who's in charge up there?"

"It seems Nalon is a general. Her people seized control. I asked her to release all of the humans. She said most of the kids are terrorized Knoonk?"

"Terranized-Knoonk," Elena corrected. "They're genetically adapted to Earth. What about Reese, Tara, Maggie, Chrissie, and the others?"

"Nalon asked them to decide about the children. No mother would give up hers, and there's a stormy debate on abortions and what to do with children faithful to Zurbiz."

Elena winced at the mountain of issues they faced. "We can't bring them to Earth. They'd be like Dr. Jekyll and Mr. Hyde. Still, it's unfair." Elena realized it would be up to those in the caves to decide. Her responsibilities were here. She approached Daniel and Rosemary, who were talking with the tracker.

"It's okay," Daniel said. "Lieutenant Salis is with us. I contacted her in Washington."

"Thanks," Elena said.

Salis smiled. "We owe you everything, Elena. You were the first to see us as individuals and the possibilities of working together. When you refused to kill a guard, it signaled a beginning. Then you didn't turn Rosemary in to save yourself."

"I realized turning the couple over would allow Gorg to destroy Earth."

Salis nodded. "You got Thelma out of the caves so she could confront Gorg and Viv. We have a chance thanks to you. It won't be easy, but together we can succeed."

Elena wasn't comfortable with the attention and was glad when Marc led her to a private cove.

>====>

After a dinner of fish, Elena wandered down the beach. She played her harmonica and watched moonlight dance on the receding tide.

Thelma joined her. "I love to hear you play."

"Thanks." Elena still marveled at how a commander and a young girl could occupy the same body in harmony. "It must be hard for you to accept Marc."

"If you accept him, that's good enough for me," Thelma said. "I almost forgot. I have something for you." Thelma handed over a sealed plastic case.

Inside the case was the crumpled picture of her father. Elena stared at it for a long time, thankful that she'd gotten to see him again. Then she handed the picture back. "I have all the images I need in my heart and in you." Elena hugged her sister. "One of my biggest regrets was having to kill Major Narn. She helped me when I needed it most. She deserved better."

"It's General Narn, and don't feel bad. If you hadn't, Gorg would have tortured her. She helped arrange the fight and surrendered so you could fight her instead of Gorg. She staged her death as a means to help you get us to Earth."

"Staged? She almost killed me."

"She had to make it look convincing, or Gorg would have fought you herself."

"I wish I could have gotten to know her," Elena said.

Thelma frowned. "How would you like that opportunity?"

"What are you saying? I watched her die. Gorg would never give her resurrection."

"I'm sorry," Thelma said. "The plan was for me to carry her resurrected soul."

"No, you're too young. Tell me you didn't."

"You were so insistent that I wait that I couldn't and then…"

Elena rubbed her belly. "You put her inside of me?"

"I'm sorry. I thought when you were with Marc that you were giving consent."

"Marc's baby, not an implant. How dare you?"

"I'm sorry," Thelma said. "It was all my fault."

"Thelma, you can't decide things for other people like that."

"I know, but we need General Narn and it was either you or me. The child will still be Marc's and yours. She'll have your DNA and love you as I've grown to love you. I'm sorry; there was no way to ask permission. Please don't hate me."

Elena sighed. "I don't hate you, hon, but you can't make these decisions for other people."

Embracing her sister, Elena felt strange about raising a Terran-adapted Tracanor child, yet General Narn had been good to her and Elena owed Narn for helping her and Thelma get to Earth. Besides, they needed all the help they could get. Maybe General

Narn would improve their chances.

Massaging her belly, Elena wondered if she could accept the responsibility for the child and all that carrying her would mean. Her trickster coyotes faded away. She vowed to be more attentive when they returned.

PEOPLE/TERMS

TERMS
Tracanor: Entire race of aliens.

Knoonk: Group of alien renegades who lost their Civil War and who have taken over an outpost in our solar system to regroup.

Terran-adapted Knoonk (TK): Knoonk who have undergone transformation to human form.

CREW & PASSENGERS
Dr. Elena Sweetwater Pyetrov: Senior scientist on a planned mission to Europa. Lost her father on a similar mission eighteen years earlier. Driven to follow his passion.

Marc Russell: Elena's on-and-off fiancée, marine, finagled his way onto shuttle with strings attached.

Reese Paswitch: Shuttle's navigator, she planned to marry on the moon and retire from the service.

Tara L'Enfant: Electronic whiz, passenger who wanted on this mission and has to deal with the consequences.

OTHER HUMANS
Dr. Alexis Pyetrov: Elena's father, whose ship disappeared near Jupiter eighteen years earlier.

Thelma Pyetrov: Elena's half-sister (same father), traumatized, speaks cryptically.

Senator Jorgensen: Vocal opponent of Elena's mission on Senate Committee.

Mason Crenshaw Devereaux: Billionaire owner of MCD Enterprises that financed Elena's mission.

ALIENS
Supreme Commander Viv: Knoonk who has assumed human form through adaptive transformation to lead her people on Earth.

General Gorg: Fierce Knoonk warrior with ambitions to replace her commander. She lost her sister (also a warrior) on a routine mission on Earth and vows revenge against humans.

Commander Zurbiz: Gorg's commander, loyal to Viv, but Gorg sees her as incompetent for rejecting a rescue mission for Gorg's sister.

Nalon Krok: Faithful servant to Zurbiz and first contact for Elena and crew.

Major Narn: Possible member of alien opposition.

Daniel Rykner: Half of Royal Opposition hiding on Earth.

Rosemary Beloit: Half of Royal Opposition hiding on Earth.

Lieutenant Telet: TK tracker whose mission is to locate the Royal Opposition and support Supreme Commander Viv.

OTHER STORIES BY LANCE ERLICK

REGINA SHEN: RESILIENCE (Regina Shen book 1)

Outcast Regina Shen is forced by the World Federation to live on the seaward side of barrier walls built to hold back rising seas due to abrupt climate change. A hurricane threatens to destroy what's left of her world, tearing Regina from her family.

Global fertility has collapsed. Chief Inspector Joanne Demarco of the notorious Department of Antiquities believes Regina holds the key to avoid extinction. Regina fights to stay alive and avoid capture while hunting for her family. Does she have the resilience to survive?

REGINA SHEN: VIGILANCE (Regina Shen book 2)

Regina Shen is pursued by the notorious Department of Antiquities for her unique DNA. She jumps the Barrier Wall into the Federation to find her kidnapped sister. Stuck on a heavily guarded closed university campus in the mountains, she must use her wits to escape and rescue her sister without letting either of two rival Antiquities inspectors capture her.

REGINA SHEN: DEFIANCE (Regina Shen book 3)

Outcast Regina Shen has DNA the Federation believes can reverse a global fertility collapse. Rival Federation agents fight over capturing Regina to gain power amidst turmoil over who will become the new World Premier. Regina has to flee from Virginia through desert and wilderness to Alaska to hunt a treasure big enough to barter for her freedom and that of her sister.

THE REBEL WITHIN (Rebel Series book 1)

Annabelle Scott lives under the iron rule of a female-dominated régime that forces males to fight to the death to train the military elite. When pressed into service as a mechanized warrior to capture escaped boys, Annabelle stays true to herself by helping some escape. Her defiance endangers everyone she loves and thrusts her to a place of impossible life and death decisions.

LANCE ERLICK

THE REBEL TRAP (Rebel Series book 2)

Despite being a military recruit, Annabelle Scott rebels against her female-dominated régime by refusing to kill a handsome boy she fancies and helping him escape. Auditory implants and cameras allow her commander to watch her 24-7. Can she help the boy free his brother from a heavily guarded geek institute without destroying her family or getting killed?

REBELS DIVIDED (Rebel Series book 3)

The first time Geo sees Annabelle, they meet as enemies and she doesn't kill him, which mystifies them both. It's after the 2nd Civil War with the nation divided into an all-female Federal Union and a warlord controlled Outland. The Outland warlord kidnaps Annabelle's sister and kills Geo's father. Can Annabelle and Geo overcome mutual distrust and work together to rescue her sister and gain justice for his father's murder? Will their feelings for each other derail or further their goals?

Written as a standalone story, *Rebels Divided* is also part of the Rebel series, three years later.

SHE-DEVIL ROCKS (novelette)

Inspired by *Lord of the Flies*.

Bullied as the smallest of thirteen boys in his class, Bradley is on a plane that crashes on a remote island with a bully who is out of control. Bradley meets a mysterious tomboy who shouldn't be there. He has to learn to survive on the hostile island, deal with the tomboy, and come to terms with the bully.

REGINA SHEN: SALVAGE (novelette)

Living on the seaward side of barrier walls built to protect against rising seas, the only means of survival for Regina Shen is underwater salvage, which is banned by the World Federation. After a storm takes a friend's family and home, Regina is determined to help by defying the Federation

MAIDEN VOYAGE (short story)

Security Chief Nina Rekovic keeps the peace on the all-female Maiden's Ark that left Earth five years before. Distress signals say Earth is lost, stranding lunar colonists. While balancing Returners she sympathizes with, a dictatorial captain, and an estranged lover

ii

who betrays her, can Rekovic solve the conspiracy before she's imprisoned or killed?

WATCHING YOU (short story)

At the intersection of pervasive networks and the Patriot Act, we have the ability and some say the obligation to know everything about everyone. Can privacy survive? Can the individual endure?

Harold is a second-class citizen and a low-level worker in a government surveillance system charged with reviewing "criminal activity." He has private thoughts about a woman he's forbidden from approaching. He will not be deterred.

ABOUT THE AUTHOR

Lance Erlick writes science fiction thrillers for young adult and adult readers. He is the author of *The Rebel Within*, *The Rebel Trap*, and *Rebels Divided*, three books in the Rebel series. In those stories, he explores the consequences of Annabelle Scott following her conscience. He authored the Regina Shen series—*Regina Shen: Resilience*, *Regina Shen: Vigilance*, *Regina Shen: Defiance*, and *Regina Shen: Endurance*. This series takes place after abrupt climate change leads to the Great Collapse and a new society under the World Federation. A related short story is: *Regina Shen: Salvage*. His latest novel is *Xenogeneic: First Contact* about encounters with an alien race aiming to take over Earth. Lance is also the author of unrelated short stories.

Find out more about the author and his work at LanceErlick.com. Go to that website to sign up to receive occasional email newsletters with links to free short stories and updates on new releases and other writing developments.

www.ingramcontent.com/pod-product-compliance
Lightning Source LLC
Chambersburg PA
CBHW070809180626
46818CB00001B/183